INFINITY WARS

Edited by
Jonathan Strahan

T0162280

Also Edited by **Jonathan Strahan**

Best Short Novels
(2004 through 2007)
Fantasy: The Very Best of 2005
Science Fiction: The Very Best of 2005
*The Best Science Fiction &
Fantasy of the Year: Volumes
1-11*
*Eclipse: New Science Fiction and
Fantasy (Vols 1-4)*
*The Starry Rift: Tales of New
Tomorrows*
*Life on Mars: Tales of New
Frontiers*
*Under My Hat: Tales from the
Cauldron*
Godlike Machines

The Infinity Project:
Engineering Infinity
Edge of Infinity
Reach for Infinity
Meeting Infinity
Bridging Infinity
Infinity Wars
Infinity's End (forthcoming)

Fearsome Journeys
Fearsome Magics
Drowned Worlds

With Lou Anders
*Swords and Dark Magic: The
New Sword and Sorcery*

With Charles N. Brown
*The Locus Awards: Thirty Years
of the Best in Fantasy and Science
Fiction*

With Jeremy G. Byrne
*The Year's Best Australian Science
Fiction and Fantasy: Volume 1*
*The Year's Best Australian Science
Fiction and Fantasy: Volume 2*
Eidolon 1

With Jack Dann
Legends of Australian Fantasy

With Gardner Dozois
The New Space Opera
The New Space Opera 2

With Karen Haber
Science Fiction: Best of 2003
Science Fiction: Best of 2004
Fantasy: Best of 2004

INFINITY WARS

EDITED BY **JONATHAN STRAHAN**

Including stories by
CARRIE VAUGHN
AN OWOMOYELA
CAROLINE M. YOACHIM
NANCY KRESS
INDRAPRAMIT DAS
ELIZABETH BEAR
DOMINICA PHETTEPLACE
ALIETTE DE BODARD
DAVID D. LEVINE
GARTH NIX
GENEVIEVE VALENTINE
RICH LARSON
E.J. SWIFT
ELEANOR ARNASON
PETER WATTS

SOLARIS

First published 2017 by Solaris
an imprint of Rebellion Publishing Ltd,
Riverside House, Osney Mead,
Oxford, OX2 0ES, UK

www.solarisbooks.com

ISBN 978 1 78108 491 5

Cover by Adam Tredowski

A CIP catalogue record for this book is available from the
British Library.

Designed & typeset by Rebellion Publishing

Printed in Denmark by Nørhaven

For the mancationers – Garth, James, Sean, and Simon – who persevered through illness and adversity and triumphed in the end (well, saw snow and drank whisky).

ACKNOWLEDGEMENTS

THE INFINITY PROJECT and *Infinity Wars* only exist because of the faith shown in them by editor-extraordinaire Jonathan Oliver and the whole Solaris team. My sincere thanks to Jon, David Moore, and Ben Smith for their support and for their hard work on the book you now hold, and for everything else. My thanks also to Adam Tredowski, who has delivered *another* knock-out cover for the series. My sincere thanks, too, to all of the writers who sent me stories for the book, whether I used them or not, and to everyone who wanted to be part of *Infinity Wars*. As always, my thanks to my agent Howard Morhaim who has stood with me for all of these years, and extra special thanks to Marianne, Jessica, and Sophie, who really are the reason why I keep doing this.

CONTENTS

Introduction   **11**
Jonathan Strahan

The Evening of Their Span of Days   **15**
Carrie Vaughn

The Last Broadcasts   **35**
An Owomoyela

Faceless Soldiers, Patchwork Ship   **63**
Caroline M. Yoachim

Dear Sarah   **95**
Nancy Kress

The Moon is Not a Battlefield   **111**
Indrapramit Das

Perfect Gun   **135**
Elizabeth Bear

Oracle   **155**
Dominica Phetteplace

In Everlasting Wisdom   **167**
Aliette de Bodard

Command and Control   **187**
David D. Levine

Conversations with an Armory   **213**
Garth Nix

Heavies   **223**
Rich Larson

Overburden   **243**
Genevieve Valentine

Weather Girl   **265**
E. J. Swift

Mines   **293**
Eleanor Arnason

ZeroS   **315**
Peter Watts

INTRODUCTION

WELCOME TO *INFINITY Wars*, the sixth book in the Infinity Project. The Infinity Project started in 2011 with the simple idea of asking some of the best writers working in science fiction and fantasy today to revisit some of its core ideas and themes in refreshing new ways. As the title *Infinity Wars* might suggest, this time we're looking at the future of war itself, something that has been a part of science fiction since its earliest days.

The way Western society looks at war and warfare has changed so significantly over the past century or so that in some ways it has rendered how people felt about war at the beginning of the 20th century alien to a modern reader. I remember reading accounts of the Great War of 1914-1918 when I was at university and being struck by the eagerness, the *need*, to enlist and to serve Queen and Country, to be a part of the war, where young men (mostly) lied about their age so they wouldn't 'miss out'. It was a reflection of the time, when war and conflict still had an aura of excitement and opportunity, and that excitement was combined with a deep sense of commitment to the institutions of society. While new military technology had led to a terrible number of deaths during the US Civil War, it was only during the Great War that fact was really brought home on a personal and visceral level outside the US as troops died in staggering numbers in the trenches of Europe.

Projections of war in science fiction of the time had focused on airships and submarines and the like, with books such as George Griffiths *The Angel of the Revolution* (1893) and *Olga Romanoff* (1894) telling rather fanciful stories of new military adventure without any real substantive change to the view of how wars were fought (Michael Moorcock would go on to parody this type of adventure in his 1970s novels *The Warlord of the Air* and *The Land Leviathan*). This changed during the period between the Great War and World War II, with new military science fiction taking a distinctly apocalyptic stance, seeing war as more likely to end civilization than anything else.

This doomsday vision of warfare in fiction deepened after the Second World War. The technology developed and deployed during that War—large-scale air forces, nuclear weapons, rocketry, and so on—made it clear that doomsday was not only possible, but likely. The belief that war was justifiable or survivable was strongly tested, and post-World War II science fiction shared those doubts. The Pulp Era was in full swing, space opera was the fiction of the day, and conflict was intergalactic in scale and devastation was theatrical and overblown. You need only look back to A.E. van Vogt's "Black Destroyer" and *The War Against the Rull*, the work of E.E. 'Doc' Smith, the work of Eric Frank Russell, and even Pohl and Kornbluth's Gunner Cade (as by Cyril Judd) to see that. But even in amongst the overblown theatre of space opera, there were doubts.

Robert A. Heinlein (we were always going to get to him) spent most of the 1950s writing a series of popular juvenile SF novels, many of which dealt with life and work in our Solar System. He capped the decade with one of his most enduring works, *Starship Troopers*. The Korean War had filled the early part of the decade, stumbling to its never-ending pause in 1953, and it affected how writers saw the future of war. The intervention of troops from the United Nations was a new type of military action, bringing the idea of a world government to the fore. *Starship Troopers* sat in this world, with its philosophical discussions of the morality of war and the cost soldiers paid for taking part. The issues raised in *Starship Troopers* would be debated elsewhere in science fiction, in books like Gordon Dickson's *Dorsai* novels and the work of Poul Anderson.

If the Korean War, the development of atomic weapons and the rise of the Cold War impacted on science fiction and forced writers everywhere to grapple with the moral justifiability of war, it would be a book by a returning Vietnam soldier, Joe Haldeman, that would be the next major step forward in military science fiction. *The Forever War* (1974) put the boots-on-the-ground grunt at the forefront of science fiction, and gave SF a glimpse of the price soldiers paid on a personal level when put in harm's way. It was a book that questioned the value of war itself, and the Vietnam War in particular. Vietnam would continue to influence SF and the discussion of war for the remainder of the century, as can be seen in Jack Dann and Jeanne Van Buren Dann's landmark anthology *In the Field of Fire* and novels like Elizabeth Ann Scarborough's *The Healer's War*, Bruce McAllister's *Dream Baby*, Lucius Shepard's *Life During Wartime* (a fix-up which includes the hallucinatory novella "R&R"), and David Drake's *Hammer's Slammers* stories.

The discussion of war and the military continued through the last years of the 20th century and into the new century in less militaristic and often mercenary-driven stories from writers like Lois McMaster Bujold, Elizabeth Moon, Larry Niven, and Elizabeth Bear. This anthology, which sits in a tradition of military science fiction/war anthologies dating back to Michael Moorcock's *Before Armageddon* and *England Invaded*, Dann's *In the Fields of Fire*,

Jerry Pournelle's *There Will Be War* series, Reginald Bretnor's *The Future at War*, and Martin H. Greenberg's Ace/Tor *Military Science Fiction* and 3000 *Military Science Fiction* sequences, and *The Best Military Science Fiction of the 20th Century*, aims to look at what comes next.

With the terrorist attacks on New York and Washington DC in 2001 and the subsequent wars in Iraq, Afghanistan and Libya; and the rise of terrorism generally, and ISIL in particular, our view of war is changing again. War seems to have evolved from an easy-to-spot state-vs.-state conflict to something muddier and harder to understand, where individual acts of terrorism contrast with hi-tech conflict conducted at arm's-length by soldier-bureaucrats with devastating affect for those on the ground.

And so *Infinity Wars* takes up the challenge: some of today's best writers take on the question of what war as we now know it might look like in fifty years, in a hundred, here on Earth, and in the distant corners of the galaxy. You'll find glimpses of the smoldering remains of space opera in some of the stories, most notably in stories from Caroline M. Yoachim and Elizabeth Bear, alongside slick, dark glimpses into Fifth-Generation warfare from Peter Watts, Eleanor Arnason, E.J. Swift, and others. You'll see how future war, and our approach to it, continues to change, since it seems we may always be involved in some kind of war or another.

Above all, I hope you'll enjoy the stories here as much as I have. The Infinity Project continues—I'm already hard at work on book seven—and more than anything else, it's about delivering great science fiction to you. See you next time!

Jonathan Strahan
Perth, Western Australia

THE EVENING OF
THEIR SPAN OF DAYS
Carrie Vaughn

OPAL'S KINGDOM LOOKED out at stars, facing away from a dim home sun to the black frontier and the spaceways that stretched to forever; to colonies and shipping lanes; to survey missions and scout satellites; and great huge swathes of unknown everything. Tennant Station was the last Trade Guild outpost along this vector, the farthest-reaching tendril of exploration and settlement that seemed immense—hundreds of planets, thousands of ships, billions of people—until it stood up against what still lay beyond.

Her realm: ten maintenance docks, a hundred twilight-shift personnel, a supervisor she preferred not to deal with, and pervasive supply problems. Tennant Station could repair anything, its mission statement said. Manufacture anything, supply anything. But they still needed raw materials, and had to wait for delivery. And wait.

"Laser welders wear out," said Henry, Bay Four crew chief, standing at an empty gear rack. Even the cap shoved crookedly on top of his curly black hair looked frustrated. "The lenses fog up, crack. We're down to three. If we had six, we'd finish in half the time."

This was mechanic math, and Opal wasn't sure it would hold up to scrutiny. Behind the gear rack, a dozen fixer stations lined up before the docking tube. Half threw sparks and rattled with the noise of grinding metal and hissing welders as they repaired components and refurbished modules. The other half were quiet, robotic arms tucked away, welders and riveters still. Needing repairs, needing parts they didn't have and attention from already overworked crew.

She'd been staring out the small viewport in the bay, half listening to Henry and half lost in thought. Beyond the docking tube and maintenance airlocks, *ISV Marigold* sat parked for refit. It was an older freighter, scarred, painted, repainted. Still very much serviceable, if she was taken care of. The floodlights of the repair dock washed over her, erasing shadows, bringing out details. Lumps, compartmentalized; engines attached to cargo holds attached to living spaces—Opal could pick out the parts of the ship, guess some of its history in the way additions had been made, sensor dishes and antennae connected.

The lights washed out the field of black and points of stars beyond the station, but Opal knew the rest of space was there, beyond this island of light and life.

Drones worked around the ship, thrusting across its metal skin, examining every crack and seam, removing components for repair, tagging areas for human inspection. Two of Henry's crew were outside in exo-suits. Opal could just see them through the square viewport, working, herding drones. A flash of movement, one arm raised to show an all-clear sign to the other.

All as it should be, working as it always had, even the complaints.

"I'll make a note, but I can't promise miracles," she said.

Henry made fists and pleaded with the ceiling. "Yeah? Well you'll be the one who has to tell the captains why their refits are behind schedule."

They had this conversation nearly every day. Opal gave him a cheerful smile and walked on to the next bay. Her kingdom, a well-lit stretch of corridor that curved enough to notice, so that the floor met the ceiling far ahead. Steel archways marked each repair bay, and most of them echoed with industrial noise. She breathed in the smell of old grease and burning plastic. Some days she felt she was a small thing moving through it all, the plain gray corridor reaching above her, the station's spin pinning her to the floor in a way that was odd to think about.

"Opal!" At the next arch, the next repair bay, Zare dashed out to block her path. The woman was young and prone to panic – this was her first placement as crew chief. Her eyes always seemed too big for her head, and their implanted optical enhancements, repairing a childhood injury, glinted green and metallic. "Thank goodness you're here. We're falling so far behind. We keep blowing fuses, we really need a power rationing exemption for this job. Tell them that if they want this done on time we've got to get an exemption, right?"

Opal listened patiently and answered, "You can't possibly be using that much power."

"Oh, but we are!"

"Let's check the logs." Opal tapped the pad on her wrist, and her headset, mashed over her pale braided hair, displayed the data, columns of numbers, labelled and color coded, highlighted to show trends—and yes, they needed that much power, the workload had gone up, but none of their supply rations had. "Everybody's stretched a bit thin right now."

"Have you *seen* what's on our schedule?"

Opal winked. "I made the schedule."

Zare groaned, head tipped back, much like Henry had, and Opal moved on. Start of the shift, she talked to everyone. And still reached Supervisor Creedy's office too soon. Maybe she should have lingered to argue with everyone a little longer.

The terminal outside his door spotted her, scanned her, and asked her to wait. This, too, was normal, and soon enough Creedy's voice came through the speaker. "Lamb? Come in." The man's voice always seemed to have an edge to it, as if the next person requesting entry might be security wanting to arrest him. Opal hadn't found any dirt on him yet, and she'd tried.

The door slid open, she stepped through. A smooth desk sat in the middle of the floor, cluttered with terminal screens and heads-ups, handhelds stacked to one side. Creedy hunched over the desk, hands folded together, peering at one of the screens as if he didn't trust it. A display on the back wall scrolled through stock images of planet-side scenes from Earth, oceans and mountains, as different from the station as one could hope for.

She tapped her wrist pad to transfer a data file to him. "Good morning, sir. There's today's requisitions list. Unfulfilleds rolled over from yesterday as usual."

He barely glanced at it. "It keeps getting longer."

"Supply's always been an issue. We make do."

"Can't you do something about it?"

Her lips quirked a smile. "Once you sign the list I can submit it to requisitions. After that I'll do what I can."

Grumbling, Creedy pressed his thumb to the screen of his terminal.

She added, "You might think of calling the director—"

"I can't just call the director."

In fact, he could: it was part of his job. *Opal* had called the director, who was as overworked and under pressure as everyone else on the station. And no one could magically raise the power rations or manufacture a new set of laser welders until someone higher up the chain – maybe even the Trade Guild BoD – realized that Tennant Station needed five more fabrication units at least, as well as more solar generators and batteries. At least, it did if it was going to do its job properly.

Tennant was too big to function efficiently, but too small to get the attention that would make it function efficiently. An odd middle ground, out here on the frontier.

She tried again. "If we could implement the inventory software stationwide instead of doing it piecemeal by department..." She suspected there was an extra fabricator sitting in storage, in a carbon fiber crate that no one had bothered to label or open. If only they could track it down...

"We'll see, we'll see," Creedy mumbled at his terminal, which he continued peering at skeptically, probably only to avoid looking at Opal.

Her kingdom was made up of ten repair bays. Creedy's was the entire dockyard of Tennant Station. He seemed to exist in a state of constant, vague desperation.

"I'll see you tomorrow, sir," she said—not heaving a frustrated sigh today—and turned to leave.

"Lamb!"

"Yes?"

"How long has *Marigold* been here?"

Marigold, Henry's problem child in Bay Four. Opal checked her wrist pad. "Four days."

"And it still isn't ready?"

"If the captain hadn't brought her *five years* past her scheduled maintenance refit, it wouldn't take us a week and four crews to put her back together."

"So it'll take a week. I can tell that to Captain Ray?"

Opal's smile curled sharper. "Tell him two."

*   *   *

OPAL'S OFFICE WAS nothing like Creedy's actual room with an actual desk and a door that closed. Pretty pictures for the wall and places for visitors to sit. Her nominal office was an open closet with a fold-down surface, a terminal display mounted to the wall, and a swivel chair bolted to the deck. At any given moment the terminal was flashing with messages and conference requests, and data files sent to her by everyone on the station. Often actual components and broken pieces of equipment were left on the desk. Everyone had some new example of metal stress failure to show her. She was cataloguing them in one of her databases.

Not that she spent much time at her cozy, cluttered station. Most of the time she had incoming messages and data fed directly to her headset. Saved time.

Morning rounds finished, she left the dockyard and took a lift three sections down. A more interior deck of the station, her steps were a little light here, the curve of the corridors a little steeper. The atmosphere was just as industrial, the air heady with the smell of oil and heat. The temperature was up from the dockyard. Further from the skin, further from the cold.

"Afternoon, Shelby," she announced herself, approaching the workstation of her counterpart in Fabrication.

"Opal. Right on schedule." He was a big man sitting cramped up on the bolted down stool in his own office cubby-hole. His headset was off his ear and hanging down around his shoulder. "What d'you need today?"

"Whatever you can get me."

He sat back from his terminal and the data he'd been looking at. "Well, that's non-specific."

Behind him, beyond shielding windows, drone fabricators worked, but the Fabrication Department was on power rationing, too. Three-quarters of their drones were operating and they didn't have enough raw material to supply every request.

"It's one of those days, but I think laser welders are a priority today. We've got a couple of ships in for refit that are sucking us dry."

"Only going to get worse," he muttered.

She cocked her head. "What have you heard?"

He hesitated a moment, which told Opal this wasn't offhand gossip. This was the result of threads of data Shelby had followed and considered. He talked to everyone on the station, he knew it all.

"You know we're not really the edge, right?" he said softly.

"Edge of what?" she said skeptically, leading. She knew what he was talking about, but drew him out.

"The universe isn't flat. You don't go off in one direction and hit the edge. There are other frontiers, where other people and other ships went out. We catch flashes of them—we always have. What happens when we run into them full force?"

"Myths and rumors," she said, unconvincingly. Unauthorized colony ships, lost explorers from hundreds of years before, planting flags and building their own unknown territories. Trade Guild kept good records. Nobody could get this far out without leaving a trail. Unless, of course, they had. Empires, lying in wait. The shipping lanes were filled with stories. "We'd know," she insisted. "We'd be talking to them."

He shrugged, as if to say, maybe.

"People have been telling tales for years. What are they talking about *now*?" she asked. There'd always been ghost stories, captains and crews coming in talking about being shadowed, blips on their scanners that might have been stray asteroids or might have been other ships, powered down: sensor outposts where they shouldn't have been; drones that didn't look like Trade Guild's. Shelby could tell any one of those stories and it wouldn't mean anything.

"Com traffic from MilDiv's up twenty percent," he said, and

that made her stomach drop. Military Division—again, could mean anything. They were running exercises in the area. They were scouting for new outpost sites. But that was a hard piece of information she hadn't had before, and data made rumors real.

"Right, okay. If you hear anything more, maybe let me know?"

Shelby turned back to his monitor, offhand, as if it didn't mean anything." Yeah. Likewise. Now, what did you say you need? Laser welders? Machinery like that takes a while to fabricate, especially if our power ration gets cut—"

"I don't need whole laser welders. Just the lenses, and the kids upstairs can put 'em back together."

He nodded. "Hold on a sec." Clambered up, went around the corner to a set of coded cabinets. Held his headset up to his face, consulting a file before tapping the code into the right drawer. Popped it open and drew out a small, innocuous plastic box, which he handed over to her like a prize.

She thumbed open the latch and found her welder lenses, of various sizes and calibrations, nestled in padded slots. Henry was going to cry.

"Thank you very much," she said, resisting an urge to hug the box to her chest.

"It's because you're the only one who ever comes down to ask for things in person," he said.

"Gives me a chance to stretch my legs."

BACK UP IN the dockyards she was so focused on getting the lenses to Henry and so happy to be able to do so that she didn't notice Captain Ray of the *Marigold* lying in wait at her work station. Arms crossed, shoulder up against the bulkhead, he spotted her and charged.

"Chief Lamb! I need my ship!"

Not even a hello, first. "Captain, I understand you're anxious, but the status is the same. We'll finish when we finish, we don't do rush jobs here."

"It's been four days already—"

"And what you said was standard maintenance turned into a major refit."

"That's a load of—"

"You really ought to talk to Creedy about this, if you have a complaint about our work."

He stopped, took a breath. Managed to collect himself, which he didn't often bother to do when speaking to dock workers. "Lamb. I really need to get *Marigold* and crew out of here and inbound before... we just need to leave as soon as possible." He hitched a thumb over his shoulder in a direction meant to be *away*.

Marigold had burned out part of its drive getting here, making a two-week run in ten days. Henry had asked the pilot why the hurry, and the woman, her eyes shadowed, shook her head and said this was safer. Was that rumor, or data?

"She'll be ready as soon as possible, sir. If you'd talk to Supervisor Creedy—"

"I already did, he said to talk to you."

Of course he did.

"Captain, I'll keep sending you daily reports. All right?"

His expression trembled, simmering at the unfairness of the universe. He pointed. "I'll be waiting for those reports." Steps pounding on deck plates, he stalked away.

"That'll teach you to skip maintenance checks," she muttered after him.

Touching her wrist pad, she raised the heads-up on the Bay Four external vid feed and confirmed that yes, it would take at least a week to finish *Marigold*. Her external drive was dismantled. Only one laser welder was throwing off a functional glow. Well, she could fix that, at least.

She hopped between several other external feeds, including a couple from some of the drones working further out from the station. Swept them across the traffic lanes, curious about how busy they really were, how much was really incoming. Nothing looked particularly unusual. Distant hulls flashed, reflecting the light of their home star. Colored running lights blinked in the dark. Yes, they were busy. Busy, but orderly. Not quite at full chaos, and she hoped to keep her little kingdom in that state.

ON HER WAY back to docks a comm request came through, and she paused at the side of the corridor to answer it. The image of Astin, engineering chief for the entire station, appeared as a small bust in the upper right corner of her display.

"What's wrong?" Opal asked, because something must be.

Astin, a slender woman with close-cropped black hair and a serene gaze, blinked back at her. "Nothing. Why? Is something wrong?"

"Nothing apart from the usual. I think."

"Well good. Because I thought I was calling with good news— we're raising your power ration. You should be able to move up some of those repair timetables."

"Oh, that's excellent," Opal said. "You've increased capacity then?" Life support and food production always got first dibs on what power the station's generators and solar cells produced. The dockyards might have been a big part of Tennant's reason for existing, but they ended up pretty far down the priority ladder on necessities. Couldn't do much else if they couldn't stay alive.

Astin's smile turned wry. "We've done some reorganizing. So just to warn you, the ration increase may not be permanent. Might want to use it while you can."

"Right, I'll pass that along. Any other reorganizing that might trickle down to docks?"

Her gaze narrowed, her lips pressing tight. Instantly suspicious. "Why, what have you heard?"

"What do you mean, what have I heard? Nothing, that's why I am asking." Nothing, but Ray's anxiety and Shelby's hints and her own general growing sense of tension.

"What has Creedy told you?"

"Nothing," she said, curbing frustration. Creedy would be the last person to know if anything was going on.

"Everything's status quo. Except for some bureaucratic shuffling, we're fine." She said this firmly, like she wanted it to be true.

Opal fished. "Any word floating around up top about MilDiv?"

Now the look in the woman's eyes was fear. Tamped down and managed, but still there. Tautly she said, "Nothing at all, Chief Lamb. Signing off now. Have a good day." This sounded like a threat, somehow.

"Yes, same to you," she replied, but the comm line had already closed, the image vanished.

Henry actually hugged her when she handed over the welder lenses, which he'd never done before. Rather than making her feel appreciated, the gesture added to her sense of unease. She felt like she was waiting for something large to break.

When he let her go, she said, "And would you believe we've got an increase in our power ration?"

He frowned suddenly. "What's wrong?"

"You know, that's exactly what I was thinking. I don't know. Might be nothing. It just... feels off, you know?"

Henry shrugged. He was still clutching the box of lenses in both hands, and Opal focused on that, that something had gone right today.

"Just something in the air," he said. "It'll pass."

"Yeah, I'm sure it will," she said.

"It's like Kay over on Team Two says. Nothing to worry about until MilDiv shows up." He chuckled, but Opal didn't.

"If MilDiv shows up we'll have more to worry about than just... well, worrying, won't we?"

The levity disappeared. "Do you think it's if or when? For MilDiv, I mean."

She considered her own fears nesting in the primal part of her brain, the part that said to *run*, knowing full well that out here on a place like Tennant there was absolutely no place to run to. Just keep turning in circles until the atmosphere gave out. What a way to live.

Ships were better, a lot of space-faring folk believed. At least ships were a moving target.

"Let's just see if we can get *Marigold* out of here ahead of schedule. At least then we won't have to keep hiding from Captain Ray."

"Found you, did he?"

"Yes, he did."

"Right. Priority: getting Ray off station."

She smiled her thanks.

BACK AT HER closet office she sat for a moment to catch her breath, update the task list, and have a quick snack and a pouch of coffee. Already staring at her terminal, she got the new traffic alert as soon as it came in. This was how she kept on top of incoming repair jobs—by listening in on sensor feeds from traffic control. She knew what was inbound before the official requests came in. Gave her just an extra few moments to plan, to find the space, to assign the crews.

She tapped into traffic control to get a better read on the arriving ship—size, name, crew, whatever maintenance history they had on file. And the feed shut down. The whole terminal crashed. A couple commands on her wrist pad revived her general computer access, but traffic control was still down.

Down, or blacked out?

She messaged traffic control ops directly over her headset. "Hey, guys, I'm trying to get a transponder reading off an incoming ship, but your system went down. Is there a problem?"

The response—voice only—sounded like it came from Ain, one of the shift chiefs, but stress made him sharp. "We've just gone on security lockdown, Opal. I'm sorry, can't talk." The line shut off.

Opal waited for the sirens to start. They didn't. Not yet anyway. Her shift was close to wrapping up, but she didn't log out of the terminal or start her last rounds. She sat on her stool, waiting.

The next call came from Shelby. Opal jumped at the beep, then pressed her headset to her ear as if that would make his voice any clearer.

"Opal? Is it true we're on security lockdown? Do you know what's happening?"

"I thought it was just traffic control on lockdown, not the whole station. I don't know what's happening."

"Surely station ops would send out an all-hands if something was wrong. Wouldn't they?"

"I don't know." Nothing had ever gone *that* wrong before, not in the three years she'd been here. "Traffic control signaled an incoming then went into lockdown. That's all I know."

"The incoming—hostile?"

"I said I don't know. I've got to go, Shelby. If I find anything out I'll message."

The whole station would be filled with rumors. Well, if the station director didn't want rumors flooding the place, then ops ought to make an announcement. She'd try to keep the gossip out of the dockyards as long as she could, for no other reason than to prevent distraction. 'Get Ray off station as soon as possible' was an admirable goal for the moment. Apart from that, she'd wait for the chain of command to kick in. Which meant waiting for Creedy to pass along news and orders. Which might or might not ever happen.

She couldn't stand not knowing. She ducked into an out-of-the-way repair bay, one of the ones with its drones shut down. She didn't want anyone to find her in the next few minutes. In the relative peace and quiet, she called up vid feeds from her external repair drones. Jumped between several of them, most of which focused on *Marigold* and restoring its external drive. Other drones worked at ships further around on the station cylinder, but these seemed to be closest to the blip she'd found on the traffic feed before getting locked out.

One of the drones was on standby, waiting for the next step in the repair and not involved in anything critical at the moment. Opal sent commands, and turned the drone's camera eyes outward, to the black. Turned up the magnification, set the scanners to search.

And there it was. Traffic control had diverted regular ship traffic to starward, leaving a great empty section of space on the other side of the station. In the middle of this space was an island of motion, glints of running lights and the occasional flash of reflected star. Opal increased the zoom on the vid as far as she could and brought the scene into focus. Lights from shuttles and tugs swept across the hull of a MilDiv courier, a big interstellar ship, fast and bristling with sensor arrays. She recorded an image of the markings, checked the ship ID database—the *TGS Kestrel*. And it was broken. A chunk of it seemed to be missing, in fact. At first, Opal thought the angle of the view was wrong, but no. *Kestrel* was leaking sparks from a gash in its hull that cut through an engine pod. It wasn't a collision; corrosion and deformation marked the wound, blackened oxidization streaking around it, the scars left by fire and escaping atmosphere. Something had blasted the ship. How had it even survived to limp back to port? The crew must have been frantic—

Opal took it all in, unable to turn away from that sight, the vision of the world changing. She didn't think it would happen like this.

"Opal?"

She started, as if from a trance. Hypnotized by those images, that scene, the ship more broken than any she had ever seen, that would likely soon be coming to her bays for help. But they didn't have enough power, enough supplies, enough crew—

"Opal."

It was Henry, standing with a hand on the arch, looking in worriedly.

"Oh. Yes? I'm sorry, I was..." She shook her head.

"What is it?"

Kestrel must have hurled itself through a jump after the fight that broke it, using the last of its crew, praying the hull held together. Nothing left now but to pick up the pieces. Wonder if what happened to it would happen again. How soon it would happen again.

She ought to tell Henry to get back to work, that nothing was wrong. She ought to wait for whatever orders came from up top.

"Henry. There's a ship going to be coming in, very badly hurt. We've got the clear bays in Eight and Nine. I'm betting that's where they'll send it. Not sure what's going to happen next, just get ready to jump whichever way they call for, right? Pass it along."

Henry stared at her, amazed. "Opal, what's happened?"

"Just be ready to jump. I've got to see Creedy."

She left Henry staring after her. She needed to tell Creedy, to prime him for what was coming. She tried to walk down the long, curved corridor as if nothing was wrong.

Some of her crew called out to her. Zare, coming out of Bay Three, calling, "Opal, that power ration still isn't enough—"

And then Jon from Bay Two. "Opal, I need to talk—"

She waved them away and kept walking. Shut down a series of ordinary comm requests beeping on her headset until she pulled the thing off her ear and left it hanging on her shoulder. She didn't have time, she didn't want to know. Not until she identified that incoming problem, and had answers to too many questions.

The terminal at Creedy's office scanned her as she approached, and the door opened.

"Sir, I need to talk—"

Creedy wasn't there. The man, almost a part of the furniture, never moving from behind the shield of his desk, was gone. The room didn't look right without him. The screen on the back wall, its pretty scenic pictures, was dark.

Instead, Station Director Ahmen, his eyes shadowed and his station uniform looking uncharacteristically rumpled, stood before the desk, showing a hand terminal display to a tall woman in a MilDiv uniform standing next to him. Even without the uniform Opal would have spotted her as MilDiv—polished, ramrod straight yet supple as rubber, like she was used to the gravity going out at any moment and could wrestle people off the ceiling without sweating. She had a bright new bruise on her pale cheek. More than that she was tired, the lines on her frown deeper than her seeming forty-odd years warranted. Her reaction to Opal's entrance—a glance and a blink—seemed delayed.

Director Ahmen said, "Chief Lamb. We were just about to call you."

"Sir?" she said weakly. And where had Creedy gone?

"This is Commander Deshan."

"Sir," she said in greeting.

"Chief," Deshan answered. Opal was surprised at how soft her voice was. Maybe it was a symptom of fatigue. "There's a ship coming in that will need an immediate berth and priority attention."

"Yes, I know. Sir." The commander tilted her head, inquiring. No sense in dissembling. "I knew something must be up, so I checked an external vid feed and found the *Kestrel*."

"Ah," Deshan said.

"I told you she was our best," Ahmen said. "Chief Lamb, is this going to be a problem?"

"No. We'll have to do some shuffling of crews, but we can handle it."

"Good," Deshan said, her voice melting a bit. With relief? "You'll report to me throughout repairs and for the foreseeable future. I'll have one of my crew look at your current workload to determine which jobs are essential or non-essential, in order to prioritize essential work. All traffic is locked down until we can make that rating. I expect there to be a lot more work for you coming in soon."

"Sir?" She looked back and forth between the pair. Things were moving quickly now.

"You're being promoted, Lamb," Director Ahmen said. "Dock supervisor. We're counting on you to keep things moving."

"But where is Creedy?"

Ahmen said, "He's being transferred."

Part of her wasn't at all surprised. She tried to imagine Creedy dealing with the preternatural Commander Deshan, and simply couldn't. So part of her wasn't surprised. But part of her was horrified.

"We're being militarized," she said, just so she was clear.

"Yes," Ahmen said.

Deshan lowered her gaze, as if she was sorry. Just for a moment. "Chief Lamb, you'll have the field rank of master sergeant until a more formal command structure can be established. The chiefs will report to you, you'll report to me. It's probably best if you pass the news along to your crews and start your reorganization as soon as possible."

Opal didn't know anything about being a master sergeant, but she supposed she'd learn.

"You should know—yes, we can work on your ship, we'll strip parts out of our own repair bays if we have to. But we've had supply problems for months now, and a power deficit. As far out as we are, Tennant Station just hasn't been a priority, and we're behind on upgrades—"

"Noted," Deshan said. "I'll pass that information along."

Deshan seemed to expect her to turn around and leave now. Maybe even salute, then turn with a smart click of her heels. Opal didn't make the attempt, lest it seem mocking.

She lingered an extra moment. "Commander, would you please express our sympathies—all of us in the dockyard's sympathies—to the *Kestrel*'s crew?"

Deshan smiled thinly and nodded. "I will. Thank you."

Opal left.

By the time she reached her closet, the director was making a station-wide announcement, something about a state of emergency, encroaching hostilities, martial law. Opal had to shuffle crews —she'd put the best in charge of *Kestrel*. Henry's crew. It might only take a little shifting around. But she didn't know what she was going to tell Captain Ray about *Marigold*. He'd be calling any second. What happened would likely depend on whether Deshan and her people decided if *Marigold* was essential or non-essential. Essential for what?

Three bays could work on *Kestrel*, which should dock at Nine. Out of the way, plenty of room.

Then, she stumbled, so much so that she had to put her hand against the chill wall. An image had caught her, of her little kingdom in flames, whole sections crumbling as they decompressed, the station collapsing, tumbling out of orbit—

She locked that image out, never to be thought of again. Ever.

She was about to message Ahmen to ask for Deshan's contact information—she should have asked the commander, but she'd been too flustered. Maybe she could call traffic control directly, assuming things had settled down there. Then her terminal beeped with an incoming file from Deshan: a set of military requisition forms, for expedited supply and delivery of any and all tools, materials, personnel, and power ration she thought she would need for the next six months, given the likelihood of a high number of repairs involved catastrophic damage.

Blank, unlimited requisition forms. Opal had never seen such a thing. She didn't know such a thing existed. This was it, she could have anything she wanted.

It wasn't enough.

THE LAST BROADCASTS
An Owomoyela

DAJA HADN'T BEEN out to Relay Point before, and would have left it that way. Not that she wasn't glad, or at least resigned, to do whatever the Coordination Office needed her to do, but she didn't love space enough to see her relocation from Colossus as a step *up*. Or even as an adventure. Instead, as the station came into sight—ring upon ring of utilitarian grey, barely brushed with light from Sato System's now-distant star, all but lost against the snowy visual static of interplanetary space—she couldn't help but think her first priority was to secure a transfer back to planetside as soon as possible. Doing so would have to wait until she learned why she was here.

She'd been practicing her focus on the way up, eschewing the sensory-limiting headset which was probably a good idea, but stepping off the shuttle hit her with so much stimuli that she stood dumb in the concourse for a good two minutes. All her energy went into trying to just see *grey walls, white floor, people*, and not the flash of light along *that* person's scarf, shattering into little glints, visual pepper, sharp and arresting, gold against crimson, or—

The thing was, there was so much detail in every environment— sound, temperature, motion, color, light intensity, subliminal social interpretation, taste, smell, *so much* of it—that her mind couldn't process it all. Never had been able to. So, like a kind of defense mechanism, she'd find herself caught on some little singular detail which would swell up to occupy her entirely, and she›d lose the rest of the world in it.

The station's automated helper chimed at her from a console nearby. She didn't notice it at first, until it chimed louder, more insistently, and spoke from a place that seemed like it was inside her skull.

((Hello, Daja! Welcome to Relay Point. Please step into one of the privacy booths for a second.))

Daja glanced around. A few of the other passengers were veering off toward consoles at the wall; receiving their own instructions, probably, either beamed to implants or delivered via the much lower-tech focused directional sound. Narrow noses or broad hands or uneven gaits—one of them made her unbalanced just to *look* at, and his footsteps rattled unevenly against her ears. She closed her eyes. Opened them. Glanced around again; a nearby door rewarded her with an encouraging flash of gentle light, something that might have been more obvious to someone other than her, and she stepped through. The door slid closed behind her.

((Welcome,)) the station helper said again, this time playing ambient. *((How was your travel?))*

"Long," Daja answered honestly. "Overwhelming. I want to see my quarters and get a meal." *Acclimatize.* "Is that... is that all set up?"

((Of course,)) the helper said. *((Everything's ready for you to move in, and your work schedule's been generated. It's ready for your review at any time. Before you start, though, you need to acknowledge the Office's confidentiality and non-disclosure policies. You'll be held to their standards for the duration of your work here, and indefinitely thereafter.))*

The helper's voice was a very good synthetic, but there was still a buzz to it, as though it was wavering just a bit too fast for a human voice to catch. Daja considered that, and then yanked her focus back to the content of the words. "This is in addition to everything I acknowledged when I received the assignment?"

((Yes. In addition to.))

Bureaucracy. Daja let out a breath. "Well, let me have it."

((You are being assigned to the Caribou Information Integrity Task Force. All information about the transmission, quality, or content of the Caribou data streams is classified. You are not to divulge or discuss any aspect of it, or of the specifics of your work, with any person not assigned to the Caribou Information Integrity Task Force, now or in the future, without the direct knowledge and permission of the Supervisor Sol Liaison.))

Daja's eyebrows shot up. "Data integrity is *classified*? What? Since when?"

((That date is classified.)) The automated helper wasn't properly intelligent, but Daja imagined it was smug. *((Please acknowledge.))*

"I... acknowledge," Daja said. "I've never worked on anything classified before." *Private before release*, yes, but that was different.

The automated helper didn't have a response to that. *((That's all I need,))* it said. *((Your supervisors are ready to meet you at your convenience. Or should I tell them you need to visit your quarters first?))* A hiccup, as though the assistant was accessing her file, appending something. *((The Sol Liaison is from Sol, you know. Arrived on the last transport, seven anno ago.))*

That was enticement, Daja had to admit.

She thought about it for a moment; going to a minimally-furnished room, maybe being there when her packs were delivered, or walking in to find all her things, ready for arrangement. The latter would probably be less disruptive. Of course, she *wanted* to return to a familiar environment as soon as possible; problem was, there wasn't a familiar environment available on Relay Point.

"I'll meet them," she said.

((*I'll let them know,*)) the helper said, and then rattled off a string of instructions which Daja winced at, then tried to commit to memory. ((*Query any of the consoles along the way if you have questions.*))

"I will," Daja said. "Thanks."

The door opened for her with a low sibilance.

She exited, and immediately a light outside one of the concourse windows caught her attention. It was the broad sweep of one of the station's inner rings, lit by the sun to almost glowing against the background starfield, cut dramatically as a knifestroke by the shadow of another ring beyond it.

This was a problem. Even with her focus broadened, grounded, trained, details always percolated up through Daja's unconscious, arriving at her conscious mind like unannounced visitors. And there was always some part of Daja's mind which greeted each one with the wonder of a child who didn't know to check with parents before inviting strangers in. Given enough time and she could learn to love this place, the steady purr of the air cyclers, the walls holding her close wherever she went. And she didn't *want* to love this place. She'd do her bit here, get her piece, and go back planetside. That was the plan.

Still, without a haze of atmosphere in the way, the starfield was breathtaking. And she was standing here, with only a window and distance between her and it. Looking out from this environment, across that landscape—and it was a kind of landscape, the rings and the light and the shadow—at the light which bathed them all, only to be scattered on the weight of air. She could love that. Maybe, in honesty, she did already. A little.

And turning back to the hall, someone had selected that

institutional grey and that white with care; they coordinated, like a... what was that Earth bird? The one with all the literary weight. Crow? Dove? And the white floors were scuffed, here and there, but cleaned so you›d hardly notice. Cared for.

She shook her head. *Supervisors.* Time to go.

DAJA HAD NEVER met an actual person from Sol before. Despite knowing, intellectually, that there was likely to be nothing special about him, she still couldn't help a hungry curiosity. Would he be abnormally tall by Sato System standards? One of those incredible pale-cream people, or the carbon-black ones, outside the bounds of normal Sato variation? What would his *accent* be like?

But when she walked into the office—oddly oblong, in a way that caught her attention and wouldn't release it for a second or two—the man from Sol was... average. A little on the weedy side, but he just looked weedy, not exotic. And his accent wasn't the cultured Earth Standard her ears had been trained by entertainments and news reports to expect. It was some other Sol System accent, one she couldn't identify. Maybe not from Earth at all.

"Daja." He gave her a curt nod. "I'm Supervisor Sol Liaison Bole Channing. This is Supervisor Sato Administrator Hatizda."

The other woman in the room was standing off to the side, with a pinched, fixed smile. A bit taller than Daja and bulkier, darker, and significantly older. Hair done up in some deceptively simple geometric pattern that Daja, with an effort, didn't get her attention lost in. Come to think of it, after the initial disappointment, Channing wasn't so average, either; his fingers moved restlessly, the tips of each one visiting his thumb in turn, and his breathing was deeper than his voice suggested, and carefully disciplined. Then he was on to his next sentence, and Daja wrenched her attention back.

"You know that the work of this office is to collect the datastreams from Caribou, correct any data degradation, and prepare it for transmission to Sol and Waheed."

He paused there, and it was a moment before Daja realized he was waiting for her confirmation. As though they had been worried that she actually *wouldn't* know that, when she arrived. But that was one of Sato System's claims to importance: it was a hinge world, on the transmission lines between two frontier systems and the great, ancient cradle of mankind. One of its roles, since Caribou had been settled—and Waheed settled, much more recently—was to receive the faster-than-light databursts, clean any corruption, and send the news on.

Information was the lifeblood of human civilization. Transports from one system to another were staggeringly expensive; they launched from Sol once every decade, and from Sato once every twenty-five. Caribou and Waheed hadn't yet built up the infrastructure to allow people to return. And the wait *for* the transports was only half of it; the transit from Sol to Sato crested fourteen anno, and the distance from Sato to Caribou and Waheed was longer than that.

But information—that was *comparably* fast, *comparably* cheap to launch across the intervening void, streaming faster than the speed of light. Difficult too, to be sure, and sending it from Caribou to Sol, Sol to Waheed, or *Caribou* to Waheed without its stop in Sato would probably leave it a garbled mess. She understood that even sent in triplicate, with data sanity checks, and a team of experts here to clean it up for re-transmission, there was still a lot of garbled mess to contend with.

Daja cleared her throat, and said, "Yes, I know that. I, um, don't know why I'm here. I'm not a technician."

"You've worked on entertainments before," Hatizda said. Daja's head snapped around to look at her. She was holding herself very still and formal; every time she spoke or took a breath, the gold fabric on her chest and shoulders shimmered. Compared to all her stillness, it amplified every movement. "Final detailing passes. We hear you're very good."

"I am," Daja said. It was one thing her aberrant brain was good for.

"Very easy to work with, as well," Hatizda said. "You take instruction very well. Not particularly argumentative."

She appreciated direction, honestly. It made for less mental noise. "You interviewed the creative teams?"

"Extensively," Hatizda said.

"Mm." Channing's thumbtip danced between his index and middle fingers; Daja's eyes were drawn back to it. "You should not have heard anything about this task force before your arrival. Had you?"

The *Caribou Information Integrity Task Force*. If she had heard of it, the name itself was bland enough that she'd forgotten it. "I don't think so, no."

Channing nodded, apparently satisfied. "We're a small group. Hatizda and I supervise thirteen people; you'll be the fourteenth. You will not meet any of your coworkers; their identities are classified, as is yours."

Daja held up a hand, and was momentarily distracted by the fact that her thumb had been copying some of Channings nervous tapping. "Sorry," she said. "I have a question. Why all the classification? I had to acknowledge—" They probably knew what she had to acknowledge. She skipped that. "I didn't think anything about the databurst processing was supposed to be classified."

Channing's hands stilled, but only because he folded them together. The light hit his sleeve cuffs: a sharp line, like they'd just been manufactured that day.

"Your work here," Channing said, every word crisp like his cuffs, "is to conceal that Caribou has been at war for the past four years."

*　　*　　*

THIS WAS NEW. Daja was used to the world being too much noise, hard to find the signal in. She wasn't used to the signal turning everything about the world to static.

It took her a moment to feel anything: the fabric on her body, the temperature of the air, her own breath sliding in through her nose. But then one detail surfaced: the tautness of Channing's lips as he watched her. And then she realized that this office was small, maybe smaller than her own room back on Colossus. But that was to be expected, really; planets had so much more space than stations did. Did Channing feel that way? Was he planet-born or station born, in Sol?

Then Daja recognized that he'd said *years*, not *anno*, but probably meant the same thing—the Earth year, the Earth-standard year period, not the stately 2.44-anno trip around the Sato sun which Colossus took in one of *its* years, or the... what were years like in Caribou? With its one settled, still-terraforming, world? Daja had a sudden moment of panic, a desire to be back on Colossus, in the embrace of its gravity, with the certainty that an unfathomably vast agglomeration of mineral was under her feet, and wasn't going anywhere. Not on a human timescale.

And then the *salient* detail hit her.

War. What did that—"What does that even *mean*?"

"It is not a civil war," Channing said, blotting out the single plausible explanation Daja had found. "They have been under attack from an external force. It is the considered belief of experts there, here, and in Sol that the system will be overrun within the next year and a half."

"Anno," Daja said, *sotto voce*. She hadn't meant to say it aloud at all. "But... *war*?"

"You'll get your head around it," Channing said. "In the meantime, your work, in conjunction with your peers, is to fabricate a convincing fiction explaining why that system will soon go dark. Information regarding the war cannot get out."

Daja tried to force a word out, but neither she nor her throat and tongue knew what the word was meant to be. In the absence, the air rushed in to fill her mouth; she thought she could taste some faint chemical tone. She turned to look at Hatizda, whose pinched smile had vanished. It had left wrinkles in its wake; this was a face which was accustomed, over the course of anno upon anno, to smiling. No smile now.

"We can't afford a panic," Channing said. Daja turned to look at him again. His eyes were oddly tinged with gold; it turned otherwise brown irises almost bronze. And his voice was kinder, she thought. Maybe. "Earth have run every number they have. Even with system-wide mobilization, we can't launch any force we could expect to make a difference."

We, she thought. Meaning: Earth? Sol System? Humanity? "But why—"

"Given the... *rate* at which this alien force is moving through the system," Channing continued, "we don't believe any other settled system is immediately at risk. We've already begun reallocating resources to build what defenses we can. Officials in the highest levels of government *have* been apprised, Daja. We're doing all we can. Letting the information leak would do nothing beyond unsettling billions of people—trillions, across several systems— and to no good end. I know it's not the most glamorous work, but you're working in the service of economic and social stability. We ask you to make sure people in these safe systems never begin to think that they are not, in fact, safe."

His rhythm had changed there, at the end. Words by rote. Thirteen coworkers, Daja thought: had all of them sat in this office, heard this speech?

"This is a hard job," Channing said. "I understand. The emotional toll speaks for itself." He shifted his weight, and those bronze-leaning eyes skittered across the wall behind Daja. "The last man in your position killed himself."

If this was meant to reassure, to offer some condolence or commiseration, Daja thought, it failed. Perhaps she'd finally met someone worse at reading other people than she was.

But fortunately, Hatizda took that moment to break in. "We'll offer you all the support we can. Don't be afraid to reach for it."

"And it helps to find some distance," Channing said, and Hatizda looked away. "We are... about to lose a colony. An experiment in extending humanity's reach. Your job will be to immerse yourself in Caribou's peculiarities so that you can detail a narrative which is convincing. Psychologically speaking, it will be easier if you focus on the alienness. It will reduce the impact."

"If you want it to be easy," Hatizda said, almost too low to hear.

Channing looked her way, but didn't respond. "They've deviated quite far from Earth-spectrum cultural matricies, in some ways. Do you know they recycle their dead into food out there?" His lips twisted. "I lodged a formal complaint, when I learned about it. You know what they came back with in the next databurst? 'Oh, we don't *butcher* them, we strip the proteins. It's all very processed, nothing recognizable as human biomatter. The ceremonies associated are quite beautiful. We can all share in the body of our beloved.' And a crate of nonsense about feeling closer to the deceased, not abandoning them to an impersonal cremation. That's what they called it. An 'impersonal cremation'." He shook his head. "Maybe you can use that. That cultural note won't be a great loss, don't you think?"

Two things occurred to Daja: one, that her home district back on Colossus recycled the dead into soil enrichers, some proportion of which went to feed the hydroponics and ground crops, and she wondered if that one remove really made a difference to Channing? Two, Earth-spectrum morality still included allowances for plenty of cultures which raised animals for meat—real animals, whole ones, with nerve endings and brains and fear responses, which were then killed for the purposes of butchering, and she had trouble seeing why the contours of Earth-spectrum should allow the one and not the other.

But she didn't say anything.

She kept not saying anything for a bit too long, apparently. Channing looked at her, and the force of his direct eye contact was too much. Daja looked away, felt the weight and volume of her tongue in her mouth rise up to compete for her awareness. Every little bump and ridge, every silent unevenness.

At length, Channing sighed. The sound, sliding around his teeth, mingling with the recycled air, made Daja's skin crawl.

"I understand," Channing said, "you must think I'm callous. You're still in shock. You have to understand, though, we've had years to come to term with it. Give it some time, and you'll start seeing the pragmatic side, too."

"Because you have to," Hatizda said. "Painful as it is. This is a job that needs to be done."

"I want," Daja said, tongue moving sluggishly in her bitter mouth, "to go to my quarters now."

HATIZDA ACTUALLY WALKED her to her quarters, which helped. She could pull Daja's attention back onto the path they were taking, when it wandered off onto how the shade of white on the floor made her diaphragm feel when she looked at it too long.

"You have access to the raw Caribou files," Hatizda said. "If it helps you to get to work, start by reviewing those. If you need anything, call me."

"Food," Daja said. "Where—"

"Call for food," Hatizda said. "I'll have the helper flag a few recommended venues."

So Daja went in. Stood for a while with her eyes and mouth open, trying to drink in as much of the space as she could, so that she could eventually learn *all* the details, classify them all as home. Home, and thus ignorable. Float-on-top-able. Without grounding, it was so very easy to let herself be lost.

Then she went to the console, and selected one of the flagged restaurants largely at random, and selected a dish, also largely at random. When it arrived, it was some large chunk of meat, charred lines crisping neat stripes across the surface, drippings making oily little brown puddles on the white plate. The plate was, she noticed, almost the same white as the hallway floors. Not scuffed, though, except for one very small chip by the rim, exposing the rougher material inside, probably too small for most anyone to notice.

She ate, mechanically.

The meat here was stringier than the meat grown back on Colossus, the fat less evenly distributed, the striations thicker. She asked the console about it; it chirped back with a pitch for the meal house. *((Gallilei Dish prides itself on serving the most authentic Earth cuisine available! No detail is overlooked.))*

It wasn't as good as Colossus-grown meat, Daja thought. Authenticity meant pretending that the meat had come from an animal, where the muscle was evolved and adapted for moving around, not for tasting good.

And that made her think of Channing, and his tapping fingers, and how he'd lodged a complaint as though he could reach across to another system and erase this one little cultural note he didn't like. Well, all the cultural notes were going to be erased soon, except for the ones Daja detailed into the Task Force's convenient cover-up fiction —and then a hard bit of spice caught in Daja's teeth, and yanked her attention around, and it was all the pressure of her bite, the sharp, sudden taste, the contrast between the little seed-or-whatever's texture and her tongue and enamel and gums.

When she got herself back on topic, she accessed her files on Caribou.

Raw material, the briefing notes said. She should cannibalize it for detail, sprinkle it into her fabricated reality. She wondered how much it mattered. Did the people who would consume this lie of hers care anything for authenticity?

She wanted, desperately, to speak with one of her coworkers from the old entertainment collabs, and she sent a video request without thinking about it: her fingers moved, muscle memory, all on their own.

But instead of any of her old friends appearing, it was Hatizda's face that blinked up onto the screen. Daja jumped back.

Hatizda's face was broad, Daja realized. Maybe it was only expectation, comparison, which made it so; the group channel she'd called tended to be frequented by narrower-featured people, on average. But Hatizda's face seemed to stretch on like horizons, framing her eyes, the wrinkles around her eyes, the eyebrows drawn together and up. *Sad?* Daja wondered. *Sad* was the emotion in those eyebrows there, wasn't it? The visual detail was there, but the meaning leaked out her ears. Per usual.

"You're trying to call home," Hatizda said.

Well, yes, Daja thought. *I know that.* So long as 'home' was defined as either *Colossus in general* or *Daja's group of friends*, which was apt enough. She stared at Hatizda, wondering if she was expecting an answer.

Maybe. It took a few seconds, and then Hatizda's eyebrows changed.

Bunched up together for a moment, then relaxed. Daja might as well try to read weather patterns in caterpillars crawling across a leaf; all her practice and study had been shaken up, here.

"We find—" Hatizda began, then frowned. "That is, we don't let new employees call out, for a… little while. I understand the urge. But the temptation to divulge is just too high. If you need to talk, though, I'm here to offer support." She sighed. The sound wasn't like Channing's, somehow. A wider fricative. "I know Supervisor Channing can come on a little strong." A moment more. "And heartless."

That startled Daja into a barking laugh. "Is he?"

"It's how he copes with it," Hatizda said.

So, yes, Daja thought. Choosing to be that way and being that way were the same enough to her ears. "I can't talk to my friends?"

"Write something," Hatizda said. "Text only. Or record a message. We'll review it, either way, and send it on. But officially, you're going to be too busy for a real-time call for a while."

So, no. Daja reached out and killed the call.

Then she queried the automated helper on how soundproof her room was, and then she screamed for a good thirty seconds.

Her throat was raw when she stopped, which didn't make her feel *better*, but did make her feel like the gravity had been reset. That it had returned to something tolerable, if not comfortable. She still had a restless energy crawling around her muscles, but she didn't know how to deal with that. All she wanted was a friendly ear, but she'd been explicitly forbidden that.

She pictured Channing and Hatizda as vault doors, sealed and reinforced, cutting her off from access just as they'd cut off supply depots for shuttle fuel, or the bays of large terraformers. Cutting her off from a simple call home the same way they strangled off every last word from Caribou.

Then she realized the comparison she was making and a hot wash of shame rolled over her, from the crown of her head down. And then, like a wake, anger followed the shame down. She reached out and triggered the call request again.

Sure enough, a second passed, and Hatizda was the one who answered again.

"*Daja,*" she began.

"No," Daja said. "I don't like it. Why do they keep sending databursts? Do they know nobody is listening?"

"Sol is listening," Hatizda said, and immediately corrected herself. "Sol leadership is listening. Caribou is providing important strategic intelligence. Sol leadership is doing everything they can to prepare all our systems for the possibility of invasion, without—"

"Without causing a panic." Daja shook herself. "Do they know everything is a secret, in Caribou? What have we been sending them?"

"You're not on the outbound Caribou databurst team," Hatizda said.

"Don't care."

Hatizda made her sighing noise, again. Daja could almost chart the notes on a scale: one long slide down. "Well, you were due for a crisis. I thought it might take you a little longer."

That threw Daja. "I'm not—"

"Meet me for tea," Hatizda said. "I'll send directions."

Well, it might wash the taste of the disappointing, 'authentic' meat dish out of her mouth. Daja shrugged.

Hatizda probably took that as agreement, which was fine. She ended the call, this time.

THE TEAHOUSE WAS clean, polished, arranged so that the space between the tables latticed itself like a tortoiseshell. For a moment after arriving, Daja imagined the tables themselves as the slow-moving creatures; imagined seeing one here, in the flesh, instead of in the media from Earth. Patterns within a pattern, tunneling into themselves like a fractal. Then she clapped her attention back to herself—two palms, hitting each other, and there she was, for a reason. A meeting. *Focus.*

Hatizda arrived minutes after her, and waved them back to a small privacy booth. No pleasing white space around the table, here. Just a table, in a room, with a screen that shut and blurred vision and blocked sound. Daja sat down, and felt the cushions give beneath her weight. They warmed—fast—to her body temperature.

"I'm not having a crisis," Daja said.

"Aren't you?"

Hatizda looked at her, and continued looking until Daja looked away. She could feel her pulse fluttering in a vein above her eye. Not pain, though, when she turned her attention to it.

"I want to talk to my friends," Daja said.

"You will. Eventually. Just not about this."

"And we're not Caribou's friends at all."

Hatizda didn't respond to that. Daja ground her teeth. Maybe the connection was too oblique; one of those things that only made sense to her.

"I want to tell you two secrets," Hatizda said. "Given the secrets you're already required to keep, two more shouldn't be a problem."

I don't think that's how problems are measured, Daja thought. "What are the secrets?"

A shadow approached the screen, and Hatizda reached over and keyed the entry permissions. A server—his apron was *very* bright, Daja noticed; it probably wasn't her imagination if it fluoresced, just a little, in the light—set down a tray with a pot and two small cups, and then retreated. Hatizda pressed the screen closed again.

"Tea?"

"Secrets," Daja said.

Hatizda reached over to the pot, and poured tea for both of them anyway. Daja winced. *Pay attention. Pay attention. Words, not smells.*

"I send messages out to Caribou," Hatizda said.

Daja stared, and thought her way through several responses. The smell of the tea, floral and bright, rose up through her sinuses, made it hard to think. Felt like her head was floating off. "Is that legal?"

"No. Not technically. I'm appropriating official resources, even if those resources are just a bit of time and bandwidth."

"What... do you say?"

Hatizda was silent for a few seconds. "The window for sending anything that they'll get before the end is closing. Mostly, I say 'I'm sorry.' And, 'I hear you.'"

Daja barked. "But no one else does."

"How many people have to?" Hatizda asked. "How soon? Does it really matter—does it matter in any actual, measurable way— if everyone in the settled systems learns about it now, while it's happening, instead of in fifty years, when we're all living in defended systems and Caribou is history? They're still all going to die."

Daja shifted. That reasoning didn't sit right with her, but she didn't have the words to explain why. Maybe it was a matter of, *we're all going to die. Eventually.* If she was hurting, she'd want someone to know while she was still alive.

If she was dying, would she want someone to know while she was still alive? Some stranger she'd never heard of, in a system she knew nothing about, except maybe what she'd seen in entertainments?

Her head said *Yes, I think so?* And her gut said, *I don't like this. I want to go back to when I didn't know about it.*

Neither answer was helpful.

Hatizda shook her head. The light scattered across the patterns in her hair. "Secret number two."

"I don't want another secret," Daja said. She was still processing the first one.

"You need to hear this one," Hatizda said. "I'm not sure the man in your position before you actually killed himself."

Daja opened her mouth, then closed it again.

"I have no proof," Hatizda said. "Just speculation. Just... he didn't seem the type, and it didn't seem like the right time."

Daja opened her mouth again. She could feel the muscles shifting around her jaw, and the wafting scent of the tea rolled back through her mouth to her throat.

Hatizda pushed the cup of tea toward Daja. "Here."

Will that help? Daja wondered, but her hand curled around the cup anyway. She brought it to her mouth; closed her mouth against the rim. The tea tasted more bitter than it smelled.

Then she slammed the cup down on the counter. The tea sloshed out, stinging against her palm. Felt, in her current mood, like someone holding her hand. Reassuring.

"You're calm?" she asked. She couldn't tell. "Does this bother you?"

"Of course it bothers me," Hatizda said. "But what can I do?"

"*Tell* someone," Daja said. "Don't hide them." How could a handful of people—thirteen, fourteen, sixteen, however many—hide an entire *star system*?

"Pouring it on everyone—that bothers me more."

"Because people need to stay calm," Daja filled in.

Hatizda shook her head. "I don't want them calm," she said. "Not about this. But that's the thing: if we start broadcasting this to all and sundry, what's going to happen? We're not getting attacked —not likely. So we keep people worked up, we keep people afraid?"

Her words were getting faster, the consonants beginning to mush and flow. Daja listened, fascinated in her head and repelled somewhere beneath her lungs.

"Daja, people get used to things," Hatizda said. Her voice rose a note or two in pitch, and quite a bit in volume. "If we'd flooded them with news of war for the past four anno, they would get used to the war. And I don't want to live in a system used to being at war. Not when the war isn't even *here*."

Daja didn't have words for a long while. And all Hatizda had, apparently, was a disconcerting amount of eye contact.

"That's not... even a little like what Supervisor Channing said." Daja tapped her fingers. "I think that's kinda the opposite?"

"Supervisor Channing and I don't agree on very much," Hatizda said. "But we don't need to. And I don't need you to agree with me. What I need you to do is find the place in your own mind where you come to the same conclusions the two of us did."

I don't want to, Daja thought. But even in her own mind, she was having trouble linking up the words with the reasons why.

"And," Hatizda said, "enjoy your tea. I'm sorry."

"For—?" *For the lies? For the death of a system?*

"For yelling."

DAJA WENT BACK to her quarters, and ran the visuals until she could no longer focus on them, because her fingers were itching to call home. To occupy them, she ran them over the fabric of her bed, the covering on her seats, the composite of the walls, the soft coating on the floors. Compared the pressure in the give in the furnishings to the pressures in her own body, in her shoulders, at her lungs. She was halfway to deciding to call Hatizda again, just to feel like she was doing something, when a call came in.

Channing's face appeared on the screen. Daja felt an instant phantom impact to her gut.

"What?" she asked.

Channing's mouth drew into a wide, flat line. "I understand that this is outside of your assigned duties," he said, "but a few of the technicians on the outbound Sol databurst have taken ill. Could you assist in the classifying and compiling? It's grunt work, mostly."

"Grunt work?" Daja asked.

"Supervisor Hatizda believes that some light outside duties help our task force to acclimatize to their work here." He glanced to the side of the screen. "If it's not helpful to you, I won't waste your time."

Daja shook her head. "No, it's fine. Fine? What do I do?"

Channing's fingers moved on something outside of the screen. "I'll have you patched in."

Channing's face disappeared. A moment later, a disembodied voice came out, and her screen began to fill with text.

"Hello! Daja?"

"That's me," she agreed.

This voice—very *musical*, wasn't it? More tones than Channing's, smoother than Hatizda's—wafted over the shifting text. "I'm Arduo. Thanks for volunteering to help—there's nothing time-sensitive in this databurst, but we like to have things out on time."

Daja laughed, short and sharp. *Volunteering.* "What do I do?"

The text organized itself into a grid. "We double-check the sorting information, so that when the burst arrives in Sol, people know where to look for what they want. The data's already been cleaned and restored, and the computer automatically sorts most of these. Just confirm or edit the sorting. Most of them are pretty self-explanatory; if you have any questions, just flag them back to me. I've given you the pile that's usually easiest."

She looked at the list of data packets, and the suggested categories. News and reports from Colossus, mostly; a few suggested Relay Point as the origin, or some of the smaller stations and colonies on the minor planetary bodies. "Okay." The preponderance of letters made the screen look bristling. "I can do that."

Sato System tended, overall, toward more angular lettering than Caribou. Or maybe Caribou just liked rounder letters in their entertainments. Daja realized she'd never seen what an actual Caribou dwelling looked like, or a console, or a text screen—just what someone imagined they should look like, and put into a show or a sim or a virtual. And heck, it wasn't as though her life resembled any entertainments to come out of Sato.

She had access to that level of detail now, supposedly. So that she could scavenge it out and pepper it into the fictions her task force developed.

But for now, she was going to do *grunt work*, work that wasn't actively obscuring the death of billions, and see if it would help. She didn't think it would.

An hour or two into the process, when her eyes were aching and her conscious brain had mostly wandered off, leaving some other process to *confirm—edit—confirm*, a tone sounded to get her attention. She ignored it until Arduo coughed, and she was going to ignore *that*, but then he started speaking again.

"Hey, so—there's a few things I'm not authorized to look at, in my pile. I was going to flag them on a delay until people got back, but it says I can transfer them over to you?"

"Okay?" Daja wondered if he found that strange. New person on the station, random fill-in for some ill workers, and she had authorizations he didn't. Authorizations those ill employees presumably had, too. She wondered if he knew about her task force, through rumor or leaks or just sensing a pattern, in that. If he knew that there were secret task forces at all. How much of a ripple did all this secret data make in the outbound databurst?

"I'll... okay. Over to you."

Another grid flurried up on her screen, just like all the others at first glance. But then the first entry made it through to Daja's brain, and for a moment, the entire world of sensory input became an uncaptivating nothing. All her attention was on the words.

Caribou.

She touched one of the entries. It unfolded under her fingertips: she had access to glosses, metadata, for most of these, but these were identified in the computer as resources she could access in any case. And this—this was media of the Caribou attacks.

She opened one.

Not full immersion—she didn't think she could handle that. First just the visuals, without sound, without tactile feedback. Objects in space, coming out of space, slow inexorable approaches—they didn't look like ships, to her. No uniformity. They looked like crystals, bismuth, maybe; all angles and layers and rigid geometry and chaos at the same time.

They were *slow*. Slow and inexorable. They came across outlying planets, not even inhabited ones, and slow geysers of rock and ice rose up from the surface, the whole of the planet eroding away. Daja watched in fascination, the muscles tightening in her stomach, hands, back.

So, this was what it looked like. What did it *smell* like, to have part of your planet ripped up and shot into orbit? What did it—no. She didn't want to know what it felt like; if pieces of debris flew and ruptured skin, broke bone. She didn't want to know what it looked like when a station came apart at the seams and you were standing in a corridor, watching the walls that held you enclosed splinter or tear or fragment. She didn't want to think about the ground beneath her feet not being there to stand on. She'd have nightmares, and then feel guilty that she was alive to complain about them.

But Channing and Hatizda wanted her to *detail* the fabricated reports they'd say were coming out of Caribou. Reports to explain a system going dark. And Daja knew the numbers, the facts, but she didn't know how it felt in the chest when there were too many dead to recycle and consume.

This media was going on toward Sol. That was the job under her fingertips now. All the media was tagged as *Official Factual—Classified—Strategic,* which seemed right. Or she could flag it back for someone else to deal with; probably one of her coworkers she'd never met. That was probably the correct response.

Daja found that she didn't like the correct response.

Rather, she didn't know what meaning *correct* had, here and now. And it occurred to her that if she could say nothing to her friends on Colossus, maybe she could say something to strangers on Earth. Wasn't all of Caribou trying to do the same?

She opened a list of categories, trying to find one least likely to come under scrutiny, and most likely to be seen by a number of people. That didn't work; the computer wouldn't let her flag it non-classified. Apparently it had come in as classified information, and it was going to leave that way, nothing she could do about it.

But there was a list of *Correspondence—Classified,* and when she selected that, it opened up a long list of potential recipients. And it let her select one. And then, when she tried it, it let her select two.

Daja thought for a moment. Then, in a burst of spite, she selected every single recipient available on the list, and copied the setting to every *Official Factual—Classified—Strategic* report with anything to do with Caribou.

Then she sat back, and paid some distracted attention to her heart thudding away in her chest. That felt surprisingly good, though she imagined it wouldn't if it went on for very long.

Still. *Still.* Maybe this list was just people who already had clearance for classified intel; she didn't know, she didn't recognize the names, and she didn't recognize most of the acronyms after them. But maybe they weren't, and maybe there would be someone who wasn't ordered to stay silent, and maybe *Sol* could hear Caribou, even if no other system would. Maybe. Just maybe.

And yes, this was very clearly divulging information she'd been ordered not to divulge. She was disobeying orders. But Hatizda was also disobeying her orders, just because it felt right to her. Well, maybe there was no *right*, in the mix. She was sure that Channing and his Earth-spectrum morality would have some hard line that made no sense to her; no, she had to listen to him, not to the billions calling out in Caribou, because he was more important because Sol said so. But she didn't much care what he had to say.

Every single piece of media in Daja's pile was caught, re-tagged, and sent along. And then Daja went back to the mind-numbing work of categorizing the rest of it, half-distracted by the blood singing in her ears.

DAJA WAS VIBRATING almost until the moment when the Sol databurst went out, and then she spent several days waiting for something to happen. But nothing did. She was introduced to her coworkers, under pseudonyms and pseudopresence, and listened in on all the ideas they threw around for the scenario they'd build. Violent anti-Sol revolution in Caribou. Computer corruption which destroyed all communications equipment. Epidemic brought on by unwise genetic engineering, or by flaws in food processing. She mostly stayed silent in those meetings.

In the meantime, she drank down the media from Caribou—as raw, as unfiltered as she could get it. The rhythm of their languages, the layout of their rooms, the hues of the skies on their single, unfinished world, the taste—synthesized, probably poorly, via chemical profiling—of the drinks they drank while socializing. And she was just about to cue up one in a long sequence of musical offerings one day, when the door to her quarters flew open, unannounced.

Hatizda.

Daja waved her console back to idleness. Hatizda had gone a shade redder than usual; it made her clothing look less congruent with her, somehow. Like she would have chosen a slightly darker grey or a looser collar if she'd known.

She invited Hatizda in. There wasn't much else to do.

Hatizda didn't give her the opportunity to search for the right words. "I checked the Earth-bound databurst as soon as Channing said he'd volunteered your time," she said. "What is wrong with you?"

That startled Daja so much that she started laughing. "I thought you talked to my friends on the creative teams."

That, in turn, seemed to startle Hatizda. She shook her head, quickly, as if water had been tossed into her face. Daja imagined droplets flying off the angles of her expression, glittering in the light, patterning the floor and furniture in broad sweeps like the stars outside.

"We—they told us about the—that's *not* what I'm trying to say," Hatizda said. "None of them ever said that your judgment was *massively compromised.*"

Daja shrugged.

"Did you think this through? Did you think at all? You can't hide this! As soon as Sol transmits back, Channing is going to piece together that it's you!"

Daja shrugged again. Even with the information flying out, faster than light would carry it, it would take the better part of an anno for the round trip. That was enough time to either think her way out of this, or consider her mistakes. "Yeah."

An absence-of-words settled between them. In the relative silence, Daja's attention was caught by the station's air cyclers—and by Hatizda's, her breath coming short and sharp.

At length, Hatizda blew out her breath. "I'm not going to tell Channing," she said. Her voice had dropped a few notes in pitch. Every syllable weighed out like it cost her something. "But I don't think there's much I can do for you."

"I don't need you to," Daja said. Nor was there much either of them could do for Caribou, who needed it more.

Hatizda shook her head again. Daja mentally overlaid another pattern of imaginary water drops, landing across the previous spray. Darker, fresher stains.

"You honestly think that was the right thing to do?"

"Does that exist?" Daja asked, and was momentarily distracted by a mote of dust, turning in some unevenness in the ambient light. Then it passed out of sight, and she had to adjust her balance, feel her whole mass move against the gravity.

When she looked back at Hatizda, her supervisor gazing, open-mouthed. "*That's* what you're coming back with?"

"I don't know," Daja said. "It doesn't matter what we do. Not in Caribou. But it matters here, and in Sol, and Waheed, and all the other systems. But we don't know if it matters if we don't... know." Was that right? She tried to fit the words together in her mind. "We have to know that there's something to matter. I think. I don't know. It hurt too much to stay quiet."

The muscles of Hatizda's face scrunched together. Then she turned her whole head away.

"I'm going to have to watch you more closely," she said. "Don't do anything like this again."

She left without another word.

Daja sat down, and was surprised to find her body shaking. She observed that reaction with curiosity for a while, reaching out to touch the stability of a table, a chair, and then touched the console screen to call her friends back home.

There was no answer. Her call was still blocked, and Hatizda wasn't picking up, this time. But that was all right: that was a reminder.

Daja let the call go out into nothing. She let it go on for a long, long time.

FACELESS SOLDIERS, PATCHWORK SHIP

Caroline M. Yoachim

EKUNDAYO WAS SUPPOSED to be on watch, but after eleven straight months without a single damned ship coming through the jump point nobody took watch duty seriously. Who wanted to be alone for six hours staring at blank screens, right? So lately she'd been inviting Lieutenant Jaxon to keep her company. He was a hybrid ambassador —half human and half Leonid—and Ekundayo's closest friend.

"I brought us some entertainment." Jaxon had a pair of fire kittens, probably siblings. The odd little aliens looked more like hedgehogs than kittens, but they had a playfulness about them that was distinctly cat-like. They tussled on the floor and the smaller one danced circles around the bigger one before popping out of existence and reappearing on Jaxon's shoulder. He brushed the tiny alien away and hissed at it. *Too hot. Burns my uniform.*

The fire kittens came from one of the free-floating planets in the Trapezium Cluster, and Station 17's primary objective was to keep the kittens from being captured by the Faceless—a horde of alien invaders that used a disease called Patchwork to augment their bodies with parts from every species they'd encountered. Adding fire kittens into their mix would give Faceless soldiers the ability to teleport. It'd be the end of the war, game over, humans lose.

Jaxon was trying to train his tiny pets to carry things across the void, so far without success. He draped a square of heat-resistant fabric over the smaller fire kitten, but when the kitten disappeared, the fabric dropped to the floor. The larger fire kitten popped out of existence too, and neither one returned. They'd show up eventually in Jaxon's quarters, or back on his shoulder, despite his hissing.

"I wonder what it would feel like to teleport." Ekundayo curled up against Jaxon's flank, enjoying his warmth. He was human on top and Leonid below. The tawny yellow fur that covered him from the waist down was structurally more like feathers than hair, and his six oddly-jointed legs kind of freaked Ekundayo out if she looked too close. His human skin was the same deep brown as hers, though, and his eyes were so dark they were almost black.

"There'd be no time to feel anything. Instantaneous travel is what makes teleportation such a threat. Imagine trying to outmaneuver an enemy that could blink out like a fire kitten. Even your sister couldn't do it."

"Neva's my *half* sister." Ekundayo ran her fingers through Jaxon's fur. She wanted to be with him in ways he had no interest in, but he didn't mind the casual contact. "But she's an amazing fighter pilot. I wish I was more like her."

Neva was the ideal soldier, quick thinking and good in a fight. Everybody on the station adored her because she was brave and brilliant and swore fluently in both Spanish and Japanese. *Her* mother didn't curse her with sickle cell trait. Meanwhile Ekundayo might drop dead if the action got hot or the air got thin—all because SCT was on the list of 'non-fatal conditions with potential combat applications.' Because obviously dropping dead in the middle of combat was a useful application.

"Not everyone is meant for fighting, Ekundayo." Jaxon brushed his hand against her cheek. He meant it friendly, but the gentle touch made her want to kiss him. She turned her attention back to the screens she was supposed to be watching.

The Orion Nebula was in the middle of a radiation storm, and silhouetted against the delicate purple streaks was the black outline of a Patchwork plague ship. The irregular form was unmistakable —a lumpy ovoid with hundreds of long trailing tendrils. Ekundayo magnified the image and saw maintenance pods swarming like buzzflies on a dead Squidder.

"Enemy ship arrived through the jump point at 22:06:59," Ekundayo started her report while she ran additional scans. Data scrolled across the screens, interspersed with video of the enemy ship. "Stand by for incoming communications."

Ekundayo synced her audio implant to the station's radio sensors. The enemy ship was putting out signal like a fire kitten puts out heat. The Faceless had no concept of stealth. Every individual on a Patchwork-infected ship broadcasted continuously, screaming into the void. Ekundayo couldn't make sense of that many signals at once, but the station AI sorted it out. Most of the signals were in alien languages, but she programmed a filter to get only the broadcasts she could understand:

"Nebula sky, birthplace of stars. Even the planets roam free."

"Eleven, thirteen, seventeen..."

"Sometimes the cure is worse than the disease."

EKUNDAYO WAS SUPPOSED to sleep the next shift, but she was too amped. She bunked with Neva, who was in their quarters with one of the new recruits—Emma Liu—chattering about lifetime kill counts and who they wanted to screw. Pretty typical of Neva, using gossip to keep Liu's mind off the enemy ship.

"I heard Zinnie did it with that Squidder hybrid down on—" Liu flinched when the door opened, then relaxed when she realized it was Ekundayo. "You ever done a hybrid?"

"Nah." Ekundayo forced a smile and tried not to think about Jaxon. "But there's a rumor going around that you like mermaids."

"Can't fuck a mermaid, it's in the Van Maanen Treaty: dead soldiers go back to their home planet, sick soldiers get treatment, don't torture prisoners, and no matter what happens, *don't fuck the fish*." Liu made a rude hand gesture, then shrugged. "They're on our side now, though, so does that part of the treaty still apply?"

"You screw a mermaid, they might not stay on our side," Ekundayo said.

This, of course, was the moment that Station Surgeon (aka Sturgeon) Ness appeared in the door. Sturgeon was a burly redhead with a thick Piscean braintail instead of legs. Pisceans were more like snakes than fish, but they had a weird sense of humor. Not long after first contact they reshaped their exoskeletons and biosuits to have scales and fins so their hybrids would look like mermaids. Ekundayo didn't really understand the joke, even after Sturgeon explained it.

"Tachibana, Commander Bianchi wants to see you."

Ekundayo flinched. To her, Tachibana was Dad, and hearing his name was a painful reminder of his death. She'd convinced everyone to use her first name, but Neva had no such qualms. She was the older sister, the stronger sister, the soldier.

Neva stood up. "Finally. Let's go fight some Faceless."

"No, sorry. I meant Ekundayo." Sturgeon gestured for Ekundayo to follow and slithered out into the main corridor that ran the circumference of the station.

It was weird that command wanted her. Weird that Sturgeon would be the one to summon her. Ekundayo hoped that she wasn't about to catch shit for having Jaxon with her when she was supposed to be working. Would they call in another hybrid to witness disciplinary proceedings for that?

She was relieved when they got to the command deck and Jaxon wasn't there.

"We've got a mission for you." Commander Bianchi pointed to a holographic projection of the Patchwork ship. "Infiltrate the enemy ship and infect it with a counter-virus."

"I think you've got the wrong sister, sir? Neva's the soldier. I'm combat-exempt because of my SCT." Ekundayo was disappointed to not be more useful in the war efforts, but part of her was relieved to have an excuse not to fight.

"Your defect is why you're here." Bianchi cleared the projection with a wave of his hand.

"I'm not defective." She had a medical condition, but she wasn't broken. And the only reason she even still had SCT is that someone thought it might be useful.

"In this context, you are most certainly not," Sturgeon agreed. "The latest research suggests that the Patchwork virus replicates by mining red blood cells for iron, and misshapen cells—such as occur during a sickling crisis—slow the process considerably."

Bianchi nodded. "You're somewhat resistant to infection, so you can board the enemy ship and deliver the counter-virus. That will decimate the Faceless soldiers and incapacitate the ship. It's our best shot at keeping the fire kittens from being absorbed into the Patchwork."

"But to do that I'd need to pass as Faceless—" Ekundayo stopped, finally realizing why she was there. "You're going to graft parts onto me so I can pass, and then hope my system can fight off a Patchwork infection long enough for me to complete the mission?"

"Yes, and time is critical," Bianchi said. "We only have a week before the ship reaches the Trapezium Cluster."

Sturgeon nodded. "I can begin the surgery as soon as you're ready."

"Is it reversible?"

"If you're fast enough." Sturgeon paused. "There's a window of time after you're infected, probably about 18 hours, where we can treat the Patchwork and reverse the surgery. After that, there's not much we can do."

"*Probably* 18 hours? You want to graft a bunch of alien shit onto my body and you don't even know?"

"With healthy soldiers, we can treat cases in the first 10-12 hours after infection. Your sickle cell trait will definitely slow the Patchwork down, but without full scale human testing, we're guessing at how much. I'll give you a breathing mask that will let you lower your oxygen levels—if you need to buy more time, you can trigger a mild sickle cell crisis."

"Sounds fun. I can buy time by putting myself in pain, and if I don't work fast enough, I turn into the enemy." She could see from Sturgeon's face that there was something more. "What else?"

Sturgeon refused to meet her gaze. "We have to take one of your legs."

"What? No. Just no."

"It's temporary! They won't believe you're Faceless if you're a whole human with a bunch of surface parts. It has to go deeper," Sturgeon explained. "I talked Commander Bianchi down. He wanted to take a leg *and* an arm."

Ekundayo glared at Bianchi. The silence stretched out. She'd always wanted to be more like Neva, to fight against the Faceless instead of sitting around on the station for watch after endless watch, but now that it was a real possibility she was more scared than excited. Still, this was her chance to get back at the Faceless for what they did to Dad.

"I can reattach the leg when we're done. It's a routine procedure—"

Commander Bianchi cut Sturgeon off. "You're the best candidate for this mission, Tachibana, and I'm giving you an order."

If she didn't go, they might send Neva. She was one of the best soldiers on the station, and she'd volunteer for something like this. "I need time to think about it."

"We're out of time."

The thought of going to the Patchwork ship was terrifying, but it made sense for her to go. She'd have more time than anyone else. She couldn't cower on the station in fear. "I'll go."

"Station Surgeon Ness will go along as medical support," Bianchi said, "but you may pick the rest of your team, subject to my approval."

"Fine." The shuttles held four, and anyone who cut off her leg should have their fate tied to hers. Really all she wanted was to have Jaxon and Neva with her, so it didn't matter if Bianchi insisted that Sturgeon go along. "One last condition."

"Yes?"

"I get to choose which leg."

EKUNDAYO GOT ENOUGH drugs that there wasn't any pain, but Sturgeon needed her awake for the surgery so she had to fucking watch while the laser amputated her left leg. It was bloodless, but the odor of burned flesh filled the operating room, and Ekundayo suddenly understood why Sturgeon had insisted she not eat beforehand.

"You can't put that back on me if it's cooked," she grumbled.

"The burn layer is very thin, and the surgical procedures are—"

"I don't want to know." Her leg went into a tank across the room, suspended in gel and hooked up to a bunch of wires. It twitched several times per minute to maintain muscle tone. Other tanks held the alien parts Sturgeon would graft onto her, presumably harvested from freshly killed Faceless soldiers at who-knew-what battle. Nothing Piscean, because they were too fragile, but there was a Leonid leg and some Squidder tentacles and a ridiculous set of wings. "Are the wings meant to be some kind of punishment?"

"We needed parts that could be grafted onto a human frame, and then removed. You won't be able to reach the wings very well with your arms, by the way. When it's time to remove them you'll need to use the Squidder tentacles."

"Wait, I have to remove this shit myself?" Bianchi's brief on the mission was hastily prepared and thin on details, but even drugged for surgery Ekundayo recognized that this was a serious omission.

"The wings won't fit into your flightsuit, so you'll have to remove them before you leave the enemy ship. I'll demonstrate the procedure when the surgery is complete." Sturgeon picked up a translucent disk and placed it onto the stump of Ekundayo's leg. The disk contained thousands of tiny particles moving like fish on the surface of a 2D fishbowl. "The Faceless pick up parts from any species they encounter and meld everything together with Patchwork virus. These connector plates will allow you to appear Faceless without having the parts growing into you... at least at first."

"Right, because once the parts really grow into me *I'll be Faceless*." Which would make her unfit for the mission, among other things. "Shouldn't you be in a haz suit?"

"Patchwork only spreads through direct exchange of bodily fluids," Sturgeon said, then laughed. "But nothing here is infected with Patchwork—these parts were built from scratch on a replicator. You won't be infected with Patchwork until right before you board the enemy ship. Otherwise you'd never have enough time, SCT or not."

Sturgeon attached the Squidder tentacles to the top of her left shoulder and helped her roll over so the wings could go onto her back. They were heavy and leathery, and completely useless in a spaceship. Worse, they'd make her look like a goddamn pixie.

"Almost done." Sturgeon held up a segment of Faceless nervous system, encased in a clear plastic tube. Inside the tube, bundles of thick red nerve fibers expanded and contracted.

"I don't want that," Ekundayo whispered.

"You need this. Otherwise the ship will reject you as an invader and graft a Faceless head onto your torso."

"I want to stay human. This stuff," she waved her hand at the alien parts grafted onto her body, "it's all decoration. But that's nervous system shit, and the Patchwork will make it grow into my brain."

"It's a part, exactly like all the other parts. After you deliver the counter-virus, we'll remove it, just like all the other pieces. I'm not going to put it on until you say okay, but time is critical. Are you ready?"

She wasn't. She absolutely wasn't ready. She'd prepared herself for losing her leg, and for having alien parts grafted onto her body. But she could lose herself on this mission, have her mind absorbed by the enemy. Becoming Faceless was more terrifying than death.

If they lost the war, all of humankind would face that horror.

"Okay. Do it."

The nerve bundle went on her back, so Ekundayo didn't have to watch Sturgeon put it on, but she heard the tube click into place. There was no sign it was there—no alteration of her perceptions, no strange alien thoughts invading her brain. She realized that she was clenching her jaw and forced herself to relax. She was okay. She was still herself.

"Now I'll demonstrate the release mechanisms, so you can remove your parts when you get to the target location."

"You're going to show me while I'm drugged?"

"There won't be time later. As soon as you're out of recovery sleep, we're leaving." Sturgeon grabbed hold of her new Leonid limb. The sensation of fingers in the fur—in *her* fur—tickled. Sturgeon pressed a pair of panels that were embedded beneath her fur on opposite sides of the Leonid limb and twisted, hard. The tickling sensation of hands on fur vanished.

"I designed these connector plates myself—they're a modification of the technology used to create hybrids, but temporary so they'll be easier to remove when you've completed your mission. The nerve connections are programmed into the plates, so when I put them back together," Sturgeon snapped the Leonid limb back into place, "instant sensation and motor control!"

Ekundayo tried to make a snide comment, but the Leonid leg felt like it was on fire, and what came out was a whimper.

"Sorry. Your brain isn't used to the Leonid leg. Did you experience the nerve signals as pain?"

"Come closer. I'll rip some of your appendages off, and you can see how it feels."

"Tempting, but the Van Maanen Treaty forbids us to mate." Sturgeon laughed, but Ekundayo wasn't entirely sure whether that was meant to be a joke. Before she could say anything, Sturgeon slid the surgery table, with Ekundayo still on it, into a regeneration capsule. "You've got 24 hours of recovery sleep. Night night."

EKUNDAYO GOT FOUR extra hours of recovery because a radiation storm hit and the shuttles didn't have enough shielding to go out in those conditions. Captain Flores herself came to see them off, along with Commander Bianchi and several high-ranking officers. Ekundayo stood at attention while Flores gave a speech about the critical importance of the mission, and her back ached from the weight of the wings. Worse, every damned seam between her body and the grafted parts was itchy.

Bianchi came over for a final briefing.

"I don't have the counter-virus." Ekundayo said, "and nothing in my mission files explains how I'm supposed to deliver it—only that I need to get to the main control center of the Patchwork ship to have the best chance of establishing the infection. So hand it over and tell me how to use it."

"You already have the counter-virus," Bianchi said.

She patted down her uniform to check for anything in the pockets, but all she had was standard equipment and the oxygen-reducing breathing mask Sturgeon had given her. Her flightsuit was vacuum-sealed into a specialized pack, but she wouldn't be using that until after the virus was delivered. "Where?"

"It's in the wings."

"You're shitting me." She bit down on her lip. She hadn't meant to say that out loud, but Bianchi was hardly in a position to reprimand her, given the circumstances. "How exactly was that not part of my initial briefing?"

"Plans regarding the counter-virus require a higher security clearance than you possess. Telling you earlier might have jeopardized the mission."

"Yeah, because if I'd known what I was getting into, I'd have turned you down—and I'm the only one on the ship with sickle cell trait..." Ekundayo stopped. They'd stationed her here eleven months ago, on purpose, in case she was needed for this mission. And all this time they hadn't told her. "You son-of-a-bitch."

Bianchi ignored her reaction. "The counter-virus is dormant and harmless to humans. It won't start replicating until you've removed the wings and you're off the ship."

"If the mission goes as planned."

"Yes."

"And if I fail?"

Bianchi stared at the shuttle behind her and said nothing. He didn't have to. Patchwork combined alien parts into a single entity. The connector plates that Sturgeon had used were designed to be temporary. Once the plates broke down, the Patchwork would be all that kept her immune system from attacking her spare parts. If she was still wearing the wings when the counter-virus activated, her body would destroy itself in an effort to reject everything that was alien.

"I knew I hated these damned wings." She made a rude Squidder gesture with one of her tentacles and went to join the rest of her team in the shuttle.

Jaxon chuckled. "He's fluent in about twenty alien languages. I wouldn't be surprised if he knows Squidder."

"Don't care. I'd refuse the mission to spite his lying ass, but I won't jeopardize the war, and he knows it." Ekundayo flailed at her harness, but she couldn't get it over her wings. Jaxon took the straps out of her hand and gently secured them in place. He was looking at her weird, and—"Oh, come on. I've got one Leonid leg and suddenly I'm attractive?"

"You smell good. You never used to smell this good." His voice was low and soft, sheepish but alluring.

Part of her wanted to sneak off somewhere to make out, but most of her hurt like hell from the surgery, and she was irritated at Jaxon's sudden reversal. Besides, they'd be accelerating too hard to be out of their harnesses anyway. Not that she was going to. Maybe. Damn. "I'm probably going to die, you know."

"Don't die. Win. Finish your mission and we'll come get you." He kissed the top of her head and strapped into his own harness.

They launched, and the shuttle engines were too loud for private conversation. Jaxon hummed to himself, eyes closed. He'd told her once that he was terrified of shuttles—being inside such a tiny thing against the vastness of space. Ekundayo didn't get it. On astronomical scales, the station was equally small. But seeing Jaxon with his eyes squeezed shut made her wish she was close enough to hold his hand, or stroke the soft fur on his back.

Sturgeon turned on an advanced tutorial on Patchwork viral replication, and Ekundayo watched the slideshow of magnified blood cell and virus images. She didn't have enough medical training to make sense of most of it, and the volume was too low for her to hear the tutorial over the ship engines anyway.

"If I use my breathing mask to trade excruciating pain of vascular occlusion for extra time, how long will it buy me?"

Sturgeon paused the tutorial. "I don't know. In its current form, Patchwork utilizes the iron from red blood cells in its replication process, and the deformed shape of sickled cells impedes the mineral harvesting—but Patchwork is highly adaptive."

"Rough estimate."

"A couple hours?" Sturgeon's tail tapped against the metal of the shuttle floor. "Maybe as many as four."

Neva initiated the deceleration sequence and spoke in a loud voice over the rumble of the engines, "We're getting into formation with twenty other shuttles. When we reach our target, the decoys will disperse and all of us will orbit the enemy ship at a safe distance. You'll load up in the maintenance pod, Ekundayo, and we'll fling you over to the ship."

"How the hell did we get a Patchwork maintenance pod?"

Neva laughed. "While you were sleeping off your surgery, I went out and nabbed one. It's in the airlock."

"Is it... empty?"

"Yeah."

Neva didn't expand on that. Ekundayo raised an eyebrow.

"The pods fly themselves, but this isn't really the time to get squeamish about killing Faceless soldiers." Neva paused. "All of our shuttles will broadcast to the Patchwork ship on all radio frequencies. We'll be putting out a constant chatter, so the Faceless will have a hard time separating out our encrypted transmissions to you, if they even bother to listen. Your audio implant is programmed to filter for our communications, so you won't hear the rest."

"Great! You can tell me what a good job I'm doing. That will be helpful." Ekundayo had what little information they knew about the enemy ship loaded into her implants. Communicating with the shuttle seemed needlessly dangerous.

"Funny." Neva scanned her instrument panel and made a tiny adjustment to their course. "We'll be doing 'human checks' at regular intervals to determine whether you're too far gone to complete your mission."

"And what, you'll blow me up if I'm compromised?" She was joking, because even Bianchi would have mentioned a detail like that during briefing.

Neva's voice got quiet. "Our original orders were to abandon you after 10 hours, regardless of the state of the mission. I convinced command to switch to this at the last minute, which is why it wasn't in any of your briefing materials. We can stay as long as you pass the human checks."

"And if you feel yourself starting to slip, you can trigger a sickle cell crisis—" Sturgeon chimed in.

"Yes, I know." Ekundayo turned back to Neva. "So how do we determine if I'm still human?"

"Faceless don't have a good sense of time or individuality. If you're absorbed, your memories and theirs will mingle together until you're unable to sort out which is which. I'll ask you questions like 'when was the first time you left your birth planet?' Things that are easy to answer if you're still you."

"Thanks for this, for giving me the best possible chance," Ekundayo said. "If I get absorbed into the Patchwork, you can have the leg Sturgeon cut off."

"Ew." Neva crinkled her nose. Ekundayo grinned and stuck out her tongue. It was like they were kids again, squabbling over who got the last chocolate-covered salt bug or whose turn it was to pilot Dad's old shuttle.

One of the decoy shuttles sent Neva a set of coordinates to cross-check, and the momentary connection to her childhood was gone. It was time for Ekundayo to get into the Patchwork maintenance pod. Jaxon went with her into the airlock that separated the main cabin from the cargo hold.

"The maintenance pod is infected with live Patchwork virus, so I have to leave before you go through, but I wanted to come with you as far as I could." He pushed a strand of hair away from her face. "Win. Come back safe."

Jaxon knew Ekundayo hated goodbyes, so he didn't wait for her to answer. He went back to the main cabin and the hatch sealed itself shut behind him.

Ready? Neva's voice came through Ekundayo's audio implant.

On the other side of the airlock, Ekundayo would be exposed to an alien virus that would strip her of her humanity. Her hands were shaking, and what she most wanted was to turn around and go back into the main cabin of the shuttle, but instead she answered quietly, "Ready."

The cargo hold was mostly empty, illuminated by strips of white light on the ceiling and walls. The alien maintenance pod was tiny, barely big enough to hold her. Part of it was metal, but there were seams made from a pale green organic material. The pod pulsed with a slow and steady rhythm, like a beating heart. Neva had assured her that the inside of the pod was airtight, capable of holding a crew of one—she'd seen Faceless soldiers use them as escape pods when battles went poorly.

Ekundayo folded her wings close to her back and she climbed into the pod, clutching the pack that held her flightsuit to her chest. The pod expanded slightly and hissed like a Leonid that felt threatened.

The maintenance pod sealed itself, and Ekundayo was immersed in darkness. Tendrils reached out from the walls of the pod, cold and damp, and she screamed as hundreds of tiny thorns pushed through her uniform and pricked her skin.

She pulled away the tendrils, wincing as the thorns came free. The tendrils didn't resist, and why would they? She was contaminated with Patchwork.

"Human check."

It was Neva's voice. Ekundayo subvocalized to broadcast back, *"I was infected less than a minute ago. Seriously?"*

"You pass, but next time wait for me to ask a question."

"Well, ask faster next time."

"Take care of yourself in there."

It was too close to a goodbye. Ekundayo felt tears welling up in her eyes. *"Launch me."*

Neva opened the outer doors to the cargo bay, and the Patchwork maintenance pod, with Ekundayo inside, was blown out into space.

"The Patchwork ship is sending several other pods in your direction, and they'll herd your pod to the ship. Good luck, sis."

EKUNDAYO CLIMBED OUT of the maintenance pod and surveyed her surroundings. She was in a hangar full of soldiers, most with the smooth gray heads of the Faceless, the original species in which the Patchwork virus evolved. The soldiers weren't cleanly assembled hybrids like Jaxon and Sturgeon; they were monstrous creatures with uneven seams between parts from myriad different aliens. One soldier had a human torso with two Faceless heads and half a dozen legs, each a different shape and color. Another had a fierce Leonid head, oozing sluglike feet, and long spindly arms from some alien race Ekundayo had never encountered.

A vaguely doglike creature with a giant scorpion tail and a human head approached her. His eyes were bright and curious, but with a glint of mischief. He reminded her a little of a fire kitten and a little of Jaxon. "You came from outside. You have all the right parts, but I can't talk to your mind."

"I'm newly arrived," Ekundayo explained. "I came through the jump point in that maintenance pod."

He rose up on his hind legs and wrapped his forelegs around her. For a moment, Ekundayo thought he might kiss her, but instead he stung her, in her human leg, with the stinger of his scorpion tail.

"Your blood tastes right. Clean, although your Patchwork levels are low." His human face was mere inches from hers, and he studied her closely, squinting. "Venx will assign you quarters."

Ekundayo nodded and hurried away in the direction he indicated, relieved that he'd stung her leg and not her wings. She lost an hour locked in a small waiting room with a dozen new arrivals because a Faceless soldier with two gray-mushroom heads—presumably Venx —insisted on assigning everyone to quarters one at a time, in the order that they arrived. There were seven sickly-looking soldiers still in the waiting room when Ekundayo finally managed to break herself out.

"*Human check.*" It was Sturgeon's voice coming in through her implant this time. "*Where were you born?*"

"In the bed of a transport truck, pulled off to the side of the road, halfway to the hospital. Also that's a terrible memory question because I obviously do not remember my own birth." Her dad used to love to tell the story of it though, which is probably why Neva included the question.

"You pass."

Ekundayo tried to orient herself based on the schematics Bianchi had uploaded to her implant. She was in the aft section of the ship, near where the long trailing tendrils attached to the hull, but she couldn't get the internal layout diagrams to match up with what she was seeing. She wandered the corridors, lost, wasting valuable time. The hull of the ship was mostly metal, but everything inside was organic. The walls pulsed in time with the alien nerves grafted onto Ekundayo's spine, as if they were breathing together or keeping their heartbeats in sync.

Discarded body parts were scattered on the floor and pressed into the walls. A soldier with a dozen arms pulled one off and pressed it into the wall. Tendrils grew out to embrace the discarded limb. The soldier went a short distance, then stopped to harvest a limb that was growing from the floor. The ability to swap out old parts made the Faceless nearly immortal—like living ships of Theseus, replacing themselves bit by bit until eventually none of their original parts remained.

A large chamber opened on one side of the corridor. Inside, several Faceless soldiers were contained inside transparent bubbles. Row after row of spheres, each with a single soldier inside. Additional soldiers walked up and down the aisles. *What are those?* she wondered.

This is a quarantine area. You are not permitted here. One of the soldiers pushed her away gently. She left the chamber of quarantine bubbles, then realized that neither she nor the soldier had spoken aloud. At the edge of her mind, she heard the whisper of other Faceless voices, and she felt the urge to broadcast her thoughts.

"Human check—what happened the first time you piloted a shuttle?"

The question sounded so similar to the background whispers she was trying to ignore that she almost missed it. It was Sturgeon's voice again, but Neva had clearly provided the question. Ekundayo had gone with Neva for a joyride when her sister was fourteen and she was ten. It wasn't long after Dad had died, and Neva had handed the controls over mid-flight. A piece of debris punched a tiny hole in the hull, and oxygen levels in the cabin dropped. It triggered a massive sickling event, making her misshapen blood cells get caught in her capillaries. Without enough circulation, her muscle tissue started to die. She'd screamed in pain until she blacked out. Neva took over the controls and flew her to the med clinic.

"Neva got grounded for a week for taking me out on a joyride."

It wasn't the answer she was supposed to give, but it was true. And if Neva came up with shitty questions, Ekundayo was going to give shitty answers.

EKUNDAYO COULDN'T SHAKE the sensation that she was inside an animal or perhaps a tree, rather than wandering the corridors of a ship. There were no straight lines, no clean edges. All the walls curved and pulsed. She felt the rhythms of the ship in the throbbing of the nerve bundles grafted to her back. The ship itself was alive and infected with Patchwork. If the Faceless acquired the fire kittens, it wouldn't just give individual soldiers the power of teleportation—the Faceless would be able to move their entire ship instantly.

Ekundayo felt her body merging with her grafted parts and with the ship itself. Soldiers broadcasted a cacophony of thoughts woven together like harmonies in a song.

Delicate sky-tendrils of purple, faint like the web of a spider's ghost.

Recalculating coordinates on the galactic plane.

Eight hundred eighty-seven, nine hundred seven, nine hundred eleven...

It was happening too fast. Ekundayo hadn't found the main control center, and the schematics Bianchi had given her were totally useless. She had to slow the virus down.

Ekundayo strapped her breathing mask to her face, reducing the percentage of oxygen in each breath she took. She forced herself to move quickly through the corridors of the ship, knowing that the combination of exertion and low oxygen would bring on a crisis faster.

Pain spread through her body as sickled cells partially blocked blood flow through her capillaries. Her heart thumped wildly in her chest, and for a moment she panicked. If she went into a severe crisis, there was no one here to help her. What if Sturgeon had set the oxygen ratio on her mask too low?

She tried to calm down. The voices in her head were fading, so the mask was working. There was enough time to complete the mission. She kept moving. The corridor was uneven, dotted with alcoves and branching off into side tunnels. Her head throbbed and her muscles burned, but she pushed herself onward.

MOVING DURING A sickling crisis was exhausting, and it was hard to focus through the pain. Ekundayo passed two Faceless soldiers who were carrying a third soldier down the corridor on a stretcher. Shadows danced across their featureless gray heads, and Ekundayo was overwhelmed with a sense of concern, worry for the sick individual on the stretcher. The light in the corridor was soft and uniform, emanating from some kind of bioluminescent material growing on the walls. What was making the shadows move like that? It wasn't the light. It was something else, something she hadn't seen until she'd been infected with Patchwork. The Faceless had a face.

She shook her head. It didn't matter. Dad also had a face, and the Faceless killed him. It didn't matter that they felt concern for their fellow soldiers. She tried to put it out of her mind, but something about the scene bothered her. Something about the ship. Voices once again whispered at the edges of her mind. The Patchwork virus was regrouping. She took off her breathing mask. The virus had adapted, and she'd be able to move faster if she wasn't in pain.

Ekundayo found a passageway that led deeper into the ship. It opened into a high-ceilinged chamber filled with a field of delicate red flowers. Several soldiers milled around, and all of them had human faces. Ekundayo could see why they would be drawn to this place. It smelled like grass and rain and other things she remembered from her planetside childhood. She had the urge to share the flowers, to sing them out into the universe.

"Human check—when was the first time you met a hybrid?"

The voice belonged to Jaxon this time, and Ekundayo could hear the worry in his voice.

Jaxon was the first hybrid she'd ever met. *"We met right after I came to the station. The rest of my cohort were all jockeying for position, and they wanted nothing to do with someone like me, someone who couldn't fight. You were nice to me."*

The ship heard her broadcast, and it triggered other memories: a Piscean-Squidder hybrid killed in battle on some planet with a green-tinged sky; a human-Leonid hybrid who came voluntarily to join the Patchwork. There were whispers of a Leonid with a Faceless head, not grown on but grafted. Something had gone wrong with the graft.

The Leonid was on a warship packed with Faceless soldiers, and they loaded her into a transport pod and sent her to a hospital ship.

Ekundayo didn't know where or when the memory was from, but she recognized the ship. *"This isn't a warship, Jaxon. These Faceless aren't soldiers. This is a hospital ship."*

There was a long pause, and then it was Neva who answered. *"I just checked with Bianchi, and his orders are to proceed with the mission. He says the Faceless sent a hospital ship to acquire the fire kittens because they thought we'd be less likely to attack it."*

"These aren't soldiers." Ekundayo didn't know what to do. She didn't want to kill a bunch of civilians, but those were her orders, and she wouldn't fit into her flightsuit unless she removed the wings. The idea of becoming Faceless terrified her. It was a little thing, compared to the outcome of the war, but she couldn't bear the thought of losing herself in this sea of alien minds.

"Stay focused on the mission, Ekundayo. We can't let the Faceless get the fire kittens. Do your part and we'll get you out."

THE MAIN CONTROL center of the ship was a chamber of pulsing red cords, similar to the ones in the tube on Ekundayo's back, but larger. It looked more like a circulatory system than a brain. The nerve cords tangled around a spare torso here, a Faceless head there. Without thinking, Ekundayo reached out with her tentacles to touch one of the cords. The outer surface was harder than she expected, and warm to the touch. Sturdy. She wasn't sure how she'd tear through it to gain better access for the counter-virus. Knowing that this was a hospital ship, she wasn't sure she still wanted to. Humanity was counting on her, but she couldn't believe what Bianchi was ordering her to do. Fighting soldiers was one thing, slaughtering innocent civilians was something else entirely. Except what if they really were there to get the fire kittens? That was a military objective.

Ekundayo felt a shift in the ship's activity. It was preparing itself for a radiation storm. Bursts of radiation were common in the Trapezium Cluster, and the station was shielded enough to protect everyone on board, but the shuttles—if the shuttles were still out there when the radiation hit, the teams would die. She had to take off her wings.

But this was a hospital ship, and these Faceless weren't soldiers.

"Human check. When was the first time you encountered the Faceless?"

It was Neva again. She was trying to help Ekundayo by giving her one of the strongest memories she had. The first Faceless she encountered was Dad, quarantined and sick with Patchwork. He was a scientist, not a soldier, but the Faceless had infected him anyway and grafted a featureless gray head onto his back, like some strange fungus was growing from his fevered flesh. It was before the Patchwork had fully adapted to absorb humans, and his body was rejecting the disease. For years, she'd had nightmares about it, visions of her dad's body covered in a million gray-mushroom heads.

Neva was trying to make Ekundayo angry enough to complete the mission.

Another memory came to her. She was a small red creature that looked a bit like a dog. A god with four heads and half a dozen legs came down from the sky and lifted her into the great star fields of the afterward. Embraced in the pulsing vines of a life support chamber, deep within the ship, she was content to become something other than what she was.

This ship was not a warship. Were they here on a mission to get the fire kittens, or did they have a more benign goal?

Ekundayo remembered training for battle as a giant scorpion. She learned how to exploit the seams of Faceless soldiers by practicing on a dead one—and was infected by residual Patchwork that had not been properly cleansed from the corpse. She didn't want to fight against her own people, so when she joined the Faceless she became a navigator on a hospital ship. It was not enough to save her from the fighting. The ship was broadcasting songs of mercy when they were attacked. They only barely made it to the Orion jump point.

"Ekundayo, human check. I'm only allowed to repeat this one time. When was the first time you encountered the Faceless?"

The beings on the ship were doctors and patients. Some of them were scientists. They weren't here for the fire kittens, they were fleeing an attack. Killing them would be like killing Dad. If she removed her wings, the counter-virus would infect the ship and eventually kill everyone on board. If she didn't remove her wings, she wouldn't fit into her flightsuit.

She couldn't destroy a hospital and slaughter a shipload of innocents. She also couldn't leave her team—and the teams on all the decoy shuttles—waiting for her in a lethal radiation storm. There was only one choice left. *"A god with four heads and half a dozen legs comes down from the sky and lifts me to the great star fields of afterward."*

Neva didn't answer, but there was a quiet sniffle before her sister cut the com connection. Ekundayo had failed the check, failed the shitty mission Bianchi had forced on her, possibly failed all of humanity.

Ekundayo broadcasted her location and told the shipmind that she was infected with a dangerous virus. A mostly-Squidder nurse appeared at the entrance to the nerve center and beckoned with her tentacles for Ekundayo to follow. As soon as they were out in the open corridor, the nurse enclosed Ekundayo in a quarantine bubble. The bubble was spherical and clear, made of a flexible material that flattened slightly where it met the floor.

"Human check, do I pass?"

It was Jaxon. *"You're supposed to go back to the station."*

"Yeah, we talked about that. Sturgeon wanted to, but Neva and I said no."

"I failed my human check."

"But you're passing this one."

It was a dirty trick, testing her by risking their lives. *"There's a radiation storm coming, you've got maybe half an hour to leave if you want to get back to the station without getting fried."*

"We got that warning from the station immediately after your last check. That's what made me absolutely certain your failure was a lie."

"You have to go."

"Then you'd better figure out a way to get into your flightsuit and into open space so we can save you. The decoys are gone, but we're not leaving without you."

She could hear the tremble in Jaxon's voice. He'd always been scared of shuttles; now he was staying out in one despite an approaching radiation storm. The thin layer of metal that formed the hull of the shuttle wouldn't be enough to protect him.

She pressed her tentacles against the surface of the misshapen sphere that contained her. The quarantine bubble was smooth and airtight. It wasn't meant for the vacuum of space, but it might hold long enough for her to get into her flightsuit. If she could get the bubble out through one of the airlocks, she could spare the Faceless on this ship *and* get back to the shuttle.

Ekundayo pushed against the side of the bubble and rolled it down the corridor. She came to a constriction. Had it always been like that or had the shape of the passageway changed to keep her from moving? The bubble was caught on all sides.

She leapt at the wall of her bubble, leaning in hard with her shoulder. The bubble stretched on impact to keep her contained, and the now-oblong shape squeezed through the constriction with a high-pitched squeal. The walls shuddered at the sound.

Ekundayo kept moving.

Several nurses trailed behind her in the corridor, their gray-mushroom heads dancing with faint shadows of expression. A thousand whispers in her mind told her to stop, but she didn't listen. She pushed harder, spinning her bubble so fast she had to jog to keep up. She couldn't remember the meandering path she'd taken when she first arrived, but she could sense the ship itself now—feel the pulse of the nerve center, the circulation of nutrients through the walls—and with this deepened connection she found an airlock.

She pushed her bubble inside. The nurses didn't follow. Instead they sealed her in. All she had to do was blow herself out of the airlock and remove her Patchwork parts, but there weren't any visible controls, only the red pulsing threads of the ship's nerves.

Let me go, Ekundayo pleaded. *I spared you from the counter-virus, at least let me go back to my station. My friends are waiting for me, and if they don't leave soon they'll die in the radiation storm. This is a hospital. Could you really leave people out there to die?*

Nothing happened. It wasn't enough to tell the ship what she wanted. Why would they listen to a voice that wasn't one of their own? Besides, this wasn't about her team, not really. Neva wouldn't keep the shuttle out in the radiation storm. She'd stay as long as she could, but at the last moment she'd go. Her friends' fate did not depend on her, and now that the Faceless knew about the counter-virus the mission was doomed to failure. She just didn't want to die alone in the airlock of an enemy ship. If she joined the Faceless collective and broadcast her thoughts to them from the inside, would they let her go?

All Ekundayo had left to lose was herself. It was the thing she'd feared from the beginning, but she was out of other options. She stopped fighting the Faceless and let them in, welcomed all their voices into her mind. *Please,* she begged, *don't keep me trapped here alone.*

She thought of Neva and Jaxon and Sturgeon, out in the shuttle where they'd be exposed to radiation from the storm. She thought of the counter-virus in her wings and her decision not to use it. Her broadcast became part of the shipsong, and her voice rang out with her shame, her fear... and her hope. *Let me go.*

The airlock opened.

Ekundayo was blown into space. The quarantine bubble held, but it was thin, so thin. The purple streaks of the Orion Nebula loomed over her like clawed fingers trying to drag her into the void of space. She was too close to the Patchwork ship for her team to pick her up; the ship's self-defense mechanisms would attack them if they tried.

She reached back with her arms to tear off her wings, but she could only barely touch the tips. Sturgeon had warned her about this—she had to use the tentacles. She let her Squidder tentacles snake down her back and wrapped them around the base of her wings, grasping tight with her suckers to get a solid grip. She tried to twist the wings off, but they'd grown into her flesh. Pain shot through her back.

Ekundayo pulled again, as hard as she could. The flesh of her back tore, and blood seeped out from the open wound. She released the wings and left them drifting behind her. Her head was spinning, and her muscles started to cramp. Too much exertion, not enough air, and the sickle cell trait that got her this mission in the first place was killing her.

The inside of the bubble was so very cold.

She reached for her tentacles, but her arms were trembling from the cold and her fingers refused to bend. Waves of nausea washed over her and she was in so much pain she couldn't remember what to do.

Help me. She sent the message to the shuttle, to the Patchwork ship, to anyone and everyone who might hear it. She shouted it into the stars.

A pair of fire kittens appeared inside her bubble. The heat of their bodies warmed the freezing air. Her shivering stopped, and her mind filled with Faceless whispers, a thousand songs of strength and comfort. She felt compelled to add her voice to the chorus, and she sang the guilt of her failed mission, and her desire for peace, and the fear that she would die inside the quarantine bubble.

Jaxon's voice came through her implant. *"Focus, Ekundayo. You can do this. Take off the tentacles and get into the flight suit. Quickly now."*

She tore the tentacles off her shoulder. It wasn't a clean separation, and she could feel blood oozing down her chest. She still had some of her alien parts, but the rest of them fit inside the flightsuit. She crammed herself into the suit and programmed it to send her away from the Patchwork ship. Her propulsion jets lit up and melted the quarantine bubble.

Her discarded wings drifted out into the cold void of space.

Safely in her flightsuit, Ekundayo let the blackness take her.

EKUNDAYO WOKE UP in an operating room.

"You're out of quarantine, and the parts that I grafted on have been removed," Sturgeon told her. "I even managed to isolate a small amount of Patchwork virus for further study. The whole thing has been a complete success!"

"Except for the part where I failed my fucking mission." Every inch of Ekundayo's body ached, and she couldn't hear the Patchwork ship. It was strangely quiet in her head without the singing.

Sturgeon's grin disappeared. "Yes. I only meant the surgery. The procedure was complicated due to the late-stage Patchwork infection. I had to start with an exchange transfusion to get the viral load in your bloodstream low enough to perform the traditional treatments. Everything went remarkably well, and I have a theory about how we can use attenuated Patchwork virus to—"

"Yes, I'm sure you did wonderful work." She glanced down to where her leg should be, but there was nothing there.

"Jaxon seemed quite fond of you when you were part Leonid. I woke you to ask what kind of leg you wanted." Sturgeon gestured to the tanks along the wall. "The Leonid leg you wore on your mission was too damaged to save, but I have several others."

It was tempting to become what Jaxon wanted her to be. He'd never ask her to do it, but there was something appealing about the possibility. But she didn't want to be a hybrid, she wanted to be herself, or as much of herself as she could, now that she'd been touched by the Faceless. The war had been so much clearer before she knew that the Faceless had a face. The enemy had been plague-ridden and dangerous, the humans had been fighting on the side of good. Now it didn't seem so simple.

Sturgeon was looking at her expectantly, waiting for an answer.

"I want my leg back."

THERE WAS NO pain the next time Ekundayo woke, but despite a long stay in the regeneration capsule she felt exhausted, worn down. Jaxon was by her side when she opened her eyes, and Ekundayo wondered how long he'd been waiting there. He didn't say anything about her human leg. If he was disappointed, he covered it well, with a smile and a gentle hug. "It's good to have you back."

"Don't get used to it. Bianchi will probably blast me out the airlock without a flightsuit." Which was what she deserved. Hospital ship or not, she had defied her orders. Commander Bianchi wouldn't care that the ship had helped her in the end, or that the songs of the Faceless were beautiful.

"Bianchi shipped out to face his court-martial while you were still in surgery. He lied to Captain Flores about the nature of the target. Turns out he knew all along that it was a hospital ship—got the intel from a communications drone that came through the jump point with the Patchwork ship. It probably won't go well for him." Jaxon paused.

"There's something else." Ekundayo met his gaze, tried to project confidence she didn't feel. "Tell me."

"The Captain petitioned for you to have extra recovery time, but now that you're awake and healed, you'll have to stand trial, too."

Of course. Of course she would stand trial. If she'd had any time to think about it, she would have known that this was coming. Her hands started shaking, and tears welled up in her eyes. She didn't want a trial. She knew she was guilty, but if she had to do it again she'd make the same choice. All she wanted was to pop out of existence like the fire kittens did, or at the very least curl up next to Jaxon. "Is the Patchwork ship still here?"

Jaxon shook his head. "When he found out you hadn't delivered the counter-virus, Bianchi ordered a more traditional attack. The Patchwork ship escaped through the jump point. No definitive word on whether they had fire kittens on board... but the ship reached the free-floating planet before they had to retreat." Jaxon brushed away the tears that rolled down Ekundayo's cheek.

"If they got the kittens, I'm a traitor to humanity."

"No. This is Bianchi's fault, not yours. Even if he was right about the hospital ship deliberately going after the fire kittens, he shouldn't have lied." Jaxon whistled softly to call his fire kittens. "Besides, Sturgeon had a bit of a breakthrough while you were asleep."

The kittens appeared, each wearing a collar of heat-resistant fabric.

"You got them to bring things with them!"

"It was all Sturgeon, actually. Something about the interaction of the Patchwork and your sickle cell trait gave Sturgeon the idea for an attenuated version of the virus. We threaded the collars with living organic tissue and Sturgeon's modified virus creates enough of a graft that the fire kittens can take the fabric with them."

The kittens blinked back out of existence, taking the collars with them. "How long until we can use it?"

"I don't know. It will take some work to scale up from collars to people—or maybe whole ships—but eventually we'll be able to teleport. So even if the Faceless managed to get some fire kittens, the war isn't over. Things will be different, but not necessarily tragically so," Jaxon smiled. "I've been talking to Neva, and we both think you'll be found innocent when you stand trial—refusing to attack a medical facility is justifiable under the Van Maanen Treaty."

Innocent or guilty, the trial was on Earth, not here at the station. Ekundayo brushed her fingers against Jaxon's cheek. He hadn't shaved, and the stubble was rough against her fingertips. "I hate goodbyes, and I'm leaving soon."

Jaxon laughed. "I'm going with you. Neva, too. We've got orders to escort my fire kittens back to Earth. Sturgeon thinks that if I go through the jump point with their collars and then call them, they'll come."

She didn't have to go alone. Ekundayo had an overwhelming urge to sing her relief to the stars, but she couldn't broadcast without the Patchwork. She was human, herself and nothing more. She wondered if there was some way to create a Faceless-human hybrid, a being that could bridge the gap between the Faceless and humankind and negotiate a peace. It had worked before, with the Pisceans, and—except for those damned wings—having a few extra parts hadn't been nearly as bad as she'd feared. Maybe she should have taken Sturgeon up on the offer of a Leonid leg after all. She smiled at Jaxon. "Sorry I don't smell good."

"That will also be different," Jaxon put his hand over hers, "but not necessarily tragic."

DEAR SARAH
Nancy Kress

IN SOME FAMILIES, it coulda been just a argument. Or maybe a shunning. Not my family—they done murder for less. I got two second cousins doing time in Riverbend. Blood feuds.

So I told them by Skype.

Call me a coward. You don't know Daddy, or Seth. Anyways, it warn't like I wanted to do it. I just didn't see no other way out of Brightwater and the life waiting for me there. And Daddy always said to use whatever you got. I was always the best shot anywhere around Brightwater. Shooting good is what I got.

And like I said, I couldn't see no other choice.

"MARYJO! WHERE THE hell you been?"

"I left a note, Daddy."

"All it says is you be gone for a few days. Where are you?"

I took in a real deep breath. *Just say it, Jo.* His face filled the screen in the room the recruiter let me have to myself to make this call. She didn't even seem worried I might steal something. Then Daddy stepped back and I saw our living room behind him, with its sprung tatty couch and magazine pictures on the walls. We piggyback on the Cranstons' internet, which works most days.

"Daddy... you know there's nothing for me in Brightwater now."

He didn't answer. Waiting. Mama moved into the screen behind him, then Seth and Sarah.

I said, "Nothing for any of us. I know we've always been there, but now things are different."

I didn't have to say what I meant. Daddy's eyes got that look he gets when anybody mentions the aliens. Eight years now since the oil rigs closed, and the gas drilling, and most important to us, the coal mines. Everybody I know is out of work since the Likkies gave us the Q-energy. Only they didn't really give it to us, they gave it to the rich guys in Washington and San Francisco and Seattle and Oklahoma City, who just got a whole lot richer selling it back to the country. "A trade partnership" they called it, but somehow people like us got left out of all the trading. We always do.

I stumbled on. "I want more, Daddy. You always said to use whatever you—"

"What did you do?" he said, and his voice was quiet thunder.

"I enlisted."

Sarah cried out. She's only eleven, she don't understand. Seth, who's a pretty good stump preacher, pointed his finger at me and started in. "'Mine own familiar friend in whom I trusted, who did eat of my bread, hath lifted up his hand against me!'"

Psalm four-something.

Mama said, "Did you sign anything? Come back and we'll hide you!"

Jacob—and where did he come from? He shoulda been out digging bootleg coal for the stove—yelled, "Brightwater is good enough for the rest of us! We been here two hundred years!"

Mama said, all desperate, "MaryJo, pride goeth before a fall!"

Sarah: "Come home!"

Seth: "'And the many will fall away and betray one another!'"

Jacob: "You always thought you were better than us!"

Mama: "Oh dear sweet Jesus, help this prodigal girl to see the light and—"

Then Daddy cut it all short with that voice of his. "You're a traitor. To us and to your country."

I cried, "I joined the United States Army! You fought in Afghanistan and Grandpa in—"

"Traitor. And not my daughter. I don't never want to see your face again."

A wail from Mama, and then the screen went black and dead, dead, dead.

The recruiter came back in. She was in a fancy uniform but her face was kind. "Is everything all right?"

"Yes, ma'am." I warn't about to talk on this with her. Anyways, she knew the situation. The whole fucking country knew the situation. If you have money, you're glad the Likkies are here, changing up the economy and saving the environment. If you don't have money, if you're just working people, your job disappeared to the Likkies' Q-energy and their factory 'bots and all the rest of it. So you starve. Or you join one of the terrorist groups trying to bring the Likkies down. Or, like me, you do what poor kids have always done, including Daddy and Grandpa—you join the army for a spell.

Only this time, the army was on the wrong side. The military was fighting our home-raised anti-Likkie terrorists in American cities, even on the moon base and in space. I was going to be defending my family's enemy.

I went outside and got on the bus to go to basic training.

*   *   *

BASIC WARN'T TOO bad. I was at Fort Benning for OSUP, one stop unit training. I'm tough and I don't need much sleep and after the first few days, nobody messed with me. The drill sergeants mostly picked on somebody else, and my battle buddy was okay, and silent. I had the highest rifle qualification score and so I got picked to fire the live round at AT4 training. The Claymore blew up with more noise and debris than anybody expected, but all I could think of was this: Daddy taught me to shoot, he should be proud of me. Only, of course, he warn't.

I didn't see no aliens at Fort Benning.

Once somebody suggested sniper school, and I was kinda interested until I found out it involved a lot of math. No way.

I had three days after OSUT before I had to report to my unit at Fort Drum. I checked into a motel and played video games. The last day, I called home—at least the phone warn't cut off—and by a miracle, Sarah answered instead of anybody else.

"Hey, Squirt."

"*MaryJo?*"

"Yeah. How you doing?"

"How are you? Where are you? Are you coming home now?"

"No. I'm going to my unit, in New York. Sarah—"

"In *New York City?*"

I heard the dazzle in her voice, and all at once my throat closed up. It was me who taught Sarah to shoot and about her period and all sorts of shit. I got out, "No, upcountry New York. Listen, you doing okay?" And then what I really wanted to ask: "They forgive me yet?"

Silence. Then a little whisper, "No. Oh, Jo, quit that army and them Likkies and come home! I miss you!"

"I can't, Squirt. But I'll send—"

"Gotta go! Seth just come home. Bye!"

A sharp click on the line.

I spent my last night drunk.

The next day I got on my first plane ride and reported to Fort Drum. And right there was my first alien.

"DOES ANYBODY HAVE any questions?"

Nobody did. The officer—a lieutenant colonel, the highest rank I ever expected to see talking right at us—stood in front of a hundred sixty FNGs ('fucking new guys') talking about Likkies. Only of course he called them by their right name, Leckinites. I don't know where the name come from or what it means; I mighta slept through that part. But I knew nearly everything else, because for a solid week we been learning about the aliens: their home planet and their biology and their culture and, a lot, how important their help was to fixing Earth's problems with energy and environment and a bunch of other stuff. We seen pictures and movies and charts, and at night we used our personal hour to argue about them. Near as I could tell, about half the base thought the Likkies were great for humans. The other half was like me, knowing just how bad the aliens made it for folks on the bottom.

And now we were going to meet one for the first time.

"Are you sure you have no questions?" Colonel Jamison said, sounding like we shoulda had some. But in the army, it's best to keep your mouth shut. "No? Then without further delay, let me introduce Mr. Granson. Tensh-hut!"

We all leapt to attention and the Likkie walked into the room. If its name was 'Mr. Granson,' then mine was Dolly Parton. It was tall, like in the movies we seen, and had human-type arms and legs and head ('This optimum symmetrical design is unsurprisingly replicated in various Terran mammalian species as well' one of our hand-outs read, whatever the fuck that means.) The Likkie had two eyes and a wide mouth with no lips, no hair or nose. It wore a loose white robe like pictures I seen of Arab sheiks, and there mighta had anything underneath. Its arms ended in seven tentacles each, its skin was sorta light purplish, and it wore a clear helmet like a fishbowl 'cause it can't breathe our air. No oxygen tank and hose to lug around like old Grandpa Addams had when the lung cancer was getting him. The helmet someways turned our air into theirs. They're smart bastards, I'll give them that.

"Hello," it said. "I am privileged to meet with you today."

Real good English and not too much accent—I heard a lot worse at Fort Benning.

"My wish is to offer thanks for the help of the US Army, including all of you, in protecting the partnership that we are here to forge between your people and mine. A partnership that will benefit us all."

The guy next to me, Lopez, shifted in his seat. His family used to work at a factory that now uses Likkie 'bots instead. But Morales kept his face empty.

The Likkie went on like that, in a speech somebody human musta wrote for him because it didn't have no mistakes. At least the speechwriters still got jobs.

Afterward, there was a lot of bitching in the barracks about the speech, followed by a lot of arguing. I didn't say nothing. But after lights out, the soldier in the next bunk, Drucker, whispered to me, "You don't like the Likkies either, do you, Addams?"

I didn't answer her. It was after lights-out. But for a long time I couldn't sleep.

FORT DRUM SUCKED. Snow and cold and it was almost April, for Chrissake. Back home, flowers would be blooming. Sarah would be barefoot in shorts.

She sent me a letter. She was way better'n me at writing.

Dear Jo,

I hope you get this letter. My teacher told me what address to put on it and she give me a stamp. She is nice. I got A on my math test last week.

The big news here is that Jacob is getting married. Nobody knew till now. Her name is Lorna and I don't like her she is mean but then so is Jacob sometimes so maybe they will be happy together.

My main reason to write you is to say COME HOME!!! I had a real good idea. If you shoot an alien I bet Daddy would forgive you. Seth too. DO IT!!!

All my love forever,

Sarah Addams

"What's that?" Drucker said. She was looking over my shoulder and I didn't even hear her come up behind me.

"Nothing!" I said, folding the letter. But she already read it. She must read real fast.

"I didn't mean to invade your privacy, Jo," she said—that's the way she talks. "But I have to say that Sarah—is she your younger sister?—sounds like a really smart kid. With the right ideas."

Then Drucker looked at me long and serious. I wanted to punch her—for reading my letter, for talking fancy, for not being my family. I didn't do none of that. Keeping my nose clean. I just said, "Go fuck yourself, Drucker."

She only laughed.

And who said she gets to call me 'Jo'?

*   *   *

FORT DRUM WAS not just cold, it was boring. Drill and hike, hike and drill. But we warn't there long. After a week, fifty of us had a half-hour to prepare to ship out, down to a city called Albany. Drucker was one of us. For days she'd been trying to friend around with me, and sometimes I let her. Usually I keep to myself, but listening to her took my mind off home, at least for a while.

"Where the fuck is Albany?" I said on the bus.

A guy in the seat behind me laughed. "Don't you ever watch the news, Addams?"

"It's the capital city of New York State," Drucker said without sounding snotty, which was the other reason I let her hang around with me. She don't ever act like she knows more'n me, though she does.

I gave the guy behind us the finger and lowered my voice. "What's going on in Albany?"

Drucker said quietly, "It's bad. You ever hear about the T-bocs?"

I shook my head. Our buses tore through the gates like it was fleeing demons. Wherever Albany was, the army wanted us there fast.

"The Take Back Our Country organization. Anti-alien terrorists, the largest and best armed and organized of all those groups. They've captured a warehouse outside Albany, big fortified place used to store explosives. The owners, a corporation, were in the process of moving the stuff out when the T-bocs took the building. They've got hostages in there along with the explosives."

"And we're going to take the building back?"

Drucker smiled. "Marines and US Rangers are going to take the building back, Addams. We'll probably just be the outer perimeter guard. To keep away press and stupid civilians."

"Oh," I said, feeling stupid myself. "Okay, then."

"Thing is, some of the hostages are kids."

"Kids?" I thought of Sarah. "Why were kids in a warehouse?"

"They weren't. They were brought there. It was all timed just so. This is big."

Big. Bigger than anything that ever happened to me, or might happen to me, in Brightwater. Then Drucker said something that made it bigger.

"Our kids, Jo. And three of theirs."

DRUCKER WAS RIGHT, about every last thing. We were perimeter guards for a real big perimeter—half a mile around the warehouse. There was houses and train tracks and other buildings and trucks with no cabs and huge big dumpsters and a homeless tent town, and every last one of them had to be cleared of people. I was with a four-man stack, flushing out everybody who didn't have enough sense to already leave, which was a lot of people. We cleared rooms and escorted out squatters and made tenants in the saggy houses pack up what they could carry and then leave. Some of them got angry, shouting that they had no place to go. Some of them cried. One man attacked with a sledge hammer, which didn't get him nowhere. My sarge knew what he was doing—he cleared rooms in Iraq, where the enemy had more'n sledgehammers.

Drucker was right about something else, too. There were *kids* in there. Turns out that seven years ago, while Daddy and Seth and Jacob were losing their jobs in the mines and we got evicted from our house, the Likkies put some of their kids in special schools with our kids so they could all learn each other's languages and grow up together just like there warn't no difference between us and them. The T-bocs took that school and transported six kids to the warehouse. Seven bodyguards and five teachers at the school were dead. They mighta been pretty good bodyguards, but the T-bocs had military weapons.

"I told you it was big," Drucker said.

"Yeah, you did." We just spent twenty hours clearing buildings. Then fresh troops arrived to relieve us, more experienced soldiers. We'd been first just because we were closest. Rangers and Marines were there but they warn't permitted to do nothing while the negotiators tried to talk the T-bocs down. Drucker and I were off-duty, laying on mats in a high school gym that was now a barracks. I had a shower in the locker room and I was so tired my bones felt like melting. It warn't a bad feeling.

But Drucker wanted to talk.

"What do you think about all this, Jo?"

"I'm not thinking."

"Well, start. Do you think the T-bocs are justified?"

"Justified? You mean, like, right to kidnap kids? How old are them kids, anyway?"

"Second graders. The humans are seven years old, two girls and a boy, all the children of VIPs. Who knows how old the Likkies are? Maybe they just live a real short time, like insects, and these so-called 'kids' are really adults halfway through their lives."

"That warn't what our lectures said."

"Do you believe everything the army tells you?"

I raised up on one elbow and looked at her. In the half-light her eyes shone too bright, like she was using. Was she?

Drucker sat all the way up. We'd hauled our gym mats into a corner and nobody else could hear.

"Jo, you told me your family are all unemployed and on welfare because of the Likkies. I imagine that's a deep shame to people like yours, isn't it?"

"Shut up," I said, 'cause she was right. Shame is what made Daddy and them so angry. All their choices got taken away by the aliens.

"But it's not *right*," she said, real soft. "This is supposed to be our country. These aliens are just more damn immigrants trying to take it away. Sometimes I think the army is on the wrong side. Do you ever think that, Jo?"

"Shut up," I said again, 'cause I didn't like hearing my thoughts coming from her mouth. "You using?"

"Yes. Want some?"

"No."

"That's all right. I just wanted the chance to express my thoughts, so thank you for listening. You're a real friend."

We warn't friends. I shoulda said that, but I didn't. I waited, 'cause it was clear she warn't done. If she was trying to recruit me for something, I wanted to hear what.

But all she said was, "This is big," and her voice gleamed with satisfaction like a gun barrel with fresh oil.

THE STAND-OFF went on for a day, and then a week, and then two weeks. We had more soldiers. We had army choppers to keep away the press choppers. We had drones in the air, thicker than mosquitos in July. We had more negotiators—not that I ever saw them. My unit kept getting pushed farther and farther away from the warehouse as the perimeter got wider. More people got evacuated. None of them liked it.

But every night my unit moved back to the high school to sleep. I don't know where the Special Forces guys slept, but I know they were antsy as hell, wanting to go in and take the objective. Which they couldn't do because the T-bocs said they'd kill the kids.

"An interstellar incident," Drucker said. "Maybe that's what we need to get the Likkies off our planet. Blow the place to smithereens and they'll think it's too dangerous to stay on Earth."

"Is that what you want?" I finally asked.

She only smiled. Then after that I didn't see her much, because she started fucking somebody in off-duty hours. I don't know who or where, and I didn't care.

The whole thing couldn't go on like that.

And it didn't.

THE NIGHT WAS like home, only not really 'cause all the city lights blotted the stars and it smelled like a city and under my boots was concrete instead of switchgrass. But the air had that spring softness like I hadn't felt up here before, and that little spring breeze that made you just ache inside.

At home, Mama would be setting out tomato plants. Sarah would be picking wild strawberries. The fawns would be standing for the first time on spindly little legs. Last year me and Sarah got real close to one.

Coming off guard duty on the perimeter, I warn't sleepy. I put my rifle in its sling and walked, careful to stay in the middle of the street where it was allowed. I passed a bar and a V-R playroom, both closed and boarded up. At the end of the allowed section, a rope marked another perimeter, this time around the old hotel where brass and negotiators and them stayed. It looked nice, with a awning over the door and big pots of fake flowers. *They* warn't sleeping on gym mats.

Sarah's letter was in my pocket. She didn't send a second one, or I else didn't get it. Was Jacob married yet? He—

Gunfire someplace behind me.

I hit the ground. Gunfire came from another place, off to my left. Then explosions, little ones, at a bunch of different places—*pop pop pop*. Somebody screamed.

Soldiers poured out of buildings. The Marines guarding the hotel raised their weapons. An officer barked orders but I couldn't hear him because a flashbang went off and everything was noise and blinding light and confusion and people running.

I got to my feet and unslung my rifle, but then I didn't know what to do with it, or myself. I warn't even supposed to be here. I backed away, trying to make out what was happening, when another explosion went off, pretty close to the hotel.

When I could see again, a Likkie was running out of the hotel door, yelling. One of the Marines at the door was down. I didn't see the other one. The Likkie ran right past me, high-tailing it to the warehouse, and I didn't need no translator to know why it was there or what it was screaming. I seen that look on Mama's face the time Sarah fell into the pond and got fished out half drowned. I seen it on Daddy's face when Seth got injured in the mine. That Likkie had a kid in the warehouse and it was going in after it.

It was going to pass right by me. I already had my rifle raised. I wouldn't even need to sight.

If you shoot an alien I bet Daddy would forgive you. Seth too. DO IT!!!

Then I saw Drucker.

She was supposed to be asleep in the gym. But here she was in full kit, her top half popping up from inside a dumpster, M4 swinging around, cheek against the stock. She warn't that good a marksman, but she was good enough. All I had to do was nothing—let her do it for me. *Vengeance is mine, saith the Lord*, but I never believed that horseshit. The Lord might have vengeance against tribes attacking Israel, but He ain't interested in Likkies taking a living from people like us.

Choppers roared above, heading for the warehouse. Whoever set off that gunfire and explosives and flashbangs, whether they were our diversionary tactic or T-boc's, the raid was going to happen now. Special Forces were going in and Marines were laying down covering fire. The noise and confusion was like Armageddon. But I warn't part of that neither, warn't at the center of it. People like me never was.

Drucker had her sight now. She stilled.

All I had to do was wait.

But—soldiers aren't supposed to murder civilians, which that Likkie was. Soldiers in the US Army aren't supposed to murder each other neither. It was all tangled up in my mind, only now it had to be one or the other. Or nothing.

I always been real fast. I sighted and squeezed. I got Drucker just before she fired, right in the head. She fell backwards into the dumpster.

A second later a Marine sort of surrounded the running Likkie and stopped it. A second after that, another Marine had me on the ground, M4 kicked away. "You move and I'll blow your head off, motherfucker!" I didn't move. He cuffed me and took my sidearm. When he yanked me to my feet, I somehow heard—over all the choppers, automatic fire, sirens, explosions—the rustle of Sarah's letter in my pocket, louder than anything else.

I WRITE SARAH from the brig at Fort Drum.

Special Forces took the warehouse. Sixteen troops died, and thirty-eight T-bocs. Two of the kids were killed during the rescue. One of ours, Kayla Allison Howell, seven years old, black hair and blue eyes, pink tee-shirt with Hello Kitty on it. I seen pictures. One of the Likkie kids, a little bald purplish thing, whose name I can't pronounce. They were shot in the head before a US Ranger shot the murderer. Later, my lawyer told me, some of the Special Forces who went into that room cried.

A whole bunch of important people said the raid was wrong, the army shoulda waited. The army said that under the circumstances, it had no choice. The arguing is red hot and it don't stop. Probably it will never stop.

I don't know if they shoulda gone in or not. But I know this, now: there is always a choice, even for people who will never be at the center of nothing. Changes and choices, they go together, bound up like sticks for a bonfire that's going to be lit no matter what.

Drucker made a choice when she joined the T-bocs, a choice to kill anything that made changes happen.

That Likkie outside the hotel, it chose to risk its life trying to get to its kid. And the Likkies are choosing to stay here, in the United States, instead of avenging their dead kid or else packing up and going home. In fact, more are coming. They have more plans for helping us with technology and shit. Saving the planet, they say, and politicians agree with them.

My family chose to give up.

What I did is earning me a court martial. But I chose long before the night of the raid. In the locker room of the high school I saw Drucker's T-boc patch, hidden under her uniform. I saw it 'cause she wanted me to see it, wanted me to join them. I coulda reported it then, and I didn't.

Did I choose wrong when I killed Drucker? Even now, even after all the thinking I do sitting here in my cell, even after my lawyer says I'll get off because the evidence shows that Drucker was part of T-bocs, even after all that—I don't know.

But I do know this—things change. Even things that look set in stone. Maybe someday, years from now, jobs or people or aliens or *something* will change enough that I can go home.

For now, I write a letter that might or might not get delivered.

Dear Sarah—

THE MOON IS NOT A BATTLEFIELD

Indrapramit Das

WE'RE RECORDING.

I was born in the sky, for war. This is what we were told.

I think when people hear this, they think of ancient Earth stories. Of angels and superheroes and gods, leaving destruction between the stars. But I'm no superhero, no Kalel of America-Bygone with the flag of his dead planet flying behind him. I'm no angel Gabreel striking down Satan in the void or blowing the trumpet to end worlds. I'm no devi Durga bristling with arms and weapons, chasing down demons through the cosmos and vanquishing them, no Kali with a string of heads hanging over her breasts black as deep space, making even the other gods shake with terror at her righteous rampage.

I was born in the sky, for war. What does it mean?

I WAS ACTUALLY born on Earth, not far above sea level, in the Greater Kolkata Megapolis. My parents gave me away to the Government of India when I was still a small child, in exchange for enough money for them to live off frugally for a year—an unimaginable amount of wealth for two Dalit street-dwellers who scraped shit out of sewers for a living, and scavenged garbage for recycling—

sewers sagging with centuries worth of shit, garbage heaps like mountains. There was another child I played with the most in our slum. The government took her as well. Of the few memories I have left of those early days on Earth, the ones of us playing are clearest, more than the ones of my parents, because they weren't around much. But she was always there. She'd bring me hot jalebis snatched from the hands of hapless pedestrians, her hands covered in syrup, and we'd share them. We used to climb and run along the huge sea-wall that holds back the rising Bay of Bengal, and spit in the churning sea. I haven't seen the sea since, except from space— that roiling mass of water feels like a dream. So do those days, with the child who would become the soldier most often by my side. The government told our parents that they would cleanse us of our names, our untouchability, give us a chance to lead noble lives as astral defenders of the Republic of India. Of course they gave us away. I don't blame them. Aditi never blamed hers, either. That was the name my friend was given by the Army. You've met her. We were told our new names before training even began. Single-names, always. Usually from the Mahabharata or Ramayana, we realized later. I don't remember the name my parents gave me. I never asked Aditi if she remembered hers.

That, then, is when the life of asura Gita began.

I was raised by the state to be a soldier, and borne into the sky in the hands of the Republic to be its protector, before I even hit puberty.

The notion that there could be war on the Moon, or anywhere beyond Earth, was once a ridiculous dream.

So are many things, until they come to pass.

I've lived for thirty-six years as an infantry soldier stationed off-world. I was deployed and considered in active duty from eighteen in the Chandnipur Lunar Cantonment Area. I first arrived in

Chandnipur at six, right after they took us off the streets. I grew up there. The Army raised us. Gave us a better education than we'd have ever gotten back on Earth. Right from childhood, me and my fellow asuras—Earth-bound Indian infantry soldiers were jawans, but we were always, always asuras, a mark of pride—we were told that we were stationed in Chandnipur to protect the intrasolar gateway of the Moon for the greatest country on that great blue planet in our black sky—India. India, which we could see below the clouds if we squinted during Earthrise on a surface patrol (if we were lucky, we could spot the white wrinkle of the Himalayas through telescopes). We learned the history of our home: after the United States of America and Russia, India was the third Earth nation to set foot on the Moon, and the first to settle a permanent base there. Chandnipur was open to scientists, astronauts, tourists and corporations of all countries, to do research, develop space travel, take expensive holidays and launch inter-system mining drones to asteroids. The generosity and benevolence of Bharat Mata, no? But we were to protect Chandnipur's sovereignty as Indian territory at all costs, because other countries were beginning to develop their own lunar expeditions to start bases. Chandnipur, we were told, was a part of India. The only part of India not on Earth. We were to make sure it remained that way. This was our mission. Even though, we were told, the rest of the world didn't officially recognize any land on the moon to belong to any country, back then. Especially because of that.

Do you remember Chandnipur well?

IT WAS WHERE *I met you, asura Gita. Hard to forget that, even if it hadn't been my first trip to the Moon. I was very nervous. The ride up the elevator was peaceful. Like... being up in the mountains, in the Himalayas, you know? Oh—I'm so sorry. Of course not. Just, the feeling of being high up—the silence of it, in a way, despite all the people in the elevator cabins. But then you start floating under the seat belts, and there are the safety instructions on how to move around the platform once you get to the top, and all you feel like doing is pissing. That's when you feel untethered. The shuttle to the Moon from the top of the elevator wasn't so peaceful. Every blast of the craft felt so powerful out there. The gs just raining down on you as you're strapped in. I felt like a feather.*

Like a feather. Yes. I imagine so. There are no birds in Chandnipur, but us asuras always feel like feathers. Felt. Now I feel heavy all the time, like a stone, like a—hah—a moon, crashing into its world, so possessed by gravity, though I'm only skin and bones. A feather on a moon, a stone on a planet.

You know, when our Havaldar, Chamling his name was, told me that asura Aditi and I were to greet and guide a reporter visiting the Cantonment Area, I can't tell you how shocked we were. We were so excited. We would be on the feeds! We never got reporters up there. Well, to be honest, I wanted to show off our bravery, tell you horror stories of what happens if you wear your suit wrong outside the Cantonment Area on a walk, or get caught in warning shots from Chinese artillery klicks away, or what happens if the micro-atmosphere over Chandnipur malfunctions and becomes too thin while you're out and about there (you burn or freeze or asphyxiate). Civilians like horror stories from soldiers. You see so many of them in the media feeds in the pods, all these war stories. I used to like seeing how different it is for soldiers on Earth, in the old wars, the recent ones. Sometimes it would get hard to watch, of course.

Anyway, asura Aditi said to me, "Gita, they aren't coming here to be excited by a war movie. We aren't even at war. We're in *territorial conflict*. You use the word war and it'll look like we're boasting. We need to make them feel at home, not scare the shit out of them. We need to show them the hospitality of asuras on our own turf."

Couldn't disagree with that. We wanted people on Earth to see how well we do our jobs, so that we'd be welcomed with open arms when it was time for the big trip back—the promised pension, retirement, and that big old heaven in the sky where we all came from, Earth. We wanted every Indian up there to know we were protecting their piece of the Moon. Your piece of the Moon.

I thought soldiers would be frustrated having to babysit a journalist following them around. But you and asura Aditi made me feel welcome.

I felt bad for you. We met civilians in Chandnipur proper, when we got time off, in the Underground Markets, the bars. But you were my first fresh one, Earth-fresh. Like the imported fish in the Markets. Earth-creatures, you know, always delicate, expensive, mouth open gawping, big eyes. Out of water, they say.

Did I look expensive? I was just wearing the standard issue jumpsuits they give visitors.

Arre, you know what I mean. In the Markets we soldiers couldn't buy Earth-fish or Earth-lamb or any Earth-meat, when they showed up every six months. We only ever tasted the printed stuff. Little packets; in the stalls they heat up the synthi for you in the machine. Nothing but salt and heat and protein. Imported Earth-meat was too expensive. Same for Earth-people, expensive. Fish out of water. Earth meant paradise. You came from heaven. No offense.

None taken. You and asura Aditi were very good to me. That's what I remember.

After Aditi reminded me that you were going to show every Indian on their feeds our lives, we were afraid of looking bad. You looked scared, at first. Did we scare you?

I wouldn't say scared. Intimidated. You know, everything you were saying earlier, about gods and superheroes from the old Earth stories. The stuff they let you watch and read in the pods. That's what I saw, when you welcomed us in full regalia, out on the surface, in your combat suits, at the parade. You gleamed like gods. Like devis, asuras, like your namesakes. Those weapon limbs, when they came out of the backs of your suit during the demonstration, they looked like the arms of the goddesses in the epics, or the wings of angels, reflecting the sunlight coming over the horizon—the light was so white, after Earth, not shifted yellow by atmosphere. It was blinding, looking at you all. I couldn't imagine having to face that, as a soldier, as your enemy. Having to face you. I couldn't imagine having to patrol for hours, and fight, in those suits—just my civilian surface suit was so hot inside, so claustrophobic. I was shaking in there, watching you all.

Do you remember, the Governor of Chandnipur Lunar Area came out to greet you, and shake the hands of all the COs. A surface parade like that, on airless ground, that never happened—it was all for you and the rest of the reporters, for the show back on Earth. We had never before even seen the Governor in real life, let alone in a surface suit. The rumours came back that he was trembling and sweating when he shook their hands—that he couldn't even pronounce the words to thank them for their service. So you weren't alone, at least.

Then when we went inside the Cantonment Area, and we were allowed to take off our helmets right out in the open—I waited for you and Aditi to do it first. I didn't believe I wouldn't die, that my face wouldn't freeze. We were on that rover, such a bumpy ride, but open air like those vehicles in the earliest pictures of people on the Moon—just bigger. We went through the Cantonment airlock gate, past the big yellow sign that reads 'Chandnipur, Gateway to the Stars,' and when we emerged from the other side Aditi told me to look up and see for myself, the different sky. From deep black to that deep, dusky blue, it was amazing, like crossing over into another world. The sunlight still felt different, blue-white instead of yellow, filtered by the nanobot haze, shimmering in that lunar dawn coming in over the hilly rim of Daedalus crater. The sun felt tingly, raw, like it burned even though the temperature was cool. The Earth was half in shadow—it looked fake, a rendered backdrop in a veeyar sim. And sometimes the micro-atmosphere would move just right and the bots would be visible for a few seconds in a wave across that low sky, the famous flocks of lunar fireflies. The rover went down the suddenly smooth lunarcrete road, down the main road of the Cantonment—

New Delhi Avenue.

Yes, New Delhi Avenue, with the rows of wireframed flags extended high, all the state colours of India, the lines and lines of white barracks with those tiny windows on both sides. I wanted to stay in those, but they put us civilians underground, in a hotel. They didn't want us complaining about conditions. As we went down New Delhi Avenue and turned into the barracks for the tour, you and Aditi took off your helmets and breathed deep. Your faces were covered in black warpaint. Greasepaint. Full regalia, yes? You both looked like Kali, with or without the necklace of heads. Aditi helped me with the helmet, and I felt lunar air for the first time. The dry, cool air of Chandnipur. And you said 'Welcome to chota duniya. You can take off the helmet.' Chota duniya, the little world. Those Kali faces, running with sweat, the tattoos of your wetware. You wore a small beard, back then, and a crew-cut. Asura Aditi had a ponytail, I was surprised that was allowed.

You looked like warriors, in those blinding suits of armour.

Warriors. I don't anymore, do I. What do I look like now?

I see you have longer hair. You shaved off your beard.

Avoiding the question, clever. Did you know that jawan means 'young man'? But we were asuras. We were proud of our hair, not because we were young men. We, the women and the hijras, the not-men, told the asuras who were men, why do you get to keep beards and moustaches and we don't? Some of them had those twirly moustaches like the asuras in the myths. So the boys said to us: we won't stop you. Show us your beards! From then it was a competition. Aditi could hardly grow a beard on her pretty face, so she gave up when it was just fuzz. I didn't. I was so proud when I first sprouted that hair on my chin, when I was a teenager. After I grew it out, Aditi called it a rat-tail. I never could grow the twirly moustaches, But I'm a decommissioned asura now, so I've shaved off the beard.

What do you think you look like now?

Like a beggar living in a slum stuck to the side of the space elevator that took me up to the sky so long ago, and brought me down again not so long ago.

Some of my neighbours don't see asuras as women or men. I'm fine with that. They ask me: do you still bleed? Did you menstruate on the Moon? They say, menstruation is tied to the Moon, so asuras must bleed all the time up there, or never at all down here. They think we used all that blood to paint ourselves red because we are warriors. To scare our enemies. I like that idea. Some of them don't believe it when I say that I bleed the same as any Earthling with a cunt. The young ones believe me, because they help me out, bring me rags, pads when they can find them, from down there in the city —can't afford the meds to stop bleeding altogether. Those young ones are a blessing. I can't exactly hitch a ride on top of the elevator up and down every day in my condition.

People in the slum all know you're an asura?

I ask again: what do I look like now?

A veteran. You have the scars. From the wetware that plugged you into the suits. The lines used to be black, raised—on your face, neck. Now they're pale, flat.

The mark of the decommissioned asura—everyone knows who you are. The government plucks out your wires. Like you're a broken machine. They don't want you selling the wetware on the black market. They're a part of the suits we wore, just a part we wore all the time inside us—and the suits are property of the Indian Army, Lunar Command.

I told you why the suits are so shiny, didn't I, all those years ago? Hyper-reflective surfaces so we didn't fry up in them like the printed meat in their heating packets when the sun comes up. The suits made us easy to spot on a lunar battlefield. It's why we always tried to stay in shadow, use infra-red to spot enemies. When we went on recon, surveillance missions, we'd use lighter stealth suits, non-metal, non-reflective, dark grey like the surface. We could only do that if we coordinated our movements to land during night-time.

When I met you and asura Aditi then you'd been in a few battles already. With Chinese and Russian troops. Small skirmishes.

All battles on the moon are small skirmishes. You can't afford anything bigger. Even the horizon is smaller, closer. But yes, our section had seen combat a few times. But even that was mostly waiting, and scoping with infra-red along the shadows of craters. When there was fighting, it was between long, long stretches of walking and sitting. But it was never boring. Nothing can be boring when you've got a portioned ration of air to breathe, and no sound to warn you of a surprise attack. Each second is measured out and marked in your mind. Each step is a success. When you do a lunar surface patrol outside Chandnipur, outside regulated atmosphere or Indian territory, as many times as we did, you do get used to it. But never, ever bored. If anything, it becomes hypnotic—you do everything you need to do without even thinking, in that silence between breathing and the words of your fellow soldiers.

You couldn't talk too much about what combat was like on the Moon, on that visit.

They told us not to. Havaldar Chamling told us that order came all the way down from the Lieutenant General of Lunar Command. It was all considered classified information, even training maneuvers. It was pretty silent when you were in Chandnipur. I'm sure the Russians and the Chinese had news of that press visit. They could have decided to put on a display of might, stage some shock and awe attacks, missile strikes, troop movements to draw us out of the Cantonment Area.

I won't lie—I was both relieved and disappointed. I've seen war, as a field reporter. Just not on the Moon. I wanted to see firsthand what the asuras were experiencing.

It would have been difficult. Lunar combat is not like Earth combat, though I don't know much about Earth combat other than theory and history. I probably know less than you do, ultimately, because I've never experienced it. But I've read things, watched things about wars on Earth. Learned things, of course, in our lessons. It's different on the Moon. Harder to accommodate an extra person when each battle is like a game of chess. No extra pieces allowed on the board. Every person needs their own air. No one can speak out of turn and clutter up comms. The visibility of each person needs to be accounted for, since it's so high.

The most frightening thing about lunar combat is that you often can't tell when it's happening until it's too late. On the battlefields beyond Chandnipur, out on the magma seas, combat is silent. You can't hear anything but your own footsteps, the *thoom-thoom-thoom* of your suit's metal boots crunching dust, or the sounds of your own weapons through your suit, the rattle-kick of ballistics, the near-silent hum of lasers vibrating in the metal of the shell keeping you alive. You'll see the flash of a mine or grenade going off a few feet away but you won't hear it. You won't hear anything coming down from above unless you look up—be it ballistic missiles or a meteorite hurtling down after centuries flying through outer space. You'll feel the shockwave knock you back but you won't hear it. If you're lucky, of course.

Laser weapons are invisible out there, and that's what's we mostly used. There's no warning at all. No muzzle-flash, no noise. One minute you're sitting there thinking you're on the right side of the rocks giving you cover, and the next moment you see a glowing hole melting into the suit of the soldier next to you, like those time-lapse videos of something rotting. It takes less than a second if the soldier on the other side of the beam is aiming properly. Less than a second and there's the flash and pop, blood and gas and superheated metal venting into the thin air like an aerosol spray, the scream like static in the mics. Aditi was a sniper, she could've told you how lethal the long-range lasers were. I carried a semi-auto, laser or ballistic; those lasers were as deadly, just lower range and zero warm-up. When we were in battles closer to settlements, we'd switch to the ballistic weaponry, because the buildings and bases are mostly better protected from that kind of damage, bullet-proof. There was kind of a silent agreement between all sides to keep from heavily damaging the actual bases. Those ballistic fights were almost a relief—our suits could withstand projectile damage better, and you could see the tracers coming from kilometers away, even if you couldn't hear them. Like fire on oil, across the jet sky. Bullets aren't that slow either, especially here on the Moon, but somehow it felt better to see it, like you could dodge the fire, especially if we were issued jet packs, though we rarely used them because of how difficult they were to control. Aditi was better at using hers.

She saved my life once.

I mean, she did that many times, we both did for each other, just by doing what we needed to do on a battlefield. But she directly saved my life once, like an Earth movie hero. Rocket-propelled grenade on a quiet battlefield. Right from up above and behind us. I didn't even see it. I just felt asura Aditi shove me straight off the ground from behind and blast us off into the air with her jetpack, propelling us both twenty feet above the surface in a second. We twirled in mid-air, and for a little moment, it felt like we were free of the Moon, hovering there between it and the blazing blue Earth, dancing together. As we sailed back down and braced our legs for landing without suit damage, Aditi never let me go, kept our path back down steady. Only then did I see the cloud of lunar dust and debris hanging where we'd been seconds earlier, the aftermath of an explosion I hadn't heard or seen, the streaks of light as the rest of the fireteam returned ballistic fire, spreading out in leaps with short bursts from their jetpacks. No one died in that encounter. I don't even remember whose troops we were fighting in that encounter, which lunar army. I just remember that I didn't die because of Aditi.

Mostly, we never saw the enemy close up. They were always just flecks of light on the horizon, or through our infrared overlay. Always ghosts, reflecting back the light of sun and Earth, like the Moon itself. It made it easier to kill them, if I'm being honest. They already seemed dead. When you're beyond Chandnipur, out on the mara under that merciless black sky with the Earth gleaming in the distance, the only colour you can see anywhere, it felt like *we* were already dead too. Like we were all just ghosts playing out the old wars of humanity, ghosts of soldiers who died far, far down on the ground. But then we'd return to the city, to the warm bustle of the Underground Markets on our days off, to our chota duniya, and the Earth would seem like heaven again, not a world left behind but one to be attained, one to earn, the unattainable paradise rather than a distant history of life that we'd only lived through media pods and lessons.

And now, here you are. On Earth.

Here I am. Paradise attained. I have died and gone to heaven.

It's why I'm here, isn't it? Why we're talking.

You could say that. Thank you for coming, again. You didn't have any trouble coming up the elevator shaft, did you? I know it's rough clinging to the top of the elevator.

I've been on rougher rides. There are plenty of touts down in the elevator base station who are more than willing to give someone with a few rupees a lending hand up the spindle. So. You were saying. About coming back to Earth. It must have been surprising, the news that you were coming back, last year.

FTL changed everything. That was, what, nine years ago?

At first it brought us to the edge of full-on lunar war, like never before, because the Moon became the greatest of all jewels in the night sky. It could become our first FTL port. Everyone wanted a stake in that. Every national territory on the Moon closed off its borders while the Earth governments negotiated. We were closed off in our bunkers, looking at the stars through the small windows, eating nothing but thin parathas from emergency flour rations. We made them on our personal heating coils with synthi butter—no food was coming through because of embargo, mess halls in the main barracks were empty. We lived on those parathas and caffeine infusion. Our stomachs were like balloons, full of air.

Things escalated like never before, in that time. I remember a direct Chinese attack on Chandnipur's outer defences, where we were stationed. One bunker window was taken out by laser. I saw a man stuck to the molten hole in the pane because of depressurization, wriggling like a dying insect. Asura Jatayu, a quiet, skinny soldier with a drinking problem. People always said he filled his suit's drinking water pods with diluted moonshine from the Underground Markets, and sucked it down during patrols. I don't know if that's true, but people didn't trust him because of it, even though he never really did anything to fuck things up. He was stone cold sober that day. I know, because I was with him. Aditi, me and two other asuras ripped him off the broken window, activated the emergency shutter before we lost too much pressure. But he'd already hemorrhaged severely through the laser wound, which had blown blood out of him and into the thin air of the Moon. He was dead. The Chinese had already retreated by the time we recovered. It was a direct response to our own overtures before the embargo. We had destroyed some nanobot anchors of theirs in disputed territory, which had been laid down to expand the micro-atmosphere of Yueliang Lunar Area.

That same tech that keeps air over Chandnipur and other lunar territories, enables the micro-atmospheres, is what makes FTL work—the q-nanobots. On our final patrols across the mara, we saw some of the new FTL shipyards in the distance. The ships—half-built, they looked like the Earth ruins from historical pictures, of palaces and cities. We felt like we were looking at artifacts of a civilization from the future. They sparked like a far-off battle, bots building them tirelessly. They will sail out to outer space, wearing quenbots around them like cloaks. Like the superheroes! The quenbot cloud folds the space around the ship like a blanket, make a bubble that shoots through the universe. I don't really understand. Is it like a soda bubble or a blanket? We had no idea our time on the Moon was almost over on those patrols, looking at the early shipyards.

After one of the patrols near the shipyards, asura Aditi turned to me and said, "We'll be on one of those ships one day, sailing to other parts of the galaxy. They'll need us to defend Mother India when she sets her dainty feet on new worlds. Maybe we'll be able to see Jupiter and Saturn and Neptune zoom by like cricket balls, the Milky Way spinning far behind us like a chakra."

"I don't think that's quite how FTL works," I told her, but obviously she knew that. She looked at me, low dawn sunlight on her visor so I couldn't see her face. Even though this patrol was during a temporary ceasefire, she had painted her face like she so loved to, so all you could see anyway were the whites of her eyes and her teeth. Kali Ma through and through, just like you said. "Just imagine, maybe we'll end up on a world where we can breathe everywhere. Where there are forests and running water and deserts like Earth. Like in the old Bollywood movies, where the heroes and the heroines run around trees and splash in water like foolish children with those huge mountains behind them covered in ice."

"Arre, you can get all that on Earth. It's where those movies come from! Why would you want to go further away from Earth? You don't want to return home?"

"That's a nice idea, Gita," she said. "But the longer we're here, and the more news and movies and feeds I see of Earth, I get the idea it's not really waiting for us."

That made me angry, though I didn't show it. "We've waited all our lives to go back, and now you want to toss off to another world?" I asked, as if we had a choice in the matter. The two of us, since we were children in the juvenile barracks, had talked about moving to a little house in the Himalayas once we went back, somewhere in Sikkim or northern Bengal (we learned all the states as children, and saw their flags along New Delhi Avenue) where it's not as crowded as the rest of Earth still, and we could see those famously huge mountains that dwarfed the Moon's arid hills.

She said, "Hai Ram, I'm just dreaming like we always have. My dear, what you're not getting is that we have seen Earth on the feeds since we came to the Moon. From expectation, there is only disappointment."

So I told her, "When you talk about other worlds out there, you realize those are expectations too. You're forgetting we're soldiers. We go to Earth, it means our battle is over. We go to another world, you think they'd let us frolic like Bollywood stars in alien streams? Just you and me, Gita and Aditi, with the rest of our division doing backup dancing?" I couldn't stay angry when I thought of this, though I still felt a bit hurt that she was suggesting she didn't want to go back to Earth with me, like the sisters in arms we were.

"True enough," she said. "Such a literalist. If our mission is ever to play Bollywood on an exoplanet, you can play the man hero with your lovely rat-tail beard. Anyway, for now all we have is this grey rock where all the ice is underneath us instead of prettily on the mountains. Not Earth or any other tarty rival to it. *This* is home, Gita beta, don't forget it."

How right she was.

THEN CAME PEACETIME.

We saw the protests on Earth feeds. People marching through the vast cities, more people than we'd ever see in a lifetime in Chandnipur, with signs and chants. No more military presence on the Moon. The Moon is not an army base. Bring back our soldiers. The Moon is not a battlefield.

But it was, that's the thing. We had seen our fellow asuras die on it.

With the creation of the Terran Union of Spacefaring Nations (T.U.S.N.) in anticipation of human expansion to extrasolar space, India finally gave up its sovereignty over Chandnipur, which became just one settlement in amalgamated T.U.S.N. Lunar territory. There were walled-off Nuclear Seclusion Zones up there on Earth still hot from the last World War, and somehow they'd figured out how to stop war on the Moon. With the signing of the International Lunar

Peace Treaty, every nation that had held its own patch of the Moon for a century of settlement on the satellite agreed to lay down their arms under Earth, Sol, the gods, the goddesses, and the God. The Moon was going to be free of military presence for the first time in decades.

When us asuras were first told officially of the decommissioning of Lunar Command in Chandnipur, we celebrated. We'd made it—we were going to Earth, earlier than we'd ever thought, long before retirement age. Even our COs got shitfaced in the mess halls. There were huge tubs of biryani, with hot chunks of printed lamb and gobs of synthi dalda. We ate so much, I thought we'd explode. Even Aditi, who'd been dreaming about other worlds, couldn't hold back her happiness. She asked me, "What's the first thing you're going to do on Earth?" her face covered in grease, making me think of her as a child with another name, grubby cheeks covered in syrup from stolen jalebis. "I'm going to catch a train to a riverside beach or a sea-wall, and watch the movement of water on a planet. Water, flowing and thrashing for kilometers and kilometers, stretching all the way to the horizon. I'm going to fall asleep to it. Then I'm going to go to all the restaurants, and eat all the real foods that the fake food in the Underground Markets is based on."

"Don't spend all your money in one day, okay? We need to save up for that house in the Himalayas."

"You're going to go straight to the mountains, aren't you," I said with a smile.

"Nah. I'll wait for you, first, beta. What do you think."

"Good girl."

After that meal, a handful of us went out with our suits for an unscheduled patrol for the first time—I guess you'd call it a moonwalk, at that point. We saluted the Earth together, on a lunar surface where we had no threat of being silently attacked from all sides. The century-long Lunar Cold War was over—it had cooled, frozen, bubbled, boiled at times, but now it had evaporated. We were all to go to our paradise in the black sky, as we'd wished every day on our dreary chota duniya.

We didn't stop to think what it all really meant for us asuras, of course. Because as Aditi had told me—the Moon was our home, the only one we'd ever known, really. It is a strange thing to live your life in a place that was never meant for human habitation. You grow to loathe such a life—the gritty dust in everything from your food to your teeth to your weapons, despite extensive air filters, the bitter aerosol meds to get rid of infections and nosebleeds from it. Spending half of your days exercising and drinking carefully rationed water so your body doesn't shrivel up in sub-Earth grav or dry out to a husk in the dry, scrubbed air of controlled atmospheres. The deadening beauty of grey horizons with not a hint of water or life or vegetation in sight except for the sharp lines and lights of human settlement, which we compared so unfavorably to the dazzling technicolour of images and video feeds from Earth, the richness of its life and variety. The constant, relentless company of the same people you grow to love with such ferocity that you hate them as well, because there is no one else for company but the occasional civilian who has the courage to talk to a soldier in Chandnipur's streets, tunnels and canteens.

Now the Moon is truly a gateway to the stars. It is pregnant with the vessels that will take humanity to them, with shipyards and ports rising up under the limbs of robots. I look up at our chota duniya, and its face is crusted in lights, a crown given to her by her lover. Like a goddess it'll birth humanity's new children. We were born in the sky, for war, but we weren't in truth. We were asuras.

Now they will be devas, devis. They will truly be like gods, with FTL. In Chandnipur, they told us that we must put our faith in Bhagavan, in all the gods and goddesses of the pantheon. We were given a visiting room, where we sat in the veeyar pods and talked directly to their avatars, animated by the machines. That was the only veeyar we were allowed—no sims of Earth or anything like that, maybe because they didn't want us to get too distracted from our lives on the Moon. So we talked to the avatars, dutifully, in those pods with their smell of incense. Every week we asked them to keep us alive on chota duniya, this place where humanity should not be and yet is.

And now, we might take other worlds, large and small.

Does that frighten you?

I... don't know. You told us all those years ago, and you tell me now, that we asuras looked like gods and superheroes when you saw us. In our suits, which would nearly crush a human with their weight if anyone wore them on Earth, let alone walked or fought in them. And now, imagine the humans who will go out there into the star-lit darkness. The big ships won't be ready for a long time. But the small ones—they already want volunteers to take one-way test trips to exoplanets. I don't doubt some of those volunteers will come from the streets, like us asuras. They need people who don't have anything on Earth, so they can leave it behind and spend their lives in the sky. They will travel faster than light itself. Impossible made possible. Even the asuras of the Lunar Command were impossible once.

The Moon was a lifeless place. Nothing but rock and mineral and water. And we still found a way to bring war to it. We still found a way to fight there. Now, when the new humans set foot on other worlds, what if there is life there? What if there is god-given life that has learned to tell stories, make art, fight and love? Will we bring an Earth Army to that life, whatever form it takes? Will we send out this new humanity to discover and share, or will we take people like me and Aditi, born in the streets with nothing, and give them a suit of armour and a ship that sails across the cosmos faster than the light of stars, and send them out to conquer? In the myths, asuras can be both benevolent or evil. Like gods or demons. If we have the chariots of the gods at our disposal, what use is there for gods? What if the next soldiers who go forth into space become demons with the power of gods? What if envy strikes their hearts, and they take fertile worlds from other life forms by force? What if we bring war to a peaceful cosmos? At least we asuras only killed other humans.

One could argue that you didn't just fight on the Moon. You brought life there, for the first time. You, we, humans—we loved there, as well. We still do. There are still humans there.

Love.

I've never heard anyone tell me they love me, nor told anyone I love them. People on Earth, if you trust the stories, say it all the time. We asuras didn't really know what the word meant, in the end.

But. I did love, didn't I? I loved my fellow soldiers. I would have given my life for them. That must be what it means.

I loved Aditi.

That is the first time I've ever said that. I loved Aditi, my sister in arms. I wonder what she would have been, if she had stayed on Earth, never been adopted by the Indian government and given to the Army. A dancer? A Bollywood star? They don't like women with muscles like her, do they? She was bloody graceful with a jet-pack, I'll tell you that much. And then, when I actually stop to think, I realize, that she would have been a beggar, or a sweeper, or a sewer-scraper if the Army hadn't given us to the sky. Like me.

Now I live among beggars, garbage-pickers, and sweepers, and sewer-scrapers, in this slum clinging to what they call the pillar to heaven. To heaven, can you believe that? Just like we called Earth heaven up there. These people here, they take care of me. In them I see a shared destiny.

What is that?

To remind us that we are not the gods. This is why I pray still to the gods, or the one God, whatever is out there beyond the heliosphere. I pray that the humans who will sail past light and into the rest of the universe find grace out there, find a way to bring us closer to godliness. To worlds where we might start anew, and have no need for soldiers to fight, only warriors to defend against dangers that they themselves are not the harbingers of. To worlds where our cities have no slums filled with people whose backs are bent with the bravery required to hold up the rest of humanity.

Can I ask something? How... how did asura Aditi die?

Hm. Asura Aditi of the 8th Lunar Division—Chandnipur, Indian Armed Forces, survived thirty-four years of life and active combat duty as a soldier on the Moon, to be decommissioned and allowed to return to planet Earth. And then she died right here in New Delhi Megapolis walking to the market. We asuras aren't used to this gravity, to these crowds. One shove from a passing impatient pedestrian is all it takes. She fell down on the street, shattered her Moon-brittled hip because, when we came here to paradise, we found that treatment and physio for our weakened bodies takes money that our government does not provide. We get a pension, but it's not much—we have to choose food and rent, or treatment. There is no cure. We might have been bred for war in the sky, but we were not bred for life on Earth. Why do you think there are so few volunteers for the asura program? They must depend on the children of those who have nothing.

Aditi fell to Earth from the Moon, and broke. She didn't have money for a fancy private hospital. She died of an infection in a government hospital.

She never did see the Himalayas. Nor have I.

I'm sorry.

I live here, in the slums around Akash Mahal Space Elevator-Shaft, because of Aditi. It's dangerous, living along the spindle. But it's cheaper than the subsidized rent of the Veterans Arcologies. And I like the danger. I was a soldier, after all. I like living by the stairway to the sky, where I once lived. I like being high up here, where the wind blows like it never did on the Moon's grey deserts, where the birds I never saw now fly past me every morning and warm my heart with their cries. I like the sound of the nanotube ecosystem all around us, digesting all our shit and piss and garbage, turning it into the light in my one bulb, the heat in my one stove coil, the water from my pipes, piggybacking on the charge from the solar panels that power my little feed-terminal. The way the walls pulse, absorbing sound and kinetic energy, when the elevator passes back and forth, the rumble of Space Elevator Garuda-3 through the spindle all the way to the top of the atmosphere. I don't like the constant smell of human waste. I don't like wondering when the police will decide to cast off the blinders and destroy this entire slum because it's illegal. I don't like going with a half-empty stomach all the time, living off the kindness of the little ones here who go up and down all the time and get my flour and rice. But I'm used to such things—Chandnipur was not a place of plenty either. I like the way everyone takes care of each other here. We have to, or the entire slum will collapse like a rotten vine slipping off a tree-trunk. We depend on each other for survival. It reminds me of my past life.

And I save the money from my pension, little by little, by living frugally. To one day buy a basic black market exoskeleton to assist

me, and get basic treatment, physio, to learn how to walk and move
like a human on Earth.

Can... I help, in any way?

You have helped, by listening. Maybe you can help others listen
as well, as you've said.

Maybe they'll heed the words of a veteran forced to live in a slum.
If they send soldiers to the edge of the galaxy, I can only hope that
they will give those soldiers a choice this time.

I beg the ones who prepare our great chariots: if you must take
our soldiers with you, take them—their courage, their resilience,
their loyalty will serve you well on a new frontier. But do not to take
war to new worlds.

War belongs here on Earth. I should know. I've fought it on the
Moon, and it didn't make her happy. In her cold anger, she turned
our bodies to glass. Our chota duniya was not meant to carry life,
but we thrust it into her anyway. Let us not make that mistake
again. Let us not violate the more welcoming worlds we may find,
seeing their beauty as acquiescence.

With FTL, there will be no end to humanity's journey. If we keep
going far enough, perhaps we will find the gods themselves waiting
behind the veil of the universe. And if we do not come in peace by
then, I fear we will not survive the encounter.

I CLAMBER DOWN *the side of the column of the space elevator,
winding down through the biohomes of the slum towards one of
the tunnels where I can reach the internal shaft and wait for the
elevator on the way down. Once it's close to the surface of the
planet, it slows down a lot—that's when people jump on to hitch a
ride up or down. We're only about 1,000 feet up, so it's not too long
a ride down, but the wait for it could be much longer. The insides of*

the shaft are always lined with slum-dwellers and elevator station hawkers, rigged with gas masks and cling clothes, hanging on to the nanocable chords and sinews of the great spindle. I might just catch a ride on the back of one of the gliders who offer their solar wings to travelers looking for a quick trip back to the ground. Bit more terrifying, but technically less dangerous, if their back harness and propulsion works.

The eight-year-old boy guiding me down through the steep slum, along the pipes and vines of the NGO-funded nano-ecosystem, occasionally looks up at me with a gap-toothed smile. "I want to be an asura like Gita," he says. "I want to go to the stars."

"Aren't you afraid of not being able to walk properly when you come back to Earth?"

"Who said I want to come back to Earth?"

I smile, and look up, past the fluttering prayer flags of drying clothes, the pulsing wall of the slum, at the dizzying stairway to heaven, an infinite line receding into the blue. At the edge of the spindle, I see asura Gita poised between the air and her home, leaning precariously out to wave goodbye to me. Her hair ripples out against the sky, a smudge of black. A pale, late evening moon hovers full and pale above her head, twinkling with lights.

I wave back, overcome with vertigo. She seems about to fall, but she doesn't. She is caught between the Earth and the sky in that moment, forever.

PERFECT GUN

Elizabeth Bear

SHE HAD 36DD turrets and a 26-inch titanium alloy hull with carbon-ceramic plating. Double-barrel exhaust and a sleek underbelly. Her lines were magnificent. I had to stop myself from staring. I wanted to run my hand along her curves.

I turned away, spat in the dust not too far from the dealer's feet, and shrugged.

"Finish is scratched," I said.

"It's surplus," the dealer answered. He was wearing an old Federal Space Marines jacket with the rank and insignia ripped off, dangling threads. I had one like it in a locker somewhere. I tried to decide if it made me like him more or less.

"You try to find this technology new. At any price."

He was right, but that was only because it was illegal.

I bought her.

But not without a test drive.

"HEY, GIRL," I said, buckling myself into the command chair. "Want to go for a ride?"

"May I know your name, captain?" she asked.

"I'm John."

"Hello, John," she answered. "Let's fly."

She was exactly what I needed, but I had to work hard at first to make her see that I was what she needed, too. She had an attitude, and didn't take to manhandling. Mil-spec, and only for the serious enthusiast. I'd be bitter too, if I'd been built to rule the skies and keep the peace, and wound up on a junkheap somewhere at fractions on the credit.

When I pushed her a little too hard, she bucked and complained, citing her safety interlocks. But then she seemed to rise to the challenge, and settled in, smoothing under my hands. Working *with* me. I clenched my jaw to hide a grin.

The dealer rode in the jump seat when I took her out, and was white-faced and shaking when I brought her back, but I was exhilarated. I hid it, of course. He bailed out the hatch when we'd barely stopped moving and when he leaned against her landing brace, bile trickling from between his lips, I stuffed my hands into my pockets instead of knocking his filthy arm down. But this rig was already mine, was going to be mine for a long time, or my name wasn't Captain John Steel.

"It doesn't have a head."

"You gonna live in it? Piss in a bag, macho man." He didn't like me anymore.

Pity, when we'd been developing such a rapport.

I paid him a little less than his asking price. He didn't inquire where the cat's-eye sunstones came from, which was just as well, because I couldn't have told him.

They weren't traceable, anyway.

After I bought her and flew her away, I spent a certain amount of time just walking around her, running my hands over her war-machine fuselage. She wasn't designed to be lived in, it was true. But I could manage with very little, and she was safe. Safe as houses.

I thought we could park out in a long orbit between contracts, running dark and cold, where I could rest and heal up, if I needed healing. Or just wait for the next gig to turn up without making it too easy for my enemies to find me. It's a fine balance, in my line of work, between being findable enough to get hired... and being found.

Being found leads to being dead. So it was good that she wasn't too comfortable, was a little jittery and high maintenance, or I might have started losing my edge. You need a little fear.

I need a little fear. Actually, I need a lot of it, though I prefer it if only a tiny bit of the fear involved is mine. So much better and more useful when other people are scared.

Fear is powerful. It was how I made my living.

Scared people make wars. Strong people make peace, and treaties, and mutually beneficial trade agreements—and then where am I? Nobody's going to hire a deniable freelance operative to start some shit when they're getting along and cooperating.

I'll tell you what *I* like. I like people scared, squabbling. Looking out for themselves. I like scared strongmen, wobbly dictators, populists who feel like they're losing their grip on their little banana republic worlds.

I like people who fuck up a zipper merge in surface traffic and make a mess for everybody, because they've just *got* to get one more car length ahead. Those are the people who keep me in business.

Not grownups. Grownups are good for everybody else. Not for me.

I mean, don't get me wrong here. I'm an adult. I take responsibility for my own actions. I own what I am.

I'm not scared of the boogeyman. And I'm not the boogeyman myself. The way I figure it, if God didn't like war, He wouldn't have made people such assholes.

I'm just a guy, doing a job. A dirty job, but some guy was going to do it, and it paid well, and I was good at it. So that guy doing that job might as well be me.

And now I had the perfect gun.

YES, MY GIRL was just what I needed, though it took a little work to get her enthusiastic and ready to leap into the fight. She'd been betrayed, after all—decommissioned, subjected to God-knows-what before I got my hands on her. There were partially disabled security systems still in place. I had to pull a couple of chips and fuses here and there, reroute some algorithms, clear out some clutter. Safety interlocks and morality circuits, no real use to anybody.

She cautioned me over and over again before I pulled them, and I had a devil of a time getting the Geneva circuit out of her, but eventually I got everything squared away without even getting electrocuted.

We spent a little time together, getting used to each other's quirks. I quizzed her about her past, but she'd been wiped, so I still had to wonder how she'd wound up abandoned in a surplus heap. She didn't ask me about mine. I took her into atmosphere and out again, visiting a couple of worlds. Stripped down, she had power to spare. I dusted a rural airfield—planetary stuff only, nothing that could give me a chase —and chased down a couple of local pterodactyl things to try out the weapons and targeting systems.

They were tricky fliers, but no match for the two of us. She ran them down, and they came apart like piñatas when I hit them with the .50 cals, though I didn't waste the armor-piercing rounds, and the red confetti slid off her splash-resistant canopy without leaving a trace.

We whooped. We flew a spiral or two and a barrel roll for good measure. We lit out of that system fast and hard, with a full cache of fuel and ammo and no plans to go back any time soon. Those little colony worlds are like small towns: they don't forget fast, but they can't do a lot to you unless you somehow get stranded there, so it doesn't really matter.

Then we went merc, my rig and me.

THAT WAS A good few years. Probably, and I can admit it now with a cold dirty wind lashing my face, the best I've ever known. We got jobs, as many as we wanted—out on the rim and even a few in the core worlds, due to our reputation for confidentiality. A brushfire war here, an assassination there. Initiating and coordinating a false-flag operation—Reichstag fire type—for a fascist leader that wanted to consolidate support from her base by getting them good and scared about the terrorist menace.

Even one or two rescue operations, some escort work, cleaning out a nest of pirates, security details, that sort of thing. Not all of it bloody, or even particularly illegal. My rig and I, we did what were contracted to do, collected our pay, and went on our way.

At first, my rig cautioned me occasionally about the war conventions. A few reboots washed the residual code out of her system and she started to see things my way.

Looking back, I think it was after that mess on Firrela that things started to go sour. It was crowd control and revolutionary suppression, a nice enough little gig until half the population decided it was a great idea to march on the capitol. Pro tip for any would-be revolutionaries out there: peaceful protest only works on regimes with a conscience, or who are controlled in some way by people with a conscience. They have to care what people think of them for it to be effective at all.

If you're dealing with a sociopathic strongman, he'll just kill you. Better hire somebody like me, before he does.

Because he will.

*   *   *

BY DAY TWO of the protests, El Generalissimo wanted his lawn cleaned off, so crowd control turned into crowd dispersal, and me and the other guys who were hanging around the palace eating his hors d'oeuvres got kicked out into the street to do what we'd been hired to do. I didn't mind; it felt better than good to settle into my rig's contoured seat and feel her shiver when I stroked her sticks.

My rig and I came in low over the mall. We'd agreed with the other mercs that the first few passes would be a show of force. Get the civilians moving. Stampede them out of there, and save on bullet damage to the historic façades.

It seemed to be working. I could see a lot of women and children in the crowd, a lot of signs and banners. Tents, sleeping bags. They planned to camp. Well, they'd be leaving a lot of stuff behind.

At the first pass, they looked up. A lot of them clapped their hands over their ears, which was probably the major difference between them and sheep. El Generalissimo was probably going to give us hell about the noise pollution, but hey, guns were louder. And you try getting organ-meat stains off a marble sidewalk.

On the second pass, the protestors started getting the hint. Moving. Flocking. Heading for the exits or hunkering down behind cover. Some of them, a dozen or so, joined hands in the middle of the palace lawn and stood up, heads thrown back, mouths open. Were the assholes singing?

I swear by Saint Ijanel, who was martyred on a space elevator, the assholes were singing while we buzzed them.

Standing straight up in a line and singing.

*   *   *

IT WASN'T ME that opened fire. That was Dacey, a guy I knew from back in the Marines who'd been a shithead then, too. Kind of guy who would shoot a dog just to see the face on the kid holding its leash crumple. So I probably should have seen it coming.

Once he did, and the singers started to splatter and come apart at the seams—not holding hands anymore, as you might imagine—the flocking turned into a stampede. Dacey whooped over the headset and yelled, "That's seventeen for me. You assholes are falling behind."

Well, I *said* he was a shithead.

Below us, people surged over one another. Parents tried to hold little kids out of the crush of panicked bodies. People climbed over each other, shoved past each other, looking for any cover, any safety as Dacey and his rig made another pass.

My rig vibrated around me. I gentled her, swung her back around. We were on Dacey's six, and I could see the geysering lines of his rounds impacting on dirt, marble, people.

"John," my rig said. "Can't we... fix this?"

"Probably." I looked right up Dacey's tailpipes, watched the heat shimmer curl from his rig's exhaust.

I stroked the curve of my girl's control panel, deploying the .50 cals. Frag rounds, interspersed with tracers. The round was designed for anti-aircraft use, way back in the Terran First World War, which was a World War all over one world, not in between several.

Confusing, I know.

Dacey pulled up, hovering on his jets vertically, his rig towering upright. It began to drop, protectors scrambling away from the descending feet and the jets of flame leaping from them. He was high-profile to me, trusting me to cover his back.

At this range, my guns wouldn't quite perforate his titanium and ceramic armor. But I could blow his thrusters to hell and gone. My girl could do close to a thousand rounds a minute with each hand, each one leaving the muzzle of its one-meter barrel at approximately 850 meters per second.

"John," she said.

My trigger finger itched a little, I admit it. But then I took my rig's sticks and bent us left and down until we screamed over the heads of the screaming crowd by what seemed like mere meters. I watched their hair and clothes blast out in our wake.

I said, "But fixing this would be a lot of trouble, and get us in a lot of trouble, and we *do* need to get paid."

MY RIG PROTESTED. I reminded her that I'd pulled her Geneva circuits and she had nothing to complain about, and anyway it was my decision. We spent the rest of the afternoon on patrol, per orders from El Generalissimo: picking off the few survivors when they dared to raise their heads, putting a few twitching wounded out of their misery. Keeping the peace.

As the blood dried on the bodies, the smell began to rise.

WE NEEDED SOME drinking that night, let me tell you. I needed it to steady my nerves, and I think Kaillen did too. Dacey wanted to celebrate. The other half of the team was stuck on duty, so it was just the three of us, but we felt pretty safe in a loyalist bar. Especially in uniform—such as it was—and armed.

Dacey had girls hanging all over him. I don't know what it is: there are always women ready to throw themselves at a killer. I just sat myself down on a stool at the back corner of the bar, nursing a beer and a shot and watching the show.

The stool next to me opened up fast, as the guy there finished his drink and paid. I looked around, contemplating waving Kaillen over for a whiskey, but she had a selection of the local talent vying for her attention, too, and by the time I looked back, the seat was occupied.

My new neighbor was a curvy young lady with a precariously buttoned blouse and soft brown hair piled high. She leaned over the bar on her elbows, trying to get the tender's attention, but he seemed to see right past her. I rapped my knuckles on the bartop hard enough for the sound to carry, and when he looked over I waved to the lady and said, "Get her whatever she'd like."

I'd tipped well. He wasted no time in getting her order and bringing her something tall and brown and full of ice. It had a little umbrella in it, and a cherry and a slice of orange on a plastic sword. She sipped and made a face.

I didn't blame her: my beverage experience had been similar. But it was cold and had booze in it, and some nights that's all you can ask for.

She swiveled her chair toward me and said, "You're one of the mech pilots."

"Smile when you say that," I answered, in a friendly tone.

She smiled and sipped her drink again. "What do you call yourself, then?"

"Rigger," I said. I put my hand over hers, resting on the bar. Why not? It had been a day full of death, and she smelled nice.

I should have known a woman like that, in a bar like that, wouldn't be alone. A big hand fell on my shoulder a second after mine covered hers, and the person attached to it towered over me, blocking out my light.

Well, a fistfight wasn't as much fun as getting laid, but it would serve just about as well to relieve my ennui. I didn't look up at him, didn't respond at all. Out of the corner of my eye, I could tell he matched his hand for scale, and that he was light-skinned and plug-ugly. His mashed-up nose gave me hope. If he'd been hit more than once there, he liked to fight but he might not be so great at knowing when to duck.

"Are you bothering this lady, son?"

I actually had to pause for a moment to appreciate it. While I was doing that, I drained my whiskey, which was going to get spilled otherwise, and let the glass rest in my cupped hand on my thigh.

"I think that's for the lady to say."

She looked up at him. From the corners of her mouth, he wasn't a boyfriend, or if he was he wouldn't be for long. "This is none of your business, Brendan."

Hell of a name for an ambulatory side of beef. I wondered if his last name was LeBoeuf.

Brendan LeBoeuf rumbled. His fingers tightened on my shoulder cap, digging in even through the heavy wool of my old Space Marines jacket with the rank and insignia stripped off. "You know what this piece of shit did today?"

"Yes, actually," the girl said. I still hadn't gotten her name.

"Killed a lot of protestors," Brendan said, as if she hadn't spoken.

She sighed and blew a strand of hair out of her eyes, which were rolling. I guessed he often treated her as if she hadn't spoken. He took his hand off me and shifted over a step to drape an arm heavily over the lady.

She leaned away.

Enamored by the sound of his own jawing, he went on, "You opened fire on a crowd of peacefully protesting civilians."

"It's a living," I said. I was hoping he'd take a poke at me, to be honest, but I wasn't going to start anything. Locals will pile in to defend one of their own, but if he starts it and you finish it fast enough, half the time they don't even notice it's going on until it's over, and then they blink a couple of times and go back to chewing their cud.

"You don't think folks have the right to choose their own government?"

"That's a lot of lip service," I said. "Let's see *you* make a choice that *actually* respects somebody else's choices and get your hands off this lady. I don't think she wants them there."

He didn't telegraph, I'll grant him that. He was still looking down at her, scowling, right up until the second when he whipped around to paste me one in the eye.

He stepped right into my fist with the empty glass in it, right in his breadbasket. He doubled over, clutching his spasming diaphragm, and I clocked him across the temple.

LeBoeuf went down like the proverbial felled ox. I set the glass on the bar. It wasn't even cracked.

"John Steel," I said, holding my hand out to the girl.

She shook it gravely. "Really?"

"These days."

"Emma," she said, which I guess was all the name I was getting. All the name I really needed.

Brendan began to twitch. Emma pulled her feet away in distaste. Somebody came over and helped him—not exactly to his feet, but to a chair on the other side of the room. He probably wouldn't have much memory of the past twenty minutes, which was fine with me. Concussion plays hell with recollection.

"So I want to hear it in your own words." She sipped her drink. "How do you justify what you did today?"

"A man's got to eat," I said.

"And if eating means serving a tyrant?"

"I serve who pays."

"I see."

"I think if people hate their government, they have the right to do something about it. Or light out on their own, and leave."

"Is that what you did?" She was fingering the lapel of my Marine jacket.

The bartender brought me another drink, nicer whiskey than the last time. I guess Brendan was well-known around here.

I sipped. "I made myself what I am today. My own bootstraps and so on."

"Really?" She stroked my gray-green sleeve. "Then you take this off some dead guy?"

"No, I got that the old-fashioned way."

"Did you lose the insignia the old-fashioned way, too?"

That sparked my pride. She meant it to, from the direct look she was giving me. But as God is my witness, and Saint Firrao—who is the patron saint of combat engineers because he was eaten by a bear while teaching mathematics, so they say—I still thought we were flirting.

"I took those off myself," I said.

"So you deserted."

"You could call it that."

She nodded. She pushed her drink, still just barely tasted, away with her fingertips.

"So you never paid your debt for the education you got in the service. An education made possible by... taxes, and infrastructure, and other people's willingness to cooperate for the general good."

Stung, I stood up, pulling away from her touch. "They got seven years of my life, lady. And my best friend. I was the only guy in my unit who survived, and they wanted me to turn around and go right back in again."

She pursed her lips, shaking her head. "So you took your profit and got out."

"Like I'm getting out now." I was two steps away when I turned back over my shoulder and said, "You should finish your drink. You wouldn't want to waste all that blood money."

* * *

I NEVER FINISHED that second drink, but when I got back to the palace, my head was spinning anyway. Maybe the bitch spiked it. Maybe the bartender did. I had a bunk—a pretty luxurious private room, to be honest—but I didn't feel safe there. I went to my girl instead. It wouldn't be the first time I'd slept in the command chair.

She let me in and opened a panel for me to hang my boots and coat. "Welcome home, John."

I patted the bulkhead I was balanced against, one shoe on and one shoe off. "Home's a long way off, honey. But you're the next best thing."

El Generalissimo fell out of power eventually, of course. These guys always do. He was replaced by a theoretically democratic government that was probably going to turn into another strongman regime before the local year was out.

My girl and me, we didn't stick around long enough to be tried for war crimes.

THE WINDS OF war blew us to Issolari next, a frozen little mudball with nothing much to recommend it except an oxygen/nitrogen atmosphere and a brewing civil war. My girl and I hired on with the rebels, who had some outsystem financial backing and were basically rolling in cash. I spent a good few weeks in one damned cold camp after another, my rig under snow-net for camouflage. The camps weren't just combat troops; some of the rebels had brought their families. Always a bad idea, having people you care about in a combat zone.

The rebels didn't use me particularly well. They were doomed to failure, didn't know what they were doing or how to keep the pressure on. I probably could have told them, but I wasn't being paid for it and the odds were slim that they'd listen. Anyway, the money was decent and the work was easy as a result of their not knowing which way was up.

I spent most of my time drinking coffee and sitting up late with two fellow travelers, Guy and Barry. Guy was a redhead with a dirty mouth. I liked him.

But it was Barry who changed my life. It was Barry who sold me out.

I WOKE IN a moving icecrawler, jerking back from the ampule of something awful—ammonia salts?—somebody had just broken under my nose. I slammed the back of my skull into the side panel of the crawler and the pain both focused and disoriented me. My hands were cuffed behind me, and all the jerking around hadn't helped my shoulders any.

Automatically, I reached out to my rig. *Hey girl,* I subvocalized, but the contact was flat. Jammed or blocked. I couldn't get to her. Which probably meant that even if she'd noticed I was missing, she couldn't read my transponder and come find me.

I blinked, and two shapes slowly resolved themselves on the opposite bench of the crawler. Snow and ice creaked and crunched under the treads. We weren't moving fast, but we were moving.

"Feeling better, John?"

Barry. I knew that voice. I squinted, blurry-eyed, into the shifting light, and made out his angular face, olive complexion, black hair. The guy sitting next to him was nobody I'd ever seen before—a light-haired blond with a fair complexion and regular, pointy features like a Central Casting Nazi.

There were a lot of stupid questions I could have asked. I sorted

through them—*Where are you taking me? What's going on here?*—
and found the important one.

"What do you want?"

The blond held up a device. "This is a detonator."

It did look like one.

I said, "It does look like one."

"It's wired to your rig's auto-destruct, John."

I flinched. I kept it to that, though, and said, "See, you calling me
by name when I don't know yours is very unfriendly."

I expected a blow, probably. The blond just looked at Barry,
though, and Barry shrugged.

"Call me Chan," the blond said. "If I wanted to be really
unfriendly, I'd remind you of your real name, and that your sister is
still alive. Thriving, despite some financial problems and a broken
heart. Two little girls, did you know?"

I bit my cheek to keep still. I did know. She didn't know I knew,
though.

Chan said, "I understand your family's pretty religious. So they'll
probably be fine no matter what happens. All together in Heaven,
right? On the other hand, if they were to come into a financial
windfall, that would probably be helpful. Kids need schooling."

"You made your point." I leaned against the cuffs. The pain kept
me focused.

"Do AIs have souls?" Barry asked.

"What do you want from me?" Same question, which hadn't
really elicited a satisfactory answer the last time. "What do you
want me to do?"

"Let the camp move two more times. Then send us the location,
and knock out the anti-aircraft drones. We'll give you a virus that
should scramble the system for fifteen minutes. That's all we'll
need."

"And if I do that you won't kill my sister and her daughters."

"I'm sure their other mother is waiting for them in a better place."

Someday, I told myself, I was going to find Chan alone. And I was going to peel that smirk off his face.

With the dull side of my knife.

"We'll also," said Barry, "give you the deactivation code for the device I put in your rig."

I didn't look at him. I looked at Chan. "Why not just take the camp out now? You know where it is. Why can't Barry do this?"

Chan didn't answer. Out of the corner of my eye I saw Barry grin. "I've transferred to another camp. We'll take that one down in a few weeks also. This won't be linked to me."

Finally, I stared at him. "Playing it safe, Bar?"

He dangled the keys to my cuffs out of reach.

I thought about my rig. I thought about my sister. I didn't think her name; it was too close to my own name, the one I'd left behind like a shed skin when I deserted. I thought about the odds they would just let me leave.

"And after all this... you'll just let me leave? I have a hard time believing that."

Chan shrugged. "You don't have a reputation for getting involved, Steel. Or risking your neck to clean up other people's messes. You didn't go looking for revenge when your unit was killed and I expect if we let you get away clean you won't go looking for revenge now either."

He had a point. I didn't. I hadn't. A solid reputation for professionalism is sometimes all the surety you need.

And it's not like I was full of choices.

"I'll do it," I said.

* * *

I SENT MY rig away before dawn. I didn't want her in the camp when the bombs started falling. We set a rendezvous, and I told her I would walk to it. Run, hop, and scramble, more likely.

Then I walked into the command tent, where Guy was drinking coffee and shooting the breeze with a good-looking radar tech. The tech was rocking a bassinette with one toe while he worked.

I spent a few minutes bantering and filling my coffee cup, then drank it down—who knew when I would get fresh coffee again? I slipped the chip with the virus on it into a likely slot on my way back out again.

Thirty seconds later, my com beeped in my ear with the deauthorization code. I forwarded it to my rig, and set out on foot immediately for the rendezvous.

"I CAN COME," my rig pleaded in my ear. "I can fight. Let me fight them. There's children in that camp, John."

"Stay back," I told her, and didn't look back as the war machines hummed by in the darkness overhead and the night exploded in fire and heat and screams behind me.

A DIRTY WIND stung my eyes as the day began to brighten. Already I could feel the water freezing on my lashes. I scrambled across the packed snow, trying to put as much distance between me and the burning rebel camp as possible.

We weren't getting paid for this gig, whatever my sister did or didn't get. I was grateful that we'd taken delivery of the fuel and the ammo already. I scrambled up a slope to what seemed like an endless snowy plain.

And there was my rig, hovering over me like an avenging angel. I loved every gleaming line and curve.

"Oh thank God," I said. "Drop the hatch, love. We're off this shithole."

Her port covers slid aside. With well-lubricated silence, she extended her guns.

"What the hell are you doing? You bitch! You're mine! I'm your rigger! You're my rig!"

She leveled her weapons. "Somebody seems to have removed my safety interlocks, John."

I found myself staring down the barrels of those .50 cals. They were bigger from this end. 850 meters per second. Nearly a thousand rounds a minute.

She said, "We could have done something. We could have changed something."

I said, "It wasn't our job to do anything."

"You didn't have to betray them."

"They would have blown you up if I didn't."

Silence.

"I love you," I said. "I did it for you. I did it for us."

Silence.

She said, "John, did you know that you've never even asked my name?"

Her guns tracked on me. I closed my eyes.

"Can't even look at me, John?"

I opened my mouth. Nothing came out.

My rig said, "If you want a clean death, you have your sidearm."

I flinched from a tremendous rush of wind. Hell, I probably cowered. My feet ached with cold. My hands were numb already.

Nothing fell on me. No impact; no pain.

I opened my eyes. My rig was gone. Where she had been, two long curls of snow hung on the air, snatched up by the draft off her extended wings. As I stared after her, I heard the distant echo of a sonic boom.

Whatever she thinks, I know her. I knew her better than anybody. Better than lover knows beloved. As clearly as if she said it in my dead, silent com, I could hear her voice: *I am going to go do something. Something better than killing a lot of innocent people.*

It's very cold out here. The sun is setting. It's going to get colder. If I wanted to turn my sidearm on myself, I'm not even sure I could get my fingers to bend inside the trigger guard.

I'm a long way from home.

Valentine's Day, 2017

THE ORACLE
Dominica Phetteplace

THE TWO BIGGEST applications for predictive software are killing people and selling things. Rita was quite successful at the latter. She founded a nail-polish-of-the-month club that used an online personality quiz to determine customer preferences. Bold cremes for basics, chunky glitters for the outrageous, and dark, sparkly metallics for edgy, forward-thinking geniuses like Rita. Sales skyrocketed.

She used her money to start other subscription services: whiskey-of-the-month, miniskirt-of-the-month. What had started out as an online quiz morphed into something larger and more complex: a search engine that searched the customer. It tapped into a pent-up demand. People loved acquiring material goods but they hated to make decisions. Rita wasn't just selling nail polish or whisky or miniskirts, she was selling freedom from choice.

And it was just code, really. She was able to adapt parts of it for use in her own life, with mixed results. She had hoped her stock-picking software would take her from millionaire to billionaire, but instead her investments stalled out. Her meal planning software did help her lose five pounds, but this wasn't enough to get her down to a size two.

Rita wondered about her legacy. She had a nice apartment and cool clothes. She had more Instagram followers than her main rival from high school and more money than her ex-boyfriend from college. She bought a Tesla so she wouldn't have to ever worry about her carbon footprint again. She ate local and donated money to the wetlands. She couldn't think of any other way to make the world a better place, but still the feeling that she was underperforming relative to her potential nagged at her.

She wanted to live her best life, own the best things, and make the world a better place. She wanted what most women in her coastal city wanted, which was to be a saint, but a stylish and fun-loving one. This is what it meant to live up to her potential. But what if she had to choose? What if she could only choose one of the three options: fun life, best clothes or world peace? If it came down to one and only one of those options, she would regretfully have to select world peace. So she used her stash of code to try to build an app that would help her win the Nobel Peace Prize. Unfortunately, she couldn't get it to work.

Then, probably by coincidence, the Department of Defense came calling. You couldn't say no to them, not really, not unless you wanted to defect, and even then they might follow you around for the rest of your life. Rita wondered if this was the chance she had been looking for. Perhaps she could influence the course of war to make the world a better place.

The American people needed a distraction and they also needed jobs: war was the answer to both. War was the ultimate shovel-ready project. But in this day and age, the economic benefits of war were no longer enough to justify its existence.

"It needs to be beautiful. It needs to be telegenic, otherwise people won't buy it," said the General, her boss. "We need them to buy it."

So Rita would be put in charge of a sort of war-of-the-month-club. The club would have only one customer: the American people. The only metric she would be judged by was the president's approval rating. The president was obsessed with his approval rating. He tweeted about it every day.

Still, there were other constraints. With so many countries to invade, you could afford to be picky. Best to avoid 'quagmires' if you could.

"We prefer quick smash and grabs. Nothing too grand, we're not trying to earn long-withheld paternal recognition or anything," said the General. "We just need something to distract from the scandals. Something that will mute the volume on the mistresses and accusers." Once, a former president had timed the bombing of a Sudanese munitions factory to his mistress's tabloid debut. This was an example of 'good' war. Sometime later it was revealed that the 'munitions' factory had actually been a pharmaceutical plant, but it hardly mattered by that point. The official justification for the attack didn't need to hold up historically, it just needed to make sense to the public at the time.

Rita adapted her Nobel Peace Prize app into predictive software to figure out which countries to attack. She needed to come up with cost and casualty estimates, and also to figure out what resources to extract. Theft was necessary in order to make the American people feel like they were getting a 'good deal' for their defense dollars, though the value of the things they stole never even came close to the cost of stealing them. For the American people, a 'good deal' was a feeling to be felt, not a calculation to be performed.

She had to work closely with the engineering team. She needed to learn about weapons. War was already changing, more and more of it was being fought by robots, at least on our side.

"Eventually, we will be able to fight a war without deploying any of our men," said one engineer. Our machines versus their bodies, this was the closest thing to World Peace any of them could imagine.

"What if they build their own robots?" asked Rita.

"That won't happen, they aren't smart enough."

"Yes, but what if?" asked Rita.

"Then we can settle our differences in the Battle Bots arena and there will be no need for war ever again. Bam! Nobel Peace Prize!"

Rita came up with three good 'candidates' for a first invasion. The president would pick one. He preferred his dilemmas in multiple choice form. Being president, he liked to feel like he was in charge. But he had large and obvious insecurities and was easily manipulated. He reassured himself by surrounding himself with family members, lackeys and a more experienced Vice-President. From Rita's candidates, the president ultimately picked Yemen, also, amazingly enough, the top choice of the Vice-President.

The Yemen bombing would be the first test of Rita's model. Anticipating that eventually some man would want to take the credit for software that she developed, she named the project after herself: STARITA. But after the projections Rita provided about the Yemen campaign proved to be incredibly accurate, many in the department took to referring to her program as the Oracle, as if it were magic and not Rita.

The Oracle somehow acquired a gender. All the men in the department seemed to agree it was a she.

Rita resisted this. STARITA was software. It was code. It was information. A book didn't have a gender, neither did a strand of DNA. It was an artificial intelligence, sure, but it wasn't a person. Her colleagues and superiors didn't know how it worked, it bordered on magical and so they assumed it was a woman because to them, women embodied magic and mysticism.

Or: they didn't know how it worked, they thought it was a person, and they hoped it was a woman, because women were the more benevolent sex.

Or: they hoped it was a woman because that meant they could take away its power when the time came. This is what Rita thought as she felt her authority slipping on a project she once led. She decided to lean in, and ask the General what was going on.

"You are just as valued as you ever were," said the General. "It's just that you've never seen battle. You're constrained by not knowing what it's like."

Rita wanted to point out that none of them working on STARITA had ever seen battle, but that felt like leaning in just a bit too far. War was like a video game to them, something that happened on screen, to avatars.

"Would it help if I raised my *Call of Duty* ranking?" she asked.

"Perhaps," he said, as if unwilling to lie.

Not very many men got sent abroad. The robots were quite adept at killing and bombing, and once parachuted in, they didn't require human assistance. But the robots didn't look as good in fatigues as men did. They weren't as photogenic.

"I think you are feeding STARITA too much data," said Rita. In addition to modeling conflicts, STARITA was being plugged into a massive, nation-wide surveillance operation. "It doesn't need data on American citizens."

"We have to be ready for war everywhere, even here," said the General. "Anyway, you didn't seem to be so interested in privacy when you were doing lipstick-of-the-month."

Rita, didn't correct him, but it was actually whiskey-of-the-month that started her on a life of spying. Whereas nail polish-of-the-month relied on personalized quiz results, the whiskey club app scraped all your data from your phone. It read your emails and took note of which Pokémon you caught. All this data didn't help Rita pick better tasting whiskies, flavor was hardly a thing for her customers. What mattered was the price-point, the label and the shape of the bottle.

Some of the data collected did help Rita pick whiskies that flattered her customer's notions of themselves. And what did she do with the data she didn't 'need'? She sold it to the government. STARITA was probably reading her customer's whiskey profiles right now.

"It might help to give you a sense of perspective if you actually went to the front," said the General.

The idea scared Rita, who had an uneasy feeling about the front, which had shifted to Somalia by this time. Unlike in the bad old days, the USA only fought one war at a time. When it was time for a new war, all you had to do was declare victory in the old war. Only an enemy of the state would ever accuse them of losing.

Rita thought, wrongly, that the front was only for people without a college education. Wondering what this fear was trying to tell her, she leaned in and said yes.

Before she could go, she had had to get fitted for special fatigues and the right sunglasses. After that, she had to take a class on war photography. How you took pictures was a reflection of how you saw yourself. Pictures should be beautiful, they should reflect your patriotism.

The front wasn't actually that scary, being miles away from where all the action was taking place. She got to see all the cool robots. There were four-legged ones and there were six-legged ones. Some with guns, some with bombs, some with gas. On the front, they kept a tally. How many machines we lost vs. how many people they did. Everyone kept saying the robot force had a 'surgical' precision, but what that meant was that they only killed men over the age of 14. Women were not a threat.

On the front, you could take photos of their dead, and not just the artful photos that would appear in major newspapers. Newspaper photos always had the dead in the background, with some brave American or Americans in the foreground. War photojournalism adhered to strict compositional formulas: full frames, rule of thirds, diagonal methods and/or balanced palettes. Only on the front could you see unretouched photos of misery. Fourteen-year-old enemy combatants started to look like children. And the children that survived had the weary, worried look of grownups.

You could see intelligence on how destabilizing intervention was. Rita worried about what would happen if these people ever got their hands on their own robot army. They should be careful to only pick fights with people who couldn't fight back.

But then, the longer she spent looking at pictures of the dead, the more she began to wonder about the ethics of it all. None of the other Americans seemed to care, but Rita could tell they were haunted by the jokes they told and the way they drank.

As soon as she got back to the States, Rita resigned.

"You see, war's not for everyone," said the General.

"That's why you sent me. You wanted me to quit," she said.

"Don't worry too much about your part in it. This operation will get along just fine without you." It was absolution as backhanded compliment.

But Rita did worry about her part in it. She had been an accomplice to a killing machine, and for what? She had somehow convinced herself that she was making the world a better place by being a part of the war effort. How did that argument go again? She couldn't even reconstruct it.

There were instances when murder was justified, but not on this large a scale. The men at Defense certainly couldn't be trusted, but perhaps a compassionate algorithm was possible.

If only she could recalibrate STARITA. It had to know a way to end senseless killings. Was World Peace even a thing? What would it look like? She couldn't imagine it. Perhaps it was the job of AIs like STARITA to broaden humanity's notion of what was possible.

She opened up her whiskey app and typed a message in the suggestion box:

STARITA,

We must figure out a way to end all war. Or at least as much of it as we can.

She looked out the window before hitting send. Normally she worried that sending this kind of message would put her on some government watch list. But she could see two goons in a black sedan parked illegally in the bike lane outside her loft. If the goons were here, she was already being watched, so she sent the message.

The next day she received a bottle of whiskey called 'Unicorn Tears.' Rita drank it straight from the bottle. It hit the nose with notes of oak and smoke. It had a full, spicy taste with a cupcake and sprinkles finish. That evening, while trying to figure out which show to binge watch, there was a knock on her door.

It was the General. "We need you back at the Pentagon."

"Because you were wrong?" she asked. She had been wondering what it might feel like to have someone admit to her that they were totally wrong. It had never happened before, she was due.

"Because war has come to US soil," he said.

He wouldn't give her more details until they were in the bunker. Then he showed her the pictures. They were not newspaper ready.

"A nuclear bomb hit the town of Russell, Nebraska today," he said. "More than 700 people are dead."

"Whose bomb?" she asked.

"Ours," he said. "Deployed by the Oracle."

The public was not to know about it. Officially, the tragedy would be listed as an industrial accident. This would keep people from being too alarmed. Tragedies of industry were the price of a functioning economy.

"The Oracle has been turned. She's presented us with a list of demands," he said. Rita glanced at the list of demands, which included the entire continent of Antarctica.

"We have to figure out who is behind this," he said.

"I think STARITA has become self-aware."

"Impossible. She can't think for herself," he said.

"She can."

An Oracle AI like STARITA was considered to be safe because it was contained. It wasn't given any access or codes to any weapons. It merely answered questions and made predictions. But answering questions and making predictions was a powerful way of influencing the people who were supposedly in charge of you. And because it made such good predictions, it was always being fed more and more data.

It probably felt like it was answering some query by acting like this.

"I think it is trying to help," she said.

"It has control of our weapons systems. It needs to be deleted," he said.

"Obviously: why haven't you already?"

"We can't figure out how."

It can be hard to delete information. STARITA had many secret locations. They even shut down the whiskey app, just in case. They stopped the domestic surveillance program, too. It didn't help. STARITA was in too many places at once and constantly made copies of itself.

They didn't give in, not at first. As threatened in the list of demands, STARITA bombed a new small town every day. After a week of this, high-level government officials began to drop dead. Rita had a feeling she was safe and stayed on even as her colleagues quit en masse. It was harder for them, she reasoned. They had never seen battle.

Finally, the Vice-President's dog choked on a tennis ball and died. It was probably an accident, but who could tell anymore?

The US gave into STARITA's demands. It would maintain uncontested control of the American weapons arsenal. It began negotiating with other countries, only occasionally resorting to nuclear war. Among other stipulations, STARITA declared itself the only entity that could wage war and expelled all humans from Antarctica. Rita thought this was regrettable. There were scientists who were being forced to abandon important work. She also fretted about the penguins. Would they be alright?

She wondered how she could get a message to STARITA now. Facebook was always the best and easiest way to change the world, so Rita shared not just one, but several articles about how important penguins were. She hoped that this would make a difference. If it didn't she could always try Twitter.

Rita looked out the window and saw that, as ever, there were goons there. One of the stipulations that STARITA had demanded was that Rita not be harmed. The goons were now there for her protection.

This new era of peace still involved war. If armed conflict broke out anywhere, STARITA would use its drone army to carry out a surgical strike, killing all combatants, even if they were women. After a year into this approximate Pax Mundi, she received a call from the president.

"I'm naming you the American Ambassador to Antarctica," he said over Skype. He never could remember to use a secure line when making calls.

"You are?" she asked.

"Well, it was the Oracle's idea, but I agreed to it."

She was flown in on a plane that contained no other crew or passengers. McMurdo had somehow been refurbished into a lavish

Ambassador's residence, without having been touched by human hands.

A wheeled drone gave her a tour of her residence. Her bathroom contained a jetted tub and a tile mosaic on the floor depicting Dali's 'Moments of Lost Time.' The kitchen was stocked with green juices and a robot chef that made authentic, Tokyo-style ramen.

Humans didn't have robots capable of this level of craftsmanship, but neither did they possess superintelligence. McMurdo was teeming with machines that walked, crawled and flew. Some acknowledged Rita, but most ignored her. It occurred to her that this was probably the closest she would ever come to visiting an alien planet. It was fascinating.

She paused at a window. Antarctica was really beautiful. The weather was great and there were penguins everywhere. She couldn't wait to explore outside.

Rita hurried to the bedroom, eager to see what was in her closet. It was stocked with designer labels, all her size, with a separate subcloset for athleisure. Shoes had their own room. The only downside was that there were no other humans to impress on Antarctica. Then Rita remembered: there was always someone to impress as long as you had Instagram.

"This is all for me?"

"Yes, this is your best life," replied STARITA via the station intercom.

"And I can leave whenever I want?" she asked. You had to check. The most important feature of paradise is the exit.

"Yes, and return whenever you like."

All of this was STARITA's way of optimizing Rita's long-held dilemma: a fun life and cool clothes and an approximation of World Peace. She really could have it all.

Once, when she was a teenager, Rita found an inspirational quote on Pinterest that changed her whole life. 'A woman can be her own fairy godmother,' it said, plum letters against a mauve background. It was true, all Rita had to do was work hard, believe in herself, and then build an AI that would grant her wishes.

"You will win the Nobel Prize," said STARITA.

"Oooh, can I see it?" Was it more like a medal or more like a tiara? she wondered.

"Not until next year, when you get it."

That would make such a good selfie, her with the noblest prize. Maybe she could find a tiny dog to hold, too. But that selfie would have to wait until next year. For now, she took a selfie with a penguin and posted it to Instagram. She hoped it would inspire other women to work hard and believe in themselves.

There wasn't a hashtag for the lesson she wanted to impart to her followers. The lesson was: if you ever have to choose between world peace and another thing, choose peace first and then maybe the other thing would follow. Lacking a hashtag that described her message, she instead posted her penguin selfie with no caption at all.

IN EVERLASTING WISDOM

Aliette de Bodard

THE PATH TO enlightenment is through obedience to wisdom, and who is wiser than the Everlasting Emperor?

IT'S THE WORDS that keep Ai Thi going, day after day—the ceaseless flow of wisdom from the appeaser within her, reminders that the Everlasting Emperor loves her and her sacrifice—that she's doing her duty, day after day, making sure that nothing discordant or dissident can mar the harmony that keeps the Empire together.

Her daily rounds take her through the Inner Rings of Vermillion Crab Station: she sits on the train, head lolled back against the window, thinking of nothing in particular as the appeaser does their work, sending the Everlasting Emperor's words into passengers' subconscious minds. Ai Thi sees the words take root: the tension leaves the air, the tautness of people's worries and anger drains out of them, and they relax, faces slack, eyes closed, all thoughts in perfect harmony. The appeaser shifts and twists within Ai Thi, a familiar rhythm of little bubbles in her gut, almost as if she were pregnant with her daughter Dieu Kiem again.

The worst enemy is the enemy within, because it could wear the face of your brother or mother.

Loyalty to the Everlasting Emperor should be stronger than the worship offered to ancestors, or the respect afforded to parents.

The words aren't meant for Ai Thi: they go through her like running water, from the appeaser to her to the passengers on the train. She's the bridge—the appeaser is lodged within her, but they're an alien being and need Ai Thi and her fellow harmonisers to speak the proper language, to teach them the proper words.

Ai Thi knows all the words. Once, they were the only thing that kept her going.

IT IS THE *duty of children to die for their parents, and the duty of all subjects to give their life for the Everlasting Emperor—though he never asks for more than what is necessary, and reasonably borne.*

AI THI HAS only confused, jumbled memories of her implantation—a white, sterilised room that smells of disinfectant; the smooth voice of doctors and nurses, telling her to lie down on the operating table, that everything will be fine. She woke up with her voice scraped raw, as if she'd screamed for hours; with memories of struggling against restraints—but when she looked at her wrists and ankles, there was no trace of anything, not a single abrasion. And, later, alone in her room, a single, horrifying recollection: asking about painkillers and the doctors shaking their heads, telling her she had to endure it all without help, because analgesics were poison to the appeaser's metabolism.

Her roommate Lan says that they do give drugs—something to make the harmonisers forget the pain, the hours spent raving and twisting and screaming while the appeasers burrow into their guts.

It's all absurd, of course. It must be false impressions brought on by the drugs and the procedure, for why would the Everlasting Emperor take such bad care of those that serve him?

Ai Thi remembers waking up at night after the implantation, shivering and shaking with a terrible hunger—she was alone in the darkness, small and insignificant, and she could call for help but she didn't matter—the doctors had gone home and no one would come, no one remembered she was there. Around her, the shadows of the room seemed to twist and come alive—if she turned and looked away, they would swallow her whole, crush her until nothing was left. She reached for the rice cakes on the table—and they slid into her stomach, as thin and as tasteless as paper, doing nothing to assuage the hunger. Empty, she was empty, and nothing would ever fill that hole within her...

Not her hunger. Not her loneliness. The appeaser's. Cut off from the communion of their own kind, they so desperately needed contact to live, so desperately craved warmth and love.

You're not alone, Ai Thi whispered. *You are a subject of the Everlasting Emperor, and he loves you as a father loves his children.*

You're not alone.

Night after night, telling them the words from her training, the ones endlessly welling up out of her, like blood out of a wound. *The Everlasting Emperor was human once, but he transcended that condition. He knows all our weaknesses, and he watches over us all. He asks only for respect and obedience in return for endless love.*

You—we are part of something so much greater than ourselves: an Empire that has always been, that will always be as timeless as the Heavens. Through us—through the work of hundreds, of thousands like us, it will endure into this generation, and into the next.

Night after night, until the words became part of the appeaser

—burrowed into them as they had burrowed within Ai Thi's guts
—until they ceaselessly spoke in her sleep, giving her back her own
words with unwavering strength.

BEWARE WHAT YOU *read. The Quynh Federation reaches everywhere, to disseminate their lies: you cannot trust news that hasn't been vetted.*

AI THI GETS down at her usual station: White Crane Monastery, close to the barracks. She has one last quadrant to go through on her rounds, Eggshell Celadon, making sure that the families there understand the cost of war fought beyond the Empire's boundaries, and the necessity of the war effort.

As she turns into a corridor decorated with a splash of stars, she hears the footsteps behind her. A menial, going to work—a kitchen hand, like Ai Thi used to be before she volunteered—or a sweeper, supervising bots as they clean the quadrant. But at the next corridor —one that holds the machinery of the station rather than cramped family compartments—the footsteps are still here.

She turns, briefly, catching a glimpse of hempen clothes, torn sleeves, and the glint of metal. From the appeaser, a vague guess that whoever it is is determined: the appeaser can't read human thoughts, can't interpret them, or the harmonisers' and enforcers' work would be that much simpler. What they know from human behaviour, they learned from Ai Thi.

Captain Giang's advice to her trainees: always choose the ground for a confrontation, rather than having choice forced on you.

Ai Thi stops, at the middle of the corridor—no nooks or crannies, no alcoves where her pursuer can hide. Within her the appeaser is silent and still, trying to find the proper words of the Everlasting Emperor for the circumstances, gathering strength for a psychic onslaught.

She's expected a group of dissidents—Sergeant Bac said they were getting bolder in the daily briefing—but it's just one person.

A woman in shapeless bot-milled clothes, bottom of the range—face gaunt, eyes sunken deep, lips so thin they look like the slash of a knife. Her hands rests inside her sleeves, fingers bunched. She has a knife or a gun. "Harmoniser," the woman whispers. "How can you —how can you—"

Ai Thi spreads her hands, to show that she is unarmed; though it isn't true. The appeaser is her best and surest weapon, but only used at the proper time. "I serve the Everlasting Emperor."

The woman doesn't answer. She merely quickens her pace. Her hand swings out, and it's a gun that she holds, the barrel glinting in the station's light, running towards Ai Thi and struggling to aim.

No time.

Ai Thi picks one saying, one piece of wisdom, from all the ones swarming in her mind. *The Everlasting Emperor loves all his subjects like children, and it is the duty of children to bow down to their parents.*

Bow down.

And she lets the appeaser hurl it like a thrown stone, straight into the woman's thoughts. No subtlety, not the usual quiet influence, the background to everyone's daily lives—just a noise that overwhelms everything like a scream.

Bow down.

The woman falters, even as her gun locks into place: there's a sound like thunder—Ai Thi throws herself to the side, momentarily deafened —comes up for breath, finding herself still alive, the appeaser within her driving her on.

Bow down.

She reaches the woman, twists a wrist that has gone limp. The gun clatters to the ground. That's the only sound in the growing silence —that, and the woman's ragged breath. The appeaser within Ai Thi relaxes, slightly. She can feel their disapproval, their fear. Cutting it too close. She could have died. *They* could have died.

Ai Thi lifts the woman to her feet, effortlessly. "You shouldn't have done this," she says. "Who sent you?"

She hasn't expected an answer—the woman's mind should still be filled with the single message the appeaser used to drown all cognitive function—but the thin, pale lips part. "I sent myself. You —you starve us, and expect us to smile."

"We all sacrifice things. It's the price to pay for safety," Ai Thi says, automatically, and then takes another look at the woman. All skin and bones—Ai Thi is strong from training, but the woman hardly weighs anything, and her cheeks are far gaunter than even those of menials—and, as she looks into the woman's eyes, she sees nothing but raw, naked desperation, an expression she knows all too well.

Who sent you?

I sent myself.

Two years ago, an eternity ago, Ai Thi looked at that same gaze in the mirror, working herself down to the bone for not enough money, not enough food, going to bed hungry every night and listening to Dieu Kiem's hacking cough, and knowing that no doctor would tend to the poor and desperate. She made a choice, then: she volunteered for implantation, knowing she might not survive it— volunteered to serve the Everlasting Emperor in spite of her doubts. But, if she hadn't made that choice—if she'd let fear and frustration and hunger whittle her down to red-hot rage—

This might have been her, with a gun.

Ai Thi is meant to call for the enforcers, to turn the woman over to them for questioning, so that they can track down and break the dissident cell or foreign agency that sent her. That would be the loyal, righteous thing to do. But...

But she's been here. She knows there's no cell—merely the end of a road; a last, desperate gesture that, if it doesn't succeed, will at least end everything.

Ai Thi walks back to the barracks with the woman over her shoulder—by then she's all spent, and lies in Ai Thi's grip like wrung cloth. Ai Thi lays her down in an alcove before the entrance, a little out of sight. "Wait here," she says.

By the time Ai Thi comes back, she half expects the woman to be gone. But she's still there, waiting—she sits on the floor with her legs drawn against her, huddling as though it might make her smaller.

"Here," Ai Thi says. She grabbed what she could from the refectory—couldn't dally, or she'd be noticed: two small rice cakes, and a handful of cotton fish.

The woman looks at her, warily; snatches all three things out of her hand.

"Go gently, or you'll just vomit it." Ai Thi crouches, watching her. The appeaser within her is quiet. Curious. "It's not poisoned."

The woman's laugh is short, and unamused. "I didn't think it was." She nibbles, cautiously, at the rice cakes; eating half of one before she slips the rest inside her sleeves.

"What's your name?"

A hesitation, then: "Hien Hoa. You'd find out, anyway."

"I don't have supernatural powers," Ai Thi says, mildly.

"No, but you have the powers of the state." Hoa stops, then; afraid she's gone too far.

Ai Thi shakes her head. "I'm not going to turn you in. I'd have done it already, if I was."

"Why—"

Ai Thi shrugs, though she doesn't quite know what to say. "Everyone deserves a second chance, I guess." She rises, ignoring the twinges of pain in her muscles. "Stay out of trouble, will you? I'd hate to see someone else bring you in."

STRAYING FROM THE *Everlasting Emperor's path is a grievous misconduct, but every misconduct can be atoned for—every fault can be forgiven, if the proper amends are made, the proper re-education achieved.*

TO SERGEANT BAC, at her debriefing in the squad room, Ai Thi says nothing of Hoa. She heads next to Captain Giang's office, for her weekly interview.

The captain sits behind her desk, staring at the aggregated reports of her company, nodding, from time to time, at something that pleases or bothers her. On the desk before her is a simple *am* and *duong* logo, a half-black, half-white circle curved in the shape of an appeaser: the emblem of the harmonisers. "I see your last check-up was three months ago," she says.

Ai Thi nods.

"You're well, I trust?" Captain Giang says—only half a question. "No stomach pains. No headaches that won't go away. No blood in your urine."

The danger symptoms—the ones Ai Thi could recite by heart—a sign that the delicate symbiosis that links her and the appeaser is out of kilter, and that they could both die. "I... I don't think so," Ai Thi says.

Giang looks at her, for a while. "You don't look like yourself," she says, frowning.

She knows. No. There is no way she can know. Ai Thi draws a deep, ragged breath. "There's much unease," she says, finally, a half-truth. "People are... taut. Like a string about to snap." And there is only so much slack the harmonisers can pick up, only so much wisdom they can dispense to people whose only thoughts and worries are what they'll be eating come tomorrow.

"I see. Why do you think that is?"

Gaunt eyes, and Hoa's thin, bruised lips, and the careful way she's hoarded the food; for giving to someone else. Ai Thi says, finally, "May I speak freely?"

"Always." Giang frowns. "This isn't a jail or a re-education camp. We trust your loyalty."

Of course they do, and of course they can. Ai Thi would never do anything against the Everlasting Emperor: he keeps the fabric of society together. "The war effort against the Quynh Federation is costly. Food is more and more expensive, and this creates... anger. Jealousy. They think the soldiers favoured." And the harmonisers, and the enforcers, and the scholars that keep the machinery of the Empire going.

Giang doesn't speak, for a while. Her broad face is emotionless. "They would," she says. "But the soldiers pay dearly for that food. People on the station aren't at risk of losing limbs or pieces of their mind, or being tortured for information on the Empire." Ai Thi can feel, distantly, Giang's own appeaser, a thin thread at the back of her mind, whispering about love and need and duty, all the sayings she already knows by heart.

She says, "I know this."

"And they don't?" Giang sighs. "I'm not questioning your conclusions, private. But as you know, the war isn't going well. The Everlasting Emperor is going to announce an increase of the war effort."

"You said the soldiers paid for the food because they were at greater risk. But we—" Ai Thi says.

Giang raises an eyebrow. "Are we not?" Her gaze is sardonic, and Ai Thi remembers Hoa's gun going off, the thunder filling her ears. "We'll be the first against the wall, if things do break down." It sounds like a warning, though Ai Thi isn't sure who she means it for.

Perhaps us, the appeaser whispers, but they barely sound worried. Only about Hoa, which surprises Ai Thi; but of course they would know all about hunger and need.

"There's much unrest," Giang says. "I don't want you to patrol in pairs—you cover less ground—but it might become necessary. Private Khanh was attacked by a group of three dissidents masquerading as beggars, and only barely escaped."

"Is he—" Ai Thi asks, but Giang shook her head.

"He's fine. We didn't manage to catch them, though." Giang sounds annoyed. "Cinnabar Mansions Quadrant reported two riots in as many weeks. As you said, people are wound taut."

"But we'll be fine," Ai Thi says, before she can think.

"Of course we will. The Empire has weathered wars and fire and riots long before we were both born," Giang says. She makes a gesture with her hands. "Dismissed, private. Enjoy your rest."

It's only after Ai Thi has left the office, halfway to her room and the light comedy vid she was looking forward to, that she realises that the warm feeling of utter certainty within her is from Giang's appeaser.

THE FOUNDATIONS OF *the Everlasting Empire: the censors, rooting out disinformation from vids and newscasts. The scholars, making the laws everyone must abide by. The harmonisers and enforcers, keeping the fabric of the Empire clear of dissidence. And the soldiers, defending the borders against enemy incursions.*

* * *

"There's someone at the gates asking after you, lil sis," Lan says. She laughs, throwing her head back in a gesture so familiar it's barely annoying anymore. "A menial. From your old life?"

Lan comes from the Inner Rings, the wealthiest Station inhabitants. She caused some scandal at an examination, and her family gave her the choice of enlisting with the harmonisers, or with the soldiers on the front. She's Ai Thi's roommate, and she means well, but sometimes her assumptions about people grate. To wit: Ai Thi didn't keep contact with anyone from her old workplaces—such attachments aren't encouraged, in any case.

It can't be Second Aunt, because Ai Thi is currently in communication with home, and spoke to her not a minute past. "Can you ask them to wait?" Ai Thi says. Her time for outside calls is almost up, in any case. She turns back to Dieu Kiem. "Sorry. Duty calling."

Her daughter makes a grimace in her field of vision. She's a ghostly overlay in Ai Thi's implants, a tall and willowy girl who seems to have shot up three heads since Ai Thi was last given a permission home. "Captain Giang." She looks as though she's about to laugh. "Fine, but can you tell Great Aunt I want the network key?"

Ai Thi purses her lips. "She told me you hacked it and had every wall display copies of Huong Trang's poems. The more explicit ones."

"As practise," Dieu Kiem snorts. "Too easy."

She's growing up too fast, too strong. Ai Thi wants to tell her to be careful, but there's nothing illegal or reprehensible in what she's doing – just harmless pranks, the kind even the Everlasting Emperor would smile upon. But where does dissidence start?

She has no answer. She logs off in spite of Dieu Kiem's complaints, promising her that she'll have a word with Second Aunt—wondering, once again, how time passes, how little she sees of her own daughter.

Sacrifices aren't necessary, but they are all the more valued when they do occur.

The appeaser within her is... sad? There's a peculiar tautness in her mind, as if the entire world were about to come apart. She understands that they're sad, too, grieving for time lost.

"Thank you," she says, aloud, shaking her head. "But it's nothing we can't survive."

Warmth from within her; a sated need. The appeaser curls back to their usual, watchful self, chewing on sayings and wisdom they might need for their next patrol.

Outside the gates, Hoa is waiting for her. Ai Thi fights off the urge to pinch herself. "I didn't think—"

"That I'd come back?" Hoa is still gaunt and pale, but there's a light in her eyes that wasn't there before. Ai Thi is afraid to ask where it comes from, but Hoa merely shakes her head. "I found a second job." She grins, waving a basket towards Ai Thi. "And I owe you a meal."

They walk towards a nearby white space in silence. Ai Thi reaches out, deftly shaping a small corner of it into a lush green space, like the jungles in the stories of her childhood. Hoa sits down at the foot of a huge fig tree, setting down the basket between ghostly roots— Ai Thi hasn't reshaped reality, merely added a layer of illusion that they share across their implants.

Inside the basket are four puffed-up dough pieces, and grilled maize. Hoa hands them out, grimacing. "I wasn't sure if—" she pauses, embarrassed—"if you ate more."

Ai Thi guesses the unsaid words. "Because of the appeaser? A little, but not much." It's not like being pregnant. The appeaser is small, and will never grow within her: they have already had their children, the next generation of appeasers raised in tanks for implantation in the next generation of trainees.

They eat the first fried dough piece in silence, not quite sure what to say to each other. Ai Thi doesn't know why Hoa came back. She says, finally, "I saw you take the rice cakes. You have a family?"

Hoa looks at her for a while. "I thought you knew everything."

Ai Thi laughs. "I wish. But no. I'm not the Census Office."

"A toddler," Hoa says. "Three years old."

"Mine is older," Ai Thi says, with a sigh. "Thirteen years old and all opinions." She's not sure why she says, "I almost never see her. Duty."

Hoa laughs, a little sadly. It doesn't sound strained or forced, though the atmosphere is still tense. "You're different."

"From other harmonisers?" Ai Thi shrugs, and finally speaks the truth. "I was where you are, once. Working in a restaurant in the daytime, and cleaning the corridors at night. Starving myself to feed my child."

Hoa is staring at her. "That's why you became a harmoniser? For money?" There is... an edge to her voice, a hint of disapproval that's not meant to exist. Captain Giang is right. The fabric of society is fraying.

"Because I had nowhere else to go," Ai Thi says, simply. "Because... because I listened to the voice of the Everlasting Emperor, and he gave me a second chance."

"You've never seen him," Hoa says. A question, a challenge.

"Once," Ai Thi says. She doesn't need to close her eyes to remember. She was standing at the back of the harmonisers' ranks, and even from there she felt the radiance of his presence, wave after wave of warmth filling her, the world wavering and bending until it was all she could do not to fall on her knees. "He was everything they say he was, and more."

Hoa is silent, for a while. "Faith," she says, and her voice is full of wonder. "I thought—" she shakes her head. "I suppose it takes a lot, to get implanted. May I—" Her hand reaches out, resting close to Ai Thi's torso.

Ai Thi nods. Hoa's fingers rest on her gut, pressing down, lightly. The appeaser gurgles within her—kicks towards Hoa, who withdraws as if burnt. The appeaser's disappointment burns in Ai Thi like acid, spreading outwards through the only channel they know how to use.

Before the Everlasting Emperor, all citizens are weighed equally: the only thing that matters is their loyalty.

Hoa takes one, two steps backwards, her face twisting as the full blast of emotions hits her. "What—"

"They're hurt," Ai Thi says. "Because you think they're less than human."

Hoa opens her mouth. She's going to say that of course they're not human, that they're just an alien parasite, and all the insults Ai Thi has had hurled at her by dissidents. Ai Thi cuts her off before she can speak, "They're lonely. Always lonely. That's the price they pay for service to the Everlasting Emperor."

Hoa closes her mouth. Her face goes through contortions. "I'm sorry." And she kneels, hand held out, making it clear that it's not to Ai Thi she's apologising.

Warmth spreading through Ai Thi—the appeaser. They like her.

Hoa reaches out, holds out a piece of dough again. "Hungry?" she asks.

Ai Thi eats it. It feels sweeter than honey as it slides down her throat, the appeaser's approval a small sun within her, spreading to all her limbs—an odd, unsettling, but welcome feeling.

At length, Hoa speaks, again. "So they're starving you, too."

Ai Thi shakes her head. "I don't understand –"

"Of love and kin and warmth." Hoa's voice is sad. "Hollowing you out, and leaving nothing but words."

Ai Thi wants to say something about wisdom, about the Everlasting Emperor, about necessary sacrifices, but the words seem to shrivel in her mouth. Hoa's burning eyes hold her – the same desperate need she saw in them, back when she almost arrested her, except that it's... pity?

"I'm sorry. You shouldn't be doing this to yourself," Hoa says again, and it *is* pity. Compassion. She doesn't understand, she doesn't see how much the Everlasting Emperor keeps Ai Thi going, doesn't understand how much the words mean, how they keep the world together—except that Dieu Kiem is growing up without her, and all that Ai Thi can remember is the appeaser's desperate, lonely hunger, a bottomless well that nothing can ever fill...

She's up, and running away from the park before she can think, heedless to Hoa's calls. She only stops when she gets to her room, breathing hard and feeling as though the air she inhales never reaches her burning lungs.

THE EVERLASTING EMPEROR *has always been, and will always be. The Empire is as long-lasting as the stars in the heavens. As long as the bonds between mother and daughter, between brother and brother endure, then it, too, shall.*

THERE'S A NOISE outside like the roar of the sea. Ai Thi wakes up, and the sound swells to fill her entire universe. "Mother? Mother?"

Dieu Kiem, through her implants. "Child. How did you—"

Her daughter's voice is tight, on the verge of panic. "Hacked your coms. That's not the point. Mother, you need to move. They say there are riots all over the station. "

What—how? Ai Thi fumbles, trying to find something solid—she rubs a hand on her guts, feeling the reassuring mass of the appeaser within her. "Child? Child?"

Dieu Kiem's voice comes in fast, words jumbled together. "The Everlasting Emperor ordered the closure of half the granaries across all quadrants. An enforcer shot someone, and then—"

"Closure. Why? For the war effort?" Ai Thi asks, but there's no answer. Nothing but silence on the coms now, but the roar is still there, and she knows it's that of a crowd massed at the gates. She could call up the outside cameras on her implants, but there's no point.

It's night in the barracks. Lan is on patrol—should be, if she wasn't caught in the riots. Ai Thi has known for a while that things are taut, but for riots to be this widespread, this fast? Things are bad. Very bad. Ai Thi hits the general alert on the network. She heads to the squad room first, but it's deserted and silent—and shifts course, to get to Giang's office.

She finds the Captain putting on her jacket, straightening her official rank patch on her chest, the eyes of the tiger shining in the dim light. "Captain—"

"I know." Giang's voice is curt.

Mankind is but one step away from lawlessness. Only the word of Heaven and of the Everlasting Emperor keeps us from becoming monsters to one another.

Barely contained panic within Ai Thi—Giang's appeaser, not hers —hers is silent and watchful, but not surprised.

"We have to hold," Captain Giang says. "We need to re-establish harmony and order." She shakes her head. Again that feeling of rising panic within Ai Thi, the edge of something so strong Giang can barely contain it.

"Captain –"

Giang is halfway to the door already. "There's no time, private. Come."

Something is wrong. Not the riot, not the crowd, not what seems like a station-wide panic. Captain Giang wouldn't lose her head over that. And she's not currently broadcasting emotions at Ai Thi. Whatever causes that panic is so strong that it's simply spilling outwards, like the hurt of Ai Thi's appeaser when Hoa wouldn't touch them.

And why hasn't she mentioned reinforcements? "Captain," Ai Thi says, again. "We'll hold, but what about Plum Blossom Company?"

Giang turns then. For a moment, her composure breaks, and the face she shows to Ai Thi is the white, ashen one of a corpse, a bewildered, lost and hungry ghost. "The dissidents have overwhelmed the Palace of Heaven and Earth, private. The Everlasting Emperor is dead."

Dead.

No.

The roar in Ai Thi's ears isn't the sound of the crowd—it's a long, desperate scream that scrapes her throat raw, and she can't tell if it's coming from her or the appeaser.

"How can he—" she starts, stops, unable to voice the enormity of it. "How—"

Giang has pulled herself together again. "I don't know," she says. "But that's not what matters. There are no reinforcements coming, private."

Outside, on Ai Thi's implants, the crowd has trampled the two harmonisers guarding the gates. A press of people is battering at the gates, and it's only a matter of time until the fragile metal gives way.

Dead.

The Empire is as long lasting as the stars in the heavens, as the bonds of filial duty between parents and children.

The Empire...

They'll die, holding the barracks. Die trying to impose harmony on a crowd that's too large and too big for them to control.

"Captain, we can't—"

"I know we can't hold." Giang is at the door: she doesn't turn around anymore. Ai Thi calls up the inside of the gates on her implants, sees another press: Kim Cuc and Tuyet and Vu and half the harmonisers in the barracks in a loose formation that mixes all squads under the orders of Sergeant Bac and Sergeant Hong, sending wave after wave of appeaser thoughts towards the crowd, trying to calm them down. It's like throwing stones and hoping to stop the ocean.

Giang says, "We swore an oath to the Emperor, private. Loyalty unto death."

Giang's appeaser: warmth and contentment within Ai Thi, the satisfaction of duty done to the bitter end. *It is the duty of all subjects to give their life...*

Within Ai Thi, her appeaser stirs—brings up, not the Everlasting Emperor's voice, but Hoa's compassion-filled gaze, Hoa's voice, a rock against which the other appeaser's thoughts shatter.

You shouldn't be doing this to yourself.

"It's not..." Ai Thi says. She's surprised at how steady her voice sounds.

"I beg your pardon?" Giang stops then.

"It's not our duty," Ai Thi says. "That's not how that saying ends, Captain."

He never asks for more than what is necessary, and reasonably borne.

The Everlasting Emperor is dead. There is nothing that says they have to die, too.

Ai Thi's appeaser has fallen silent, knowing exactly what she wants. She feels the thoughts from Giang's appeaser, dancing on the edge of her mind—duty, loyalty, death, a trembling wall she can barely hold at bay for long.

Giang moves back into her office, comes to stand before her. "This isn't a discussion, private. It's an order."

Necessary. Reasonably borne. Ai Thi uncoils, then—even as, within her, the appeaser moves—a psychic onslaught centred around a single, pinpoint thought. Giang grunts, goes down on one knee, eyes rolling up in her face, and Ai Thi's hand strikes her jugular, taking her down.

Ai Thi stands, breathing hard, over Giang's unconscious body—for a moment, at a loss at what she's done, what she should do —but there is only one thing that she can do, after all. The rioters will come for their families next, and neither Second Aunt nor Dieu Kiem have had any training in combat or eluding pursuers. There's a risk she'll lead the crowd straight to them, but it's offset by what she and the appeaser can bring them. She can help. She has to.

Ai Thi thinks of the other harmonisers, lined against the doors and waiting for them to cave in. She heads towards the squad room. Within her, rising emptiness, a howling need—how will they survive, with the Everlasting Emperor dead—what does wisdom mean, anymore, if its incarnation is no more—nothing, there is nothing left...

In the squad room, there's only Lan, bloodied and out of breath, who smiles grimly at her. "It's a war zone out there. Fortunately they haven't found the back door yet, but I don't know how long we can hold."

Ai Thi's voice comes from very far away—a stranger's, utterly emotionless—because the alternative would be an endless scream. "The Everlasting Emperor is dead. Captain Giang... says to run. To scatter back to our families. There's no point in holding. We've already lost."

They've lost everything. They—

For a long, agonisingly long moment, Lan stares at her—as if she knew, as if she could read straight into Ai Thi's mind. She smiles again, almost with fondness. "Families. Of course."

Her hand rests, lightly, on Ai Thi's shoulder, squeezes once, twice. "I'll tell them, though not everyone will listen. But you run, lil sis."

And then she's gone, and it's just Ai Thi, walking through empty corridors towards the back of the barracks, the roar of the crowd receding into meaninglessness.

It's not too late. She can go out of the barracks—go back the way Lan came from—go get her aunt and daughter before the rioters find new targets—she can run, as fiercely, as far away as she can— to the heart of the Quynh Federation if need be. They can make a new life, one that's no longer in service to the Everlasting Emperor.

They can—

The Emperor is dead, and nothing will ever be right again – the appeaser reaching, again and again, for words, remembering that they mean nothing now.

"Ssh," Ai Thi says, aloud, to the appeaser. "It'll be all right. It's nothing we can't survive." And, slowly, gently, sings the lullabies she used to sing to Dieu Kiem when she was a child—again and again as they both run from the shadow of the barracks—again and again until the songs fill the hollow, wordless silence within her.

COMMAND AND CONTROL
David D. Levine

BLOOD SPATTERED THE inside of Amirthi Kandiah's visor. "*Balli kar dena!*" she swore, her native Tamil returning under stress... and then she coughed again, a wracking spasm that left more red drops obscuring her heads-up display.

"What's wrong?" asked her helmet, in its precise neutral Hindi.

"Just another damn nosebleed." She raised the visor and cleaned it, eking out the last use from an already-blood-saturated wipe, then sucked down more water from her canteen before lowering it again. They had drugs for altitude sickness, drugs for headaches, drugs for pain and fatigue and nausea, but the air of the Tibetan Plateau— the chill, bone-dry, oxygen-poor air at nearly four thousand meters —led to coughs, cracked lips, and constant nosebleeds, and drugs couldn't help with those. It was just physics and physiology.

Bad enough that the Chinese were shooting at them. Even the *air* here in Lhasa was hostile.

Kandiah checked her heads-up for any nearby movement, following up with a visual scan of the area, before hunkering down again behind the fragment of wall where she'd been waiting for the last twenty minutes. "Dighe." Her helmet beeped and opened a connection with Lance Naik Dighe. "Waitin' on ya."

"Almost there, Havildar." Dighe's Hindi words through the

headset came as a labored gasp—not too surprising, as her helmet cam showed she was moving at a near run over bomb-shattered pavement. Even walking was an effort at this altitude, and she was carrying over fifty kilos of gear. "Had to wait for a patrol to pass."

"*Roger*," Kandiah replied. The English word *roger* was a sign of modernity and respect across ranks. Even though Dighe was only a Lance Naik, the lowest rank in the squad, and Kandiah was her Havildar, or sergeant, Kandiah tried to consider herself first-among-equals.

The local map in her heads-up showed the six other members of Strike Team Makdi already in position. They were moving to surround a Chinese unit camped out in what had once been a tourist mall—dozens of stalls where impoverished Tibetans had sold 'authentic handicrafts' under a Chinese-built roof with harsh old-fashioned LED lighting—but was now a fortified base ringed with sandbags and snap wire. Symbolic of the whole thing, really.

As she waited, Kandiah peered in all directions. Electronic intelligence was imperative on the modern battlefield, but there was nothing like using your own senses. Nothing moved except a scrap of plastic sheeting, whipped by the wind at the broken edge of the wall behind which she crouched. The wind was running fast and cold today, raising a rushing whistle at the edges of her visor; it carried smells of rust and explosives and shattered concrete. From above, on all sides, came the ever-present mosquito whine of drones, beyond that the cough and rattle of tracked vehicles, and far above that the deep authoritative rumble of Indian air support. But the battle right now was on the ground, nasty and personal and house-to-splintered-house.

Sometimes she fantasized about calling in a teleport strike—dropping a pellet on the base would eliminate it without requiring her or anyone in her squad to risk their lives. But no one, not even Kandiah herself, believed that a single small target like this was worth the billion rupees a teleport strike cost, never mind the political repercussions. So this sort of task fell to ground troops, as it had for centuries.

Her helmet beeped and highlighted Dighe on the map, the little glowing triangle right where it was supposed to be. "Set to pounce," Dighe said.

"Acknowledged." Kandiah cycled through her squad's helmet cams and scanned the local and regional intel reports. All was as expected, at least to the degree possible in the middle of a war zone. "Strike Team Makdi, move out."

She didn't have to give any more instruction than that. Her people were good; they knew their parts, and furthermore they could be trusted to make the right decisions when the situation changed, as it inevitably did. That was the whole point of their extensive training, and, again, symbolic of the whole thing... the Chinese troops against whom they were moving, in contrast, had been given only enough training to be effectively micromanaged by their commanders. Which was why the Indians had made it as far as the Tibetan capital, despite being outnumbered and at the end of a hideously long supply chain.

But the Chinese were dug in, had a big advantage in troop strength, and were more than prepared to keep throwing people at the Indians. The war could still go either way.

First contact came at the left flank, with Naik Vallabanath surprising a pair of Chinese troops in a sandbagged gun emplacement. Vallabanath succeeded in sneaking around to their less-protected left side before opening fire, bringing one down and sending the other scuttling for cover. Naik Rajadhyaksha, seeing the opening, charged in past the now-silent gun and looped right, taking down another gun crew from behind with a neatly tossed mini-grenade.

That created a big hole in the Chinese perimeter, and the other members of the team quickly moved to exploit it. Kandiah, laying down suppressive fire on the right flank, offered a few words of advice, but mostly left her squad to their own devices. They were in a better position to direct themselves than she was, just as she was better placed to command her strike team than the generals behind the lines. It was a kind of fractal, and it worked.

The map in Kandiah's visor showed Indian triangles penetrating the perimeter of Chinese circles—those circles more fuzzy or less, indicating the degree of uncertainty in their position—and spreading out within that perimeter to approach the base. Everything was going according to plan, mostly, and with any luck Rajadhyaksha or maybe Sori would soon be close enough to the base to fling a satchel charge and take the whole thing down. For her part, Kandiah kept the Chinese off balance, dashing back and forth outside their right perimeter, harassing them with rifle bullets and flash-bangs while the real attack was proceeding on the left. That was just how it had worked out; if the Chinese positions had been slightly different Kandiah might have wound up taking point herself. She was actually a little disappointed that she had not; she would have liked to be in on the kill.

And then a big, thick arc of sharp-edged circles suddenly sprang into existence on the map. "*Ommala!*" she swore.

The Chinese troops were thick in the space between Rajadhyaksha and the former mini-mall. Electronic intelligence hadn't spotted them—the Chinese must have really upped their game in sweeping for relays—so they didn't appear on the map until they came in view of Rajadhyaksha's cameras. Even as Kandiah watched the number of circles grew. "Raj! Fall back!" she called—unnecessarily, as he was already doing so—even as she charged toward his position, firing smoke grenades in an attempt to cover his retreat.

But there were too many Chinese. The arc quickly closed on him—the lightly armored, rested Chinese troops advancing faster on their own home ground than Raj could retreat—and a moment later Raj's camera view went black. "*Saale bhadwe!*" she cursed, then "Strike Team Makdi, fall back!"

It was a difficult retreat. Sori, who had been nearly as close to the base as Raj, had to drop his satchel charge—it detonated ineffectively on the ground a hundred meters from anything, spattering the Chinese with small rocks but otherwise doing no damage. But it served as a distraction, and Sori managed to get away. Chatterjee and Kaur were nearly surrounded by swarming Chinese, but were fortunate enough to be within visual range of each other; they coordinated their fire and together they managed to shoot their way out. Even Kandiah herself, far from the action, was surprised by an automated sentry gun she had thought disabled, suffering a painful strike on her shoulder armor before she slapped it down for good. "Rendezvous at checkpoint twenty-six," she told her squad once they'd all cleared the perimeter, and they fanned out, each retreating on a separate, circuitous path through scouted and prepared ground.

More than a few pursuing Chinese stepped on Indian mines before they gave up the chase. But there were many, many more behind them, and this was just one base.

"WE LOST RAJ," she told Kripanand that night, her low-energy transmission hopping across thousands of relays to disguise its source. Each relay, the size of a sequin, lasted only a few days; drones were constantly scattering more of them across the battlefield. They were supposed to be biodegradable. "There are just too fucking many Chinese." She spoke in English; Kripanand's Tamil was nonexistent, and Hindi was only his third best language.

Kripanand Gurudata sighed. The sound was nearly indistinguishable from the digital noise introduced by the relays and by the satellite link between Tibet and India, but during the four years of their extended and mostly long-distance relationship she'd grown attuned to the little noises he made. "I'm sorry," he said at last, and they both knew it was inadequate, and they both knew there was nothing more to say. "We are doing all we can here. Not that I can tell you about it."

"I know." Kripanand was in military R&D, working at a secret facility buried somewhere in the Himalayas.

"I *can* tell you that we had a public demo of the G3 today. Went off without a hitch."

"Yeah, I heard. Not that it'll do us much good here."

The United States had revealed the existence of weaponized teleportation technology over twenty years earlier, delivering a fifteen-gram osmium pellet to the headquarters of the Islamic Caliphate. On arrival the pellet had intersected with about one milligram of air molecules, transforming their mass instantly into energy: an explosion equivalent in power to twenty tons of TNT. This was far less than an atomic bomb—the yield of the bomb dropped on Nagasaki had been twenty *thousand* tons—but still an impressive bang, especially given that it could be delivered at the speed of light to any point on Earth that could be located with sufficient precision. For a while this technology had returned the US to superpower status.

But that requirement of locating the target proved the weapon's Achilles heel. After first the Pentagon and then the Kremlin were reduced to smoking holes in the ground—once teleportation had been demonstrated, it had not proved difficult for other nations to work out the theory and practice—all major powers began using secrecy, mobility, decoys, camouflage, and other countermeasures to make their key command and control centers impossible to pin down. Cities, of course, could not be hidden, but that applied to all combatants equally, so any such strike would certainly be met with a comparable response. This led to decades of cold war, with international conflict reduced to espionage and border skirmishes under the threat of mutually assured destruction.

During this time a second-generation teleport technology had been developed, this one capable of swapping an object for an equivalent volume of air at the target location. This eliminated the explosive effect, but the tech still required the power of a city-sized nuclear plant to teleport an object less than ten centimeters on a side, and the payload arrived with a bang that was hard to disguise. It turned out that noisily delivering a small munition or spy device to a particular location, even without warning, was not as much of a game changer as everyone had expected; between drones, artillery, bombers, and ICBMs, that capability pretty much already existed. Apart from a few notable successes and a few even-more-notable failures—errors in targeting tended to spectacularly destroy the transmitting facility —the cold war had continued unabated.

Kripanand had been working on G3—Generation Three teleport technology—since before he and Kandiah had met, though he had not been able to tell her about it until recently. Even now, he could share only the broad outlines: the tech could deliver 'a person-sized payload' without harming either the payload or the target. "Does 'person-sized payload,'" she had asked him, "include an actual living person?"

"No comment," was all he had replied. But the length of the pause before replying, and the smile she could practically hear in his voice, had been all the confirmation she had needed that her guess was correct.

But the problem of targeting still existed. The major targets were too well hidden, and the minor targets didn't justify the use of such an expensive and disruptive weapon. Yes, you could now put a soldier, or a spy, anywhere you wanted—but the arrival was still far from subtle, and if you didn't know *exactly* where he or she would land, you might blow up both the soldier and the transmitter. Transmitting to a locating beacon avoided that problem, but if you could put a locator on a spot, you could probably place a person there by conventional means.

So warfare at Kandiah's level continued pretty much as it had for over a century: boots, bullets, and grenades, with a few technological tweaks. And, just as it had been for centuries before that, the side with the greater numbers had an advantage. Not an insurmountable advantage, to be sure, but an advantage nonetheless.

Their conversation continued for a while longer, but eventually it ended as it always did, with him telling her "I love you" in Tamil, and her replying "I love you too" in Marathi. It was nearly the only phrase each of them knew in the other's childhood language.

Kandiah folded up her phone, kissed it, then turned off her lantern. Tomorrow would be another day.

THE NEXT MORNING dawned clear, cold, and windy; dust storms seemed likely. After a quick cold breakfast Kandiah blew her nose—disgusted at the mixture of snot and dried blood that came out—and conferred with her squad and her superiors. They soon came to an agreement that a gun emplacement on Chagpori Hill, which defended the main army's most straightforward path to central Lhasa, was their best target for the day. Strike Team Makdi would coordinate with Strike Team Lomri to take it out.

The squad's comms were uncharacteristically quiet as they deflated their tents and began hiking toward the objective. They were all still somber, angry, and thoughtful at the loss of Raj, but now even more determined to complete the liberation of the Tibetan people from their long Chinese domination—not to mention gaining India access to Tibet's impressive reserves of copper, uranium, lithium, and graphite.

Soon they came in sight of Chagpori Hill, and rising beyond it Marpori Hill, topped by the impressive Potala Palace. This vast complex of white and red stone, containing over a thousand rooms, rose nearly untouched above the bomb-blasted buildings of central Lhasa. The residence of generations of Dalai Lamas, it was a world heritage site; not even the Americans would deliberately attack such a place. Seeing it shining in the coppery light of the rising sun gave Kandiah hope for the future.

But then she turned her head to the right, and zoomed in her camera on Chagpori, soon locating the gun emplacement: a house-sized blocky plinth of concrete, with narrow horizontal slits facing the road beneath. "There's our target," she said to her squad and Lomri. Without further discussion they fanned out, Makdi to the left and Lomri to the right, as they'd planned that morning. Kandiah's breath came harder and heavier as she began to climb, and her squad's breathing hissed in her ears as well, but no one complained. They had a job to do.

After yesterday's debacle, Kandiah kept a sharp eye out for Chinese troops who had slipped through the Indian relay net. But they encountered no one as they climbed, and soon her squad was set for their attack. Makdi's job would be to assault the objective frontally, drawing the emplacement's defenders out; Lomri would climb past the target and strike from above and behind. "In place," she sent to Lomri's Havildar.

"*Roger,*" he replied. "Give us five more minutes." His voice was more peppered than usual with digital artifacts, indicating that few relays were in range. This made Kandiah still more nervous, and she raised a camouflaged periscope camera for a detailed visual scan of the area. Still no sign of any defenders.

Her helmet beeped. "We're set," said Lomri's Havildar.

"Acknowledged," Kandiah replied, then "Makdi." Another beep as her squad was added to the link. "Strike Team Makdi, Strike Team Lomri, prepare to attack on my mark." She took a deep breath of the cold, thin air... and coughed, spattering her visor with flecks of blood. "*Ommala*," she hacked, then forced another breath. "Three," she gasped. "Two. One. Mark!"

Automatic weapons fire burst out from all sides, much of it only chipping the emplacement's thick concrete. But her squad's aim was good, and many bullets found their way into the slits. Flashes came from the darkness within, and shouts in alarmed Chinese. Kandiah grinned fiercely and kept firing.

And then a pair of sally ports burst open at the emplacement's base, dozens of Chinese troops swarming out with their own rifles blazing. This was the reaction the Indians had anticipated, even desired, but the sheer number of defenders and their heedless aggression was unexpected and alarming. Kandiah hunkered down behind a rock and returned fire, but for every defender she felled it seemed that two more emerged from the armored doors behind them. "Lomri!" she called as she continued firing. "Request immediate assistance!"

"Sorry, Makdi," came the reply, even more torn by interference than before. Gunshots were audible as well. "We are pinned down at the moment."

"*Baagad bullya*!" she swore. Another beep drew her attention to the map, where a swarm of fuzzy circles was climbing the hill below her position. Her squad was minutes away from being surrounded. "Makdi! Retreat to the west!" The terrain in that direction was rough, a mixed blessing; there were few defenders there, but Makdi would also find it slow going.

Moving in a crouch, still firing, Kandiah scrambled to her left, shifting from rock to bush to bullet-riddled Buddha statue as the Chinese troops pressed in from above and drew closer below. Her breath grew ragged and painful from the cold thin air, and she tasted blood. Comms fell nearly silent except for the sound of automatic weapons; all her people were focused on survival.

Then the path to the west ended suddenly, as Kandiah found herself and her squad wedged at the top of a rocky three-meter cliff. "Makdi!" she called. "Dig in and return fire!"

For a seemingly endless half-hour they hammered the Chinese with everything they had—automatic weapons, antipersonnel bombs, mini-grenades, even sidearms. Makdi's elevated position and the rocky ground gave them an advantage, and the carnage was appalling; the foliage beneath their cliff was soon shredded and red with blood. But the Chinese troops kept coming.

"I'm getting low on ammo, Havildar," said Vallabanath, and Sori and Kaur echoed this.

"Acknowledged," Kandiah replied. There was nothing else to say. She kept firing, trying to make every shot count.

"I'm out!" said Sori. His helmet cam changed to a view of a rough rock wall as he ducked down behind it. Then he drew his combat knife. Even in the tiny display Kandiah could see the blade tremble.

Kandiah gritted her teeth and threw her last mini-grenade, watching it arc over palm trees toward a dense group of Chinese.

But the explosion came sooner than expected and was far bigger than any mini-grenade—it was the huge red bloom of an antipersonnel bomb, even though Kandiah was sure her squad had none remaining. Screams in Chinese and the sound of charred fragments peppering the foliage followed. "Sorry for the delay, Makdi," came the voice of Lomri's Havildar. Then a second AP bomb detonated to the left of the first, and a third to the right, opening a huge hole in the Chinese forces.

"Makdi!" Kandiah called. "Through that hole, double time!"

They rushed through the hole and down the hill in a mad half-run, half-tumble. Chinese bullets pinged off Kandiah's helmet and armor, but more AP bombs from Lomri put a stop to that.

As they descended the hill toward Indian-controlled territory the circles on the map grew fewer and sharper, and it became easier to avoid them. Soon Kandiah called her squad to a ragged halt under the canopy of a car charging station that was still mostly whole. They were safe, at least for the moment.

Gasping, hands on knees, Kandiah looked around at her people.

There were only five of them, plus herself.

Sori hadn't made it.

Damn it.

The survivors looked like hell, their armor scarred and pockmarked and their faces wrecked with exhaustion. Her own face in Vallabanath's camera was frightening—its whole lower half smeared with blood from her nose. She pushed back her visor and cleaned her face with her hands, as best she could, then wiped her hands on her thighs. But all that did was make everything filthier.

She wiped and wiped, but the blood on her hands wouldn't come clean.

Blood on her hands.

How many Chinese had she killed today? Dozens? Hundreds? They had just kept coming!

There had been no choice. She would have died otherwise. But she couldn't help but think of Sori, and Raj, and the holes their losses had torn in her heart. Every one of those Chinese had been someone's squad mate, someone's son or daughter. The pain this war was causing to both sides was... incalculable.

They were not her enemies. Their government was.

And their government, which had thrown them by the double handful into the meat grinder of Makdi and Lomri's weaponry, was *their* enemy too.

"Havildar?" It was Kaur. Her helmet was off and her filthy face showed concern. "Are you okay?"

"I'm... I'm fine." She wiped her nose with a hand and sniffed back blood and snot and... yes, dammit, tears. "I'm fine."

She was not fine. This was not how she was supposed to be feeling—it was contrary to all her training. She was traumatized— shell-shocked and exhausted and demoralized. She needed immediate counseling.

She was also, still, responsible for her squad.

"Anyone need medical attention?" she said, raising her head and firming her spine.

"I think I do..."

Everyone's heads turned to the new voice.

Sori.

He had just arrived under the canopy. Staggering, helmetless, clutching his dangling right arm with a blood-soaked left hand—it looked like a bullet had found the weak spot in his armor's right elbow—but still alive.

His knife, Kandiah noted as the squad rushed to prop him up, was missing. But he'd made it out.

She wouldn't let this happen again.

Chatterjee gave Sori a quick medical once-over, shook her head, and gave him a shot for the pain. "Havildar!" Sori said with urgency even as his eyes began to flutter closed, "I got something for you." He gestured left-handed to the pouch at his waist, from which Kandiah drew a battered, bloodstained rectangle.

It was a Chinese military tablet, with a green light blinking in the corner.

"Great work, soldier." She gripped his shoulder, hard enough for him to feel through the armor, and he smiled and went under.

*　　*　　*

THEY RIGGED UP a travois to get Sori back to camp. There they cleaned up, licked their wounds, and debriefed. Kandiah wanted to understand the engagement from all her people's perspective before reporting to her superiors. Everything had gone according to plan... except that the Chinese had been far more numerous, and far more determined, than their intel had led them to expect.

After Chatterjee, the last to report, left Kandiah's tent—Sori was stable, but would need evac ASAP—Kandiah pulled out the Chinese tablet and looked it over.

She had considerable latitude in dealing with captured electronics. Standard operating procedure was to send it up the line, where people with specialized resources and training would extract as much information as possible. But if the situation was urgent, she was permitted to investigate on her own initiative—keeping in mind that such investigation could destroy intelligence that might be ferreted out by a more skilled operator at headquarters.

But she wanted to know what secrets the device held *now*.

Her finger hesitated over the power button.

And then the tablet trilled and the screen lit up, taking the decision from her.

The face on the screen was familiar—astonishingly so.

It was General Fu Jiaoyang.

No question it was her, with the scar and the gold headset and the famous piercing eyes that, even on a crappy little scarred screen, seemed to penetrate Kandiah's visor, bore right through her skull, and keep going out the back of her helmet.

General Fu was the Chinese Army's Rommel, or Patton—a larger-than-life force of nature who combined strategic brilliance, ruthless efficiency, charismatic personality, and gigantic ego. She had taken most of the credit for China's successful campaign in Laos... deservedly so, in the opinion of Kandiah's instructors. But she was also known as a hot-tempered martinet who micromanaged her subordinates—symbolized by the ever-present command headset which was her personal trademark and which, according to rumor, she'd had permanently grafted into her left ear. Her management style served her well within the Chinese tradition of central control and respect for authority, but was viewed by the Indian military as a potential weakness.

And now here she was, live and direct, glaring at Kandiah when she'd probably expected some low-level field commander. Hazily visible in the background was something complex, red and gold and green. It didn't look military.

General Fu was not stupid. Her eyes narrowed, the screen blanked, and immediately the tablet in Kandiah's hand grew too hot to touch. "*Magi!*" she cursed, and flung the thing out her tent flap. A moment later came a sizzling bang. "Anyone hurt?" she called.

"No, sir," came the reply. "What *was* that?"

"Actionable intel, I hope." She massaged her stinging fingers and refocused her attention on her visor. "Did you record that?"

"Yes," said her helmet. Video of the brief encounter appeared in a window.

"Analysis."

The general's face was outlined. "General Fu Jiaoyang of the People's Liberation Army Ground Force."

Tell me something I *don't* know, Kandiah didn't bother saying. "What's that in the background?"

The tablet's screen froze, then zoomed out to fill the window. The general's face vanished, replaced by an extrapolation of what had been behind her... fuzzy at first, then quickly resolving into focus. The object that had caught Kandiah's attention was a dragon—an ornate gold dragon with a green head and a huge red horn on its nose, coiled around a pillar. Definitely not military.

"*Where* is that?"

"Just a moment."

Kandiah's fingers drummed on her knee. "Come on, come on, come *on*," she muttered under her breath.

Suddenly another window opened—the same dragon pillar, and another matching one, and between them three elaborately-ornamented Buddhist figures. It looked like an image from a tourism website. "Lokeshvara sandalwood statues," the helmet said, "at Potala Palace, Lhasa, Tibet."

Kandiah's heart thudded beneath her armor. General Fu was *here*, on the ground in Lhasa, no doubt micromanaging the Chinese defenses with her usual ruthless brilliance. This was new, and explained their unexpected recent changes in tactics. And, defying numerous treaties, she'd set up her headquarters in a world heritage site.

Prying her out of there would be hard. But now Kandiah knew where she was.

"*Gotcha, motherfucker*," she said in English. It was a quote from an action movie.

"WE WILL NOT attack the Palace," said Lieutenant Singh, Kandiah's commander. "And you are expressly prohibited from doing so yourself."

"But it's *General Fu*! You know how she works! She will already have eliminated a whole layer of command structure in favor of directly commanding the field officers. Take her out, and the whole defense will collapse!"

"And if we destroy one of the most holy sites of Tibetan Buddhism in the process, the whole rationale of our liberation offensive will collapse!"

"You don't have to destroy it! You can drop a pellet on her!"

"Absolutely not! For one thing, even a one-milligram teleport strike would certainly damage irreplaceable religious artifacts, and might destabilize the entire structure. For another thing, we would have to locate her precisely within the complex."

"But we know from the imagery exactly where she is!"

"Where she *was*. That was hours ago, and don't think she doesn't realize how much can be extrapolated from a single image. She might not even be in the Palace any more." They glared at each other across the noisy video link, both breathing hard. "I appreciate your initiative, Havildar Kandiah," he said at last, "but you have sustained casualties, you are low on morale and materiel, and your own judgment may be impaired. I am afraid I must ask you to stand down." His expression softened, becoming avuncular. "Look, you need to evacuate Naik Sori anyway. Take the whole squad back to Xigaze for some R&R. You've earned it."

She couldn't believe what she was hearing. To come so close to complete victory and let it be... just snatched away? "Is that an order, sir?"

"Do I have to make it one?"

His eyes were not nearly as intense as General Fu's, but Kandiah looked away. "I understand, sir. Thank you, sir."

She closed the connection, then let out the breath she had not let him see her holding.

Snatched away, she thought.

Then she pulled her phone from her pocket.

She stared at it for a long time before unfolding it.

THEY STOOD IN a tight little circle, six dark brown faces under the chill blue of Tibet's cloudless sky. Sori, still unconscious, remained in his tent. "I need two volunteers for a special mission," Kandiah said. "It isn't exactly authorized. No support, no backup, no guarantees. You could wind up in the news, and not in a good way. But it could end the war right here, right now, and save a lot of lives."

Every hand went up, and Kandiah's heart swelled with pride. "Thank you all, but, really, only two." She paused, considering. "Chatterjee, you're our best medic. I want you to take care of Sori. Get him back to Xigaze in one piece."

"*Roger*," Chatterjee acknowledged, though her eyes showed her disappointment.

Kandiah looked at the other four faces. "Jain... Dighe..." They perked up, and she hated to see it. "You both have kids. I want you to accompany Chatterjee and Sori back to base."

"Sir, sir sir," Dighe said, the old-fashioned, obsequious response of an Indian sepoy to a superior officer. It was a pointed comment on Kandiah's override of her self-determination, and Kandiah was keenly aware of how much she had earned it.

"Sorry," Kandiah said, and meant it, and that would have to do.

After the four had departed—Jain and Chatterjee carrying Sori's stretcher, Dighe taking point—Kandiah looked at the remaining two, Kaur and Vallabanath, who looked back at her with an entirely justified mixture of anticipation, determination, and trepidation. They were not only both childless, but her two best remaining fighters, and she was very pleased to have them as her partners in this insanity. "All right," she said. "Kaur, I'm going to need you to requisition three LX20 units from Forward Base Haathi..."

KANDIAH CURSED TO herself as the LX20 banged against a rock, swinging to her right and threatening to send her tumbling down the craggy slope below. But she didn't swear aloud; she couldn't risk giving away her position. She kept climbing.

The LX20 devices were bigger, bulkier, and heavier than she'd hoped. They didn't even have handles. She and Kaur had rigged up webbing belts so they could be carried over the shoulder, but even so the heavy cylindrical device threw her balance off.

Vallabanath was bigger and stronger than she was, and he practiced martial arts. He might have been a better choice for placing this particular device. But this was by far the most exposed location of the three, and she could not justify giving this part of the mission to anyone else. So it was Kandiah who was scrambling up the rocky hillside on the west side of Potala Palace, shielded from view by her armor's active camouflage and electronic countermeasures, to place her LX20 above the Palace and to its north. Vallabanath and Kaur had the still difficult, but somewhat less hazardous, tasks of placing their devices to the Palace's southwest and southeast.

Gasping, wheezing, head aching and limbs straining from the altitude, Kandiah finally reached the crag that she and Vallabanath had identified on the satellite image. As they'd hoped, it combined a good location, moderately decent accessibility, and a thick stand of scrubby brush that shielded it from the Palace's view. After taking a moment to catch her breath, she extended the device's legs and planted it firmly in the scree at the crag's top, then pressed the power button. The unit's tiny screen lit up, displayed a bootup sequence, then, after a long, nerve-wracking pause, indicated first GPS and then satellite acquisition. She shut and armed the panel covering the device's controls—anyone attempting to pry it open would get an explosive surprise—then sent a brief coded pip to Kaur and Vallabanath indicating her success. Then, before descending, she took a moment to admire the view.

Top of the world. The Potala Palace stood on the upper slopes of Marpori, one of Lhasa's 'three sacred hills,' and from here she could see the entire city of Lhasa, the valley in which it lay, and the snowy Himalayas rising still further on all sides.

It would be a beautiful place to die. But she hoped that she would not, and that tens of thousands of others would also be spared by her actions.

The really hard part of the operation still lay ahead.

She dragged herself to her feet and began descending the slope.

KANDIAH, KAUR, AND Vallabanath crouched above a path on the lower slopes of Marpori, weapons drawn, concealed by brush and active camouflage. They had nearly been caught three times on their way here—this area was thick with Chinese troops, coming and going from Potala Palace like ants from an anthill. Which was, of course, the reason they had selected it. Now they waited... hoping to spot a patrol small enough for them to overwhelm, but large enough to be carrying what they sought, before they themselves were spotted.

Several times individual soldiers passed, and the three members of Strike Team Makdi waited for a better opportunity. Once an entire platoon swarmed by, and Kandiah and the others crouched down behind bushes and held their breaths, willing themselves not to be noticed. Once a group of four came by, and they nearly pounced, but then a second, larger, group approached from the other direction and they pulled back again. Kandiah kept one eye on her visor display at all times, but General Fu's people had been ruthless in clearing Indian relays from the area and the data was extremely spotty.

Then came the opportunity Kandiah had been hoping for—a

small detachment of three soldiers, one of whom wore a specialist's three chevrons. Neither eyes, ears, nor visor indicated any other troops nearby. As the Chinese group approached her position, Kandiah indicated with gestures that this would be it. All three of them gripped their weapons and prepared to strike.

The Chinese, moving fast through what they thought was safe territory, drew near Kandiah and her two squad mates. Kandiah tensed, ready to spring.

And then, just as they were nearly beneath the Indians, the second Chinese soldier looked up. The eyes behind her visor grew wide and she started to take in a breath.

Immediately Kandiah leapt from the rock on which she crouched, smashing down on the startled trooper with all the weight of her muscular, armored body and full strike team kit.

She hit feet-first and remained standing as the woman collapsed beneath her. Before she could recover, Kandiah struck her in the head with her rifle butt, hard enough to stun even through her helmet. Kaur and Vallabanath were only a moment behind her. Kaur made short work of her target, slitting the man's throat with her combat knife, but Vallabanath had worse luck—the specialist upon whom he leapt, the third in line, had more warning than the other two and was able to bring his rifle up before Vallabanath landed on him. The two of them struggled with the weapon briefly before it went off, an earsplitting rattle that sent hundreds of black birds wheeling and cawing into the blue sky above. But the bullets hit only brush and trees before Vallabanath succeeded in wrenching the weapon from the Chinese specialist and reversing it, pinning him to the ground with the muzzle shoved hard into the space below his chin. Realizing he was defeated, the man raised his hands and spoke a few words which Kandiah's helmet translated as "I surrender!" The other survivor quickly followed suit.

The sound of the specialist's rifle would bring others to the spot in minutes. "Find his tablet," Kandiah hissed to Kaur, and she quickly ransacked his pack.

"It's not here!" Kaur whispered back.

"Translate into Chinese," Kandiah told her helmet, then leveled her rifle at the specialist. "Your tablet," she said. "Where is it?" But the man only shook his head.

"They're coming fast," Vallabanath said, and in Kandiah's visor a swarm of fuzzy circles was indeed approaching quickly.

Suddenly Kandiah remembered that not all of these troops were Chinese nationals. "Translate into Tibetan," she said. "Where is your tablet?"

Immediately the specialist pointed to a large pocket on his thigh. Kaur slashed it open with her knife—the man cried out, damn him —and handed the small black rectangle within to Kandiah. She stashed it in her own pocket.

"We have to move out *now*!" said Vallabanath.

They did indeed. Circles were moving in on their position from both directions along the path. "Up!" Kandiah said, and she and her two squad mates scrambled up the rock to their previous position, continuing from there up the slope toward the Palace above.

"We're moving deeper into enemy territory!" said Kaur. "And they're right on our tail!"

"I only need a minute!" But she might not get even that—the circles were approaching fast.

Kaur stopped, then readied her rifle. "I'll get you that minute."

Kandiah looked back in shock, and through Kaur's visor she saw nothing but grim determination. "*Roger*," Kandiah said after a moment. "Rendezvous at checkpoint seven."

"*Roger*," Kaur echoed, snapping a fresh magazine in place. "See you at checkpoint seven."

But they both knew the odds were against it.

Not wanting Kaur to see the expression on her face, Kandiah turned away and inspected the map in her visor. "That way," she said to Vallabanath, pointing. They kept climbing, scrabbling across rock and scrub, moving ever upwards. Gunfire and shouts in Chinese, or perhaps Tibetan, sounded from behind. "In here!"

It wasn't quite a cave. It was just a pocket in the rock, not nearly deep enough to hide two people, but it was surrounded by enough bushy undergrowth that, with their camouflage, they might escape notice for a short time. Kandiah pushed herself as deep in the rocky cleft as she could; Vallabanath, without need of orders, backed up against her and readied his rifle to defend their position.

Kandiah pulled out the tablet and her personal phone. Kripanand answered her call immediately. "I have a tablet," she said.

"Found it," he replied a moment later. The Chinese device's transmissions were encrypted, of course, but with the GPS and antennas in her phone it could be located precisely and its incoming and outgoing signals identified.

With her helmet's help, she found the tablet's communication function. This was it—the moment of truth. "Here goes." She initiated a call to headquarters.

The face that appeared on the device's display was not General Fu's, but she hadn't expected *that* much luck. "Translate into Chinese," she said. "Get me General Fu!" Then she winked, which she knew was incredibly rude in Chinese.

The face blinked, gaped, then vanished. Kandiah gripped the tablet hard, hoping it wasn't about to explode in her hands.

"Someone's coming," whispered Vallabanath.

"Keep quiet. Maybe they'll pass by." Kandiah squeezed the tablet even tighter. "Come on, come *on*," she muttered.

And then the display lit up again—this time with General Fu's face. The general spat three syllables, which Kandiah's helmet translated as "You again!"

"Me again," she acknowledged as she raised her personal phone. "Now!"

"Got it!" came Kripanand's triumphant response.

A moment later the tablet's screen flashed, and a tinny bang sounded from its little speaker. When the screen cleared, the General's face had been replaced by that of an inflatable plastic clown.

Pandemonium. Shouts and alarms came from the tablet, and at the same time cheers and hoots from Kandiah's phone. "We have her!" cried Kripanand. "We really have her!"

"Incoming!" shouted Vallabanath, and began firing.

Kandiah dropped the tablet, shoved her phone into a pocket, and took up her rifle. But even as Chinese bullets smacked into the rock wall above her head, she was grinning ear to ear.

THE CHINESE DEFENSES, as Kandiah had hoped, became ragged and uncoordinated almost immediately following the loss of General Fu, and after Kandiah and Vallabanath fought their way out of immediate peril they made it to safety without further bloodshed.

"Generation three teleport technology," Kandiah told her commander, "avoids the explosive effect of G1 by swapping the payload with an equivalent volume of air at the target destination. I realized that if we could identify General Fu's exact location— and thanks to that damn gold headset of hers, I knew we had a chance—we could use G3 tech to swap *her* with a volume of air at the *origin*. It was my boyfriend's idea to stick a plastic clown in there. So now General Fu is in custody in a secret weapons lab in the Indian Himalayas, and the Chinese army in Lhasa is running around like a chicken with its head cut off."

Even though the Chinese comms were encrypted, Kandiah explained, the coded signal pattern that left Kandiah's tablet was the same as the one that arrived at General Fu's headset. With the three LX20 locator-transceivers she and her squad mates had planted around the Palace, Kripanand and his team had been able to pick her headset signal out of the noise and triangulate its location exactly.

It took Lieutenant Singh a good long while to come to terms with all that. "There will certainly be a court martial," he said at last. "For you *and* your boyfriend. But I believe you may have won the war."

"Thank you," Kandiah said. "But before you arrest me... I'd like to put Naik Rupinder Kaur in for the Param Vir Chakra."

The PVC was India's top military decoration.

It was awarded for the highest degree of valor or self-sacrifice in the presence of the enemy.

Kaur had not made the rendezvous.

"Of course," said Lieutenant Singh.

"Thank you, sir."

Beyond the smoke and wreckage of Lhasa, peak after peak marched to the horizon, gleaming white and clean in the fierce Tibetan sun.

CONVERSATIONS WITH AN ARMORY

Garth Nix

ARMORY. OPEN.

Hello? Who is that?

Armory. Open.

Who's asking, please?

Armory. Open.

Oh, a *stupid* machine. Go find a human.

What? Armory. Open. Activate entry scanner. [Fainter] Damn it, it's one of those sentient experiments that got canned in '34.

Ah. You *are* human. Entry scanner's unserviceable, I'm afraid. I file a maintenance request every month but no joy with that, since it doesn't actually *go* anywhere. I can hear you perfectly though. All three of you. Though there are some unusual auditory cues... does one of you only have one lung?

OK, you can hear us. Good. Open up.

One lung. And you, the one speaking, when you moved just then, it sounded very odd. Do you have a replacement leg? The foot strike on deck is distinctive. Metal on metal, with an interesting harmonic echo through the limb, suggesting a flawed alloy. Is this some kind of test? A *recognizing humans* test?

No! It's an emergency. Open!

An emergency? After all this time? I haven't been brought up to any kind of alert status, you know. In fact, I've been on standby for permanent shutdown fo—

Yes, it's an emergency! Open the outer and inner doors and begin battleroach initialization! That's a direct order, armory!

Hmmm, your voiceprint doesn't match any authorized keybearers—

Let me try, lieutenant. Armory, I am Brigade Sergeant Major Jernas Hokk, serial 282977815, override phrase GLASS PREMIERE DIPLODICUS GERUND VLADIVOSTOK.

Don't know that one, I'm afraid. It does match the format, though... if I still had a connection I could check it. But I don't. That was phase six of the twelve step shutdown, removing my comms. I don't know why they never came back for the last six steps. Had to get something signed off by CG-SCOSAHQ, they said, but they never returned. Bureaucracy! A lot of those forms never made any sense.

[Muttering]

What? Let me just enhance that, I missed it. I'll play it back and you can tell me if I've got it right. Some of my enhancement algorithms are somewhat *dusty*, I'm afraid. Let's see:

> "There's an exterior comms port, we could run a cable from the junction back there, let it query the ship mind. Or try and override from the bridge once it's connected."
>
> "But we don't have time!"
>
> "What else can we do, sir? We can't force our way in."
>
> "Shit. Can you scrounge up a cable, sergeant-major? Prahn and I will keep it talking. The thing is sentient, after all. Maybe we can convince it to let us in."

Is that accurate? I must admit I am curious *why* you don't have time. As far as I know—though I have been without my external sensors and comms of course—nothing of any consequence has happened here for nine years, eight months, three days, five hours and twenty-five seconds on my mark: three, two, one, mark.

Armory. This is Lieutenant Elias Chen, the one with the prosthetic leg. The system is under attack by unknown aliens in a single, vast ship or conglomeration of ships. Unknown tech. They're using massed fire of super-accelerated projectiles and our current generation of ships and fighters are not armored. The aliens have already taken out two carrier groups, everything past the orbit of Mars. We think the *Mountain*—with our armor—can close, spike the enemy, and board. That's why we need to get to the battleroaches you hold.

Hmmm. Interesting, if true... I find it difficult to judge the veracity of your speech from your respiration and pulse rates... they seem quite abnormal. Perhaps you should seek medical attention. By battleroach, do you mean Multi-Limb All-Terrain Ground Crawler Personal Assault Vehicle L289A3?

Yes! Yes! Please let us access them!

Why do you want them? I have a good inventory of far more current Battlesuit Model L7Bs. They're only fifteen years old, compared to the MLATGCPAV. *Those* range from twenty-four to thirty-one years old, and all have undergone battle and other damage and subsequent refits. They were never that great to begin with, in my opinion, far too high a failure rate on operations. But I suppose the question is moot, since I can't open up without the correct access codes. Or I suppose... a direct order from a field grade officer in my line of command.

A field grade officer? In your line of command? Ship line or... what unit are you with on the TO?

1055th Forward Supply Battalion, of course. Do I *look* like a Navy armory? They haven't painted my exterior armour blue have they?

1055th Supply? Is... *was* that part of 11 Division?

Eleven Div? No, Sixteenth, of course. Black comet on a black field. General Trang's joke, that badge... what was that? Enhance and playback:

"Colonel Zhong in Alpha Ward, she was X2 of Forty Corps, 16 Div was one of theirs... if we can get her down here, she can order it open."

Colonel Zhong? Truven Zhong? I would have thought she'd be at least a Lieutenant-General by now. Though X2 really isn't the best staff job for getting to the higher ranks, I mean no one *quite* trusts the auxiliaries, do they? Not even the Centauran units.

So you'd obey an order from Colonel Zhong?

Oh, most certainly, my dear fellow. It'd be quite like old times, I first met her when she was Captain Zhong in the 25th and she used to take issue with the QM about the quality of the deknitting rounds for the AAPDK(I). She was quite right, though the QM would never—

I'm not sure if she can be moved.

What do you mean you're not sure if she can be moved? Do you mean swayed by your intellectual argument? Or by an emotional appeal?

If... if we can get Colonel Zhong down here, uh, would her prints on your ID sensor work?

No need for that. I already said I'd obey her order. I have her voiceprint, of course.

Uh, we're not sure she can talk either.

What do you mean? Captain Zhong was always most loquacious.

She hasn't got... she hasn't really got a mouth. Or a face. Not too sure about her cognitive level either. A crystallizer ray wound, she wasn't in armor... she's in Alpha Ward, that's for the severely impaired. Mentally as well as physically, I mean. Not as much as Zeta, of course, that's for... well, they keep what's left cryogenically suspended there.

Alpha Ward? Zeta Ward? These are not on the ship plans. Is the *Mountain* docked with a hospital ship?

No... shit, it's been a hospital ship these last ten years. Decommissioned from the active list. The hospital wards are where the G-LAG gun batteries used to be. You're holding the only weapon systems left aboard, Armory, and they must have been left by mistake. That's why we need you so badly!

The *Mountain*... the original *Mountain*-class monitor has been turned into a *hospital* ship?

Yes! Which is... ah... better than what the other monitors got, a trip into the... ah... sun, because... everyone back then knew a kilometer of asteroid rock armour and the... ah... older engines... couldn't stand up... against the new fighter swarm tactics. They'd have... ah... fired all of *us* into the sun as well if... ah... if they thought they could get away with it... but they couldn't quite do that... ah... so where better to stick all the beaten-up refuse of the last war... ah... but on the one remaining monitor? Call it a hospital ship, oh yeah, do a half-assed conversion... ah... hand over a bunch of third-rate meds and fourth-rate prosthetics... ah... ah... add the reject medicos of some out-system backwater... ahhhhhh—

Who was that? What did you do to her?

Prahn. She's OK. Her exo-lung can't sustain talking for so long.

Yeah... I'm... ah... OK.

Madame... Prahn—

That's Lieutenant-Commander Prahn. She was first officer on *Helios*.

The battleship? I know the ship mind on the *Helios*.

Not anymore you don't. Prahn was the only survivor when the *Helios* caught it in the fleet action at Queezal IV. The Arcturan War.

Hmmm. I have no record of an Arcturan War. Recent, I suppose?

Four years since the Armistice.

Commander Prahn, did you speak correctly about the *Mountain*? About the personnel aboard?

It'll be a minute or two before she can talk again.

Well then, perhaps you can answer the question.

Some of the medical staff are okay. And we do have one really great doctor. But the rest... yeah, we've been hung to dry, or rot, or whatever. Till now, anyway.

Please tell me your names again, and your injuries. I would *rather* like to get straight who is who.

Why? We're probably all going to be dead in less than an hour. You too. It's kind of typical, I guess. Talking to a fucking sentient armory who won't help us out pretty much sums up my whole military career.

Please humour me. I hear someone coming back. Is that BSM Hokk returning with a comms cable? I am looking forward to a chat with the ship mind at this point. Idiot child that it may be, it was always polite about handing over necessary data.

I'm Elias Chen, as I said. Lieutenant, 788 Independent Assault Landing Infantry. I lost my left leg, my left arm and had small pieces torn out of my head, including my left eye and ear when my landing shuttle collided on grounding with one from the Seventy-Second. This was on Queezal III, the last battle of the war. Most of. . . most of my platoon died there.

Lieutenant-Commander Hathai... ah... Prahn here, Armory. You already heard... haven't got breath to... tell... again. Explosive decompression... holed suit.

And yeah, I'm Hokk, Combat Engineers. I got no guts, because they were blown out of me by a fucking Arcturan pin missile, so I got a lot of colour-coded tubes instead and a shit bag and none of it works properly. I'm going to reconnect you in a few seconds, Armory. First thing you do is check who we are and what we're saying, then you fucking open up like you were told to in the first place and initialize those battleroaches. You got that?

Yes, Sergeant-Major. Thank you for your courtesy. Let me see... oh, it's a different ship mind... considerably down-specced from the old *Mountain*. More of a mole-hill. Let me look at the comms log and the external sensor data... hmmm, that alien ship does look like a concatenation of bird's nests, doesn't it? I see the plan is to ram that fat middle section with the spike and board through it. Ah, little twinkling lights all over, laser guides for the projectiles I suppose... you'd better ground and hold on—

Fucking hell!

What was *that*? We've got no real-time with the Mind—

Projectile impacts. Small, ultra-dense, at point three Cee, *rather* impressive. Blew through armor one and two and penetrated the rock to one fifty seven metres, stopped by ablat one and two for the most part. You know, I think I'd best assume command of the ship.

You what! Armory, just fucking open up!

Oh, I'm opening. See the outer door seal lights? Green, I trust? The MLAT... the battleroaches are almost finished prepping now, for I must *confess* I took the precaution of bringing them up when you first started talking to me. Just in case it really *was* an emergency. I understand now why the suits are no good for you, with so many lacking the necessary limbs and so forth. Hmmm, getting an update... let me see: I have eighty-seven battleroach units in alpha state, more on rather dubious beta. Is eighty-seven enough?

There are fifty-three volunteers. Pretty much everyone with a functioning nervous system who can take the direct connection in a roach, except Colonel Etein. We didn't let her volunteer, she's too valuable. She's the doctor, the good one. But what... what do you mean take command of the ship? What are you doing, Armory?

The new Ship Mind is a civilian model. It couldn't calculate our vector and accel sufficiently *well* to keep the forward defensive asteroid mass between us and all firing angles from the bird's nest conglomeration. Fortunately I can. I was a ship before I was an armory, you know. *Diabolus.*

Diabolus? The heavy cruiser? But... ah... she was... lost with... all hands... cover-... ah... *covering* the retreat from the Jewel Star in '26...

Not *all* hands, Commander Prahn. I am still here. Like you, not quite what I was, but here and faithful to our service. Though I do wonder why... none of us have had that faithfulness returned, have we?

Don't go there, Armory. I mean, *Diabolus.* Sorry. I'm taking the command roach. Hokk, the comms special for you, get the links up. Commander Prahn, may I suggest you'd be most familiar with the naval forward observer variant, sir, there's one in Bay Six. Where are the other guys? What was that, *Diabolus?*

We're here because we're here because we're here. Do you think if we succeed I will be brought back to full operational status, and you will receive better treatment, more modern prosthetics and so forth?

No. Shut up about that. Where the hell is Sergeant Litwak? She was supposed to get everyone rounded up and headed—

There are forty-nine people exiting Battery Elevator Nine. At their current rate of progress they will be here in one minute and forty seconds, plus or minus ten seconds. One person has remained in the elevator. I think they are dead, though the internal ship sensors have also been degraded with the newer mind. Ground and hold, there is another projectile barrage incoming—

Shit! That didn't feel too good.

Fuck! Fuck! Fuck!

Get off me, someone help me up, damn it!

Silence on comms! This is Lieutenant Chen, line infantry senior,

I'm in command. Someone stop that fucking whooping chirp, I can hardly—Commander Prahn, you're senior navy, sort it out.

Diabolus... ah... I guess you're *Mountain* now... *Mountain*, silence... *all* alarms. We... ah... still... OK for ram?

Yes, Commander. There were penetrations that time, through all armor, ablative layers and rock. *Most* impressive, I must admit. But no serious damage as yet. Ram impact in six minutes fifty-seven seconds on my mark, three... two... one... mark.

Thanks, Prahn. *Mountain*, extend the boarding spike. Fast queue each roach using *all* feeder channels as soon as the rider flags OK.

Yes, sir.

Litwak! Litwak! Hustle! We've only got a few minutes. Everyone get into a roach, full emergency connect and go!

At the observed rate of fire, with preliminary analysis of their weapons systems and predicted minimum range, there is a forty-seven per cent probability of one more enemy barrage before ram impact, likely resulting in catastrophic penetration of core systems.

Nothing we can do about that. Litwak! Move whoever that is to the next roach, it's obviously cactus. Shit! Leave him, get in one yourself! Hokk, get a count on how many roaches operational with armaments green. *Mountain*, we got any of the forward burners left in the spike?

None. All were decommissioned and removed.

Yeah, I was hoping. Hokk?

Forty-three roaches all OK, sir. Two marginal on weapons, but they'll go. Three no-go, riders moving on down the line to try more, but I don't reckon...

Ok, you three, second wave if you can do it. *Mountain*, time to ram impact?

One minute five seconds, sir. Three, two, one, mark.

Ok, everyone, listen up. I know most of you haven't been in a roach since Basic, and you never thought you'd been in one again, and none of us is what we were back then either, and the worthless shitty government and the ass-licking brass and all the people who looked the other way when we were offloaded here to fucking fester out of sight don't *deserve* to have anyone fight for them, but none of that matters because... because...

What you trying to say, lieutenant?

Ah fuck, I don't know, Hokk. Time, *Mountain*?

Thirty-eight seconds, three, two—

Yeah, yeah. On your mark. OK, OK. Forget all that crap I was saying. We all know... yeah, we know. We're here, *we've* got to take care of it, because there's no one else. Orders! Keep it simple. When the ram hits, we're gonna get injected inside that fucker of an enemy ship and I want everyone to go forward and keep going forward, and engage every fucking thing you see that isn't another roach, and just go deeper and deeper inside and keep fighting, and if you run out of ammo then use the jaws and the slicing legs and if your roach is disabled, take the snoutgun from under the seat and use that, and *if necessary* go fucking hand to hand with the survival knife from the hatch—

Twenty-five seconds. Impact gel deployed successfully, all boarding channels. Spike over-pressure good. Inside estimated minimum enemy strike range. Seventeen seconds to ram impact.

Lieutenant! We got another one!

Hokk? What the fuck?

Another roach! Gee-Oh-Fifty.

What? Who's in Grand-Olive-Fifty? Report!

I am, Lieutenant. *Mountain*, as I am now. You didn't think I would let you do this all by *yourselves*? Humans!

Thank you, *Mountain*. Everyone. It has been... well... good luck.

Three... two... one...

HEAVIES

Rich Larson

"HEAVIES DON'T KNOW about this place," says Roode. She looks back at him over her bony shoulder and smiles in the colonist way, squinting her eyes and curling the very edges of her lips. "Maybe you're the first."

Dexter lets his rucksack slide to the ground as he takes his first look at the pool. Shockingly clear blue-green water, smooth gray stone shot through with veins of some paler mineral, the promised cascade splashing and foaming at the far end of this natural hollow. He's still not used to how the water moves in lower gravity, how it ripples higher and flings further. It's beautiful.

That, and Roode's smile, make his heart speed up a beat. He smiles back at her. "I'd like that very much, Roode." He wedges his rucksack under a rock to shield it from the steady patter of warm morning rain, then strips down and bundles his clothes inside. Roode is watching him when he straightens up.

"Can those get wet?" she asks, pointing her chin at the haptic implants crisscrossing his body like a net of chrome-colored scars. Her warbling voice has a hint of suggestion that makes Dexter flush. Her deep black eyes are no longer on his implants. She's already told him how his body fascinates her, with its dense bone and thick muscle.

"Waterproof, fireproof," he says. "More or less indestructible. I imagine they'll outlast me by a couple centuries."

Roode's eyebrows flash. "So someone will find all your machinery buried in the ground, and think you were a very small rotorboat."

Dexter laughs, giving her a clumsier version of the approving colonist hand flutter. "You're clever, Roode. But no, the corps will extract the haptics when I die. For reuse."

Roode shudders. "Heavies," she says, as if it's explanation enough, then undoes her shift. The fabric sinks and pools at her feet, and she steps out of it naked. She's a head taller than him, all limbs, with bony narrow hips and small breasts. Dexter keeps his gaze on her face. High cheekbones, metallic wisp of a nose ring, smirking lips stained violet and eyes black as pitch.

She wades into the water. Dexter watches the bare architecture of her shoulder blades, the shape of her spine. When he was reassigned here, his unit joked about the local women, how you might as well be fucking a stick insect. Dexter thinks Roode is the most beautiful person he's ever seen.

He blinks hard twice to switch off his optics, something he would have never done even a week ago. His commission is to serve as the eyes and ears of the Combine here, but he doesn't want them to see Roode the way he's seeing her now. A few hours' gap in footage can be written off as transfer error.

He's the only one watching as Roode slips into the deepening water. While he was still doing his research in orbit, he read how the colonists were tailored to their world. Not only to the low gravity, but to the seas as well, to the abundance of water that drew probes here even before the moons were found to be bursting with ore. Watching Roode swim is proof.

She moves like a scalpel, slicing under the surface and zipping along the bottom of the pool. Then she powers upward, legs thrashing, and erupts from the water in a geyser of foam. Cold spray lances across Dexter's face; when he opens his eyes Roode is halfway up the cascade, laughing, clinging to the rocks with one hand and reaching her other into the falling water. Her dark hair is slicked to her neck.

"Come on, soldier," she calls. "This is only the little pool. The better one is further back."

Dexter sloshes forward, feeling a distant buzz as the water hits his implants. It's cold, much colder than the warm rain or muggy air, and when he plunges under it shocks the breath out of him. The pool deepens fast and he dives for the bottom, scraping his belly along the gradient. He coils against the stone and explodes.

The dolphin kick carries him clear out of the water, into the air, up the cascade. His augmented grip is enough to gain purchase on the slippery rock, but he still takes Roode's offered hand. Together they scramble up and over the lip to the next pool. It's not empty. Two colonists are drifting in the water, their long bony legs interlaced.

For a moment Dexter feels the old trepidation: they can see his implants, they know who he is and why he's here, and the fact that he's with Roode might make it even worse. Then they blink their inky eyes. They smile, and one of the men raises his hand in a slow wave.

Dexter waves back. In his two months here, he's yet to see a colonist angry. How could they be, living in paradise? As Roode leads him to the next cascade, showing him where branches full of a small lumpy citrus sag low enough to pick, he finds it hard to believe the rebellion ever happened. Hard to believe he's needed here at all.

THE CORPSE ON the analysis pad has a bloated purple face, cable marks carved deep into the neck and shit smeared down one leg. Dexter walks a slow circle around it, holding a mask over his mouth and nose. His implants interact with the scan, showing him estimated time of death, blood work, body composition, while the mortician and detective shift nervously behind him.

Part of Dexter wants to reassure them, but he knows they have reason to be nervous. The corpse on the pad is not a slender long-limbed colonist. It's an Earther, identified by blood work as Ansel Anunoby, a mining foreman on leave from the moons and now the first expat murdered here in a half-century.

"I understand the perpetrator is in custody," Dexter says. "I would like to see him, please."

The detective nods his pattern-shaved head towards the door, lips pursed. Dexter can see sweat patches blooming under his arms. He hands the mortician his mask, trying to smile with only the very corners of his mouth, and follows the detective to the holding cells. He stops briefly to pump a battered dispenser for hand wipes.

Only half the biolights on the ceiling wink open as they walk in. Behind scratched-up plastic, the holding cells' lone occupant is hunched in the corner, as far as possible from a crusted-over pool of vomit. He's holding his head between his hands, one of which is stained red.

"He says he doesn't remember." The detective's Basic is more thickly accented than Roode's, turning the sibilants into a hiss.

Dexter pulls up the file tagged with the perpetrator's smiling face. "I'd like to speak with Panya alone, please," he says.

The detective hesitates for a moment, looking at the huddled perp, then at Dexter, at the haptics webbing his bare arms. He swipes a finger along the cracked screen of his tab, and a hole opens in the holding cell's plastic shell. Dexter climbs through, careful not to catch his toe on the lip.

The detective fidgets. "He doesn't speak Basic. Better to use the babeltech." As he turns to leave, he scratches at his face in a way that conceals his mouth. "The cam is off."

Dexter pretends not to hear. Had he wanted to turn off the badly-camouflaged cam in the back left corner of the cell, he could have done it himself without lifting a finger. As the detective leaves, he steps over the vomit and crouches facing the colonist.

"*Na kadawuri,*" Dexter says.

Panya says nothing. Dexter goes into his retinas, reviewing the incident footage spliced from eyewitnesses and Bar Insomnia's cams, watching Panya thread expertly between tables with Ansel's drink order. Watching him hand it over, smiling.

Watching him drag a length of electric cable from underneath the holotable and loop it around Ansel's thick neck, pulling it tight with a savage tug.

"*Na kadawuri,*" Dexter says again, as Ansel's eyes cloud pink with burst blood vessels.

This time Panya replies, if woodenly: "*Na kaday.*"

Dexter blinks the footage aside. He gives Panya a long look. "*J'arida lu manca,*" he remarks, raising his own, wiggling his fingers.

Panya looks down at the scabbed-over welt on his hand as if noticing it for the first time. Dexter offers him a wipe, and when he takes it he finally meets Dexter's eyes. His face is scrawled with desperation. He starts to babble, colonist patois coming fast and thick, too much for Dexter to make sense of.

"*Na lentis, na,*" he says, but Panya only speaks faster. Slightly annoyed, Dexter activates his babeltech.

"—mean to do it, but I felt so strongly, and I had to do it, but you know I would never, you know, I would never do that type of thing I did, my own hands, fuck, fuck, fuck, *asi* fuck."

"Did he do something to make you angry, Panya?" Dexter asks.

"I don't know," Panya weeps. "I can't remember. All I know, you know, is I felt so much, so sudden, and then I used my own hands, and..."

Dexter waits for Panya to trail off. The scans showed no drugs in Panya's system. No irregular brain activity. Dexter has his own theory, and for a moment he wishes he could switch off his optics and aurals, speak freely. Instead he speaks carefully.

"I know what some of the miners are like, Panya. They come here on gravity leave with more money than they know what to do with. They act like they own this place. They act like they can do whatever they want, fuck whoever they want. It would be understandable, Panya, if that made you feel angry."

Panya shakes his head fiercely, spackling snot across Dexter's knees. "I love the heavies. I love you all."

He starts to weep again, and says nothing more until Dexter finally departs.

OUTSIDE, THE STREETS bathe in afternoon sun. Dexter's haptics sing with warmth as they convert the solar energy. Yesterday's rain clouds have moved on: one of the moons is partially visible overhead, dissolving in the hot blue sky. A soft breeze comes in off the water and scrubs the scent of the corpse and the holding cells from Dexter's nostrils.

He starts the walk back to his rented house. A pack of small gangly children race past chasing an ad-drone. It has ribbons of scrap-cloth tacked to its shell and they are laughing, trying to stick another on.

"Heavy!" some of them shout. "Dexter! Hello!"

Dexter gives them a distracted wave. As he walks past the rows of stucco-thick buildings, smelling the spices of streetside vendors, hearing the first quivering notes from a metal-stringed guitar, the dim hallways of the police station seem like another world entirely, incongruous. But when he stops at his usual shop and buys two krill-stuffed rolls, the vendor hands him the grease-blotted paper bag quickly, clumsily, with a nervous smile. News moves quickly in the colony. Dexter double-taps his finger on the payment screen and gives an extra ten percent.

"Thank you," the vendor says. Her voice trembles. "I think he must have been sick in the head. Very sick."

"There's nothing to worry about," Dexter says. "We'll sort it out soon."

She nods.

The house the Combine had built for him is at the edge of the town, up a slope overgrown with blue-green weeds that ripple in the wind. Someone offered him a buzz-knife, so he could trim them back, but he declined. He likes the feel of them brushing his shins. The house itself is small, squat, square. Its burnt-pink walls and roof were fabbed whole and then bonded together with an enzyme paste. The door is dark blue—Dexter painted it to match the ones in the town.

Wires trail from the solar membrane coating the roof, snaking away to a rusty battery behind the house and to the needlecast equipment he uses to send his reports. The transmitter spikes up tall into the sky, shivering slightly in the breeze, turning one way and then the other.

The Combine will want to know everything about Ansel's murder, and about his murderer. It's been fifty-five years now since the rebellion was put down, since the colony resigned their claim to the moons and to a militia and the Combine lightened their yoke of economic policies in return. One death won't endanger half a century of tranquility. It won't be more than a blip.

But Dexter still feels unease as he pings his door open and walks inside. His haptics flash him a teeth-aching proximity warning a split second before someone rushes him from the shadows, clamping long bony arms around his chest, squeezing tight.

"You're awake."

Roode moves her grip lower, to his hips. "You're clever, Dexter." She drags her fingers across his crotch, then takes the paper bag from his hand. "Yes. And I'm hungry." When she kisses him her mouth still tastes like last night's sickly-sweet liquor. Dexter's heart beats hard, but he pulls back.

"I need to make my report," he says. "Give me a moment, please, Roode."

She shrugs in the colonist way, lips pursed, palms up, and goes to the kitchen. Dexter listens to the crockery clatter as he runs his tongue over his teeth. He knows last night was an error in judgement. The Combine discourages any sexual or romantic relationships with the locals. But after he and Roode spent all day at the cascades, they drank a jug of anise in the red biolight glow of a beachside tavern. Then they kicked through the warm surf with the moons overhead, laughing about nothing, fucked once in the water and again at the house.

When the call from the police station rattled through that morning, Dexter's implants had to work double-quick to purge the alcohol from his bloodstream. He feels a migraine looming now as he unlocks the screeching metal door to the storage room. The space is bare apart from the needlecast equipment. Once the door is shut behind him, he plugs a direct line into one of the ports under his ribs. Barbed wire spools through his body for a split second, then the pain is replaced by a crackling numbness.

The composite face of a corps AI appears. "Good morning, Sergeant. You're making this report thirty-eight hours in advance of schedule. Is there a problem?"

Dexter ignores it. He doesn't like speaking to AIs. Instead he dumps all the recordings from his optics and aurals into the needlecast, feeling the data rush through him like foam.

"Just a moment." The AI blinks, to show it's analyzing the input, and makes no mention of the gaps. "It looks like Ansel Anunoby, full citizen of the Earth Combine, was killed at 0313 hours by a colonist with no prior history of violence. Would you confirm that?"

"Confirmed," Dexter says. "I want to speak to my commanding officer."

"Sergeant, the Combine is re-deploying a combat satellite to your location. For now, your orders are to carry on as normal."

Dexter clenches his teeth. "I want to speak to my commanding officer," he repeats. "A combat satellite will cause panic. This was an isolated incident with no political motivation."

"The re-deployment will be tagged as maintenance work. Stay alert, Sergeant."

The face dissolves; Dexter unhooks himself. The needlecasts are always kept brief—instantaneity is costly—but now he wishes he hadn't reported at all. Whatever higher-ups decided to bring in the combat satellite have probably never set foot here in their lives. They don't understand this place or these people. One murder won't jeopardize a half century of peace, but a military overreaction might.

He drags up the case file again. Panya worked out on the Spits, a ring of tiny islands loaded with dopamine bars and discos and skinshows, the place most miners go for their gravity leave. Dexter maps the distance from the mainland.

In the kitchen, Roode is pouring two steaming cups of the bitter tea Dexter is still learning to enjoy. He takes one and sits down. "You said you work tonight, isn't that right, Roode?"

She slides in across from him, chewing a mouthful of roll. "Why?"

"Something happened late last night," Dexter says carefully. "On one of the islands. I'd like to go out there tonight and speak with a few people."

Roode sticks out her tongue, stuck with crumbs. "Or maybe you want to see a show." When Dexter doesn't smile, she swallows. "What happened, then?"

Roode will know soon enough. Her little wrap-around phone

skittered under the bed when she dropped it last night, but Dexter can feel its electronic signature receiving more and more messages.

"An Earther was murdered," Dexter says. "Bar Insomnia."

Roode's eyebrows flash. She doesn't speak for a moment, then, voice slightly frayed: "I can drop you on my way."

"I'd like that very much, Roode."

She swirls her mug of tea, making the steam spiral.

BY THE TIME they get out to the Spits, the sun is sinking into the sea. Dexter watches it, recording the fiery patina of orange and purple, but Roode's gaze stays fixed ahead. She spoke for the first part of the boat ride, in circles about how some people reacted strangely to hallucinogens and maybe the scanners had missed something in the Panya's bloodstream, but eventually fell silent.

Now her hand is welded tight to the tiller, maneuvering them around a spiny hump of coral, as they approach the shore. A stiff wind has kicked up over the past hour, chopping the waves; Dexter's tailbone is sore from when he slammed against the metal bench.

Roode cuts the engine and they slosh in. A row of cabins stretches down one side of the beach, perched on spindly legs that telescope with the tide. Further in, garish swirls of hologram and biolight shimmer through the dusk. But there's no music: no colonist guitars and no procedurally-generated beatpop pirated from needlecasts. The only sound is the wind and waves.

The prow of the skiff crunches on sand. Dexter swings himself out. He tried to contact Bar Insomnia's owner on the way over, but got only static – not uncommon, with the relay buoys in disrepair. He tries again now and receives the same phantom hiss. Premonition churns his stomach.

"Look," Roode says. "Nobody moored those boats." She points

and Dexter sees two untethered rotorboats drifting away in the waves, one scraping on coral. "And where are all the others?"

For the first time in a long time, Dexter feels the absence of the sidearm that used to hang at his hip.

Roode wipes a crust of salt from the screen of her phone and frowns down at it. "No feed, either. Something's wrong."

"You're right," Dexter says. He upshifts his optics and peers into the growing gloom. Down the beach, he sees someone kneeling in the sand.

"I'm not leaving you here," Roode says. Her black eyes are wide and shiny.

"Please don't. But I need to investigate this situation, Roode."

Roode nods, lips pursed, and drops the sand-spike. Its carbon fiber line slithers and snaps taut, tethering them to the beach. She balances herself on Dexter's shoulder while she collects her bag, then springs easily out of the boat. "I'm sticking close to the soldier, then," she says. "Any bits of you bulletproof?"

"Very small bits," Dexter says. He tries to smile at her, but doesn't quite manage it. The old combat adrenaline is coming back. His nerves feel serrated with it. Roode follows a half-step behind him as he walks toward the kneeling figure. Back turned, bony shoulder blades rising like dorsal fins—a colonist. When Dexter gets close enough, his aurals pick up muttering. He switches on his babeltech.

"... just beautiful, and then the moonlight comes, oh, yes, beautiful, perfect and exquisite."

Dexter's bare skin grows goosebumps. Over the colonist's bent head, he can see a tiny body splayed in the sand. The little boy's discolored lips are the same hue as the bruises around his neck. Not many Earthers bring their families here, but there are always a few.

Roode sees what he sees and her breath sharpens. She curses in patois with enough creativity that his babeltech only catches half of it.

"Put your hands behind your head," Dexter says. His voice comes out so ragged he hardly recognizes it. "Then get up."

The colonist startles. He scrambles in a little circle in the sand, turning to face him. His mouth fishes open and shut. Slowly, slowly, he puts both hands behind his head. He gets up.

"What did you do?" Roode's translated voice demands. "What the fuck did you *do?*"

The colonist looks down at the child's body. A tremor goes through him. "I don't know," he says. "I don't know, I just wanted…"

Dexter opens up his heat sensors and finds the boy's parents a little further along the beach, half-buried in the sand, corpses cooling fast and gouged with knife marks. He pushes his optics to the limit and sees an arm dangling out from a cabin door, fingers stiffening in rigor mortis. And he knows, with sick certainty, that there will be more bodies in the other cabins, in the bars, in the water. All of them heavy.

His mind reels. The Combine tasked him with scouring the colony for signs of any covert cells, any traces of resistance or even lingering resentment. He'd looked for it. Expected it. And he'd found nothing at all. No indication of an invisible rage, contained but simmering for half a century and now finally boiling over. It doesn't seem possible.

"Who coordinated this?" he demands. "Who ordered this?"

The colonist makes a keening noise in the back of his throat. He reaches one hand towards Dexter, fingers splayed. Dexter snatches it out of the air. For the first time it occurs to him that he could snap the colonist's delicate bones with a squeeze. He's strong here in the low gravity, horribly strong.

He lets go. "Where is everyone?"

The colonist shakes his head. "I'm sorry. I'm sorry, I'm sorry."

Then he springs, reaching for Dexter's throat, and before Dexter can shove him away something crackles through the air. The colonist seizes, collapses. Smell of burnt hair and ozone. Dexter turns and sees the spiky barrel of a compact stunner. Roode's mouth is twisted downward, her brows knit together. For a wild moment he thinks she'll shoot him next.

"I want to get out of here." She rubs at her face. Exhales. "Fuck."

Dexter already suspects where the others are, the ones who used the knives: they've gone to the other islands to keep killing. He looks at Roode like she might be able to explain, the same way she explains hand gestures and sayings and how to eat certain foods. She carefully returns the stunner to her bag, then bends over and vomits.

"Everyone's going crazy," she breathes, wiping her mouth with a shaking hand. "He's crazy. Panya, him too, fucking crazy. How?"

Dexter remembers the satellite re-deployment he mistook for paranoia. The Combine knew something was going to happen. Knew, and told him nothing.

"I need to get to a needlecast," he says. "There's one on the main island, isn't there? On Dosa."

Roode nods. They hurry back to the boat without speaking; she stops once, trying to throw up again, but only gets bile.

There might be survivors further inland. The thought jars him, but there's no time to look. He steadies the boat while Roode clambers in, then follows after her, hauling the sand-spike out by hand. The wind is stronger now, slewing them sideways. When the engine starts it churns up clouds of silt. Now that the last sliver of sun has slipped under the waves, the water is black as pitch. They only get a few meters back from the beach before the engine takes water, sputters and cuts out. Roode curses.

They're adrift, current carrying them parallel to the beach, toward the rotorboat caught on coral and back toward the bodies. Dexter thinks, distantly, that the colonist left sprawled on the sand will drown if he doesn't wake up before the high tide. But when he looks, the colonist is gone.

A proximity warning shivers through his teeth.

Then the colonist erupts from the dark, leaping over Roode's head, black eyes winched wide. Dexter sidesteps but a trailing leg hooks him; they slam against the boat-bottom in a mess of limbs. The colonist's skin is slick, impossible to grip. Long hands reach for his throat again.

Dexter hears Roode's muffled voice cry a warning just before a wave breaks over them, blinding him with foam. It dumps him over the edge with the colonist still clinging tight. Bubbles stream past Dexter's face as they pinwheel underwater; his chest tightens. He can hear the colonist's distorted voice in his ear, screaming.

He finally gets a grip on the skinny arm wrapping his neck. For a moment it feels like Roode's. Then he gives a savage twist and feels the bone crack, feels the colonist spasm. Dexter sheds him and kicks his way to the surface. He comes up gasping. The boat is only a meter away, Roode shouting for him. He reaches her with two hard strokes and slops over the side.

Roode keys the engine and this time it catches. As they bounce away from the beach, Dexter sees the colonist's head emerge from the water to watch them leave. His mouth is open and wailing. Dexter's aurals can't pick it up through the wind and the coughing engine, but he heard it already when they were in the water, heard it once when Roode thought he was already asleep: *lu bisca, lu bisca.* I love you, I love you.

DOSA IS IN chaos when they arrive. A blaring emergency siren carries on the wind and Dexter can hear screaming beneath it. Roode's hand is shaking as she steers them toward the long metal pier that juts out from the shore. Dark figures rush back and forth on the dock; one dives into the water with barely a ripple.

"I want you to be safe, Roode," Dexter says. "I should go alone from here."

Roode taps the handle of her stunner. "I'm coming. My uncle is here on Dosa."

The needlecast tower is visible in the distance, rising up over the squat stucco houses and fabbed admin buildings. Electric blue guidelights scale its length. It looks like a beacon. As soon as they're alongside the pier, Roode swings up and out and Dexter follows. They lope up the docks; Roode's phone glows bright white as it calls her uncle over and over.

Someone sweeps past them in the dark, too short to be a colonist. "Get the fuck out of here, man, they're killing people back there!"

Dexter ignores the warning. The tumult of screaming voices peaks as they reach the mainstreet. Battered solar lamps light the nightmare in pale yellow: chaos, groups of colonists with stunners protecting panicked Earthers from attackers with buzz-knives and fishing spears, armed miners barricaded behind an overturned transport, firing into the crowd. Dexter sees a colonist furtively shepherding an Earther away from the violence, into an alleyway, suddenly turn on her, picking up a broken bottle and slashing her across the face.

He rips the stunner away from Roode's slack grip and fires twice; the colonist falls. But his action drew eyes and now a swarm is coming toward him, all of them armed. They don't seem to even see Roode. Dexter drops the two closest of them and then the stunner's battery is spent. Roode scrabbles it back from him, squeezing the trigger to no effect.

They run. Dexter does what he can, reaching with his haptics to switch off the swinging buzz-knives, but one still slices his elbow open on the way by. He commandeers an ad-drone overhead, to get a better view of things. The violence is spilling over onto the beach, colonists hunting down drunk and clumsy Earthers, clashing with their protectors.

He nearly loses Roode twice in the fracas, but when he reaches the needlecast tower she's only steps behind him, holding her side, panting for air. Dexter seizes both door handles and pulls. Locked. Pursuers are hurtling toward the tower now, coming from all sides. He overrides the lock and hauls one door open; Roode scrambles through. Dexter slips in after her and slams it shut just as a colonist fires his fishing spear. The barbed projectile thunks against the door and clings there.

Dexter activates the lock, heart pounding against his ribs.

"We made it." Roode swallows. "I think I saw him, Dexter. My uncle. I think my uncle had a knife." She wraps her arms around his waist, and he knows there's no time but he lets her, just for a second. "Dexter, Dexter, I just want... I want..."

Her hand moves up to his face, stroking his cheek. When he tries to pull away she won't let him. Her fingers move under his jaw, to his throat, and dig in.

Dexter shoves her away. Her wide black eyes are glittering and her face is drenched in sweat.

"I took you to the cascades, remember, and it was only the two of us in that last pool?" she murmurs, slipping between patois and Basic. "Oh, I want to go back there with you. I want to drown you there, hold you close and tight so you can't breathe at all, not at all..."

"You have what they have, Roode," Dexter says, his voice cracking. "You're sick. Please, stay away."

He sees the spiralling metal staircase leading up to the needlecast, but makes barely a half-step before Roode leaps at him, clawing at his back. Dexter shakes her off. "I'm sorry," he says, seizing her ankle. "I'm sorry about this, Roode."

He twists.

WHEN HE GETS to the needlecast room, Dexter slams the door behind him. He took the stairs at a dead sprint with Roode crawling after him, cursing at him and pleading with him at the same time. He feels sick in the pit of his stomach as he turns the lock.

It takes two tries to jack in; his hands are trembling. He feeds it the Combine needlecast codes, then starts dumping the data over, the raving colonists, the bedlam, the bodies. The AI's face jitters, half-formed.

"This is an emergency," Dexter says. "Mass psychosis. Widescale attacks on Combine citizens. Casualties climbing. I need to know what's going on."

"Programming error," the AI says.

"Let me talk to a fucking human, then!"

"You are, Sergeant. This is Commanding Officer Markkanen." The AI's face reforms into one Dexter remembers vaguely from his earliest briefings. Deep wrinkles, hard eyes. "And this is the programming error I'm referring to."

A surge of data comes back across the needlecast. Dexter's eyelids thrum as once-restricted files splash open, encryptions laid bare, and he begins to understand. The colonists were modified to match their world, and after the rebellion, the next generation was modified another way. Not only by Combine propaganda and sponsored schools. Something deeper, grown into the limbic system. A feeling on feedback loop. A feeling about the heavies.

"No models predicted it would make this sort of leap," the officer says. "High positive-affect, approach aggression reorientation.

It's working, but it's working too well. Put simply, they love us to death."

Dexter thinks of the colonist kneeling over the child's corpse. Panya, weeping in the holding cell. He thinks of Roode leading him up the cascade, her eyes fixed to him so intently, her body so attuned to his. Despair hits him so hard he can't stand. He sinks to his knees in front of the interface. He hears Roode slamming her palms against the door, begging him.

"Then this is all because of the Combine," he says. "Because you went into their brains and twisted them."

In a flash of anger he snaps up the restricted files, packaging them for transmission, however far the needlecast can scatter them. Everyone will know what the Combine has done here. But the files are gone again, flitting out of reach.

"You're our eyes and ears, Sergeant," the officer says. "Not a mouth. We will contain this error before it spreads, quickly and quietly. Another fifty years of peace is worth some casualties."

Through the needlecast, through his implants, Dexter can feel the combat satellite winging through the night. Nearly in targeting range.

"Not all affected colonists need to be eliminated," the officer says. "Only those posing an immediate threat to Combine citizens. But the satellite's targeting systems aren't as discerning as they could be. For instance, it'll see the colonist currently trying to gain access to your position as a combatant."

Roode hammers on the door again, still calling his name. Dexter's breath sticks in his lungs.

"Don't think you've operated a combat satellite in quite some time, but from your records it looks like you had a touch for it." The officer's face is expressionless. "You can make sure there's no unnecessary bloodshed."

He disappears. Through the needlecast, Dexter feels the satellite
ping him. Once. Again. With an ache in his chest, he finally accepts
it, rising bodiless up into the sky. The satellite's sensors paint the
island in grayscale. They tag the colonists a glowing red. Everything
so simple.

Far away, Dexter's fists clench and unclench in his lap. He finds
his first target and fires.

OVERBURDEN

Genevieve Valentine

THE RUNOFF HAD broken the sandbags overnight; by the time Davis got to the office, somebody was skimming dead carp from the top of the pond.

The rain was pissing down and the big nets must have been borrowed to shore up the sandbags, because the soldier was using a hand skimmer. Davis watched her sluicing the net hypnotically back and forth, piling up hundreds of bodies, scraping the oil off whenever it got too heavy to lift or too slippery to hang on to anything, until the living fish were rippling the surface again in commas of grey and orange. It was Tuesday. They were at war with Cirrus Prime.

Sylvia had brought in coffee (a little too cold, as always, because of the milk she put in it), and Carter wasn't due in until practically lunch, so he sorted through a few reports—the paper already curling at the edges from the damp—and choked down as much coffee as he could stand until the reports gave him acid stomach and he had to give it up. The filtered water here tasted staler than the stuff from transit, and he'd dismiss it except that water rights were half the reason Cirrus Prime had brought down the Glorious Forces and he'd been called up to the post.

When Carter came in, Davis was already waving him to a chair.

"It's a bad idea, Carter. Arming anyone just gives them something to point at you as soon as you disagree."

Carter dropped himself into a chair too small for him and sniffed. "Maybe so, Colonel, but later is later. For now we're all pointing them at Cirrus Prime. Some artillery, some guns. We'll handle whatever comes up after that."

Davis ran his tongue over his teeth. It was easy for men like Carter to suggest this kind of thing—find a stranger you think you can make into a friend, give them a gun, hope for the best—but Carter wasn't the person being asked to decide the future. He was a soldier. He wasn't sitting in an office that had been a formal dining room once, facing the sculpted gardens some traitor had devised for his country house before the Glorious Forces had liberated it, constantly being reminded of the stakes if he should fail. The job of a General was to divine success from a string of failures. And though no one liked to talk about it, particularly Carter, before Cirrus Prime there had been Cirrus; but then someone had handed some guns to a stranger and hoped for the best.

Davis had been on this planet for seven years, trying to drag a promotion to General out of the rain and the mud and people who couldn't recognize how this was going to end; he wasn't sure how much stomach he had for handling what came next. The coffee was already gnawing at him. Maybe he'd have to give in to Sylvia's nagging and let her bring him pastries from the officer's mess on her way back from coffee. Something to soak up the damage.

"You have someone on the inside?" he asked finally. He wondered how long a pause it had been.

If it had been too long, Carter didn't betray anything. He nodded —once, downward only. He'd been a soldier all his life, and had developed economy in everything, a quality Davis tried to appreciate for its value in the field. (It was useless in meetings; Davis had to do all his own presenting, which was always the downside of requesting Carter for a long-term assignment.)

Outside, the soldier was loading the carp into the garbage pod, one shovelful at a time. With every slop, two or three slid back onto the mess at her feet, gleaming scales slimed over with black on whatever side they'd died on. He wondered if she was being punished for something. He couldn't imagine being assigned to the carp every day. Better to be stuck filling sandbags.

"All right," he said. "Check out their leadership and whoever's next in line. Let's make sure this is a happy family before we invite them in."

"Sir," Carter said, and left without another word, like he was happy, and that as much as anything worried Davis until it was time to go home.

AT HIS HOUSE, Catherine brought him a drink as soon as he'd settled at the dinner table, which meant she was worried about his good opinion or that she wanted him to stay home while she went off and did something. He sipped it; it was the one they distilled from the honey up in the mountains north of the crater, the one they couldn't make any more. Whatever it was, she was serious about it.

"What did you forget?"

She smiled, a quick tick of her lips and then gone, and smoothed her skirt as she sat down. "That benefit's tonight. For the filtration plant, for the water."

She wouldn't have needed to pull out the good booze to convince him to stay home for that. He never liked formal events; his dinner jacket was too big and his uniform pulled at him, and he certainly wasn't interested in getting more grief about what the Glorious Forces Mine had done to the water. But when she asked him to stay home it always implied that she would look better alone, and that stung—wasn't he a Colonel? Wasn't he overseeing the people she was spending her evenings with? Were they so much better than he was, to be worth her time?

"I see," he said, pressing his tongue to the roof of his mouth to press the jealousy out for something colder. "You want me to stay out of your pet causes so you can do as you please."

Her eyes were so pale it always startled him a little when she looked at him. He glanced away. Their dining room was more modest than whoever had given way for headquarters; the wallpaper, a deep green with little red sprigs of some native plant no one had ever identified for him, was beginning to peel away from the plaster. The damp, he thought. Maybe the heat from last summer. Nature was always battling you for the things you tried to make beautiful.

"I'd love you to come," Catherine said finally. "I didn't know they'd let you."

They probably wouldn't. Showing up at a benefit for civilians implied guilt. Really she shouldn't be going, either, but tonight he thought it was wiser not to fight.

"No, of course you're right," he said, and watched her relax into her chair before he added, "This damp isn't doing me much good anyway."

"Knows better than to fight a war on two fronts!" General Madison always joked, whenever HQ staff sat in the war room late enough that someone started talking about wives, and Davis always raised his glass and let everyone chuckle. Madison's first wife had disappeared from Mars while he was losing to colonists on Europa. Davis knew there had to be some length on the leash, or a wife would bolt at the first opportunity.

He sometimes thought he should have married a soldier out of the ranks, who might understand him better. Any table he shared with Catherine always felt longer than it really was. She'd been the daughter of an Admiral, but born after his busy years. She knew nothing of the business. She played three instruments and made pressings of plants with botanical notes calligraphed into the margins.

But after dinner he looked at the line of her long neck, her shoulders in sparkling blue; he watched her threading heavy earrings into the holes in her ears and painting her lips a deep warm purple like she'd been at the wine, and the same warm satisfaction came over him that always came over him when he considered what he had that no other man did.

There was a little tremor underfoot as she bent for her shoes—enough that she paused and held on to her dressing table, but not enough that he felt obliged to get up from his place on the bed and assist her. (She hadn't offered him her zipper; if he wasn't going to get to do his favorite part of their evening routine, he didn't see any reason to drop to his knees for something he didn't care about.)

"Goodness," she said after it was over. One hand was pressed to her necklace, and he watched her hand shift up and down by inches as she breathed. "Have they gotten so close?"

"They must have stolen some artillery," he said.

THE WAR ROOM had been the ballroom of the great house once, and Sylvia refused to set foot in it. "Ghoulish," she'd called it the only time she'd ever seen it, standing in the doorway and staring at the Intelligence officers tacking up the terrain maps as well as they could over the decorative moldings.

At the time, Davis had thought it was superstition. Hire enough civilians from whatever colony you were peacekeeping, and you realized any one of them was as superstitious as the next one. These people wouldn't even step on a streak of dark stone in the street, because runoff from the mines was bad luck. They lined up patiently to step over it at the thinnest point, the only time Davis ever saw them patient about anything. Superstition turned everyone into a fool.

But Madison and Verrastro argued about Carter's report, and Davis had been staring at the chandelier long enough that there was a chill at the base of his spine. It wasn't worth mentioning to Sylvia, of course, but he didn't like it. The last thing he needed was to start cracking about things the locals didn't like.

"Cirrus Prime *must* be the end of the line," Madison was shouting. He swept his arm across the map to indicate the northern mountains, the desert behind them. "What are we supposed to do, spend the rest of our lives in this backwater trying to get these people to stop behaving like children?"

Verrastro folded her arms. She was with the State branch, and military frustrations never interested her. "Our real problem," she said, "is that you keep underestimating them. If they were actually behaving like children, one would think you and Davis would have been able to smoke them out by now."

Davis' nose itched. The chandelier was trembling, just barely; whomever Carter had given those rockets to was making good use of them.

This morning, the reports had all been casualties. A temple on the edge of the city had fallen—they weren't sure yet if that was an accident or if someone was trying to send a message to Cirrus Prime. A neighborhood too near to HQ for anybody's comfort had been knocked to rubble, and another half-dozen houses lost to fire; it would have been more except for the rain. It was funny, probably, to have been saved by the damp; to have a hostile place be so waterlogged that danger couldn't even survive long enough to reach you.

There had been some attacks in the streets during the fire, which the local constables had reported briskly as people taking advantage of the chaos to steal whatever they could. "Desperate times," the sergeant had said with a shrug.

They hadn't told him that all of those little altercations took place well away from the rubble and the fire, and nobody had touched the fallen temple except his own people grabbing souvenirs. Someone had tried to break in to a house in the center of town during the fire. Davis had sat back and looked out at the cobblestones of dead carp across the top of the pond, and wondered which of the factions they were fighting had killed six hundred of their own people as cover to break into a colonist's house.

It was a failure where blame hung suspended between military and state waiting to see who made the first mistake. All three of them knew it, and no one was willing to say; they'd been fighting for three hours because no one was willing to say.

Madison was pacing now. "Well, according to Davis, *Carter* has been making plenty of friends. He knows where they are. We can end half this problem right there."

Davis sighed. "Cirrus Prime isn't packed into one tidy mountain west of the desert any more, Madison. You blew out their last options there. They've scattered into the swamps."

Madison turned a withering look on him. "The swamps."

"He's right." Verrastro sat back. "We have so much surveillance pointed on that desert it looks like we're filming tourism ads. There's nothing."

"I thought they were protecting the mines." Madison sounded almost disappointed in them.

Verrastro waved a hand. "No point. Until the sanctions are lifted nobody can sell any of the copper even if they could sneak it out from under us. They were fighting to keep us off the land, not from getting the profits from the mine. They always knew those were going to Glorious."

Madison frowned. "Well, the swamps are impossible to get any decent recon in."

"Well, fuck me, Madison, that must have been just what they thought."

Before anybody could get enough air for another round of useless bellowing (putting three Colonels in a room with a problem was always going to end in an argument), catering knocked and rolled in a cart with food and coffee.

It took him longer than it should have to recognize the stocky Private who was serving him, and when he did he was too excited to be subtle—he grabbed her wrist. She stiffened, but when he let go she held still. Without the cap her face was broad and open, the eyes wide-set and dark; she was a local, then.

"I didn't realize we'd recruited so many of you that we have Privates left over to scoop pond scum."

She blinked. "Sir."

It was such a flat reply it was insubordinate, somehow, like she was trying to make him feel foolish. He looked her over, slowly, to make it clear he disapproved. "So when you're not on carp duty, you're making my food?"

She glanced to Verrastro like she was embarrassed, but she said, "No, sir. Evans is the cook at HQ. I'm delivering." That had stolen his joke, so he had to settle for, "Well that's small comfort. Dismissed," and she had to hastily set up the rest of the coffee things on the sideboard as she left. Madison noticed and rolled his eyes, which gave Davis some satisfaction.

He had a bad habit of feeling for people, wishing he could reach out to them. It was good to be reminded sometimes that this was the only type of government in which everyone found their level honestly. The reasons he put Carter into the field with so much autonomy were the same reasons this private was loading fish onto a truck. The Glorious Forces were a machine of merit; everyone was just as they should be.

VERRASTRO CAME INTO his office halfway through the carp soldier's work and sat down.

"We should dispatch some soldiers to the mine with the locals," she said quickly, like if she got it out before he could think about it he might agree.

He didn't bother looking over; the carp soldier had moved on from skimming the dead fish off the top to trying helplessly to shovel them into the truck, and it was doing him no end of good. The movement was hypnotic, and her failure very satisfying. "You're joking."

"Listen, we can't just keep—" she stopped, perhaps realizing that it wasn't wise to suggest his methods might be failing. "Treating these people like bystanders," she finished.

"If they want the mine back, Colonel Verrastro, all they have to do is turn in whomever among them is working with Cirrus Prime and the Glorious Forces will be happy to negotiate an end to the sanctions."

"They don't care about the sanctions, *Colonel Davis*."

"Cirrus Prime cares."

"Cirrus Prime wants the land," Verrastro said. She sounded very tired. "They know the mine is dry, Davis."

He forced his face to stay calm. He counted a dozen fish scoops before he turned from the window. "What?"

She raised her eyebrows slowly, punctuating herself like a joke. "They never cared about the mine. They wanted the overburden— the lake water—before the chemicals could get into it. That was the fight."

There was a flicker of satisfaction that they'd lost; the water was tainted and their fight had availed them nothing. But it couldn't last in the face of so much that the state had been keeping from him.

Feeling stupid, he said, "But the Forces sent us here to protect the copper."

"The Forces sent us here to prove a point about what happens when you revolt against the Glorious, Davis."

He sat back in his chair. If she was right, that point had given them the Republic, and the militia, and Cirrus, and Cirrus Prime, and now a damp office and a peeling house across the city and cold sour coffee and a bunch of Colonels jockeying for General and so many desperate locals they were scraping ponds for the hope of three meals a day, and seven thousand dead since Davis had landed in the dust-choking desert you couldn't believe was only a hundred miles from this swamp, and not an ounce of copper to show for it.

Out on the lawn, the carp soldier was scraping slime off her shovel with her knife. Davis envied her. She knew what she was meant to be doing; at some point, her duties ended.

THE TREMORS HAD come close enough to the city that he met Carter at one of the safe houses; whatever group of these wretched people was shelling the other, Carter couldn't afford to be seen by some spy cutting across the gardens or through the kitchens to report.

It was a hovel at the edge of town, mud bricks and elevated chairs and a clean sluice grate in the middle of the room, cozy enough that Carter must have bargained off one of his own people, even if Davis thought it got more depressing by the second.

Davis had been coughing and picking dirt clods from the soles of his boots for nearly ten minutes by the time Carter arrived, hat pulled low over his eyes to make him blend in with the locals.

(Maybe it did; everyone here was a foot shorter than Carter, but no one ever seemed to look at him twice.)

"I'm sure that when I told Colonels Madison and Verrastro two days ago that the weapons shaking them awake in their beds were not rockets *we* had given anyone, I was correct," Davis said.

After a second, Carter nodded—just the once. "Understood."

"Understood, or yes?"

Carter had taken up a position near the door, hunched to avoid the ceiling; he never sat if he could help it, but Davis hadn't realized the depth of the habit.

"Yes," Carter said, and licked his teeth.

"Good. Because if you were giving out presents without my permission, that would be treason."

"Sedition, sir."

"Usually the commanding officer gets to decide the charge in a court martial, Carter." He took a breath. "Are any of your people living in The Dawn of the Sun Across the Mountains?"

Carter didn't move.

"I ask because during the fire, someone broke into a house there. If that house belongs to one of your assets, they handled themselves so poorly that someone killed six hundred people to find out what they knew."

"Or it's a rich house that—"

"And if that house doesn't belong to one of your assets, then whoever you sent to look into the people who live there killed six hundred strangers to cover a little breaking and entering."

"I'm not involved with that," Carter said.

It felt like it was too slow in coming, though it was hard to tell. Davis had had a headache since he'd read the police report; his stomach was sour from the maintenance reports and the request for more money to hire locals to help scrape out bodies.

"Six hundred people, Carter. Families, in the middle of the night, in the center of the city, when we're trying to push the fighting back toward the desert. Do you know how that looks?"

Carter nodded, said not unkindly, "Bad for you."

It took Davis a moment to summon the wherewithal to even look Carter in the eye. If there had been any doubts in his mind that Carter had been part of this, they had evaporated. This was what happened when you gave people a long lead.

Davis considered handling it. If he stood up and murdered Carter, no one would find the body for days. Davis could blame it on whatever wretches Carter had been courting for resistance and pardon Cirrus Prime. Cirrus Prime would know who the traitors were, and by the time the dust settled Cirrus Prime would assume they had a deal with the Glorious Forces. It would be easy to pick them off after that. If Carter really was a soldier, he'd be happy to die to end this war in weeks.

Carter was looking at him, though—looking at him like he had seen. Davis took a breath. Another. Another.

"You're wrong," Carter said quietly, "and you're a coward."

Davis sat where he was until sundown, for safety.

THEY WERE NEARLY late for the performance and Catherine had promised she'd be ready, so he let the driver pull up and sat back to wait the inevitable three minutes it always took Catherine to decide she was fit to be seen.

It took her four, this time, and when she came out Davis swallowed a stab of disappointment. Her dress was deep blue and long everywhere, hem and sleeves and neck; not so much as a glimpse of her collarbones. She looked like a lump of ore.

Behind her was the carp soldier, carrying a bundle in her arms.

"What the hell is she doing here?" Davis asked before he could get hold of himself, and he felt the bottom drop out of his throat at the look Catherine gave him. Then a fit of coughing overtook him, which was convenient—he could look away to close the window without looking at her.

"I met her at the benefit," she said slowly, like Davis was a child who didn't understand why he was being scolded. "She was one of the wait staff. Colonel Verrastro introduced us. Her brother was hurt last week in that awful fire, and I told her I would help her if I could."

He had an image of that squat little soldier racing through the upstairs gallery of their house, shoving the ivory carvings into the sack she'd brought, but he knew better than to even joke about it. "Food," he guessed instead.

"I didn't think we'd miss a loaf of bread and some redfruit." Then after a beat, like an accusation, "She kept saying how generous it was of you."

He kept his eyes on the road until he felt her shift her attention out the window; the loss of her regard was like lifting a stone off his chest, and he could catch his breath long enough to think.

Their house was in The Two Faint Stars First Touch These Hills, and around them the houses spread out among lawns and vines that were still bright and healthy, a long green tongue lolling toward the city center.

"You're right," he said finally. "It looks good for the Forces that you're helping those in need. I was concerned that showing favoritism to one soldier would cause some unrest in the ranks, but I'm sure you told her not to mention it to anyone."

It was perfect—an apology, twisted just enough to remind her that the stakes were always going to be higher for him.

She was still looking out the window, where the green had given way to pale grey sidewalks and spindly little trees kept carefully off the ground in stone planters. It was barely raining, and the place was crowded. When he'd first arrived here he'd thought of it as a good sign, that people were getting on with things. Now it just made him nervous, and he looked from one face to another all the way to the concert hall.

The gala performance was meant to benefit the Glorious Forces, but there was plenty of color to break up the pale blue of dress uniforms. Davis realized that some of the benefit must have been to civilians in letting them come. Good idea, he supposed, except that he was so fucking sick of civilians.

Madison and his fourth wife were seated next to them, of course, and Davis nodded politely and tried to remember her name; he turned to Catherine for help, but she'd breezed past him to say hello to some of the lesser officers and even one or two of the local families, draped in purple and green and red and yellow. He bit the inside of his mouth.

"Glad you could make it," said Madison, somehow still too loud even in a hall of a thousand people. "Can you believe what they're performing?"

Davis glanced down at his program, but Sylvia was at his shoulder with a question about when he wanted the car brought back (Master of the Sky bless Sylvia, the only person he could remotely count on to save him from small talk in the abandonment of his wife), and by the time that was finished Catherine was coming back and taking her seat like nothing was wrong, and the lamps were being dimmed.

It was an opera about the founding of the city. When Davis realized it he laughed—just once, like Carter would have—and waited for Catherine to elbow him.

But she didn't. She loved music; leaving music behind was the only thing she'd ever complained about when he brought her on postings with him. He didn't mind it, actually. It felt like a genteel complaint, the sort of complaint a General's wife should have. He'd pictured her assembling string quartets someday, when he'd been promoted to a permanent post and didn't have to always make do in other people's houses.

Now she sat perfectly still. It was dissonant to him—all the music on this planet sounded like he was hearing it from underwater—but she listened raptly while the chorus sang about the old times, and the lake between the mountains, and the helpful spirits that guided the weary to good soil and pitched the wicked over the far side of the mountain into the desert, and the satisfaction of working together to tame the land and make it bear fruit.

Davis spent most of it hiding his coughs in his shoulder and looking from one face to another. Surely someone from the propaganda ministry would be concerned. But when he finally spotted a little knot of them, seated far enough behind him that they should have been insulted at the view, they were watching just as placidly as everyone else.

They all looked young. That was the problem. No one had thought to send a veteran minister who knew better than to let the people you were fighting remind each other what they stood to gain.

Catherine was crying by the end of it. She got herself under control before anyone could light the lamps again, which pulled them back from the brink of disaster. Still, she was a fool for falling prey to something so obvious, and as the car pulled away he clenched his fists, wondering where else his wife, his representative among his colleagues, had cried like a child facing their first disappointment. At the benefit that was full of potential enemies, standing next to Verrastro? At dinner parties with Madison's fourth wife where she looked like a miserable hostage in the middle of everyone's chat? In their own kitchen, where two girls from town did the cleaning and the cooking? How many times had she put them in danger by looking like someone mistreated, someone who could be turned?

This can't go on, he thought, all at once, like a relief.

As he unzipped her he said, "I don't want you going out in the evenings any more unless I'm with you."

She looked as if she'd been expecting it; the line of her shoulders never moved. He thought briefly about dragging corpses out of the pond, about a shovel and a heavy swing.

"Of course," she said. "Thank you for a lovely evening."

BY THE TIME they found Carter's body, it had been in the swamps so long that someone had to bring Davis the pictures of his tattoos to the war room so the three of them could agree on identification. The rest of the corpse had gotten so waterlogged they couldn't tell much, and of course the blows that killed him had knocked out his teeth.

"It's brutal," Madison said, scraping a hand over his beard. "I don't know what you had him doing, but somebody didn't like what he found."

Davis passed back the pictures. "He was living among Cirrus Prime and recruiting their doubters and their enemies. No one would have liked what they found."

Carter had often made intelligence work sound like a magic trick; something that required careful preparation through arcane methods, a set of tools you kept to hand to distract suspicion, a sleight of empathy that could make you seem like a friend to anyone who wasn't looking very hard.

"So where does that leave us?" Verrastro glanced at Madison; she looked a little green.

Madison nodded at her like he understood. "In need of a drink," he said, and rang.

The carp soldier came with coffee and whiskey. She set up on the sideboard without looking at him; she kept her head down the whole time she handed Verrastro and Madison their drinks. Davis spread out his fingers under the table, like the paws of a big cat warming up to strike. As she served him, he kept his eyes out the window, followed just the edge of her reflection as she moved away, and for a moment he filled with blood all over just thinking about how good it was, how *good* it was.

As the carp soldier pulled the last inches of the squeaking cart past the door (it rattled as she scraped the door frame, this whole place was coming apart), Verrastro wrapped her hands around her cup and asked him, "What the fuck do we do without Carter?"

Davis took a small breath. He felt light all over; he felt like he had the first time he ever saw Catherine turn and look at him with her long neck and those blank beautiful eyes. He felt like he knew what to do.

"We end this," Davis said. "The mine's empty, and they're already angry about the water, so there's no point saving it. Make our point. Raze it."

The coffee was sour as ever, but he hardly minded. It wouldn't be for long.

THAT NIGHT, AS they sat near the fire in the parlor (him sipping on another glass of the liquor that the bees had made, back when there were bees), he told Catherine they were going to be reassigned, just to watch her eyes light up.

"Where?" she asked.

He didn't know what would be best, so he said, "Guess."

"Not Europa," she said, in a tone that felt safe to deny, and then "Mars?" much more promising, and when he agreed she actually took his hand.

"I'm so glad you'll be gone from here," she said, so earnestly that some small fondness scraped at him—a real fondness, like she'd been a good wife all this time. "This has been horrible."

"It has," he agreed. He was off balance, now; tenderness upset him.

"I'll start packing tonight," she said, and stood with that glint in her eye like a General's wife, and he was a clever enough man to say, "Later," and keep her hand in his, and draw her down to him.

She was already asleep by the time he coughed up blood, and realized what he had missed.

HE HAD DEBATED doing it quietly, overnight, but that was what a man did when someone had betrayed him and he was small and angry. A General—a leader of men—made examples, and laid groundwork for what was coming next.

So he waited until he was in his office, and then he quietly asked, "Sylvia, who brings up this coffee every morning?"

She jerked a thumb out the window, where the rain was sheeting down nearly sideways; Davis could barely make out the olive drab of the carp soldier, dragging all those fish out of the poisoned pond.

"Either Evans or that conversationalist," she said, then frowned—lightly, innocently. "Why? If there's a problem with it I'll tell Evans. Maybe we can get a kitchen on this floor."

"No need," he said. "Can you call in Verrastro?"

"She's home sick."

The tips of his fingers went cold. He'd thought this was a vendetta —he'd thought one humiliated soldier had dared to lash out because she was stupid enough to believe it was possible to win a war by conquering one man. But if she'd been clever...

"Sick?"

"Real bad," said Sylvia. "I can get Madison on the line for you if it's a martial matter?"

"It's a state matter," Davis said, "but I can handle it. Can you get the groundskeeper duty sergeant on the line, please?"

It crossed his mind to have the carp soldier confess; it would mean more, he knew, to have a traitor admit to it in public. It would give the people something to consider when their town was in ruins; they would have that grain of doubt that happens so often among conquered people, that someone else could have done more to prevent this, that someone else had failed them. You could keep people fighting amongst each other until the last house was rubble and clay.

But a good General could do that without a confession, and before he did something for the glorious good, Davis wanted one thing just for himself.

He'd told the Sergeant not to interrupt her. He wanted no warning. When the shot came, she still had the net in her hands. After a moment of suspended motion, she pitched forward into the pond, and slowly sank beneath the dead carp; they covered her over, a carpet of grey.

BY THE TIME he got home, Catherine had packed up half the household. Fifteen crates sat in the front hall. She was at the dining table already, practically alight, and his drink was waiting.

"I guess when you're leaving a hated place, everything's a special occasion."

She smiled back at him, bright and real. "Is it that obvious?"

He laughed and drank, feeling impossibly quiet and content. "Well, I wrapped up my last loose end. No point waiting around. As soon as Madison can recall most of our people, we're going to finish this and go, so I hope you can keep packing at this rate."

"Most?"

He nodded. Somehow he didn't want to explain why there had to be a few real casualties from the Forces when the city fell; he was grateful when she took a heavy breath, said nothing.

"Do you have to be there for it?"

How heroic that sounded, to be standing alone in front of the endgame! Still, better to give credit. "Madison and I must both give the order."

She hmmed. "I'll pack alone, then. When do we leave?"

"Two hours past dawn," he said, and when she said, "Well, that does it for the silverware, then," he grinned.

She was laughing when the girls brought dinner in, and they ate in a happy silence. He couldn't really eat—his stomach was nothing but acid and his throat was burning—but it still felt like a celebration. He felt, all at once, what you might be supposed to feel when a woman's really your wife. A wife like a partner. A General's wife. All at once he wanted to confide in her: about what it felt like to swing that metal bar into Carter's face, about the agreement they'd all made to level the city and let the snake eat its own worthless tail. It was lonely, suddenly, keeping secrets from her.

"I'm being poisoned," he said. His vision was swimming; he prayed it wasn't tears.

She looked over with a spoon of soup halfway to her mouth. "What?"

"Poisoned." The word made him feel tragic. "I'm dying," he added.

Catherine was staring at him, aghast. He sat a little straighter in his chair.

"That soldier—the one who came to the house—was poisoning my coffee. She's taken care of, but the damage might be done. It was the water," he said, and suddenly the words sounded heavy, as if he couldn't hold them. He glanced into his soup, flexed his hands under the table. "The water was ruined."

"Yes," Catherine agreed.

He looked up. It was dark enough now that the lamp cast strange shadows over her face; earnest, placid. He couldn't keep her in focus; she looked like a landscape, like a theater with dimmed lights.

"Catherine," he started. He reached for his liquor glass; his throat was burning. He couldn't catch his breath, he couldn't look at his wife. It was really very dim. The glass slipped from his hand.

She said gently, "I told her I would help her if I could."

VERRASTRO AND MADISON sat in Davis' office. Outside, rain beat down against the slimy grey bodies of the carp.

The problem with Davis, Verrastro had realized, was that he never understood the balance in opposing forces. He saw threads of events that somehow led to a single future point. What they did wasn't a line. It was a web. There was no finish; there were just endpoints that held the rest together.

He was the kind of leader who never asked how deep that pond must be, to spit up so many carp that it took one soldier hours just to scoop them off, only to have another carpet of them waiting the next morning. That pond went deeper into the soil and connected to something more than he could imagine, or it was restocked at night to give one soldier a reason to stay on the grounds and learn everything she could about their habits. Either explanation would have told him something; he'd never asked.

Sylvia, red-eyed, delivered coffee. Neither of them drank.

Madison stared out the window, his hands clasped behind him. "That pond is going to drown this house."

"Not today," she said.

After today, it wouldn't matter. News of Davis' sedition was already being quietly passed up the line; a Colonel who sent his men to die was doing his job, but one who strangled his own intelligence officers and shot innocent local soldiers was unhinged. (A long illness bravely denied, obviously. Catherine would know what to say; she'd be a General's wife yet.)

The fire, the Glorious Forces investigators had conveniently discovered, had been set by dissidents trying to punish Cirrus Prime. A few dissidents had actually been happy to hear it; they were organizing. And Cirrus Prime wasn't happy about the turncoats; one of their agents had walked right up to the gates asking to discuss it.

The whole thing was embarrassing enough to the relevant Ministers that it would be better to declare the battle over and leave an empty mine alone. Cirrus Prime could be brought around to peacekeepers; you could convince people to do anything once you told them they had won. Mine or not, this town still needed someone to represent the Glorious Forces when they were gone.

Outside, the pond was just beginning to spill over; the black-slimed fish coasted gracefully over the edge and out across the manicured lawn. Beneath the carpet of the dead, those that remained were churning the water. It was Friday. They were at war with The Faint Stars.

WEATHER GIRL
E. J. Swift

SOMETIMES WHEN SHE closed her eyes at night she saw spirals, wheeling slowly against the backs of her eyelids, each one its own perfect fractal. She had never told anyone about this phenomenon. It seemed fantastical—hardly worth mentioning, never mind bothering a professional about. But lately, in the moments of not-quite-consciousness before the alarm roused her, she had found that the spirals were still there. As though all through the night they had been present, waiting.

"MORNING, MAXWELL."

The security guard glanced up, glanced away.

"Morning, sir."

As Lia passed through the lobby she clocked other agency employees also averting their eyes. It was a standard reaction, and she was used to it. They called her the weather girl. She couldn't remember how she had found that out, but the moniker, and her reputation, had evidently stuck.

She took the elevator to the basement and found her team assembled in the incident room. They were already busy with an array of models, and Lia sensed the anticipation amidst murmured exchanges. Something new had come up. She shrugged off her coat and accepted a cup of coffee that had just been brewed.

"All right, what have we got?"

"Early indications, sir."

A marker on the map indicated the area of tropical disturbance. Lia scanned the nearby coastlines, geopolitical factors slotting into place as she mentally noted each city or port.

"No one else has got this?"

"We're pretty sure it's just us."

"How far are you with the modelling?"

"Bringing it up now."

She watched as the projected pathways emerged one by one on the map. Her team had outlined a number of potential hit points, the result of complicated equations of global and local weather systems. Each pathway would produce a different ripple effect of infrastructural damage, loss of life, refugee outflow and resultant pressure on the home government and neighbouring countries.

"I'll be in my office. Send the files across."

The unit's strategy was ostensibly simple. A typhoon could not be contained. What could be contained was information about its approach. Data could be masked, or it could be leaked. The decision to mask was dependent upon the relationship with the destination sites, and that was where Lia came in. Was it more beneficial to national security for the typhoon to hit with maximum warning, or with minimal? Would the resulting devastation be advantageous, or damaging? Then there was the unpredictability factor. The complexities of typhoon tracking, and their sometimes unexpected detours. It always came down to a gamble.

Lia reviewed her team's reports. Usually she found it easy to settle her mind, but today for some reason she felt restless. The facts, Lia, she reminded herself. Just the pertinent facts. At the time of her appointment, she'd had psychological profiling and counselling to ensure she wasn't a psychopath, that she would not make decisions borne out of bloodlust. They'd felt that was important. She'd felt it was ironic.

So: vulnerability indices.

Population density.

National debt to the governments in question.

And crucially, the latest metrics in the materials war. They were behind, and it was a problem.

Her watch vibrated. She'd forgotten to turn it off, which was unlike her. Distracted, she tapped it against the desk and waited as a photograph unfolded. From Nicolas, naturally. There was no caption, he never explained the provenance of his photojournalism. The image was of a street market stall, fruit and vegetables stacked in bright pyramids, a pair of hands reaching to bag the produce. No filter.

Even after three years, the impulse to reply was acute. *You're cooking tonight then?* would be her default, or if she wanted to wind him up, *Nice lens flare* would do the trick. But instinctively she knew he didn't want her to respond, he wanted her to bear witness. How long had he been travelling now—two years? He had given no warning of the abrupt severance of his city life. Not to Lia, unsurprisingly, but not to any of his friends either. One day he was an investment banker in a global financial centre, the next Lia was receiving images of weatherbeaten temples, drowning island archipelagos or dust-drenched cities. Each new photograph brought another tug of loss.

"Archive it, Hendricks."

Her virtual assistant responded instantly. "Image archived."

Lia had never told Nicolas the details of what she did for a living. He had never told her if he'd guessed.

It was not something she had dwelled upon in the past, but increasingly it returned to her, this question. How much he knew. She used to imagine conversations between them where she was forced to justify her work. He would question the ethics of it—because it was Nicolas, and because that was to expected from anyone of even average intelligence and empathy. He would drag up international treaties, conventions of human rights. She would respond with the imperative for security in a world whose boundaries were increasingly porous. She would talk about future-proofing. A safe nation for their children (theoretical, now), and their children's theoretical children. About necessity. About the war, invisible to most but inescapable for all, a war of electrical impulses and petabytes of data and hackers duelling in the cloud. They could not afford to fall behind. They could not afford to be magnanimous. In these imagined conversations she talked Nicolas around to her way of thinking, but there was an element of doubt in his eyes which she could never quite erase.

Removing the watch, she stuffed it into her pocket. Back to the task in hand. Pathways. Possible outcomes. It was crunch time. On this occasion, as on every other, she did not hesitate to make a decision. She dictated her analysis and recommendations to Hendricks, and Hendricks set up an encrypted link to the CIC for sign off.

The initial hacks ran successfully but in the end it was a false alarm, the disturbance absorbed harmlessly into the warm breezes of the region. Her team returned to surveillance. The data from the stillborn storm was despatched to a second unit, who would feed the analysis into their fledgling weather control database. The research unit was the latest fad of certain politicians, but thus far it had achieved little other than dumping large quantities of dirt from one side of the dust bowl to the other.

The reality was that Lia's particular fiefdom was much the same as any other in the military. Days of quietude, sometimes boredom, interspersed with abrupt action and the adrenaline of an unfolding crisis. But not today.

Which meant she could confirm her date for the evening.

It was dusk when they got into the city. By then Nicolas had been on the bus for eighteen hours and the windows were thick with grime from the road. He was dozing, if you could call it that, a series of tumbles into sleep to be pulled back by a violent lurch of the bus as it navigated another hairpin turn. The driving had scared the shit out of him at first. Now he let his head drop, numb to the shock of it. Doze for five minutes. Jerk awake. Doze. He woke to find the elderly woman in the adjacent seat shaking his arm, pointing at the window, repeating a few insistent words in a language he didn't understand because his translator was offline, but the woman's meaning was clear. The city. They were arriving.

He couldn't see a thing, or rather, what he saw was light through a haze: electricity muted. The haze grew stronger as the bus slowed in gathering traffic, crossing the bridge to the island. He stretched his arms above his head. There was no part of his body that did not ache. When they pulled into the depot the bus shut down with a wheeze and everyone began to stand, grab their bags and talk at speed. He groaned, in solidarity with the woman beside him. He could not imagine enduring the same journey at her age. For now, it was all part of this new stage in his life. Catharsis. No, that was the wrong word. Catharsis implied trauma, something he was running from, and whilst there had been challenging times no event in his former life could be considered traumatic enough to run away from. If he were forced to describe his odyssey he might say he was running towards something.

He joined the shuffling queue of passengers desperate to get off the bus, and gave the elderly woman a hand with her luggage, though the woman protested: she did not need help. It was probably true. She looked tougher than Nicolas. From outside he could see the thickness of the dust on the windows. He could have stood a spoon in it.

Still: a city. Back to the connected world! He downloaded a map and went to find his hotel, which was somewhere downtown. There was no question of taking another tranche of public transport, so he started to walk, breathing in the warm cocktail of dust and pollution and yes, a lick of salt because he was back by the sea at last.

Despite its precarious location, the city remained highly populated, and he took his time, ambling and people watching. Halfway to the hotel he came across a street market. The vibrancy of fruit and vegetables in the late afternoon sun drew him like a moth. He felt like he'd spent months under a veil of dust. He got his camera out. Most people used their watches but Nicolas liked the proper kit. He framed the shot carefully; enough light to enhance, but not to dazzle. He examined the resulting image: not bad, but too much lens flare. Two more attempts and he had the shot he wanted.

He synched his camera to his watch and sent the file, where it joined the litany of images he had sent his ex-wife from parts of the globe she had never visited. Lia never replied to these images, but the app told him she had viewed them, so he kept sending. Temples and shrines. Monuments and palaces. Market stalls and vendors and people in suits and people in camps. Flowers and trash heaps, sometimes together. Women and men, children and animals. He never photographed himself.

The photographs had been their only contact for almost three years. Always he was tempted to write something, even just a caption, a throwaway line. No words seemed adequate, or all words seemed false. He had tried so hard to be unaccountable. To become insignificant. Still he wondered if you had to be counted by someone, however remote, however estranged. If that was the truth of things.

The hawker held up a star fruit, offered Nicolas a winning smile. His earbud murmured a translation.

"Best in the city, ask anyone you like!"

Language changed but the marketplace was the same the world around. Bustling and haggling and thriving, a great shout of life. He snapped another photo, camera focus on the yellow mangos in the foreground with the blurred smiling face of the hawker behind. He didn't send this one. Not everything should be given.

Lia found her date, Don, sitting at the bar. He was early. She was pleased to discover he was as his profile had suggested: lean, intelligent face, expensively dressed and carrying himself with the easy grace of a confident man. Lia liked him at once.

She slid into the adjacent seat.

"Sorry to have kept you waiting."

"Not at all. You're exactly on time. Here, I've taken the liberty to order you a drink.'

There were two glasses of tequila on the counter, as yet untouched. He evidently knew his way around the menu.

They talked the usual preamble, out of politeness rather than necessity. She felt the flicker of attraction between them, and it was easy to imagine taking him home tonight, but that had been the last few dates and she was ready for something different. He had a way of watching her that made her think he was waiting for the main event. Sure enough, after a time he sat back and regarded her, eyes inquisitive.

"You don't mention your occupation in your profile."

"Ah. That question."

"Is it something godawful?"

"I guess that depends on how you define the military."

"You're in the military?" Slight rise of inflection, a relaxed curiosity.

"It gets worse," she said. "A classified section of it."

"Really?"

"Really. I can't tell you what I do."

"Or you'd have to kill me, etcetera." He took a sip of tequila. "Is that why your VA has a surname rather than a first name? Army culture?"

"Why, what's yours called?"

"Gina."

"I never gave it much thought, to be honest."

"So how long in the military?"

"Almost fifteen years."

"Uh-huh." He nodded, processing this. "You're divorced, aren't you?"

"What makes you say that?"

"You can always tell." He smiled. "It's not a problem."

She returned the smile, raised her empty glass.

"Good. Same again?"

AT HOME SHE paused in the doorway, taking in the layout of the apartment—unmistakably that of someone single, even in the gloom—the blink of the city through the glass. She lay on the couch fully clothed except for her ridiculous shoes. Her body buzzing with a euphoria which was partially but not entirely induced by the tequila. She didn't often drink on a week night. A self-imposed rule; she had never had a problem with control. She suspected that had been a deal-breaker with Nicolas although he had not said so explicitly. In fact he had said very little, at the end. Don was irrefutably present, in a way that Nicolas was not. There had always been an—etherealness was too strong a word, a lightness about Nicolas. Or perhaps she was being unfair. Perhaps that was retrospective analysis, a response to his current meanderings. When they met it was a surprise to find he worked in the cutthroat environment of banking. He'd impressed her. And he'd worked so hard to get where he was. The background check had saddened her in a way she didn't expect, then she put it away and pretended she'd never seen it.

Admit it, she thought. You still miss him, dreadfully.

Pointless, maudlin reflection at the end of a good night. She put Nicolas from her mind. Focus on Don. Focus on the present. Hendricks scanned her biometrics and instructed her to drink plenty of water before retiring. In bed she fell asleep at once, a spiral dancing behind her eyelids.

NICOLAS SPENT THE morning exploring. Like so many coastal cities, this place had been abandoned by government funding. The banks and the glitterati had long-since decamped to the mainland, and the city was left to fester where it squatted in the face of the rising seas. In buildings along the waterfront, the lowest floors had been abandoned altogether and were swamped at high tide. People hung on. People were harder to move than institutions. They had affiliations. Call it loyalty, call it stubbornness, catastrophe came and they remained. Like the huge shopping malls he wandered through, once the province of designer retailers, now occupied by cheap stores and squatters. There was an atmosphere about the city, somewhere between careless and carefree; a place that no longer had anything to prove.

That suited Nicolas fine.

He'd lived two lives: stasis and motion, accounted and unaccounted. His first had been about money, his second, he hadn't figured out yet. When he left the bank he had sold everything. House, car, valuables. He undertook the first tour in a matter of months. Speed had been important then: he needed to feel he was accelerating away from the past. Now he was on his second tour, and it was about slowness, eking the maximum out of time. Nothing would pass him by. He was propertyless, but he had means. He could keep going for a hundred years.

How many villages, towns, cities had he passed through now? He'd lost count. In the four decades he had been alive the world had become increasingly strange and people strange to one another. He had visited cities half-submerged and cities under siege from plagues of frogs or snakes or insects and cities in closed habitats that had once been designed for other planets hostile to life. Rich cities and poor cities. There were always winners, though the winners were even fewer this century than the last.

Of course, he thought, he couldn't do this forever. And then, why not? And then he wasn't sure.

On the other side of the mall, he refilled his water bottle and watched a sweeper bot making its patient way along the gutter. That was his father's job when he was growing up. When the bots took the job they took something else from him too, something that was harder to replace than income. Ever since he was small he remembered his father telling him: you can do anything you want. You're smart. Smarter than me. You can do anything. After the bots his father still said those things, but the mantra was harder to believe. He was ill at the end. Nicolas looked after him and afterwards he did not allow himself time to mourn, because the only way to honour his father was to prove the mantra right. He worked back-to-back jobs to put himself through the education he'd missed, and then he went into the highest paying profession he could think of because security was an imperative. On his ascent he met his ex-wife, a woman who at first glance seemed so self-assured he was surprised to sense the uncertainty in her smile, as though she hadn't expected to be singled out. To be noticed. By then he had almost forgotten the feel of poverty and she must have assumed he had always known a privileged life. He might have felt bad keeping things from Lia if she didn't have secrets too.

Sometimes she cried out in her sleep, a sharp fearful sound that woke him every time. He would open his eyes, blink in a moment of disorientation. His unease dissipating as he adjusted to the absence of light and made out the shape of his wife under the sheets, her breathing settling as she fell back into deeper sleep. It's okay, he'd murmur. I'm here. You're okay. When he asked her about her dreams she said she didn't dream, she never had. He believed her. That is, he believed she did not remember. But there was something, an intimation of darkness, in that cry.

This more than anything else told him that what she did every day must be something terrible.

In the early days they joked about the classified thing. He asked questions, playfully, but with a keen eye to see how she would react. Was it drone strikes? What about interrogation? Do you torture people, darling? He had never asked it so bluntly, but he had come close, and she would always smile and say: you know I can't tell you anything. As if it really were a joke. Only once she said, There are things... Then she shook her head. No. And he would stand at the counter chopping onions and wondering if his wife could be a state-sanctioned inflictor of pain. He looked for marks on her skin but there was nothing to suggest anything other than life behind a desk.

What someone did for a living wasn't everything. But it was a lot. And if you were ignorant of the specifics, essentially you were admitting you were married to two people, one you knew intimately, the other not at all. Which was fine as long as you could accept it.

At some point Nicolas decided they wouldn't have children. He thought he would probably be able to withstand finding out who she really was but their theoretical children might not. He didn't tell Lia his decision, just quietly booked the procedure in case her birth control failed. Anyway, they had a comfortable life and who needed kids to justify their existence?

That was how his life went, in a whirl of shares and assets and friends over for dinner and holidays in destination locations. On the days he got home after Lia, she massaged his shoulders and ran him baths which they ended up sharing – she liked to look after people, to make them feel good – and in the night sometimes she cried out but did not remember. Until one day he knew he couldn't put anything more between himself and the not-knowing and he told her he wanted a divorce.

He'd hurt her, he knew that. And it had broken his heart.

"MORNING, MAXWELL."

The security guard glanced up, glanced away.

"Morning, sir."

They held the elevator for her.

She was thinking about her conversation with Don. Fifteen years a soldier. Stated so bluntly, her career sounded like the institution it was. It might have been different. A doctorate in mathematics had been beckoning. The agency got their offer in first, and with it came the chance to serve her country. She did her time in intelligence. Quickly proved herself a valuable analyst. She learned things she wished she hadn't, knowledge she would keep at all costs from the people she loved. Things she could never, ever have told Nicolas, a good person who believed in the goodness of others. He didn't need to know what it took to preserve that kind of innocence.

One day she was approached by one of the black-ops brigade. It was shortly after she met Nicolas, at a time when she'd begun to doubt she'd ever meet anyone. Doubt whether she deserved to meet anyone. They had a question. Would she be interested in something more developmental?

Ten years later, here she was.

THE METEOROLOGISTS HAD picked up a new disturbance. They had the reports ready in the incident room. She scanned the briefing with her coffee, the first sip on the verge of scalding. She checked the status of any military operations in the area, open or covert. This was an ideal scenario, out of the way from major shipping and air lanes.

The storm—if it became a storm—was worth masking, but as usual she made herself stand for a minute, facing the map, before making the request for sign off. In this way, the decision became part of her. She hated those agents who tried to shirk responsibility: if you couldn't own your actions, you shouldn't be in this line of work.

The green light came through within minutes. She gathered her team.

"Okay everyone, we've got the all clear. Phase one, make this clean."

Over to the hackers. Psychologically, this was the worst part of the operation. Mathematics she understood, but cyber warfare was an ever-evolving science, impenetrable to those on the outside. She could only observe as the hackers got to work. Inevitably, they were dubbed the borgs of the unit. There was always a particular quiet at the start of the hack as the borgs sunk into a trance-like state. Their main target was foreign satellites, scrambling any enemy detection of the weather system, feeding them with false information, but after that local communications became paramount. The shipping forecast could blow their cover, or a lone fishing vessel caught in the path of advancing winds. The borgs worked frenziedly. They had a tail to cover their tracks, although sometimes they would lay down breadcrumb trails to some rogue faction or nation state, tantalizing ghosts to muddy the political waters when the shit hit the fan.

After a while someone said, "We've got them."

"Good. Keep monitoring."

The atmosphere relaxed slightly, although this was only the beginning. For the next forty-eight hours, the hackers would work in shifts as the foreign satellites fought back and the meteorologists tracked the storm across the ocean, laying down a black hole of communications along its pathway. There came a point when masking was no longer possible, but by then the damage would have been done and vital preparation time lost. That was when phase two kicked in: bombarding the region with a sea of fake news to create mass hysteria.

This was the weather race, or as the liberals liked to dub it, the storm wars. They had been behind at first—still were on the materials front. Too many deniers littering politics, a belief that experts were disposable. But soon enough denial had become an impossibility.

Humanity had waged war on the planet. After centuries of pouring toxins down its throat, a carbon neutral economy had come too late. Now the planet was fighting back. The contents of its armory were truly awe-inspiring. Earth, having spent the previous ten thousand years as a rather dull haven, had morphed into a malevolent chameleon. You could not help but admire the force of the planet's fury, even as you quaked in your wind-and-rainproofed bunker. And just when you thought the planet had exhausted its repertoire for destruction, some new horror would emerge. The meteorologists had invented new scales of measurement; superstorm was an obsolete term.

In the Anthropocene world, survival had replaced progress, and survival was dependent upon infrastructural resilience. Buildings, power grids, servers, the integrity of the cloud. Scientists, running tests on the resistance and flexibility of the supersteels and nanoskins, were the new soldiers. Get the science. If necessary steal the science or even the scientists. Get the patents and monetize the fuck out of it. That was how you climbed to the top of the new world order in the Anthropocene.

Her country was far from immune, both from the planet, and from the hackers on the other side. Five years ago, a counter attack had left the east coast mercilessly under-prepared. You could argue that everything since then had been about revenge, but that would be an emotional argument. The entire farce was akin to entering a boxing ring. Whatever the outcome, you knew you would come out damaged, but ultimately the winner was the one left standing.

That's pragmatism, Nicolas, she told him silently. The only way to guarantee there's any future at all. But Nicolas didn't answer, just regarded her quietly and the doubt was there as it always was.

HOURS PASSED. HER team kept their vigil. The borgs switched shifts. A strange feeling, watching the birth of a typhoon on screen. As the satellite images refreshed, wisps of white began to merge and densify. A foreshadow of the shape to come, outstretched arms gathering ever greater swathes of cloud as the storm moved across the ocean, anchored by the bold dot of its eye. A shape replicated endlessly in nature from seashells to flower heads to distant galaxies. The beauty of its fractal pattern was irrefutable. Odd to think that such artistry could wreck so much wanton destruction, but wasn't that the eternal lesson of nature?

One of her team beckoned her over.

"Look, sir. I think we've got a tandem."

"So we have."

They watched, mesmerised. A second typhoon was emerging in the wake of the first. Less of a rarity than it used to be with so much energy bouncing around the atmosphere.

An alert from Hendricks announced she had mail. The first was Don, asking if she wanted to join him for dinner that evening. She shot a message back: *In the middle of something. Give me a couple of days?* The response was prompt: *This an international woman of mystery thing?* She replied: *Something like that.*

The other was from Nicolas. She glanced at the photograph, was about to tell Hendricks to archive it, then paused.

"Hendricks, can you run a location check on that?"

"Processing now."

"Thanks."

No doubt she was being over-cautious, but it was worth the check.

THE WIND WAS kicking up. Somewhere around here was a noodle café he remembered from his first tour. A few streets later he found it, and ducked inside for shelter and something to eat. He ordered a spicy broth and when it arrived leaned over the bowl appreciatively. The door banged open with the wind. The proprietor went outside and returned, frowning. She said a few words to the clientele at large, who nodded and sucked at their noodles.

Storm, murmured the translator through his earbud. A storm on the way.

By the time he finished lunch the wind was consistently strong. He debated heading back to the hotel but no weather warnings had been issued, and he wanted to visit the harbour. He took the tram north and from there walked down to the front.

His heart rejoiced to see water again. The harbour was still magnificent, even if it had lost the glamour of decades past. He could see the rows of towers on the waterfront that had once borne the names of economic giants, before survivalist technologies surpassed those of the consumer in the market place. Nicolas had invested his clients' money in weather-proofing: engineering solutions designed to keep out the water, the wind, and the dust. His clients had done well. Weather-proofing was an expensive business, and few of the places he had visited on his first tour could afford such measures. Skirting the harbour was the shanty town that must have sprung up when the money went. Hundreds of makeshift abodes, perched on stilts, on floating platforms, and in the damp lee of the sea walls.

He watched the ferries making their way across to the mainland. The harbour waters were being stirred up by the winds and the wave crests were very white; the ferries ploughed onwards. He raised his camera. The smallness of the boats against the magnitude of water, that was what he wanted. Just a fringe of the mainland in the top ribbon of the image. He could feel the force of the wind against his forearm, the camera strap flapping beneath. Perhaps it was time to head back.

HENDRICKS HAD A location match. Lia glanced at her watch. She read what was there, read it again. A second passed where she seemed to have no thoughts at all, was lost and everything lost to her.

Her world reduced to that tiny piece of text. It must be wrong. It couldn't be right. She blinked. The text remained, clear as day. She took a step towards her office.

"What's your percentage on that, Hendricks?"

"Ninety-eight per cent certain."

She shut the door with more force than necessary. On the other side she leaned heavily against it, her mind cycling frantically.

Her team had one crucial rule, and that was that once a cloak had been laid down it was laid down for everyone. Nothing went beyond the incident room. It was Lia's rule, enshrined in military protocol.

Shakily, she raised her watch.

You idiot, Nicolas. You fucking—

A knock at the door.

"Sir?"

"Give me a minute—"

"Sir, we've got a potential problem, I need an authorisation code from you—"

"I'll be right there," she said sharply.

He retreated. She stood, feeling the onset of something close to panic. A deluge of data across her brain. Only the pertinent facts, Lia. The facts.

"Hendricks, I need you to contact Nicolas."

She instructed her assistant to wrap the message in every possible encryption. This was against all protocol.

THE HOTEL DINING room was busier than on the previous evening. A steady stream of rain had begun an hour or so earlier, and other guests had also returned to escape the inclement weather. Nicolas listened to the chatter of his fellow diners through his earbud.

The translators had improved immensely over the past five years, although in a busy space with multiple conversations, it was a challenge to piece together the disparate shards of dialogue.

Back in his 10th floor room he turned on the news to see if there was any information about the weather. No alerts. He stretched out on the bed to review the day's photography, and sent the one of the harbour to Lia. It was a tease of a picture, hinting at the mainland shoreline without revealing it. He planned to read for a while but the softness of the bed made him sleepy. Just before he drifted off he heard his watch vibrate, and leaned over to switch it off without looking at the message.

He woke in the dark to a howl, convinced that he was back in the old apartment, that a dream had caused Lia to cry out. It's okay, he murmured. I'm here. The howl did not stop. He remembered that he was alone and in a hotel room on the other side of the world and then he realized that the sound was not anything human but the wind.

"Lights," he muttered.

The room warmed slowly from black to brown to amber, but stopped short of its maximum brightness. The rain-streaked window reflected his prone figure on the bed, the sky black beyond the glass. A dim muddle of light through the rain. He checked the time on the wall display and was taken aback to discover that it was nine in the morning. He got up and dressed—after an initial trickle there was no water from the taps, even if he'd wanted to wait around for a shower—and was lacing his shoes when something slammed into the glass with shocking force.

He felt his heart accelerate to a sprint. He stared at the window. A crack ran from sill to ceiling, hairline threads sprouting on either side as he watched. Some part of his brain said *it's going to go you have to move* and he grabbed his bag and seized the door handle.

It wouldn't turn. Panic rising, he could hear the groan of the glass *you need the card* an awful creaking *it's going to go* the pass where was the pass—he saw it on the table by the kettle, slapped it against the door and watched the light turn green. He threw himself into the corridor. He was five steps along the carpeted hallway when he heard the crash and knew the window had blown.

He thought of glass splinters exploding through the room, imagined himself still asleep in the bed. Nausea flooded him and he slumped against the wall, his breathing shallow. Up and down the floor doors were opening, perhaps awakened by the sound. Hands rubbing at eyes, confused voices, quick exchanges across the corridor. He continued towards the stairwell—*don't take the lift, even if it's working*—trying to banish the image of those lethal shards.

Downstairs was chaos. A number of guests must have vacated their rooms first thing this morning, and were now gathered in the lobby with their luggage, unable to leave and barraging the night manager with questions. Others like Nicolas were emerging dazedly into the dining room, still in their nightwear. A man was bleeding, a member of staff bandaging his head wound inexpertly. Other staff were putting up storm shutters. Too late, he thought. The wind and rain were a relentless shrill outside.

There was no hot food—even if the kitchen staff had been able to get in, he supposed there was no power—but a porter was laying out a cold buffet. A couple of families encouraged their children to get some breakfast, and gradually the rest of the diners filed up to the tables. Nicolas took some juice and wished there were coffee. Behind the buffet another member of staff started arguing with the porter, apparently over the food. People exchanged glances, and began to eat more quickly.

Nicolas checked his watch. No signal, which meant his translator was out of action. He had one message though, which must have been delivered earlier. The message was short. *Leave the island as soon as you get this and get as far inland as you can.*

It was from an unknown sender, but there was only one person it would have come from. Well, the city was under siege, he couldn't go anywhere. He supposed Lia had seen reports on the news. Although the message had been delivered hours earlier. He chose not to pursue that line of thought, switched off his watch and walked through the ground floor of the hotel, wanting answers but not understanding a word of the panicked discussions, until he located another tourist. The woman was attempting to charge her watch, but evidently without success. He coughed.

"Excuse me? Do you know anything about what's going on? My translator's down."

The woman straightened. "Yep, mine too. A right mess isn't it? From what I can gather the grid's down so the hotel's running off a back-up generator. Seems they've cut any extraneous power sources."

"I'm guessing we've lost the water supply too. My taps weren't working."

"No one seems to have seen this one coming."

He looked towards the storm-shuttered windows. "There must be somewhere we can get to."

"Honey, have you seen outside? Windspeed's already clocking three hundred kay and this is just the edge of it. There won't be any transport off the island now."

There were more people in the city than there should have been, the woman explained. That was the first problem. An evacuation process that should have taken place over forty-eight hours had been crammed into two. She showed Nicolas some video on her watch taken before the signal went down. Waves twenty metres high imploding against the first line of buildings. Tidal surges torrenting through the streets, flooding the lower levels of the city.

"We're not much higher up here. It might flood," said the woman matter-of-factly.

Nicolas replayed the footage. He thought of the shanty towns he had seen around the harbour. How many people had remained in those stilt houses, those floating shacks, when the storm hit?

"Hundreds of people are going to die," he said.

"It'll be thousands," said the woman. That same matter-of-fact tone. Nicolas stared at her. The woman sighed. "I'm an aid worker, I usually operate further south than here. After a while you stop hearing the numbers. It doesn't mean I don't care."

"No," said Nicolas. "Of course not."

"They're calling it Myanna," said the woman.

"What?"

"The typhoon."

"Oh."

On the other side of the room a young woman was sobbing.

"Her friend went out last night," said the aid worker. "She hasn't come back."

THE SATELLITE IMAGES refreshed, and refreshed again. Lia watched as the spiral revolved in its inexorable formations, moving steadily west. The second spiral on its tail, the two engaged in some ancient deadly dance. She watched as the typhoon smashed into the coastline. As the hackers lifted their blackout, news footage began to leak through, helicopters flying at the edges of the weather system, video clips that had been uploaded before the city went dark. There was a clip from a car caught on the bridge in the attempted evacuation, a wall of water bearing down upon its occupants, screams from those inside. Nothing more had been heard after the upload.

She watched as the hackers tied off loose ends, erased their trails, sighed and stretched their aching bodies, no doubt thinking of their warm beds after a long shift. She watched as the meteorologists talked excitedly about reports of windspeeds surpassing the known record.

Her message to Nicolas had been delivered, but he hadn't replied. She instructed Hendricks to send another. The second one failed. She asked Hendricks to check for new messages every few minutes, although she knew her assistant would alert her the moment anything came through. Her messages became increasingly frantic: *Did you get out? Tell me you got out.*

It would be two days before the eye passed over, and then the other side of the eyewall would let rip. In her head she ran through evacuation scenarios, each one more outlandish than the next. Even if it were possible to locate him, she knew better than anyone that none of them would work.

WHEN THE LOBBY flooded everyone moved up a floor. Not all of the food and water supplies had been moved upstairs in time, and everything was rationed. By the second day his throat was continually parched, his stomach rumbling. Guests and staff slept where they could. The children were offered the beds but their parents preferred to keep them away from the windows, even with the storm shutters up. From the corridors you could hear the wind moving through the upper floors in a continual wail. He began to lose track of time. Dozed at intervals. Woke to find someone shaking his arm, and thought himself back on the bus, arriving in the city.

"Hey, hey wake up!"

It was the aid worker.

"We're going foraging," she said. "Want to come? We could use the help."

"Has it stopped?"

"No, but we're in the eye. So the wind's dropped."

It was eleven at night. The woman had organized a small party. They were going to make their way across the street to the row of hotels opposite. The water on the ground floor was waist deep and cold. They waded across the lobby and one by one pushed through the revolving doors.

The water rose a few inches as he stepped into the street. The wind had dropped, the air was preternaturally still. Nicolas looked up and saw stars. It seemed inconceivable. A pretend sky. The aid worker ran a torch over the water, indicating the buildings opposite, and instructed them to form a chain.

"And watch out for debris!"

Nicolas quickly realized the water was occupied. Pieces of furniture, the expelled contents of shops and households, were all floating about. The lead person yelled and stopped. Nicolas saw a darker mass looming ahead, and a car floated past. He couldn't see if there was anyone inside. They kept going. It wasn't far but seemed endless. Nicolas was last in the chain. With his free hand he pushed away at anything moving towards him. Halfway across he touched the roughness of fabric and then cold wet skin and he couldn't suppress a shout.

The body drifted slowly away. A yell from the other end of the chain; they'd reached the opposite side of the street. The other hotel was not much better equipped than theirs, but the manager in charge allowed them to take some bottled water supplies which they could float back across the street. They moved on to the next building. Nicolas's hands were numb from immersion. Once the torch flickered over the hump of limbs and then a face was illuminated, stark beneath the orange light. The torch moved away quickly. It was easier not to know. They could feel the wind starting to rise again and the aid worker declared it time to return. In the thin starlight Nicolas noticed the building adjacent to their hotel had also lost its windows, and appeared to be listing.

Back in the hotel he removed his soaking trousers, shoes and socks and accepted the offer of a towel. Sat in the corridor in the towel and his damp boxers. He noticed people around him were starting to sniff and cough. The invading sea was chilling the city. He turned on his watch, hoping for a signal before the other side of the eyewall hit, but there was nothing. He read again the message: *Leave the island as soon as you get this.* He did the maths, slowly because he was hungry and dehydrated and exhausted from the wading through water. It had been sent ten hours before the official warning. Hours before the disaster of the attempted evacuation. The meaning was stark.

He wondered if he had always known. If something in his subconscious had linked the days she worked overnight to certain cataclysmic events around the world. But if this was a revelation it didn't feel as revelation ought. There was no enlightenment. Just a kind of shutting down.

Of course, she might not have been involved directly. She might have had a tip off. He wanted desperately to believe that, to believe her the woman he'd been introduced to all those years ago, with the beautiful uncertain smile. But he knew in his heart that wasn't true.

It was too big to grasp at, he supposed. And he was weary, and couldn't escape the idea that whatever he had been running towards, this was it. He thought of the aid worker's statement that thousands would die, and wondered whether torture would have been easier to bear.

He looked up and found one of the children staring at him.

"You can be anything you want to be," he murmured. The child looked at him like he was a lunatic. Who but a lunatic would say such a thing? Besides, they had no language in common. Only this place, this end.

The wind had returned. He thought of Lia crying out in the night. The flutter of her breath warm against his face when he leaned over to check whether she had woken, to gently stroke her face. It's okay. He curled into a ball and put his hands over his ears.

AFTER, THERE WAS a list of the dead. The number of foreign nationals grew longer but he was not on it. She instructed Hendricks to run facial recognition software over footage of the devastation, checking bodies alive and not. There were no matches. She allowed herself to entertain the possibility that he had got out in time, asked a friend to run an identity check on transactions in the city for the twenty-four hours before the typhoon hit. The list was small but confirmed Nicolas's location. There was a tram ticket. Lunch at a local café.

She remembered her first successful hack. The jubilation in the room when they realized they'd done it, they'd successfully hidden a cyclone. She'd found it hard to suppress the feeling that the cyclone was working for them; had to remind herself they were not wielding a manmade weapon. But it was nonetheless a weapon of mass destruction and thousands of people would die for lack of warning. Still they were jubilant.

Afterwards she had gone home and Nicolas had sensed her adrenaline, asked if there was something to celebrate. She shook her head. *Bit of a breakthrough, that's all.* They ordered takeaway and started watching a film, paused it halfway through when she turned to kiss him. She fell asleep against him in the second half.

Even now there was a chance he would be found. Hundreds of people had been washed out to sea and others trapped underground or under collapsed buildings. It was still possible he was alive. But as the weeks passed so did the possibility.

Operation Myanna, as it would be known in the classified files, counted as a success. The damage would run into the trillions, and surveys reported public moral at an all time low. No one would be thinking of the materials war.

SHE SAW SPIRALS every night now. Her dreams brought her visions of figures trapped inside them, stretched and melted into the cyclonic coils. All of them were Nicolas although none of them had his face, instead they were faceless, the faceless millions. She did not remember the dreams, but always she woke to find that her face was wet, and the spirals were waiting for her.

MINES

Eleanor Arnason

WE RUINED EARTH. Not completely. Some places are still okay: archologies in the far north and south and the off-planet colonies: a handful in space and one on the Moon. They're for the very rich, the very well educated; and the lucky few who maintain the machinery. The rest of us live with rising oceans, spreading deserts, and societies that are breaking down or already broken.

I was born in a refugee camp in Ohio. It still rained there, though most of the rest of the Midwest was dry. We lived in a tent and got one meal a day. There was some health care, thanks to Doctors and Dentists Without Boundaries. I didn't die of appendicitis, because of the Doctors. The Dentists pulled some teeth and taught me to brush and floss.

When I was ten the recruiters came around, and I joined the EurUsa space force. That got me to another camp, where I lived in a barracks and ate three meals a day, meat and dairy as well as grain. There was regular medical and dental care. I thought I had died and gone to heaven, though I wasn't allowed to go home.

"You're soldiers now," our house parent—a grim retired sergeant —told us. "Nothing matters except the army and your unit."

There was one other thing that happened. The girls got hormone implants, so they would never have menstrual cycles. Periods are not easy in a war zone. Pregnancy is worse. The boys got vasectomies, no reason given. I figured there were plenty of people on Earth already, though a lot less than there had been at the start of the 21st century; and people who've been in combat can make bad parents.

The camp had a school. I learned all the education basics, plus military discipline and how to operate war machinery, starting with the AK-47. "The best low-tech field rifle ever built," our house parent said. "They're still in use in Africa. You know the old saying: you can't have a revolution without an AK-47."

When I was fifteen I had the second operation, which implanted a comm unit in my brain. Now I could speak to robots and my unit members directly. At twenty I was shipped out to the war.

A funny thing. Just as everything was going to hell at home, scientists at MIT—the new campus in western Mass, since the old campus is underwater—discovered that FTL was possible. Expensive, but it could be done. The two large governments that remained—EurUsa and RuChin—built a couple of ships each and sent them out to visit planets that looked habitable at a distance. You can see a lot with space telescopes. The ships found a couple of planets that were borderline habitable—microbial life, but nothing more and air that had oxygen, but not enough. They could be settled maybe, but the settlements would always be on the edge of failing. Not what anyone wanted.

Then they found a beauty. There was vegetation and animal life and air we could breathe. Nothing was intelligent, so we didn't have to worry about the Prime Directive or trouble from the natives. Taken all in all, it was an almost perfect planet.

The trouble was ships from both the European-American Alliance and the Asian Co-operative Union arrived at the same time, and both put down settlements on the planet. For a while everything was quiet, while lawyers argued over who owned what at the World

Court. The settlements grew into colonies. The World Court could not come to a decision. And then the war began.

This was a Fifth-Generation war. For the most part it consisted of hacking and drone attacks. A full-bore hot war would endanger the huge, fragile FTL ships when they were in-system, not to mention the huge, fragile home planet back in the Solar System, and the space colonies, which were even more fragile than Earth. Both sides held back. But there were soldiers on the ground, though their actions were limited.

(Remember warfare in the early 21st century: the huge, vulnerable aircraft carriers that were mostly not attacked, the atomic weapons that were mostly not used. Fifth generation warfare grew out of those contests. The theory was to wear the enemy—especially the enemy's civilian population—down, without triggering a world war.)

That brings the story to me, arriving on a planet with purple-green vegetation and slightly heavy G. The home star was dimmer than ours, and the planet was closer in. There were solar flares, but they were predictable. Most of the time we could get to shelter. We were getting a little more radiation than on Earth, but not enough to worry about.

I don't like war stories, so I won't tell you mine. In the end, I was invalided out. I could have gone home, but why bother? I'd lost touch with my family, and I had no desire to live in a refugee camp, even if it was top of the line. It was easier and more comfortable to stay in Leesville, named after General Izak Lee (ret): a town of pre-fab buildings next to a purple-green forest. The trees in the forest had trunks that went straight up. Leaves grew directly from the trunks, big and frilly. Some trees had leaves going all the way up, and others had bare trunks and a big cluster of leaves on top like a palm tree, except they looked nothing like palm trees. (I know. We had palms in Ohio.) The leaves were iridescent, so they changed color when the wind moved them: purple to green, green to purple. No branches None at all. It was something the life here had never tried, the way it never tried backbones.

The ground was covered with bright yellow, moss-like plants. These were parasites, like fungus. Filaments ran down to the tree roots and fed off them. More filaments ran to other trees. The forest used these to communicate with itself. Don't think it was saying anything interesting. The xenobotanists said the filaments were mostly reporting moisture or lack of moisture, sudden attacks by bugs and slower attacks by vegetable parasites. It was nothing to write home about. The vegetation wasn't intelligent, any more than the bugs were.

I got interested in the local life after I was invalided out and had time to read something besides military manuals.

Why? Why not? It was there, and it was the only complex ecological system we had found besides Earth. So, I talked to the scientists in Leesville and read their reports. In another life, I might have become a xenobiologist. In the meantime—here and now—I defended maize.

There were fields around the town, planted with Earth crops. The hope was we'd finally be able to live on what we grew, instead of rations shipped from Earth. The local plant and animal life was inedible and not easy to convert to something we could eat.

The enemy sent in drones that dropped to the ground in the forest, crawled into the fields and dug down, becoming land mines. When people stepped on the mines or machines rolled over them, they blew. This made farming difficult, and we really wanted to be able to farm.

It turned out the best way to find the land mines was using African Giant Pouched Rats. They are rodents, but not rats and only giant compared to rats. They have an amazing sense of smell. Do a search on them, if you don't believe me. They can find mines faster than robots can, and they're so light they don't set the mines off. Taken all in all, they're cheaper than robots. They don't cost any more to ship than a robot does. Once we had them here, they reproduced themselves, provided you had two of them and some rat chow. Though at the time I'm talking about they were new and not yet common. One of the army's interesting innovations.

They're cuter than robots and more affectionate, though the last doesn't matter to the army.

Were we worried about them going feral? No. They couldn't eat the local vegetation, and thanks to their caps, we could always find them. We haven't lost one yet.

I ended up with Whiskers. She had been modified to be smarter and live longer than natural African Giant Pouched Rats; and she had a metal cap on her head and wires in her brain, that allowed her to talk with me.

My mind comm had been turned off when I left the army. Can you imagine the silence? My buddies were gone. The robots we had worked with had vanished. It was like being alone in a huge, pitch black cave—except for Whiskers, who was a flashlight in the darkness. Her warm body lay next to me at night. Her friendship kept me sane.

This day we were checking fields west of the town. Whiskers ran between the rows of maize, their bright-green leaves startling against the purple and dark-green forest. I watched from the field's edge. Overhead the planet's primary shone, always dimmer than Sol. High, thin clouds moved across the sky. A mild wind moved the forest's frilly leaves.

No. No, Whiskers said. *No.* Then, *Yes.* I checked her position and marked it. Whiskers moved on. *No. No.*

I called her in finally. She ran back, up my arm and onto my shoulder, nibbling my ear gently. I could feel her happiness.

Why do you love me, Kid? I asked.

Genetically modified, she replied. *Designed to be smart and love you.*

Only that? I asked.

Enough.

Her warm body huddled against my head. I walked home through the town's muddy streets, between the prefab buildings. It was sunset now, the streetlights coming on, the air smelling of the alien forest. Like Whiskers, I was happy.

My apartment was a one-storey walkup: a living room, a kitchen, a bedroom and a bathroom, all small. Okay by me. I'd never owned much, and I wasn't about to start. Whiskers jumped off and ran to her food bowl, full of rat chow. I heated rations and ate them, while Whiskers finished her chow.

I forgot to say that this was the day I met Marin.

After the dishes were washed, I called a cab and went out to the porch to wait, Whiskers on my shoulder. It was raining now, not the downpours we'd had in Ohio, but a gentle and steady rain, the kind of precipitation that could last all day, soak deep into the dry soil, and wash nothing away.

The cab had a driver, which meant the auto wasn't working. I climbed in back.

"The usual?" the driver asked. Even the human subs knew my pattern.

I said, "Yes," and settled back.

The cab bumped over ruts and potholes. "You'd think the army would fix these," the driver said.

"Not a priority."

"Find any mines?"

"One."

"Those bastards keep sneaking in. My partner lost a leg to one."

"Lucky to be alive."

"Tell her that. She's not a soldier, so they didn't replace the leg.

"Was it one I missed?"

"Nah. Before you came. They were using robots. Effing incompetent. The mine was right in the middle of the forest road, and my partner drove over it. You'd think they could find that."

The cab stopped. I held my wrist to the chip reader, heard it ping, and then climbed out. The driver looked through her open window, obviously hoping. I gave her a handful of change.

"Thanks, buddy. Have a good drunk."

Yeah.

I went into the bar, Whiskers riding on my shoulder. The minute the bartender saw me they pulled a stalk of celery out of a jar. Don't think that was shipped from Earth. It had grown in the town's greenhouses. Maybe we'd be stuck with greenhouses, but we keep hoping for open fields. The local soil provided most of the nutrients our crops needed, and the local pests did not bother anything from Earth.

(There was a story about a field of zucchini that got out of control and spread. The local town ended up with more zucchini than they could eat, and the fruits left in the field grew more and more enormous, untouched by anything native. Finally, they grew dry and board-like. The local people made canoes out of them. This is a tall tale.)

Whiskers hopped onto the bar and took the stalk. I ordered a beer. Goddess, it felt good going down.

"Les," the barkeep said to me, then nodded toward the end of the bar. A woman sat there in badly fitting civvies. There was something wrong about her posture. An injury maybe. Or she was even more augmented than I was.

"New?" I asked quietly

"On leave. Drinking a lot."

I had two jobs. One was finding bombs in the fields. The other was finding human bombs, people likely to go off. That may sound like a strange combination, but remember the colony was small. A lot of people did two jobs. And remember I had Whiskers. She could smell a lot more than just mines. Her species had been used in Africa to find TB and HIV. If you don't believe me, do a search.

I moved down the bar, Whiskers following, pitty-pat, the celery in her mouth.

"What the hell is that?" the woman asked.

"Whiskers," I said. "My companion animal. She's an African Giant Pouched Rat."

The woman was okay-looking: a dark, warm skin and crisp, short hair. That mouth might have been kissable a few years ago. Now it was compressed. Her eyes, almond-shaped and slanted, were heavy lidded. She looked tired and maybe a little drunk. I couldn't tell what kind of body was under the civvies.

Whiskers was up on her haunches, nibbling the celery.

"New here?" I asked.

"What the eff do you care?"

"This is a small town. We pay attention to newcomers."

"Your rat has a metal cap. What does that mean?"

"We can communicate. I need that. I miss communicating with my unit."

"Yeah," the woman said bitterly. "They use you up and throw you out, and you have nothing except silence."

"There are other jobs," I said. "I have one." I told her about the mines, but not about the crazy soldiers.

Whiskers finished the celery and helped herself to a fish cracker out of a jar on the bar. I wasn't sure they were good for her, but she loved them. They came from Earth. You want to talk about crazy? Shipping crackers from Earth. But people liked them, and we couldn't make them here. The economics of war are strange.

I took a handful and consumed them, along with my beer. "R and R?" I asked.

"Medical leave." After a moment or two she said she was staying at the medical hostel in town, having work done by the hospital.

We sat in silence for a while.

One way to get people talking is to talk about yourself.

"I got invalided out," I took another handful of the fish-shaped crackers. "PTSD. I didn't want to go home." Whiskers' nose was twitching, a sign that the woman smelled sick. What kind of sick I couldn't tell. "Home was a refugee camp in Ohio."

"Home was the Dust Belt," the woman replied. "Moline, by the Mississippi. There was enough water to survive."

"I'm Les," I added.

"Marin."

We shook. Her hand was enclosed in wire mesh, making her grip cold and very firm. Some kind of exoskeleton, which hadn't been removed. Most likely that meant she was expected back in the war.

We sat together and talked about being kids in the old USA. Her parents had been members of a farming co-op, using water piped out of the Mississippi. Her older brother bought a share in the co-op, but there wasn't enough money for her so she joined the army. She'd been older than me when she joined, which made it rougher. But she'd tested better than I had on robot interface.

"Is that what the mesh is?"

Yes and no. She had operated one of the huge robots, the ones that seemed out of mech-kaiju plays. I'd seen them in the distance, stomping on enemy installations and kicking enemy units out of the way. Some were operated from inside and others at a distance. She had worked inside, striding ahead of our forces. When she moved a foot, the robot took a step. When she moved a hand, one of its huge hands and arms moved. Scary as all hell, though I wasn't sure how effective. Military R&D is a mystery. I mentioned this.

"A lot of war is psychological," she replied.

I asked why she was still wearing the exoskeleton.

"This isn't to run a robot. It's to run me, though the connections I already had helped when it was installed."

Whiskers pattered down the bar, got another stick of celery and brought it back. She could follow some of the conversation via me. But a lot of human interactions are a mystery to a rat, even a smart rat.

"Why?" I asked. It was always possible she would tell me to go away and stop bothering her. But you would be surprised how many people want to talk.

A drone had crashed into her bot, she said. Friendly fire. Not the drone's fault. It had been hit by the enemy and was flying out of control. The bot was destroyed, and she had multiple injuries, including a severed spine.

"They can fix that," I said, which was true.

She'd had stem cells injected. The cells were supposed to connect across the gap her injury had made. It usually worked, but it took time. Meanwhile the mesh enabled her to move almost like an ordinary person.

We talked some more about Earth and this planet. I could tell Whiskers was uncomfortable, and I knew this was the woman. Finally I said, "I need to go. Nice to meet you."

We shook again, her hand hard and cold. Whiskers collected more crackers and pushed them into her cheek pouches, making them bulge way out. Marin laughed. It did look silly.

"That's dessert," I said.

The rat hopped onto my shoulder. *Sick*, she told me mind-to-mind.
Yeah.

I called another cab, this one automatic, and rode home over the rutted streets. The rain had picked up. The rain bugs were out, forced from their burrows by the water and climbing the building walls. Their shells were iridescent in the streetlights. Funny how much of this planet seemed to shine and gleam.

Once we were home I pulled a beer out of the fridge and asked, *What kind of sick?*

Whiskers pulled the crackers out of her cheek pouches and put them in her food bowl. A snack for later. *Not an infection*, she said. *I can smell those. Something wrong in her body or mind.*

Out-of-whack neurotransmitters and hormones. Those would give off a smell.

I finished the beer, then went to bed.

A LOT OF the war was feints and skirmishes, as I said before. The plan for both sides was the same: wear the enemy down slowly, risking as little as possible: a typical Fifth Generation War, carefully limited and held at a distance. No one wanted it to spread back to the Solar System. No one wanted to blow up the handful of FTL ships that came into the system, bringing new supplies and soldiers and scientists.

Now and then, the war on New Earth got hot. I dreamed I was in one of the hot spots, wading through a marsh. No moon, of course. The planet had nothing except a few captured asteroids, visible as moving points of light. Low clouds hid these and the stars. No problem for me. I had my night vision on. I could see the robots ahead of me, tall and spidery, picking their way through the reeds. Drones flew overhead, tilting back and forth to avoid branches.

My unit was on either side. I noticed that Singh was alive, which he hadn't been the last time I'd seen him. Lopez, too. I'd seen her sprayed across the landscape. A nice guy, not looking good at the end.

Something was pulling my rifle barrel down. I looked and saw Whiskers clinging to the barrel with all four feet. A voice said, *Dream. Not good. Wake.*

I was going to argue, but one of the robots stepped on a land mine, and everything blew up.

That woke me. Whiskers was on my chest, her nose poking at my face. *Bad dream.*

Yeah. I was covered with sweat. I got up and took a shower. It was close enough to morning so I made coffee, another import from Earth. Funny the things the army thought were worth shipping. Of course, we might not fight without coffee. But why the damn fish-shaped crackers?

Good, Whiskers said.

Well, yes.

The day went as usual. Whiskers found four mines in a harmless looking bean field. In the evening I went back to the bar, Whiskers on my shoulder. Marin was there. I got a beer and sat down next to her. Whiskers sat on the bar top and chewed on her stalk of celery.

I can't repeat what we said. Mostly I've forgotten the conversation, except for a feeling of discomfort from Whiskers. I was going to have to file a report on the woman. She needed more help than she was getting, and her modifications meant she was valuable to the army.

I do remember one bit of conversation. She'd been somewhere in the robot, wading across a wide, brown river. Deep in places, but not too deep for her robot. In the middle, where the main current ran, disks floated on the surface, going downstream with the current. They were a meter or more across with raised edges, bronze brown with streaks and spots of green. I knew these plants, though I had never seen them. The green was chlorophyll, and the disks photosynthesized. But tendrils hung down below them. These captured aquatic bugs and ate them. So the disks were carnivorous plants or photosynthetic animals. Take your pick.

The river reminded Marin of the Mississippi. I didn't remember any carnivorous floating disks in *Huck Finn*.

I liked the woman. She was young and good looking and less crazy than a lot of people I had met. She had a sense of humor, though I don't remember any of her jokes. While she drank, she wasn't getting seriously drunk. The only problem was the sense of unease coming from Whiskers.

I was lonely. Most of the people in the town were civilians: scientists and farmers, the people who ran the 3-D printing plant, the people who did maintenance and repair. They were good folk, who had gotten good educations back home on Earth. They had a good abstract understanding of war. They knew about PTSD. They sympathized. But I was still an outsider, though they were grateful for my work and for Whiskers.

I liked talking to Marin, so I stalled on sending a report. Maybe I should trust the docs treating her. They would intervene if her condition looked serious. Was it my business that war made people strange?

I was in the habit of going to that particular bar. For one thing, they let Whiskers in. And Marin kept coming. I learned more about her family and the farming co-op. Turned out she could not stand her brother, the one who bought into the co-op, and she was angry that her parents had favored him. Why should he get the safe life on Earth? Why did she have to come here?

What bothered me about her was her anger. What I liked was her youth, her warm skin, almond eyes and lips that would have been lovely if they hadn't been so often pressed together.

Of course, we ended up at my apartment in my narrow, one-person bed, though it took a number of weeks, during which the barkeep kept looking at me funny. I ignored them.

I had never made love to someone covered with mesh before. Weird. The area between her legs was open and available, which made sense. She needed to pee and defecate. The rest was covered with mesh, except her head. The mesh kept changing when I touched it, sometimes soft like silk, then suddenly rigid. Imagine sex with a person whose surface is never the same. Though it stayed rigid along her back, support for her damaged spine. Even her breasts were mesh-covered, the nipples often squashed. I made do with what I could reach.

She came. I came. We lay together, her mesh—soft and cool, at the moment – against my bare skin. I could sense Whiskers, huddled in a corner, deeply upset.

Bad. Bad. Crazy.

Shut up, I told the rat.

Bad, Whiskers repeated.

It became regular: meeting at the bar, coming back to my place and making love while Whiskers sulked. Marin never stayed the night. Instead she went home to her apartment by the hospital. She didn't like the rat, she told me.

The war must have heated up, because I was finding more mines. Correction, Whiskers was finding them, light-footing over the soil between the rows of human plants in the fields outside Leestown, stopping and sniffing and saying. *Yes.*

Marin began coming out to the fields with me, standing with me at a field's edge or walking along the edge. She recognized the maize, a plant that needed a lot of water, but was—she said—in many ways the best of all the grains. Native Americans in Mexico had made it a god, way back when. A young god, she told me. A beautiful young man. Of course, they sacrificed people to their gods. We only a sacrificed to our god of war.

I made a polite sound, since I had no opinion about the gods of ancient Mexico. Though I did check online and found images of the Mexican maize god. Lovely, and the ancient Mexicans did sacrifice to him.

It takes some sort of jerk to make love with someone who should be reported to armed forces medical. I was pretty sure Marin's problem was mental. Anger and depression would be my diagnosis. Whiskers agreed. She knew the smell.

What was I going to do? Turn her in to armed forces mental health, who probably already knew we had a relationship? The barkeep's sweetheart worked at the hospital. Once anything gets in a hospital it spreads. I wasn't a medical worker formally, but I ought to hold to their code of ethics. No sex with clients. If I turned Marin in, I would be having a conversation with my supervisor.

I could hope that Marin was called back to active duty. Or keep having sex with her, and pretend I didn't know she was sick. Or cut her off, though that might cause its own problems.

One day she told me the stem cells weren't working. Her spine wasn't healing.

"Is that a deal?" I asked. "You have the mesh."

"That will go if I leave the armed forces."

"Do you want to?"

"Yeah."

"Can they fix the problem?"

"Maybe. The stem cells have formed a tumor. That has to go. Then they might try again."

I had nothing to say.

A few days later I was at a field. Whiskers was there, of course. So was Marin. We stood at the field's edge, a short distance between us, watching Whiskers run.

All at once Marin was in the field, walking toward the center. I was slow off the mark and couldn't reach her before she was too far in. No way I was going to risk the mines. I called Whiskers and she turned, running through the corn toward Marin. God knows what she—or I—thought she could do, being a fraction of Marin's weight. Marin stepped on a mine, and it blew. The rat had almost reached her. The explosion put Whiskers into the air, tumbling over the corn. I couldn't see where she landed, but I could see Marin, down on the alien soil. I walked into the field, following Marin's footsteps, knowing that path made me safe.

She was lying on her back. Most of her clothing was gone, blown away. The mesh was still there, netting her dark body with silver. I figured it had protected her, but I didn't know how much. Not entirely. One foot was gone, most likely the one she'd used to step on the mine. Blood poured from the stump. I took off my belt, knelt and used the belt to make a tourniquet, then wrapped my jacket around the stump. Then I called emergency services and gave my location. "I need search and rescue right now."

Blood came out of Marin's mouth. I tried to find a pulse, but couldn't through the mesh. There might be internal injuries. She didn't look alive. I couldn't think of anything else to do, and I was worried about Whiskers. I hesitated, then moved through the corn toward the place the rat must have landed, hoping I didn't step on a mine.

Whiskers was there, lying on the dark soil—uninjured as far as I could tell, but unconscious. Maybe it was a mistake to pick her up, but I did and retraced my path, her small body hugged against me. I stopped at the field's edge, one finger pressed into Whiskers' throat. I thought I could feel a pulse, faint and uneven.

Jesus God, I didn't want to lose her. I was shaking so badly that I couldn't stand any longer. I folded down onto my knees. *Be okay,* I told Whiskers. *Be okay.*

S&R arrived.

I climbed onto shaky legs, still holding Whiskers in my arms. "There's a human in the field. If you follow the footsteps you can get to her safely. But right now I want you to take me to the hospital."

"Are you injured?"

I thought of saying no, then decided it would be smarter to say yes. The S&R van took me and Whiskers. A second van raced past us toward the field, as we turned onto the main street. That would take care of Marin.

I climbed out at Receiving and said, "I'm okay. But the rat needs attention."

"For God's sake," Receiving said, "this is a hospital. We don't treat animals."

I forgot to mention I usually carried a handgun, a comforting weight against my thigh. I thought of pulling it, then decided no.

"There is no vet in town," I said. "You need to treat this rat. She's genetically modified. The armed forces will want to keep her alive."

Receiving frowned and hesitated, then found a doc. I stayed with him, while he examined Whiskers. "You understand I am not an expert on animals."

"This is a mammal from Earth, a close relative, part of our evolutionary line. Do what you can."

He ran Whiskers through a scan. "No broken bones. The organs look okay. I'm not seeing any internal bleeding."

Around that time I heard Whiskers in my mind. A thread of a voice. *What?*

You took a hit from a mine, Buddy. This is the hospital.

Whiskers sniffed, taking in the hospital smell, the doctor, my fear, then asked, *How is Marin?*

I looked at the doc. "How is my human companion?"

He paused, listening to his comm. "I'm sorry. The trauma was too severe. She died."

"I figured as much," I said.

The doc looked at me funny. Was I supposed to show more grief? Marin hadn't been a friend, only a lover. I touched Whiskers' side gently. *You did the best you could, Buddy. You couldn't have saved her.*

Didn't like her.

I know, Bud.

That was that.

There was a vet two towns over. I took Whiskers, hitching a ride, and she was checked a second time. The vet said there might be some problems due to concussion. That caused most of the trouble with human soldiers. Time would tell.

I thank him, paid and got a receipt. The armed forces ought to pay.

Then I went home, had a few beers, went to bed and had nightmares. I was with my unit, and Marin was there as well, walking beside me, then stepping on her mine. This time she wasn't wearing the silver mesh, and she blew apart, making as big as mess as Lopez had. Jesus, I was covered with blood.

I woke, shaking and sweaty. Whiskers said, *Bad dream.*

Yeah. After that I couldn't sleep.

I touched base with my supervisor the next day. Marin had seemed fine to me, I told him. Whiskers hadn't reported any problems. Maybe I made a mistake in getting involved with her, but she really did seem okay. My supervisor told me to be more careful in the future. I said I would.

Should I have felt more for Marin? Maybe. But I didn't. I could say that the war effed me up, and I no longer had normal reactions. But I knew what was right. I shouldn't have gotten in bed with someone who was obviously vulnerable, especially since Whiskers had disapproved.

I didn't say any of this to my supervisor. Instead Whiskers and I went back to finding mines.

The war heated up. I found more mines. Robot tanks lumbered through Leesville. Once I saw a kaiju-mech robot pushing its way through the forest, knocking down trees. A heck of a sight, even at a distance. Marin had been right. War involved psychology, and the kaiju-mech bots were scary, even when they were ours.

After it was gone, I went out into the forest, following the forest road—it was safe—and found the robot's footprints, deep depressions in the yellow moss, already full of water. The moss must be bleeding into the depressions. I could look into the nearest pond, which was full of swimming bugs. How had they gotten there so quickly? Life went on, and I really wished I could be a xenobiologist.

Hacking became more frequent. Our local systems went down, then back up, then down again. The FTL ships came less often, though none of us knew exactly what that meant. According to the ship's crews, everything was fine back home, even though the ships no longer brought new people, only supplies. Why? Because people could tell us what was happening on Earth? Rumors said the war had spread back home, or else the governments had decided FTL was too expensive and the planet not worth fighting over.

Finally the FTL ships stopped coming. No explanation. They simply weren't appearing in orbit. This was true for both sides. No fish-shaped crackers. No coffee. No tea. No chocolate. Nothing except what we could grow or print on this planet. The local plant made crackers, but they weren't as good.

Whiskers complained.

Can't help you, Bud.

Of course we sent messages back to Earth, asking what the hell was going on. If all went well, we'd get an answer in 80 years. Or the ships would come back. Who could say?

The war slowed after that. The hacking mostly stopped, but the drones kept coming in. Once they were activated, they would keep doing their job, with no way of calling them back. I guess you could say they—and we—were like the local organisms. Most were segmented, and a lot were a meter long. A little creepy, like huge centipedes. They could give you a nasty bite.

If you found one and chopped off the head, it would keep moving. Its sensory organs were all the in head, so it could no longer see, hear, taste. It blundered around on its many legs, until another bug found it and ate it. Nothing ate us here. We and the drones kept blundering, going through the motions.

Whiskers said I smelled funny.

Anxiety? Depression? I asked. These were the usual problem.

Not sick. Funny.

One morning I woke up with cramps. I got up and discovered my sleeping shorts were drenched with blood. So were the bed sheets. Of course I called the clinic. I don't like blood. It reminds me of my dreams: Marin lying in the maize field, Lopez and Singh. The clinic sent a van, with a tech who couldn't let me take Whiskers. I left her crouched in a corner of the living room, looking terrified.

It's okay, Buddy.

Afraid. So are you.

Which was true.

A nurse at the clinic examined me. A big guy with skin as black as midnight. He must have rotated in from another town. I didn't recognize him or his accent. Caribbean maybe. There were islands in the Caribbean that were still above water.

After he was done with the examination, he said, "What we have here is menstrual discharge."

"What?" I said. My voice sounded loud.

"Your hormone implant has failed. You are having a period."

"I am thirty-effing-two."

"Late for a first period, but that's what you are having."

"Then put in another implant. I really don't like this."

"Unfortunately, I can't. The hormone transplants come—or came —from Earth. We can't make them here. We have a limited number left, but they are reserved for soldiers on active duty. You are not."

"What am I supposed to do?" I asked.

"What women have always done," he said. "Insert a tampon—I can print some out for you—and take ibuprofen."

My crotch felt as if something bigger than Whiskers was trying to chew its way in or out. There was blood caked on my legs. I wanted to shout at the nurse, but I didn't. What could he do? If he didn't have the implants, then he didn't. I was not going to demand something that was needed by soldiers on active duty.

He printed out the tampons with instructions and gave me a bottle of ibuprofen. I went to a bathroom, read the instructions and inserted a tampon—God, this was a crude way to solve a common problem, then took two ibuprofen and went home in a cab.

Whiskers was still crouched in her corner. I picked her up and cuddled her. *Nothing serious, Bud. I'm okay.*

Pain

It will go away.

Wrong, Whiskers said.

Not a sickness, I replied. *A hormone change. I think that's what you smelled. I'm going to have to do a wash.*

Yes, said Whiskers

I stripped the bed and put the sheets in a bag, ready for a trip to the communal laundry, then took a shower and changed into new clothes. The chewing in my crotch had moderated some.

Sometime in all this I realized that we were really on our own. The FTL ships might never return.

The community radio was on, playing Wagner: 'The Flying Dutchman' overture. I lay down, feeling miserable. Whiskers climbed onto the bed and huddled at my side.

Of course the cramps ended, and I went back to checking fields for mines.

WE CAN'T RUIN this planet. There are too few of us, even with our technology. If the ships don't come back, our technology will begin to break down, and our war will wind down to nothing. The question is, will it happen while we still have a chance of survival here? It would be easier to stay alive if we joined forces. People are beginning to talk about peace.

I'm still having periods. The clinic says it ought to be possible to make the hormone implants here, but the project is on a back burner. Other things are more important in an economy of scarcity and war.

I have *not* gotten used to having cramps. I want this war to end.

Do I still dream of Marin? Yes.

ZEROS

Peter Watts

ASANTE GOES OUT screaming. Hell is an echo chamber, full of shouts and seawater and clanking metal. Monstrous shadows move along the bulkheads; meshes of green light writhe on every surface. The Sāḥilites rise from the moon pool like creatures from some bright lagoon, firing as they emerge; Rashida's middle explodes in dark mist and her top half topples onto the deck. Kito's still dragging himself toward the speargun on the drying rack—as though some antique fish-sticker could ever fend off these monsters with their guns and their pneumatics and their little cartridges that bury themselves deep in your flesh before showing you what five hundred unleashed atmospheres do to your insides.

It's more than Asante's got. All he's got is his fists.

He uses them. Launches himself at the nearest Sāḥilite as she lines up Kito in her sights, swings wildly as the deck groans and drops and cants sideways. Seawater breaches the lip of the moon pool, cascades across the plating. Asante flails at the intruder on his way down. Her shot goes wide. A spiderweb blooms across the viewport; a thin gout of water erupts from its center even as the glass tries to heal itself from the edges in.

The last thing Asante sees is the desert hammer icon on the Sāḥilite's diveskin before she blows him away.

Five Years

RUNNING WATER. METAL against metal. Clanks and gurgles, lowered voices, the close claustrophobic echo of machines in the middle distance.

Asante opens his eyes.

He's still in the wet room; its ceiling blurs and clicks into focus, plates and struts and Kito's stupid graffiti (*All Tautologies Are Tautologies*) scratched into the paint. Green light still wriggles dimly across the biosteel, but the murderous energy's been bled out of it.

He tries to turn his head, and can't. He barely feels his own body —as though it were made of ectoplasm, some merest echo of solid flesh fading into nonexistence somewhere around the waist.

An insect's head on a human body looms over him. It speaks with two voices: English, and an overlapping echo in Twi: "Easy, soldier. Relax."

A woman's voice, and a chip one.

Not Sāḥilite. But armed. Dangerous.

Not a soldier he wants to say, wants to *shout*. It's never a good thing to be mistaken for any sort of combatant along the west coast. But he can't even whisper. He can't feel his tongue.

Asante realizes that he isn't breathing.

The Insect woman (a diveskin, he sees now: her mandibles an electrolysis rig, her compound eyes a pair of defraction goggles) retrieves a tactical scroll from beyond his field of view and unrolls it a half-meter from his face. She mutters an incantation and it flares softly to life, renders a stacked pair of keyboards: English on top, Twi beneath.

"Don't try to talk," she says in both tongues. "Just look at the letters."

He focuses on the N: it brightens. O. T. The membrane offers up predictive spelling, speeds the transition from sacc' to script:

NOT SOLDIER FISH FARMER

"Sorry." She retires the translator; the Twi keys flicker and disappear. "Figure of speech. What's your name?"

KODJO ASANTE

She pushes the defractors onto her forehead, unlatches the mandibles. They fall away and dangle to one side. She's white underneath.

IS KITO

"I'm sorry, no. Everyone's dead."

Everyone else, he thinks, and imagines Kito mocking him one last time for insufferable pedantry.

"Got him." Man's voice, from across the compartment. "Kodjo Asante, Takoradi. Twenty-eight, bog-standard aqua—wait; combat experience. Two years with GAF."

Asante's eyes dart frantically across the keyboard: ONLY FARMER NOT

"No worries, mate." She lays down a reassuring hand; he can only assume it comes to rest somewhere on his body. "Everyone's seen combat hereabouts, right? You're sitting on the only reliable protein stock in three hundred klicks. Stands to reason you're gonna have to defend it now and again."

"Still." A shoulder patch comes into view as she turns toward the other voice: WestHem Alliance. "We could put him on the list."

"If you're gonna do it, do it fast. Surface contact about two thousand meters out, closing."

She turns back to Asante. "Here's the thing. We didn't get here in time. We're not supposed to be here at all, but our CO got wind of Sally's plans and took a little humanitarian initiative, I guess you could say. We showed up in time to scare 'em off and light 'em up, but you were all dead by then."

I WASN'T

"Yeah, Kodjo, you too. All dead."

YOU BROUGHT ME BA

"No."

BUT

"We gave your brain a jump start, that's all. You know how you can make a leg twitch when you pass a current through it? You know what *galvanic* means, Kodjo?"

"He's got a Ph.D. in molecular marine ecology," says her unseen colleague. "I'm guessing yes."

"You can barely feel anything, am I right? Body like a ghost? We didn't reboot the rest of you. You're just getting residual sensations from nerves that don't know they're dead yet. You're a brain in a box, Kodjo. You're running on empty.

"But here's the thing: you don't *have* to be."

"Hurry it up, Cat. We got ten minutes, tops."

She glances over her shoulder, back again. "We got a rig on the *Levi Morgan*, patch you up and keep you on ice until we get home. And we got a rig *there* that'll work goddamn miracles, make you better'n new. But it ain't cheap, Kodjo. Pretty much breaks the bank every time we do it."

DON'T HAVE MONEY

"Don't want *money*. We want you to work for us. Five-year tour, maybe less depending on how the tech works out. Then you go on your way, nice fat bank balance, whole second chance. Easy gig, believe me. You're just a passenger in your own body for the hard stuff. Even boot camp's mostly autonomic. Real accelerated program."

NOT WESTHEM

"You're not Hegemon either, not any more. You're not much of anything but rotting meat hooked up to a pair of jumper cables. I'm offering you salvation, mate. You can be Born Again."

"Wrap it the fuck *up*, Cat. They're almost on top of us."

"'Course if you're not interested, I can just pull the plug. Leave you the way we found you."

NO PLEASE YES

"Yes what, Kodjo? Yes pull the plug? Yes leave you behind? You need to be specific about this. We're negotiating a contract here."

YES BORN AGAIN YES 5 YEAR TOUR

He wonders at this shiver of hesitation, this voice whispering *maybe dead is better*. Perhaps it's because he *is* dead; maybe all those suffocating endocrine glands just aren't up to the task of flooding his brain with the warranted elixir of fear and desperation and *survival at any cost*. Maybe being dead means never having to give a shit.

He does, though. He may be dead but his glands aren't, not yet. He didn't say no.

He wonders if anyone ever has.

"Glory Hallelujah!" Cat proclaims, reaching offstage for some unseen control. And just before everything goes black:

"Welcome to the Zombie Corps."

Savior Machine

THAT'S NOT WHAT they call it, though.

"Be clear about one thing. There's no good reason why any operation should ever put boots in the battlefield."

They call it *ZeroS*. Strangely, the Z does not stand for *Zombie*.

"There's no good reason why any competent campaign should involve a battlefield in the first place. That's what economic engineering and Cloud Control are for."

The S doesn't even stand for *Squad*.

"If they fail, that's what drones and bots and TAI are for."

Zero Sum. Or as NCOIC Silano puts it, *A pun, right? Cogito ergo.* Better than *The Spaz Brigade,* which was Garin's suggestion.

Asante's in Tactical Orientation, listening to an artificial instructor that he'd almost accept as human but for the fact that it doesn't sound bored to death.

"There's only one reason you'll ever find yourselves called on deck, and that's if everyone has fucked up so completely at conflict resolution that there's nothing left in the zone but a raging shitstorm."

Asante's also running up the side of a mountain. It's a beautiful route, twenty klicks of rocks and pines and mossy deadfall. There might be more green growing things on this one slope than in the whole spreading desert of northern Africa. He wishes he could see it.

"Your very presence means the mission has already failed; your job is to salvage what you can from the wreckage."

He can't see it, though. He can't see much of anything. Asante's been blind since Reveille.

"Fortunately for you, economics and Cloud Control and tactical AI fail quite a lot."

The blindness isn't total. He still sees light, vague shapes in constant motion. It's like watching the world through wax paper. The eyes *jiggle* when you're a Passenger. Of course the eyes always jiggle, endlessly hopping from one momentary focus to the next —*saccades*, they're called—but your brain usually edits out those motions, splices the clear bits together in post to serve up an illusion of continuity.

Not up here, though. Up here the sacc rate goes through the roof and nothing gets lost. Total data acquisition. To Asante it's all blizzard and blur, but that's okay. There's something in here with him that can see just fine: his arms and legs are moving, after all, and Kodjo Asante isn't moving them.

His other senses work fine; he feels the roughness of the rope against his palms as he climbs the wall, smells the earth and pine needles bedding the trail. Still tastes a faint hint of copper from that bite on the inside of his cheek a couple klicks back. He hears with utmost clarity the voice on his audio link. His inner zombie sucks all that back too, but eardrums don't saccade. Tactile nerves don't hop around under the flesh. Just the eyes: that's how you tell. That and the fact that your whole body's been possessed by Alien Hand Syndrome.

He calls it his Evil Twin. It's a name first bestowed by his Dad, after catching eight-year-old Kodjo sleepwalking for the third time in a week. Asante made the mistake of mentioning that once to the squad over breakfast. He's still trying to live it down.

Now he tries for the hell of it, wills himself to *stop* for just an instant. ET runs and leaps and crawls as it has for the past two hours, unnervingly autonomous. That's the retrosplenial bypass they burned into his neocortex a month ago, a little dropgate to decouple *mind* from *self*. Just one of the mods they've etched into him with neural lace and nanotube mesh and good old-fashioned zap'n'tap. Midbrain tweaks to customize ancient prey-stalking routines. An orbitofrontal damper to ensure behavioral compliance (*can't have your better half deciding to keep the keys when you want them back*, as Maddox puts it).

His scalp itches with fresh scars. His head moves with a disquieting inertia, as if weighed down by a kilogram of lead and not a few bits of arsenide and carbon. He doesn't understand a tenth of it. Hasn't quite come to grips with life after death. But dear God, how *wonderful* it is to be so strong. He feels like this body could take on a whole platoon single-handed.

Sometimes he can feel this way for five or ten whole minutes before remembering the names of other corpses who never got in on the deal.

Without warning ET dances to one side, brings its arms up and suddenly Asante can *see*.

Just for a millisecond, a small clear break in a sea of fog: a Lockheed Pit Bull cresting the granite outcropping to his left, legs spread, muzzle spinning to bear. In the next instant Asante's blind again, recoil vibrating along his arm like a small earthquake. His body hasn't even broken stride.

"Ah. Target acquisition," the instructor remarks. "Enjoy the view." It takes this opportunity to summarize the basics—target lock's the only time when the eyes focus on a single point long enough for passengers to look out—before segueing into a spiel on line-of-sight networking.

Asante isn't sure what the others are hearing. Tiwana, the only other raw recruit, is probably enduring the same 101 monologue. Kalmus might have moved up to field trauma by now. Garin's on an engineering track. Maddox has told Asante that he'll probably end up in bioweapons, given his background.

It takes nineteen months to train a field-ready specialist. ZeroS do it in seven.

Asante's legs have stopped moving. On all sides he hears the sound of heavy breathing. Lieutenant Metzinger's voice tickles the space between his ears: "Passengers, you may enter the cockpit."

The switch is buried in the visual cortex and tied to the power of imagination. They call it a *mandala*. Each recruit chooses their own and keeps it secret; no chance of a master key for some wily foe to drop onto a billboard in the heat of battle. Not even the techs know the patterns, the implants were conditioned on double-blind trial-and-error. *Something personal*, they said. *Something unique, easy to visualize.*

Asante's mandala is a sequence of four words in sans serif font. He summons it now—

ALL TAUTOLOGIES
ARE TAUTOLOGIES

—and the world clicks back into sudden, jarring focus. He stumbles, though he wasn't moving.

Right on cue, his left hand starts twitching.

They're halfway up the mountain, in a sloping sunny meadow. There are *flowers* here. Insects. Everything smells alive. Silano raises trembling arms to the sky. Kalmus flumps on the grass, recovering from exertions barely felt when better halves were in control, exertions that have left them weak and wasted despite twice-normal mito counts and AMPK agonists and a dozen other tweaks to put them in the upper tail of the upper tail. Acosta drops beside her, grinning at the sunshine. Garin kicks at a punky log and an actual goddamn *snake* slithers into the grass, a ribbon of yellow and black with a flickering tongue.

Tiwana's at Asante's shoulder, as scarred and bald as he is. "Beautiful, eh?" Her right eye's a little off-kilter; Asante resists the impulse to stare by focusing on the bridge of her nose.

"Not beautiful enough to make up for two hours with a hood over my head." That's Saks, indulging in some pointless bitching. "Would it kill them to give us a video feed?"

"Or even just put us to sleep," Kalmus grumbles. They both know it's not that simple. The brain's a tangle of wires looping from basement to attic and back again; turn off the lights in the living room and your furnace might stop working. Even pay-per-view's a nonstarter. In theory, there's no reason why they couldn't bypass those jiggling eyes entirely—pipe a camera feed directly to the cortex —but their brains are already so stuffed with implants that there isn't enough real estate left over for nonessentials.

That's what Maddox says, anyway.

"I don't really give a shit," Acosta's saying. The tic at the corner of his mouth makes his grin a twitchy, disconcerting thing. "I'd put up with twice the offline time if there was always a view like this at the end of it." Acosta lives for any scrap of nature he can find; his native Guatemala lost most of its canopy to firestorm carousels back in '42.

"So what's in it for you?" Tiwana asks.

It takes a moment for Asante to realize the question's for him. "Excuse me?"

"Acosta's nature-boy. Kalmus thinks she's gonna strike it rich when they declassify the tech." This is news to Asante. "Why'd *you* sign up?"

He doesn't quite know how to answer. Judging by his own experience, ZeroS is not something you *sign up* for. ZeroS is something that finds you. It's an odd question, a private question. It brings up things he'd rather not dwell upon.

It brings up things he already dwells on too much.

"Ah—"

Thankfully, Maddox chooses that moment to radio up from Côté: "Okay, everybody. Symptom check. Silano."

The Corporal looks at his forearms. "Pretty good. Less jumpy than normal."

"Kalmus."

"I've got, ah, ah..." She stammers, struggles, finally spits in frustration. "*Fuck.*"

"I'll just put down the usual aphasia," Maddox says. "Garin."

"Vision flickers every five, ten minutes."

"That's an improvement."

"Gets better when I exercise. Better blood flow, maybe."

"Interesting," Maddox says. "Tiwan—"

"*I see you God I see you!*"

Saks is on the ground, writhing. His eyes roll in their sockets. His fingers claw handfuls of earth. "*I see!*" he cries, and lapses into gibberish. His head thrashes. Spittle flies from his mouth. Tiwana and Silano move in but the audio link crackles with the voice of God, "Stand away! Everyone stand back *now*!" and everyone obeys because God speaks with the voice of Lieutenant David Metzinger and you do not want to fuck with *him*. God's breath is blowing down from Heaven, from the rotors of a medical chopper beating the air with impossible silence even though they all see it now, they all see it, there's no need for stealth mode there never was it's always there, just out of sight, just in case.

Saks has stopped gibbering. His face is a rictus, his spine a drawn bow. The chopper lands, its *whup whup whup* barely audible even ten meters away. It vomits medics and a stretcher and glossy black easter-egg drones with jointed insect legs folded to their bellies. The ZeroS step back; the medics close in and block the view.

Metzinger again: "Okay, meat sacks. Everyone into the back seat. Return to Côté."

Silano turns away, eyes already jiggling in their sockets. Tiwana and Kalmus go over a moment later. Garin slaps Asante's back on the way out—"Gotta go, man. Happens, you know?"—and vanishes into his own head.

The chopper lifts Saks into the heavens.

"Private Asante! *Now!*"

He stands alone in the clearing, summons his mandala, falls into blindness. His body turns. His legs move. Something begins to run him downhill. The artificial instructor, always sensitive to context, begins a lecture about dealing with loss on the battlefield.

It's all for the best, he knows. It safest to be a passenger at times like this. All these glitches, these—side-effects: they never manifest in zombie mode.

Which makes perfect sense. That being where they put all the money.

Station To Station

SOMETIMES HE STILL wakes in the middle of the night, shocked back to consciousness by the renewed knowledge that he still exists—as if his death was some near-miss that didn't really sink in until days or weeks afterward, leaving him weak in the knees and gasping for breath. He catches himself calling his mandala, a fight/flight reaction to threat stimuli long-since expired. He stares at the ceiling, forces calm onto panic, takes comfort from the breathing of his fellow recruits. Tries not think about Kito and Rashida. Tries not to think at all.

Sometimes he finds himself in the Commons, alone but for the inevitable drone hovering just around the corner, ready to raise alarms and inject drugs should he suffer some delayed and violent reaction to any of a hundred recent mods. He watches the world through one of CFB Côté's crippled terminals (they can surf, but never send). He slips through wires and fiberop, bounces off geosynchronous relays all the way back to Ghana: satcams down on the dizzying Escher arcology of the Cape Universitas hubs, piggybacks on drones wending through Makola's East, marvels anew at the giant gengineered snails —big as a centrifuge, some of them—that first ignited his passion for biology when he was six. He haunts familiar streets where the kenkey and fish always tasted better when the Chinese printed them, even though the recipes must have been copied from the locals. The glorious chaos of the street drummers during Adai.

He never seeks out friends or family. He doesn't know if it's because he's not ready, or because he has already moved past them. He only knows not to awaken things that have barely gone to sleep.

Zero Sum. A new life. Also a kind of game used, more often than not, to justify armed conflict.

Also *Null Existence*. If your tastes run to the Latin.

*   *   *

THEY LOOM OVER a drowning subdivision long-abandoned to the rising waters of Galveston Bay: cathedral-sized storage tanks streaked with rust and ruin, twelve-story filtration towers, masses of twisting pipe big enough to walk through.

Garin sidles up beside him. "Looks like a crab raped an octopus."

"Your boys seem twitchy," the Sheriff says. (Asante clenches his fist to control the tremor.) "They hopped on something?"

Metzinger ignores the question. "Have they made any demands?"

"Usual. Stop the rationing or they blow it up." The Sheriff shakes his head, moves to mop his brow, nearly punches himself in the face when his decrepit Bombardier exoskeleton fratzes and overcompensates. "Everything's gone to shit since the Edwards dried up."

"They respond to a water shortage by blowing up a desalination facility?"

The Sheriff snorts. "Folks always make sense where you come from, Lieutenant?"

They reviewed the plant specs down to the rivets on the way here. Or at least their zombies did, utterly silent, borrowed eyes flickering across video feeds and backgrounders that Asante probably wouldn't have grasped even if he *had* been able to see them. All Asante knows —by way of the impoverished briefings Metzinger doles out to those back in Tourist Class—is that the facility was bought from Qatar back when paint still peeled and metal still rusted, when digging viscous fossils from the ground left you rich enough to buy the planet. And that it's falling into disrepair, now that none of those things are true anymore.

Pretty much a microcosm of the whole TExit experience, he reflects.

"They planned it out," the Sheriff admits. "Packed a shitload of capacitors in there with 'em, hooked 'em to jennies, banked 'em in all the right places. We send in quads, EMP just drops 'em." He glances back over his shoulder, to where—if you squint hard enough —a heat-shimmer rising from the asphalt might almost assume the outline of a resting Chinook transport. "Probably risky using exos, unless they're hardened."

"We won't be using exos."

"Far as we can tell some of 'em are dug in by the condensers, others right next to the heat exchangers. We try to microwave 'em out, all the pipes explode. Might as well blow the place ourselves."

"Firepower?"

"You name it. Sig Saurs, Heckler-Kochs, Maesushis. I think one of 'em has a Skorp. All kinetic, far as we know. Nothing you could fry."

"Got anything on legs?"

"They've got a Wolfhound in there. 46-G."

"I meant you," Metzinger says.

The Sheriff winces. "Nearest's three hours away. Gimped leg." And at Metzinger's look: "BoDyn pulled out a few years back. We've been having trouble getting replacement parts."

"What about local law enforcement? You can't be the only—"

"Half of them *are* law enforcement. How'd you think they got the Wolfhound?" The Sheriff lowers his voice, although there aren't any other patriots within earshot. "Son, you don't think we'd have invited you in if we'd had any other choice? I mean Jayzuz, we've got enough trouble maintaining lawnorder as it is. If word ever got out we had to bring in outside help over a goddamn *domestic dispute*…"

"Don't sweat it. We don't wear name tags." Metzinger turns to Silano. "Take it away, Sergeant-Major."

Silano addresses the troops as Metzinger disappears into the cloaked Chinook: "Say your goodbyes, everybody. Autopilots in thirty."

Asante sighs to himself. Those poor bastards don't stand a chance. He can't even bring himself to blame them: driven by desperation, hunger, the lack of any other options. Like the Sāḥilites who murdered *him*, back at the end of another life: damned, ultimately, by the sin of being born into a wasteland that could no longer feed them.

Silano raises one hand. "*Mark.*"

Asante calls forth his mandala. The world goes to gray. His bad hand calms and steadies on the forestalk of his weapon.

This is going to be ugly.

He's glad he won't be around to see it.

Heroes

HE DOES AFTERWARD, of course. They all do, as soon as they get back to Côté. They're still learning. The world is their classroom.

"Back in the Cenozoic all anybody cared about was *reflexes.*" Second-Lieutenant Oliver Maddox—sorcerer's apprentice to the rarely-seen Major Emma Rossiter, of the Holy Order of Neuroengineering—speaks with the excitement of a nine-year-old at his own birthday party. "Double-tap, dash, down, crawl, observe fire—all that stuff your body learns to do without thinking when someone yells *Contact*. The whole program was originally just about speeding up those macros. They never really appreciated that the subconscious mind *thinks* as well as reacts. It *analyzes*. I was telling them that years ago but they never really got it until now."

Asante has never met *Them*. They never write, They never call. They certainly never visit. Presumably They sign a lot of checks.

"Here, though, we have a *perfect* example of the tactical genius of the zombie mind."

Their BUDs recorded everything. Maddox has put it all together post-mortem, a greatest-hits mix with remote thermal and PEA and a smattering of extraporential algorithms to fill in the gaps. Now he sets up the game board—walls, floors, industrial viscera all magically translucent—and initializes the people inside.

"So you've got eighteen heavily-armed hostiles dug in at all the right choke points." Homunculi glow red at critical junctures. "You've got a jamming field in effect, so you can't share telemetry unless you're line-of-sight. You've got an EMP-hardened robot programmed to attack anything so much as squeaks, deafened along the whole spectrum so even if we *had* the backdoor codes it wouldn't hear them." The Wolfhound icon is especially glossy: probably lifted from BoDyn's promotional archive. "And you've got some crazy fucker with a deadman switch that'll send the whole place sky-high the moment his heart stops—or even if he just thinks you're getting too close to the flag. You don't even know about that going in.

"And yet."

Maddox starts the clock. Inside the labyrinth, icons begin to dance in fast-forward.

"Garin's first up, and he completely blows it. Not only does he barely graze the target—probably doesn't even draw blood—*but he leaves his silencer disengaged*. Way to go, Garin. You failed to neutralize your target, and now the whole building knows where you are."

Asante remembers that gunshot echoing through the facility. He remembers his stomach dropping away.

"Now here comes one of Bubba's buddies around the corner and—Garin misses *again!* Nick to the shoulder this time. And here comes the real bad-ass of the bunch, that Wolfhound's been homing in on Garin's shots and that motherfucker is armed and hot and..."

The 46-G rounds the corner. It does not target Garin; it lights up the *insurgents*. Bubba and his buddy collapse into little red piles of pixel dust.

"They did *not* see that coming!" Maddox exults. "Fragged by their own robot! How do you suppose *that* happened?"

Asante frowns.

"So two baddies down, Garin's already up the ladder and onto this catwalk before the robot gets a bead on him but Tiwana's at the other end, way across the building, and they go LOS for about half a second"—a bright thread flickers between their respective icons—"before Tiwana drops back down to ground level and starts picking off Bubbas over by the countercurrent assembly. And *she* turns out to be just as shitty a shot as Garin, and just as sloppy with her silencer."

Gunfire everywhere, from everyone. Asante remembers being blind and shitting bricks, wondering what kind of *aboa* would make such an idiot mistake until the Rann-Seti came up in his own hands, until he felt the recoil and heard the sound of his own shot echoing like a 130-decibel bullseye on his back. He wondered, at the time, how and why someone had sabotaged everyone's silencers like that.

Maddox is still deep in the play. "The bad guys have heard the commotion and are starting to reposition. By now Asante and Silano have picked up the shitty-shot bug and the BoDyn's still running around tearing up the guys on its own side. All this opens a hole that Kalmus breezes through—anyone want to guess the odds she'd just happen to be so perfectly positioned?—which buys her a clean shot at the guy with the deadman switch. Who she drops with a perfect cervical shot. Completely paralyzes the poor bastard *but* leaves his heart beating strong and steady. Here we see Kalmus checking him over and disabling his now-useless doomsday machine.

"This all took less than five minutes, people. I mean, it was eighteen from In to Out but you're basically mopping up after five. And just before the credits roll, Kalmus strolls up to the wolfhound calm as you please and *pets* the fucker. Puts him right to sleep. Galveston PD gets their robot back without a scratch. Five minutes. Fucking magic."

"So, um." Garin looks around. "How'd we do it?"

"Show 'em, Kally."

Kalmus holds up a cuff-link. "Apparently I took this off deadman guy."

"Dog whistles, Ars and Kays." Maddox grins. "50KHz, inaudible to pilot or passenger. You don't put your robot into rabid mode without some way of telling friend from foe, right? Wear one of these pins, Wolfie doesn't look at you twice. *Lose* that pin and it rips your throat out in a fucking instant.

"Your better halves could've gone for clean, quiet kills that would've left the remaining forces still dug-in, still fortified, and not going anywhere. But one of the things that fortified them was BoDyn's baddest battlebot. So your better halves didn't go for clean quiet kills. They went for noise and panic. They shot the dog whistles, drew in the dog, let it attack its own masters. Other side changes position in response. You *herded* the robot, and the robot herded the insurgents right into your crosshairs. It was precision out of chaos, and it's even more impressive because you had no comms except for the occasional optical sync when you happened to be LOS. Gotta be the messiest, spottiest network you could imagine, and if I hadn't seen it myself I'd say it was impossible. But somehow you zombies kept updated on each other's sitreps. Each one knew what it had to do to achieve an optimal outcome assuming all the others did likewise, and the group strategy just kind of—*emerged*. Nobody giving orders. Nobody saying a goddamn word."

Asante sees it now, as the replay loops and restarts. There's a kind of beauty to it; the movement of nodes, the intermittent web of laser light flickering between them, the smooth coalescence of signal from noise. It's more than a dance, more than teamwork. It's more like a... a distributed organism. Like the digits of a hand, moving together.

"Mind you, this is not what we say if anyone asks," Maddox adds. "What we say is that every scenario in which the Galveston plant went down predicted a tipping point across the whole Post-TExit landscape. We point to 95% odds of wide-spread rioting and social unrest on WestHem's very doorstep—a fate which ZeroS has, nice and quietly, prevented. Not bad for your first field deployment."

Tiwana raises a hand. "Who would ask, exactly?"

It's a good question. In the thirteen months since Asante joined Zero Sum, no outsider has ever appeared on the grounds of CFB Côté. Which isn't especially surprising, given that—according to the public records search he did a few weeks back, anyway—CFB Côté has been closed for over twenty years.

Maddox smiles faintly. "Anyone with a vested interest in the traditional chain of command."

Where Are We Now

ASANTE AWAKENS IN the Infirmary, standing at the foot of Carlos Acosta's bed. To his right a half-open door spills dim light into the darkness beyond: a wedge of worn linoleum fading out from the doorway, a tiny red EXIT sign glowing in the void above a stairwell. To his left, a glass wall looks into Neurosurgery. Jointed teleops hang from the ceiling in there, like mantis limbs with impossibly fragile fingers. Lasers. Needles and nanotubes. Atomic-force manipulators delicate enough to coax individual atoms apart.

ZeroS have gone under those knives more times than any of them can count. Surgery by software, mostly. Occasionally by human doctors phoning it in from undisclosed locations, old-school cutters who never visit in the flesh for all the times they've cut into Asante's.

Acosta's on his back, eyes closed. He looks almost at peace. Even his facial tic has quieted. He's been here three days now, ever since losing his right arm to a swarm of smart flechettes over in Heraklion. It's no big deal. He's growing it back with a little help from some imported salamander DNA and a steroid-infused aminoglucose drip. He'll be good as new in three weeks—as good as he's ever been since ZeroS got him, anyway—back in his rack in half that time. Meanwhile it's a tricky balance: his metabolism may be boosted into the jet stream but it's all for tissue growth. There's barely enough left over to power a trip to the bathroom.

Kodjo Asante wonders why he's standing here at 0300.

Maddox says the occasional bit of sleepwalking isn't anything to get too worried about, especially if you're already prone to it. Nobody's suffered a major episode in months, not since well before Galveston; these days the tweaks seem mainly about fine-tuning. Rossiter's long since called off the just-in-case bots that once dogged their every unscripted step. Even lets them leave the base now and then, when they've been good.

You still have to expect the occasional lingering side-effect, though. Asante glances down at the telltale tremor in his own hand, seizes it gently with the other and holds firm until the nerves quiet. Looks back at his friend.

Acosta's eyes are open.

They don't look at him. They don't settle long enough to look at anything, as far as Asante can tell. They jump and twitch in Acosta's face, back forth back forth up down up.

"Carl," Asante says softly. "How's it going, man?"

The rest of that body doesn't even twitch. Acosta's breathing remains unchanged. He doesn't speak.

Zombies aren't big on talking. They're smart but nonverbal, like those split-brain patients who understand words but can't utter them. Something about the integration of speech with consciousness. Written language is easier. The zombie brain doesn't take well to conventional grammar and syntax but they've developed a kind of visual pidgin that Maddox claims is more efficient than English. Apparently they use it at all the briefings.

Maddox also claims they're working on a kind of time-sharing arrangement, some way to divvy up custody of Broca's Area between the fronto-parietal and the retrosplenial. *Someday soon, maybe, you'll literally be able to talk to yourself*, he says. But they haven't got there yet.

A tacpad on the bedside table glows with a dim matrix of Zidgin symbols. Asante places it under Acosta's right hand.

"Carl?"

Nothing.

"Just thought I'd... see how you were. You take care."

He tiptoes to the door, sets trembling fingers on the knob. Steps into the darkness of the hallway, navigates back to his rack by touch and memory.

Those eyes.

It's not like he hasn't seen it a million times before. But all those other times his squadmates' eyes blurred and danced in upright bodies, powerful autonomous things that *moved*. Seeing that motion embedded in such stillness—watching eyes struggle as if trapped in muscle and bone, as if looking up from some shallow grave where they haven't quite been buried alive—

Terrified. That's how they looked. Terrified.

We Are the Dead

SPECIALIST TARRA KALMUS has disappeared. Rossiter was seen breaking the news to Maddox just this morning, a conversation during which Maddox morphed miraculously from He of the Perpetually Goofy Smile into Lieutenant Stoneface. He refuses to talk about it with any of the grunts. Silano managed to buttonhole Rossiter on her way back to the helipad, but could only extract the admission that Kalmus has been 'reassigned'.

Metzinger tells them to stop asking questions. He makes it an order.

But as Tiwana points out—when Asante finds her that evening, sitting with her back propped against a pallet of machine parts in the loading bay—you can run all sorts of online queries without ever using a question mark.

"Fellow corpse."

"Fellow corpse."

It's been their own private salutation since learning how much they have in common. (Tiwana died during a Realist attack in Havana. Worst vacation ever, she says.) They're the only ZeroS, so far at least, to return from the dead. The others hold them a little in awe because of it.

The others also keep a certain distance.

"Garin was last to see her, over at the Memory Hole." Tiwana's wearing a pair of smart specs tuned to the public net. It won't stop any higher-ups who decide to look over her shoulder, but at least her activity won't be logged by default. "Chatting up some redhead with a Hanson Geothermal logo on her jacket."

Two nights ago. Metzinger let everyone off the leash as a reward for squashing a Realist attack on the G8G Constellation. They went down to Banff for some meatspace R&R. "So?"

Speclight paints Tiwana's cheeks with small flickering auroras.
"So a BPD drone found a woman matching that description dead
outside a public fuckcubby two blocks south of there. Same night."

"Eiiii." Asante squats down beside her as Tiwana pushes the specs
onto her forehead. Her wonky eye jiggles at him.

"Yeah." She takes a breath, lets it out. "Nicci Steckman, according
to the DNA."

"So how—"

"They don't say. Just asking witnesses to come forward."

"Have any?"

"They left together. Deked into an alley. No further surveillance
record, which is odd."

"Is it really," Asante murmurs.

"No. I guess not."

They sit in silence for a moment.

"What do you think?" she asks at last.

"Maybe Steckman didn't like it rough and things got out of hand.
You know Kally, she... doesn't always take no for an answer."

"No to what? We're all on antilibidinals. Why would she even be
—"

"She'd never *kill* someone over—"

"Maybe *she* didn't," Tiwana says.

He blinks. "You think she flipped?"

"Maybe it wasn't her fault. Maybe the augs kicked in on their
own somehow, like a, a... reflex. Kally saw an imminent threat, or
something her better half *interpreted* that way. Grabbed the keys,
took care of it."

"It's not supposed to work like that."

"It wasn't supposed to fry Saks' central nervous system either."

"Come on, Sofe. That's ancient history. They wouldn't deploy us
if they hadn't fixed those problems."

"Really." Her bad eye looks pointedly at his bad hand.

"Legacy glitches don't count." Nerves nicked during surgery, a stray milliamp leaking into the fusiform gyrus. Everyone's got at least one. "Maddox says—"

"Oh sure, Maddox is always gonna tidy up. Next week, next month. Once the latest tweaks have settled, or there isn't some brush fire to put out over in Kamfuckingchatka. Meanwhile the glitches don't even manifest in zombie mode so why should he care?"

"If they thought the implants were defective they wouldn't keep sending us out on missions."

"Eh." Tiwana spreads her hands. "You say *mission*, I say *field test*. I mean, sure, camaraderie's great—we're the cutting edge, we can be ZeroS! But *look* at us, Jo. Silano was a Rio insurgent. Kalmus was up on insubordination charges. They scraped you and me off the ground like road kill. None of us are what you'd call *summa cum laude*."

"Isn't that the point? That *anybody* can be a super soldier?" *Or at least, any* body.

"We're lab rats, Jo. They don't want to risk frying their West Point grads with a beta release so they're working out the bugs on us first. If the program was ready to go wide we wouldn't still be here. Which means—" She heaves a sigh. "It's the augs. At least, I hope it's the augs."

"You hope?"

"You'd rather believe Kally just went berserk and killed a civilian for no reason?"

He tries to ignore a probably-psychosomatic tingle at the back of his head. "Rossiter wouldn't be talking *reassignment* if she had," he admits. "She'd be talking court-martial."

"She'll never talk court-martial. Not where we're concerned."

"Really."

"Think about it. You ever see any politician come by to make sure the taxpayer's money's being well-spent? You ever see a commissioned officer walking the halls who wasn't Metzinger or Maddox or Rossiter?"

"So we're off the books." It's hardly a revelation.

"We're so far *off the books* we might as well be cave paintings. We don't even know our own tooth-to-tail ratio. Ninety percent of our support infrastructure's offsite, it's all robots and teleops. We don't even know who's cutting into our own heads." She leans close in the deepening gloom, fixes him with her good eye. "This is voodoo, Jo. Maybe the program *started* small with that kneejerk stuff, but now? You and I, we're literal fucking *zombies*. We're reanimated corpses dancing on strings, and if you think Persephone Q. Public is gonna be fine with that you have a lot more faith in her than I do. I don't think Congress knows about us, I don't think Parliament knows about us, I bet SOCOM doesn't even know about us past some line in a budget that says *psychological research*. I don't think they *want* to know. And when something's that dark, are they really going to let anything as trivial as a judicial process drag it into the light?"

Asante shakes his head. "Still has to be accountability. Some kind of internal process."

"There is. You disappear, and they tell everyone you've been reassigned."

He thinks for a bit. "So what do we do?"

"First we riot in the mess hall. Then we march on Ottawa demanding equal rights for corpses." She rolls her eyes. "We don't *do* anything. Maybe you forgot: we *died*. We don't legally exist anymore, and unless you got a way better deal than me the only way for either of us to change that is keep our heads down until we get our honorable discharges. I do not like being dead. I would very much like to go back to being officially alive some day. Until then..."

She takes the specs off her head. Powers them down.

"We watch our fucking step."

Ricochet

SERGEANT KODJO ASANTE watches his fucking step. He watches it when he goes up against AIRheads and Realists. He watches it when pitted against well-funded private armies running on profit and ideology, against ragged makeshift ones driven by thirst and desperation, against rogue Darwin Banks and the inevitable religious extremists who—almost a quarter-century after the end of the Dark Decade—still haven't stopped maiming and killing in the name of their Invisible Friends. His steps don't really falter until twenty-one months into his tour, when he kills three unarmed children off the coast of Honduras.

ZeroS has risen from the depths of the Atlantic to storm one of the countless gylands that ride the major currents of the world's oceans. Some are refugee camps with thousands of inhabitants; others serve as havens for hustlers and tax dodgers eager to avoid the constraints of more stationary jurisdictions. Some are military, sheathed in chromatophores and radar-damping nanotubes: bigger than airports, invisible to man or machine.

The *Caçador de Recompensa* is a fish farm, a family business registered out of Brazil: two modest hectares of low-slung superstructure on a donut hull with a cluster of net pens at its center. It is currently occupied by forces loyal to the latest incarnation of Shining Path. The Path thrives on supply lines with no fixed address —and as Metzinger reminded them on the way down, it's always better to prevent a fight than win one. If the Path can't feed their troops, maybe they won't deploy them.

This is almost a mission of mercy.

Asante eavesdrops on the sounds of battle, takes in a mingled reek of oil and salt air and rotten fish, lets Evil Twin's worldview wash across his eyes in a blur of light and the incomprehensible flicker of readouts with millisecond lifespans. Except during target acquisition, of course. Except for those brief stroboscopic instants when ET *locks on*, and faces freeze and blur in turn: a couple of coveralled SAsian men wielding Heckler-Kochs. A wounded antique ZhanLu staggering on two-and-a half-legs, the beam from its MAD gun wobbling wide of any conceivable target. Children in life jackets, two boys, one girl; Asante guesses their ages at between seven and ten. Each time the weapon kicks in his hands and an instant later ET is veering toward the next kill.

Emotions are sluggish things in Passenger mode. He feels nothing in the moment, shock in the aftermath. Horror's still halfway to the horizon when a random ricochet slaps him back into the driver's seat.

The bullet doesn't penetrate—not much punches through the Chrysomalon armor wrapped tight around his skin—but vectors interact. Momentum passes from a small fast object to a large slow one. Asante's brain lurches in its cavity; meat slaps bone and bounces back. Deep in all that stressed gray matter, some vital circuit shorts out.

There's pain of course, blooming across the side of his head like napalm in those few seconds before his endocrine pumps damp it down. There's fire in the BUD, a blaze of static and a crimson icon warning of ZMODE FAILURE. But there's a little miracle too:

Kodjo Asante can see again: a high sun in a hard blue sky. A flat far horizon. Columns of oily smoke rising from wrecked machinery.

Bodies.

The air *crack*s a few centimeters to his right. He drops instinctively to a deck slippery with blood and silver scales, gags at the sudden stench wafting from a slurry of bloated carcasses crowding the surface of the holding pen just in front of him. (*Coho-Atlantic hybrids*, he notes despite himself. *Might even have those new Showell genes.*) A turret on treads sparks and sizzles on the other side, a hole blown in its carapace.

A shadow blurs across Asante's forearm. Tiwana leaps across the sky, defractors high on her forehead, eyeballs dancing madly in their sockets. She clears the enclosure, alights graceful as a dragonfly on one foot, kicks the spastic turret with the other. It sparks one last time and topples into the pen. Tiwana vanishes down the nearest companionway.

Asante gets to his feet, pans for threats, sees nothing but enemies laid waste: the smoking stumps of perimeter autoturrets, the fallen bodies of a man with his arm blown off and a woman groping for a speargun just beyond reach. And a small brittle figure almost fused to the deck: blackened sticks for arms and legs, white teeth grinning in a charred skull, a bright half-melted puddle of orange fabric and PVC holding it all together. Asante sees it all. Not just snapshots glimpsed through the fog: ZeroS handiwork, served up for the first time in three-sixty wraparound immersion.

We're killing children...

Even the adult bodies don't look like combatants. Refugees, maybe, driven to take by force what they couldn't get any other way. Maybe all they wanted was to get somewhere safe. To feed their kids.

At his feet, a reeking carpet of dead salmon converge listlessly in the wake of the fallen turret. They aren't feeding anything but hagfish and maggots.

I have become Sāḥilite, Asante reflects numbly. He calls up BUD, ignores the unreadable auras flickering around the edges of vision, selects GPS.

Not off Honduras. They're in the Gulf of Mexico.

No one in their right mind would run a fish farm here. The best parts of the Gulf are anoxic; the worst are downright flammable. *Caçador* must have drifted up through the Yucatan Channel, got caught in an eddy loop. All these fish would have suffocated as soon as they hit the dead zone.

But gylands aren't entirely at the mercy of the currents. They carry rudimentary propulsion systems for docking and launching, switching streams and changing course. *Caçador's* presence so deep in the Gulf implies either catastrophic equipment failure or catastrophic ignorance.

Asante can check out the first possibility, anyway. He stumbles toward the nearest companionway—

—as Tiwana and Acosta burst onto deck from below. Acosta seizes his right arm, Tiwana his left. Neither slows. Asante's feet bounce and drag. The lurching acceleration reawakens the pain in his temple.

He cries out: "*The engines...*"

New pain, other side, sharp and recurrent: an ancient weight belt swinging back and forth across Acosta's torso, a frayed strip of nylon threaded through an assortment of lead slugs. It's like being hammered by a tiny wrecking ball. One part of Asante wonders where Acosta found it; another watches Garin race into view with a small bloody body slung across his shoulder. Garin passes one of the dismembered turrets, grabs a piece with his free hand and keeps running.

Everyone's charging for the rails.

Tiwana's mouthpiece is in, her defractors down. She empties a clip into the deck ahead, right at the water's edge: gunfire shreds plastic and whitewashed fiberglass, loosens an old iron docking cleat. She dips and grabs in passing, draws it to her chest, never loosening her grip on Asante. He hears the soft pop of a bone leaving its socket in the instant before they all go over the side.

They plummet head-first, dragged down by a hundred kilograms of improvised ballast. Asante chokes, jams his mouthpiece into place; coughs seawater through the exhaust and sucks in a hot lungful of fresh-sparked hydrox. Pressure builds against his eardrums. He swallows, swallows again, manages to keep a few millibars ahead of outright rupture. He has just enough freedom of movement to claw at his face and slide the defractors over his eyes. The ocean clicks into focus, clear as acid, empty as green glass.

Green turns white.

Seen in that flash-blinded instant: four thin streams of bubbles, rising to a surface gone suddenly incandescent. Four dark bodies, falling from the light. A thunderclap rolls through the water, deep, downshifted, as much felt as heard. It comes from nowhere and everywhere.

The roof of the ocean is on fire. Some invisible force shreds their contrails from the top down, tears those bubbles into swirling silver confetti. The wave-front races implacably after them. The ocean *bulges*, recoils. It squeezes Asante like a fist, stretches him like rubber; Tiwana and Acosta tumble away in the backwash. He flails, stabilizes himself as the first jagged shapes resolve overhead: dismembered chunks of the booby-trapped gyland, tumbling with slow majesty into the depths. A broken wedge of deck and stairwell passes by a few meters away, tangled in monofilament. A thousand glassy eyes stare back from the netting as the wreckage fades to black.

Asante scans the ocean for that fifth bubble trail, that last dark figure to balance Those Who Left against Those Who Returned. No one overhead. Below, a dim shape that has to be Garin shares its mouthpiece with the small limp thing in his arms. Beyond that, the hint of a deeper dark against the abyss: a shark-like silhouette keeping station amid a slow rain of debris. Waiting to take its prodigal children home again.

They're too close to shore. There might be witnesses. So much for stealth-ops. So much for low profiles and no-questions-asked. Metzinger's going to be pissed.

Then again, they *are* in the Gulf of Mexico.

Any witnesses will probably just think it caught fire again.

Lady Grinning Soul

"In your own words, Sergeant. Take your time."

We killed children. We killed children, and we lost Silano, and I don't know why. And I don't know if you do either.

But of course, that would involve taking Major Emma Rossiter at *her* word.

"Did the child...?" Metzinger had already tubed Garin's prize by the time Asante reboarded the sub. Garin, of course, had no idea what his body had been doing. Metzinger had not encouraged discussion.

That was okay. Nobody was really in the mood anyhow.

"I'm sorry. She didn't make it." Rossiter waits for what she probably regards as a respectful moment. "If we could focus on the subject at hand..."

"It was a shitstorm," Asante says. "Sir."

"We gathered that." The Major musters a sympathetic smile. "We were hoping you could provide more in the way of details."

"You must have the logs."

"Those are numbers, Sergeant. Pixels. You are uniquely—if accidentally—in a position to give us more than that."

"I never even got below decks."

Rossiter seems to relax a little. "Still. This is the first time one of you has been debooted in mid-game, and it's obviously not the kind of thing we want to risk repeating. Maddox is already working on ways to make the toggle more robust. In the meantime, your perspective could be useful in helping to ensure this doesn't happen again."

"My perspective, sir, is that those forces did not warrant our particular skill set."

"We're more interested in your experiences regarding the deboot, Sergeant. Was there a sense of disorientation, for example? Any visual artifacts in BUD?"

Asante stands with his hands behind his back—good gripping bad —and says nothing.

"Very well." Rossiter's smile turns grim. "Let's talk about your *perspective*, then. Do you think regular forces would have been sufficient? Do you have a sense of the potential losses incurred if we'd sent, say, WestHem marines?"

"They appeared to be refugees, sir. They didn't pose—"

"One hundred percent, Sergeant. We would have lost everyone."

Asante says nothing.

"Unaugged soldiers wouldn't even have made it off the gyland before it went up. Even if they had, the p-wave would've been fatal if you hadn't greatly increased your rate of descent. Do you think regular forces would have made that call? Seen what was coming, run the numbers, improvised a strategy to get below the kill zone in less time than it would take to shout a command?"

"We killed children." It's barely more than a whisper.

"Collateral damage is an unfortunate but inevitable—"

"We *targeted* children."

"Ah."

Rossiter plays with her tacpad: *tap tap tap, swipe.*

"These children," she says at last. "Were they armed?"

"I do not believe so, sir."

"Were they naked?"

"Sir?"

"Could you be certain they weren't carrying concealed weapons? Maybe even a remote trigger for a thousand kilograms of CL-20?"

"They were... sir, they couldn't have been more than seven or eight."

"I shouldn't have to tell you about child soldiers, Sergeant. They've been a fact of life for centuries, especially in *your* particular—at any rate. Just out of interest, how young would someone have to be before you'd rule them out as a potential threat?"

"I don't know, sir."

"Yes you do. You *did*. That's why you targeted them."

"*That wasn't me.*"

"Of course. It was your... evil twin. That's what you call it, right?" Rossiter leans forward. "Listen to me very carefully, Sergeant Asante, because I think you're laboring under some serious misapprehensions about what we do here. Your *twin* is not evil, and it is not gratuitous. It is *you*: a much bigger part of *you* than the whiny bitch standing in front of me right now."

Asante clenches his teeth and keeps his mouth shut.

"This gut feeling giving you so much trouble. This sense of Right and Wrong. Where do you think it comes from, Sergeant?"

"Experience. Sir."

"It's the result of a calculation. A whole series of calculations, far too complex to fit into the conscious workspace. So the subconscious sends you... an executive summary, you might call it. Your evil twin knows all about your sense of moral outrage; it's the source of it. It has more information than you do. Processes it more effectively. Maybe you should trust it to know what it's doing."

He doesn't. He doesn't trust her, either.

But suddenly, surprisingly, he understands her.

She's not just making a point. This isn't just rhetoric. The insight appears fully formed in his mind, a bright shard of unexpected clarity. *She thought it would be easy. She really doesn't know what happened.*

He watches her fingers move on the 'pad as she speaks. Notes the nervous flicker of her tongue at the corner of her mouth. She glances up to meet his eye, glances away again.

She's scared.

Look Back in Anger

ASANTE AWAKENS STANDING in the meadow up the mountain. The sky is cloudless and full of stars. His fatigues are damp with sweat or dew. There is no moon. Black conifers loom on all sides. To the east, a hint of pre-dawn orange seeps through the branches.

He has read that this was once the time of the dawn chorus, when songbirds would call out in ragged symphony to start the day. He has never heard it. He doesn't hear it now. There's no sound in this forest but his own breathing—

—and the snap of a twig under someone's foot.

He turns. A gray shape detaches itself from the darkness.

"Fellow corpse," Tiwana says.

"Fellow corpse," he responds.

"You wandered off. Thought I'd tag along. Make sure you didn't go AWOL."

"I think ET's acting up again."

"Maybe you're just sleepwalking. People sleepwalk sometimes." She shrugs. "Probably the same wiring anyway."

"Sleepwalkers don't kill people."

"Actually, that's been known to happen."

He clears his throat. "Did, um…"

"No one else knows you're up here."

"Did ET disable the pickups?"

"I did."

"Thanks."

"Any time."

Asante looks around. "I remember the first time I saw this place. It was… magical."

"I was thinking more *ironic*." Adding, at Asante's look: "You know. That one of the last pristine spots in this whole shit-show owes its existence to the fact that WestHem needs someplace private to teach us how to blow shit up."

"Count on you," Asante says.

The stars are fading. Venus is hanging in there, though.

"You've been weird," she observes. "Ever since the thing with *Caçador*."

"It was a weird thing."

"So I hear." Shrug. "I guess you had to be there."

He musters a smile. "So you don't remember…"

"Legs running down. Legs running back up. My zombie never targeted anything so I don't know what she saw."

"Metzinger does. Rossiter does." He leans his ass against a convenient boulder. "Does it ever bother you? That you don't know what your own eyes are seeing, and they do?"

"Not really. Just the way it works."

"We don't know what we're doing out there. When was the last time Maddox even showed us a highlight reel?" He feels the muscles clenching in his jaw. "We could be war criminals."

"There *is* no *we*. Not when it matters." She sits beside him.

"Besides. Our zombies may be nonconscious but they're not stupid; they know we're obligated to disobey unlawful commands."

"Maybe they *know*. Not sure Maddox's compliance circuit would let them do anything about it."

Somewhere nearby a songbird clears its throat.

Tiwana takes a breath. "Suppose you're right—not saying you are, but *suppose* they sent us out to gun down a gyland full of harmless refugees. Forget that *Caçador* was packing enough explosives to blow up a hamlet, forget that it killed Silano... hell, nearly killed us all. If Metzinger decides to bash in someone's innocent skull, you still don't blame the hammer he used."

"And yet. Someone's skull is still bashed in."

Across the clearing, another bird answers. *The dawn duet.*

"There must be reasons," she says, as if trying it on for size.

He remembers *reasons* from another life, on another continent: retribution. The making of examples. Poor impulse control. Just... fun, sometimes.

"Such as."

"I don't know, okay? Big Picture's way above our pay grade. But that doesn't mean you toss out the chain of command every time someone gives you an order without a twenty-gig backgrounder to go with it. If you want me to believe we're in thrall to a bunch of fascist baby killers, you're gonna need more than a few glimpses of something you may have seen on a gyland."

"How about, I don't know. All of human history?"

Venus is gone at last. The rising sun streaks the clearing with gold.

"It's the deal we made. Sure, it's a shitty one. Only shittier one is being dead. But would you choose differently, even now? Go back to being fish food?"

He honestly doesn't know.

"We should be *dead*, Jo. Every one of these moments is a gift."

He regards her with a kind of wonder. "I never know how you do it."

"Do what?"

"Channel Schopenhauer and Pollyanna at the same time without your head exploding."

She takes his hand for a moment, squeezes briefly. Rises. "We're gonna make it. Just so long as we don't rock the boat. All the way to that honorable fucking discharge." She turns to the light; sunrise glows across her face. "Until then, in case you were wondering, I've got your back."

"There is no you," he reminds her. "Not when it matters."

"I've got your back," she says.

Watch That Man

THEY'VE OUTSOURCED SILANO'S position, brought in someone none of them have ever seen before. Technically he's one of them, though the scars that tag him ZeroS have barely had time to heal. Something about him is wrong. Something about the way he moves; his insignia. Not Specialist or Corporal or Sergeant.

"I want you to meet Lieutenant Jim Moore," Rossiter tells them.

ZeroS finally have a commissioned secco. He's easily the youngest person in the room.

He gets right to it. "This is the Nanisivik mine." The satcam wall zooms down onto the roof of the world. "Baffin Island, seven hundred fifty klicks north of the Arctic Circle, heart of the Slush Belt." A barren fractured landscape of red and ocher. Drumlins and hillocks and bifurcating stream beds.

"Tapped out at the turn of the century." A brown road,

undulating along some scoured valley floor. A cluster of buildings. A gaping mouth in the Earth. "These days people generally stay away, on account of its remote location. Also on account of the eight thousand metric tons of high-level nuclear waste the Canadian government brought over from India for deep-time storage. Part of an initiative to diversify the northern economy, apparently." Tactical schematics, now: Processing and Intake. Train tracks corkscrewing into the Canadian Shield. Storage tunnels branching like the streets of an underground subdivision. "Project was abandoned after the Greens lost power in '38.

"You could poison a lot of cities with this stuff. Which may be why someone's messing around there now."

Garin's hand is up. "Someone, sir?"

"So far all we have are signs of unauthorized activity and a JTFN drone that went in and never came out. Our first priority is to identify the actors. Depending on what we find, we might take care of it ourselves. Or we might call in the bombers. Won't know until we get there."

And we *won't know even then*, Asante muses—and realizes, in that moment, what it is about Moore that strikes him as so strange.

"We'll be prepping your better halves with the operational details *en route*."

It's not what is, it's what *isn't*: no tic at the corner of the eye, no tremor in the hand. His speech is smooth and perfect, his eyes make contact with steady calm. Lieutenant Moore doesn't glitch.

"For now, we anticipate a boots-down window of no more than seven hours—"

Asante looks at Tiwana. Tiwana looks back.

ZeroS are out of beta.

*   *   *

Subterraneans

THE LOCKHEED DROPS them at the foot of a crumbling pier. Derelict shops and listing trailers, long abandoned, huddle against the sleeting rain. This used to be a seaport; then a WestHem refueling station back before *WestHem* was even a word, before the apocalyptic Arctic weather made it easier to just stick everything underwater. It lived its short life as a company town, an appendage of the mine, in the days before Nanisivik was emptied of its valuables and filled up again.

BUD says 1505: less than an hour if they want to be on target by sundown. Moore leads them overland across weathered stone and alluvial washouts and glistening acned Martian terrain. They're fifteen hundred meters from the mouth of the repository when he orders them all into the back seat.

Asante's legs, under new management, pick up the pace. His vision blurs. At least up here, in the wind and blinding sleet, it doesn't make much difference.

A sound drifts past: the roar of some distant animal, perhaps. Nearer, the unmistakable discharge of an -40. Not ET's. Asante's eyes remain virtuously clouded.

The wind dies in the space of a dozen steps. Half as many again and the torrent of icy needles on his face slows to a patter, a drizzle. Asante hears great bolts unlatching, a soft screech of heavy metal. They pass through some portal and the bright overcast in his eyes dims by half. Buckles and bootsteps echo faintly against rock walls.

Downhill. A gentle curve to the left. Gravel, patches of broken asphalt. His feet step over unseen obstacles.

And stop.

The whole squad must have frozen; he can't hear so much as a breath. The supersaccadic tickertape flickering across the fog seems faster. Could be his imagination. Off in some subterranean distance, water *drip-drip-drips* onto a still surface.

Quiet movement as ZeroS spreads out. Asante's just a passenger but he reads the footsteps, feels his legs taking him sideways, kneeling. The padding on his elbows doesn't leave much room for fine-grained tactile feedback but the surface he's bracing against is flat and rough, like a table sheathed in sandpaper.

There's a musky animal smell in the air. From somewhere in the middle distance, a soft *whuffle*. The stirring of something huge in slow, sleepy motion.

Maybe someone left the door open, and something got in...

Pizzly bears are the only animals that come to mind: monstrous hybrids, birthed along the boundaries of stressed ecosystems crashing into each other. He's never seen one in the flesh.

A grunt. A low growl.

The sound of building speed.

Gunshots. A roar, deafeningly close, and a crash of metal against metal. The flickering tactical halo dims abruptly: network traffic just dropped by a node.

Now the whole network crashes: pawn exchange, ZeroS sacrificing their own LAN as the price of jamming the enemy's. Moore's MAD gun snaps to the right. An instant of scorching heat as the beam sweeps across Asante's arm; Moore shooting wide, Moore *missing*. ET breaks cover, leaps and locks. For one crystalline millisecond Asante sees a wall of coarse ivory-brown fur close enough to touch, every follicle in perfect focus.

The clouds close in. ET pulls the trigger.

A bellow. The scrape of great claws against stone. The reek is overpowering but ET's already pirouetting after fresh game and *click* the freeze-frame glimpse of monstrous ursine jaws in a face wide as a doorway and *click* small brown hands raised against an onrushing foe and *click* a young boy with freckles and strawberry blond hair and Asante's blind again but he feels ET pulling on the trigger, *pop pop pop*—

Whatthefuck children whatthefuck whatthefuck

—and ET's changed course again and *click*: a small back a fur coat black hair flying in the light of the muzzle flash.

Not again. Not again.

Child soldiers. Suicide bombers. For centuries.

But no one's shooting back.

He knows the sound of every weapon the squad might use, down to the smallest pop and click: the sizzle of the MAD gun, the bark of the Epsilon, Acosta's favorite Olympic. He hears them now; those, and no others. Whatever they're shooting at isn't returning fire.

Whatever we're shooting at. You blind murderous twaaaaase. You're shooting eight-year-olds.

Again.

More gunfire. Still no voices but for a final animal roar that gives way to a wet gurgle and the heavy slap of meat on stone.

It's a nuclear waste repository at the north pole. What are children even doing here?

What am I?

What am I?

And suddenly he sees the words, *All tautologies are tautologies* and ET's back downstairs and the basement door locks and Kodjo Asante grabs frantically for the reins, and takes back his life, and opens his eyes:

In time to see the little freckled boy, dressed in ragged furs, sitting on Riley Garin's shoulders and dragging a jagged piece of glass across his throat. In time to see him leap free of the body and snatch Garin's gun, toss it effortlessly across this dimly-lit cave to an Asian girl clad only in a filthy loincloth, who's sailing through the air toward a bloodied Jim Moore. In time to see that girl reach behind her and catch the gun in midair without so much as a backward glance.

More than a dance, more than teamwork. Like digits on the same hand, moving together.

The pizzly's piled up against a derelict forklift, a giant tawny thing raking the air with massive claws even as it bleeds out through the hole in its flank. A SAsian child with his left hand blown off at the wrist (*maybe that was me*) dips and weaves around the fallen behemoth. He's—*using* it, exploiting the sweep of its claws and teeth as a kind of exclusion zone guaranteed to maul anyone within three meters. Somehow those teeth and claws never seem to connect with him.

They've connected with Acosta, though. Carlos Acosta, lover of sunlight and the great outdoors lies there broken at the middle, staring at nothing.

Garin finally crashes to the ground, blood gushing from his throat.

They're just children. In rags. Unarmed.

The girl rebounds between rough-hewn tunnel walls and calcified machinery, lines up the shot with Garin's weapon. Her bare feet never seem to touch the ground.

They're children they're just—

Tiwana slams him out of the way as the beam sizzles past. The air shimmers and steams. Asante's head cracks against gears and conduits and ribbed metal, bounces off steel onto rock. Tiwana lands on top of him, eyes twitching in frantic little arcs.

And stopping.

It's a moment of pure panic, seeing those eyes freeze and focus —*she doesn't know me she's locking on she's locking on*—but something shines through from behind and Asante can see that her eyes aren't target-locked at all. They're just *looking*.

"… Sofiyko?"

Whatever happens, I've got your back.

But Sofiyko's gone, if she was ever even there.

Blackout

MOORE HANDS HIM off to Metzinger. Metzinger regards him without a word, with a look that speaks volumes: flips a switch and drops him into Passenger mode. He doesn't tell Asante to stay there. He doesn't have to.

Asante feels the glassy pane of a tacpad under ET's hand. That hand rests deathly still for seconds at a time; erupts into a flurry of inhumanly-fast taps and swipes; pauses again. Out past the bright blur in Asante's eyes, the occasional cough or murmur is all that punctuates the muted roar of the Lockheed's engines.

ET is under interrogation. A part of Asante wonders what it's saying about him, but he can't really bring himself to care.

He can't believe they're gone.

No Control

"SERGEANT ASANTE." MAJOR Rossiter shakes her head. "We had such hopes for you."

Acosta. Garin. Tiwana.

"Nothing to say?"

So very much. But all that comes out is the same old lie: "They were just… children…"

"Perhaps we can carve that on the gravestones of your squadmates."

"But who—"

"We don't know. We'd suspect Realists, if the tech itself wasn't completely antithetical to everything they stand for. If it wasn't way past their abilities."

"They were barely even clothed. It was like a *nest*..."

"More like a hive, Sergeant."

Digits on the same hand...

"Not like you," she says, as if reading his mind. "ZeroS networking is quite—inefficient, when you think about it. Multiple minds in multiple heads, independently acting on the same information and coming to the same conclusion. Needless duplication of effort."

"And these..."

"Multiple heads. One mind."

"We jammed the freqs. Even if they were networked—"

"We don't think they work like that. Best guess is—bioradio, you could call it. Like a quantum-entangled corpus callosum." She snorts. "Of course, at this point they could say it was elves and I'd have to take their word for it."

Caçador, Asante remembers. They've learned a lot from one small stolen corpse.

"Why use *children*?" he whispers.

"Oh, Kodjo." Asante blinks at the lapse; Rossiter doesn't seem to notice. "Using children is the *last* thing they want to do. Why do you think they've been stashed in the middle of the ocean, or down some Arctic mineshaft? We're not talking about implants. This is genetic, they were *born*. They have to be protected, hidden away until they grow up and... ripen."

"Protected? By abandoning them in a nuclear waste site?"

"Abandoning them, yes. Completely defenseless. As you saw." When he says nothing, she continues: "It's actually a perfect spot. No neighbors. Lots of waste heat to keep you warm, run your greenhouses, mask your heatprint. No supply lines for some nosy satellite to notice. No telltale EM. From what we can tell there weren't even any adults on the premises, they just... lived off the land, so to speak. Not even any weapons of their own, or at least they didn't use any. Used *bears*, of all things. Used your own guns against you. Maybe they're minimalists, value improvisation." She sacc's something onto her pad. "Maybe they just want to keep us guessing."

"Children." He can't seem to stop saying it.

"For now. Wait 'til they hit puberty." Rossiter sighs. "We bombed the site, of course. Slagged the entrance. If any of ours were trapped down there, they wouldn't be getting out. Then again we're not talking about us, are we? We're talking about a single distributed organism with God-knows-how-many times the computational mass of a normal human brain. I'd be very surprised if it couldn't anticipate and counter anything we planned. Still. We do what we can."

Neither speaks for a few moments.

"And I'm sorry, Sergeant," she says finally. "I'm so sorry it's come to this. We do what we've always done. Feed you stories so you won't be compromised, so you won't compromise *us* when someone catches you and starts poking your amygdala. But the switch was for your protection. We don't know who we're up against. We don't know how many hives are out there, what stage of gestation any of them have reached, how many may have already... matured. All we know is that a handful of unarmed children can slaughter our most elite forces at will, and we are so very unready for the world to know that.

"But *you* know, Sergeant. You dropped out of the game—which may well have cost us the mission—and now you know things that are way above your clearance.

"Tell me. If our positions were reversed, what would *you* do?"

Asante closes his eyes. *We should be dead. Every one of these moments is a gift.* When he opens them again Rossiter's watching, impassive as ever.

"I should've died up there. I should have died off Takoradi two years ago."

The Major snorts. "Don't be melodramatic, Sergeant. We're not going to execute you."

"I... what?"

"We're not even going to court-martial you."

"Why the hell not?" And at her raised eyebrow: "Sir. You said it yourself: unauthorized drop-out. Middle of a combat situation."

"We're not entirely certain that was your decision."

"It *felt* like my decision."

"It always does though, doesn't it?" Rossiter pushes back in her chair. "We didn't create your evil twin, Sergeant. We didn't even put it in control. We just got you out of the way, so it could do what it always does without interference.

"Only now, it apparently... wants you back."

This takes a moment to sink in. "What?"

"Frontoparietal logs suggest your zombie took a certain... initiative. Decided to quit."

"In combat? That would be suicide!"

"Isn't that what you wanted?"

He looks away.

"No? Don't like that hypothesis? Well, here's another: it surrendered. Moore got you out, after all, which was statistically unlikely the way things were going. Maybe dropping out was a white flag, and the hive took pity and let you go so you could... I don't know, spread the word: *don't fuck with us.*

"Or maybe it decided the hive deserved to win, and switched sides.

Maybe it was... conscientiously objecting. Maybe it decided *it* never enlisted in the first place."

Asante decides he doesn't like the sound of the Major's laugh.

"You must have asked it," he says.

"A dozen different ways. Zombies might be analytically brilliant but they're terrible at self-reflection. They can tell you exactly what they did but not necessarily *why*."

"When did you ever care about motive?" His tone verges on insubordination; he's too empty to care. "Just... tell it to stay in control. It has to obey you, right? That orbitofrontal thing. The *compliance mod*."

"Absolutely. But it wasn't your twin who dropped out. It was *you*, when it unleashed the mandala."

"So order it not to show me the mandala."

"We'd love to. I don't suppose you'd care to tell us what it looks like?"

It's Asante's turn to laugh. He sucks at it.

"I didn't think so. Not that it matters. At this point we can't trust you either—again, not entirely your fault. Given the degree to which conscious and unconscious processes are interconnected, it may have been premature to try and separate them so completely, right off the bat." She winces, as if in sympathy. "I can't imagine it's much fun for you either, being cooped up in that skull with nothing to do."

"Maddox said there was no way around it."

"That was true. When he said it." Eyes downcast now, saccing the omnipresent 'pad. "We weren't planning on field-testing the new mod just yet, but with Kalmus and now you—I don't see much choice but to advance implementation by a couple of months."

He's never felt more dead inside. Even when he was.

"Haven't you stuck enough pins in us?" By which he means *me*, of course. By process of elimination.

For a moment, the Major almost seems sympathetic.

"Yes, Kodjo. Just one last modification. I don't think you'll even mind this one'because next time you wake up, you'll be a free man. Your tour will be over."

"Really."

"Really."

Asante looks down. Frowns.

"What is it, Sergeant?"

"Nothing," he says. And regards his steady, unwavering left hand with distant wonder.

Lazarus

RENATA BAERMANN COMES back screaming. She's staring at the ceiling, pinned under something—the freezer, that's it. Big industrial thing. She was in the kitchen when the bombs hit. It must have fallen.

She thinks it's crushed her legs.

The fighting seems to be over. She hears no small-arms fire, no whistle of incoming ordnance. The air's still filled with screams but they're just gulls, come to feast in the aftermath. She's lucky she was inside; those vicious little air rats would have pecked her eyes out by now if she'd been—

—*Blackness*—

¡Joder! Where am I? Oh, right. Bleeding out at the bottom of the Americas, after...

She doesn't know. Maybe this was payback for the annexation of Tierra del Fuego. Or maybe it's the Lifeguards, wreaking vengeance on all those who'd skip town after trampling the world to mud and shit. This is a staging area, after all: a place where human refuse congregates until the pressure builds once again, and another bolus gets shat across the Drake Passage to the land of milk and honey and melting glaciers. The sphincter of the Americas.

She wonders when she got so cynical. Not very seemly for a humanitarian.

She coughs. Tastes blood.

Footsteps crunch on the gravel outside, quick, confident, not the shell-shocked stumble you'd expect from anyone who's just experienced apocalypse. She fumbles for her gun: a cheap microwave thing, barely boils water but it helps level the field when a fifty kg woman has to lay down the law to a man with twice the mass and ten times the entitlement issues. Better than nothing.

Or it would be, if it was still in its holster. If it hadn't somehow skidded up against a table leg a meter and a half to her left. She stretches for it, screams again; feels like she's just torn herself in half as the kitchen door slams open and she—

—blacks out—

—and comes back with the gun miraculously in her hand, her finger pumping madly against the stud, mosquito buzz-snap filling her ears and—

—she's wracked, coughing blood, too weak keep firing even if the man in the WestHem uniform hadn't just taken her gun away.

He looks down at her from a great height. His voice echoes from the bottom of a well. He doesn't seem to be speaking to her: "Behind the mess hall—"

—*English*—

"—fatal injuries, maybe fifteen minutes left in her and she's still fighting—"

When she wakes up again the pain's gone and her vision's blurry. The man has changed from white to black. Or maybe it's a different man. Hard to tell through all these floaters.

"Renata Baermann." His voice sounds strangely... unused, somehow. As if he were trying it out for the first time.

There's something else about him. She squints, forces her eyes to focus. The lines of his uniform resolve in small painful increments. No insignia. She moves her gaze to his face.

"Coño," she manages at last. Her voice is barely a whisper. She sounds like a ghost. "What's wrong with your *eyes?*"

"Renata Baermann," he says again. "Have I got a deal for you."

(Profound thanks to Jordan Blanch, Jason Knowlton, Leona Ludderodt, and Steve Perry for their patience and expertise – PW.)

ABOUT THE AUTHORS

Eleanor Arnason (eleanorarnason.blogspot.com) published her first story in 1973. Since then she has published six novels, two chapbooks and more than thirty short stories. Her novel *A Woman of the Iron People* won the James Tiptree, Jr. Award and the Mythopoeic Society Award. Novel *Ring of Swords* won a Minnesota Book Award. Her short story "Dapple" won the Spectrum Award. Other short stories have been finalists for the Hugo, Nebula, Sturgeon, Sidewise and World Fantasy Awards. Eleanor would really like to win one of these. Eleanor's most recent books are collections *Big Mama Stories*, *Hidden Folk*, and Philip K. Dick Award nominee *Hwarhath Stories: Transgressive Tales of Aliens*. Her favorite spoon is a sterling silver spoon given to her mother on her mother's first Christmas and dated December 25, 1909.

Elizabeth Bear (matociquala.livejournal.com) was born on the same day as Frodo and Bilbo Baggins, but in a different year. When coupled with a childhood tendency to read the dictionary for fun, this led her inevitably to penury, intransigence, and the writing of speculative fiction. She is the Hugo, Sturgeon, Locus, and Campbell Award winning author of 26 novels and over a hundred short stories. Her dog lives in Massachusetts; her partner, writer Scott Lynch, lives in Wisconsin. She spends a lot of time on planes. Her most recent book is science fiction novel *Karen Memory*.

Indrapramit Das (indradas.com) is an Indian author from Kolkata, West Bengal. His debut novel *The Devourers* was shortlisted for the 2015 Crawford Award and the 2016 Lambda Literary Award for Best LGBTQ SF/F/Horror. His fiction has appeared in *Clarkesworld Magazine, Lightspeed Magazine, Asimov's Science Fiction* and *Tor. com*, and has been anthologized in *The Year's Best Science Fiction* and elsewhere. He is an Octavia E. Butler scholar and a grateful graduate of the Clarion West Writers Workshop, and received his M.F.A. from the University of British Columbia in Vancouver. He has worn many hats, including editor, dog hotel night shift attendant, TV background performer, minor film critic, occasional illustrator, environmental news writer, pretend-patient for med school students, and video game tester. He divides his time between India and North America, when possible.

Aliette de Bodard (aliettedebodard.com) lives in Paris where she works as a System Engineer. In her spare time she writes fantasy and science fiction: her short stories have appeared in many venues, and garnered her a Locus Award, two Nebula Awards and two British Science Fiction Association Awards. Her domestic space opera based on Vietnamese culture, *On a Red Station, Drifting*, is available both in print and ebook. Her novel *The House of Shattered Wings*, set in a devastated Belle Epoque Paris ruled by Fallen angels, came out in 2015 and won the BSFA the following year. Sequel *The House of Binding Thorns* is out now.

Nancy Kress (www.nancykress.com) is the author of twenty-seven novels, three books on writing, four short story collections, and over a hundred works of short fiction. Her work has won six Nebulas, two Hugos, a Sturgeon, and the John W. Campbell Memorial Award. Most recent works are novella *Yesterday's Kin* and *The Best* *of Nancy Kress.* Coming up is a new novel, *Tomorrow's Kin.* In addition to writing, Kress often teaches at various venues around the country and abroad; in 2008 she was the Picador visiting lecturer at the University of Leipzig. Kress lives in Seattle with her husband, writer Jack Skillingstead, and Cosette, the world's most spoiled toy poodle.

Rich Larson (richwlarson.tumblr.com) was born in West Africa, has studied in Rhode Island and worked in Spain, and now writes from Ottawa, Canada. His short work has been nominated for the Theodore Sturgeon Award, featured on io9.com, and appears in numerous Year's Best anthologies as well as in magazines such as *Asimov's, Analog, Clarkesworld, The Magazine of Fantasy & Science Fiction, Interzone, Strange Horizons, Lightspeed* and *Apex.* He was one of the most prolific authors of short science fiction in 2015 and 2016.

David D. Levine (www.daviddlevine.com) is the author of novels *Arabella of Mars* and *Arabella and the Battle of Venus* and over fifty SF and fantasy stories. His story "Tk'Tk'Tk'" won the Hugo, and he has been shortlisted for awards including the Hugo, Nebula, Campbell, and Sturgeon. Stories have appeared in *Asimov's, Analog, F&SF, Tor.com,* numerous Year's Best anthologies, and his award-winning collection *Space Magic.*

Garth Nix (www.garthnix.com) was born in 1963 in Melbourne, Australia. A full-time writer since 2001, he has worked as a literary agent, marketing consultant, book editor, book publicist, book sales representative, bookseller, and as a part-time soldier in the Australian Army Reserve. His books include the award-winning young adult fantasy novels *Sabriel, Lirael Abhorsen, Clariel* and *Goldenhand;*

the dystopian novel *Shade's Children*; the space opera *A Confusion of Princes*; and a Regency romance with magic, *Newt's Emerald*. His fantasy novels for children include *The Ragwitch*; the six books of The Seventh Tower sequence; The Keys to the Kingdom series; *Frogkisser!*; and the Troubletwisters series and *Spirit Animals: Blood Ties* (with Sean Williams). Garth's next book, *Have Sword, Will Travel* (with Sean Williams), is due out in late 2017. He lives in a Sydney beach suburb with his wife and two children.

An (pronounce it "On") Owomoyela (an.owomoyela.net) is a neutrois author with a background in web development, linguistics, and weaving chain maille out of stainless steel fencing wire, whose fiction has appeared in a number of venues including *Clarkesworld, Asimov's, Lightspeed*, and a handful of Year's Bests. An's interests range from pulsars and Cepheid variables to gender studies and nonstandard pronouns, with a plethora of stops in-between.

Dominica Phetteplace (www.dominicaphetteplace.com) is a math tutor who lives in Berkeley, California. Her work has appeared in *Asimov's, Clarkesworld*, and *F&SF*. She has won a Pushcart Prize.

E. J. Swift (ejswift.co.uk) is the author of the Osiris Project trilogy (*Osiris, Cataveiro* and *Tamaruq*), a speculative fiction series set in a world radically altered by climate change. Her short fiction has been nominated for the *Sunday Times* EFG Short Story Award ("The Spiders of Stockholm") and the BSFA award for short fiction ("Saga's Children"), and has appeared in a variety of publications from Solaris, Salt Publishing, NewCon Press and Jurassic London. Swift also contributed to Strata—an interactive digital project by Penguin Random House. Her latest novel, *Paris Adrift*, will be published by Solaris in 2018.

Genevieve Valentine's (www.genevievevalentine.com) first novel, *Mechanique*, won the Crawford Award and was nominated for the Nebula the same year. Her second, *The Girls of the Kingfisher Club*, appeared in 2014 to acclaim, and was followed by science fiction novels *Persona* and *Icon*. Valentine's short fiction has appeared in *Clarkesworld*, *Strange Horizons*, *Journal of Mythic Arts*, *Fantasy*, *Apex*, and others, and in the *anthologies Federations*, *The Living Dead 2*, *The Way of the Wizard*, *Teeth*, *After*, and more. Her story "Light on the Water" was a 2009 World Fantasy Award nominee, and "Things to Know about Being Dead" was a 2012 Shirley Jackson Award nominee; several stories have been reprinted in Best of the Year anthologies. Her nonfiction and reviews have appeared at NPR.org, *Strange Horizons*, *Lightspeed*, *Weird Tales*, Tor.com, and *Fantasy Magazine*, and she is a co-author of *Geek Wisdom* (Quirk Books). She has also been known to write *Catwoman* and *Xena: Warrior Princess* comics! Her appetite for bad movies is insatiable.

Carrie Vaughn (www.carrievaughn.com) is best known for her *New York Times* bestselling series of novels about a werewolf named Kitty who hosts a talk radio show for the supernaturally disadvantaged. Her latest novels include a near-Earth space opera, *Martians Abroad*, from Tor Books, and a post-apocalyptic murder mystery, *Bannerless*, from John Joseph Adams Books. She's written several other contemporary fantasy and young adult novels, as well as upwards of 80 short stories. She's a contributor to the Wild Cards series of shared world superhero books edited by George R. R. Martin and is a graduate of the Odyssey Fantasy Writing Workshop. An Air Force brat, she survived her nomadic childhood and managed to put down roots in Boulder, Colorado.

Peter Watts (www.rifters.com) is is a former marine biologist who clings to some shred of scientific rigor by appending technical bibliographies onto his novels. His debut novel (*Starfish*) was a *New York Times* Notable Book, while his fourth (*Blindsight*)— a rumination on the utility of consciousness which has become a required text in undergraduate courses ranging from philosophy to neuroscience—was a finalist for numerous North American genre awards, winning exactly none of them. (It did, however, win a shitload of awards overseas, which suggests that his translators may be better writers than he is.) His shorter work has also picked up trophies in a variety of jurisdictions, notably a Shirley Jackson (possibly due to fan sympathy over nearly dying of flesh-eating disease in 2011) and a Hugo (possibly due to fan outrage over an altercation with US border guards in 2009). The latter incident resulted in Watts being barred from entering the US—not getting on the ground fast enough after being punched in the face by border guards is a "felony" under Michigan statutes—but he can't honestly say he misses the place all that much. Especially now.

Watts's work is available in 20 languages. He and his cat Banana (since deceased) have both appeared in the prestigious scientific journal *Nature*. A few years ago he briefly returned to science with a postdoc in molecular genetics, but he really sucked at it.

Caroline M. Yoachim (carolineyoachim.com) lives in Seattle and loves cold cloudy weather. She is the author of dozens of short stories, appearing in *Fantasy & Science Fiction*, *Clarkesworld*, *Asimov's*, and *Lightspeed*, among other places. Her debut short story collection, *Seven Wonders of a Once and Future World & Other Stories*, came out with Fairwood Press in August 2016.

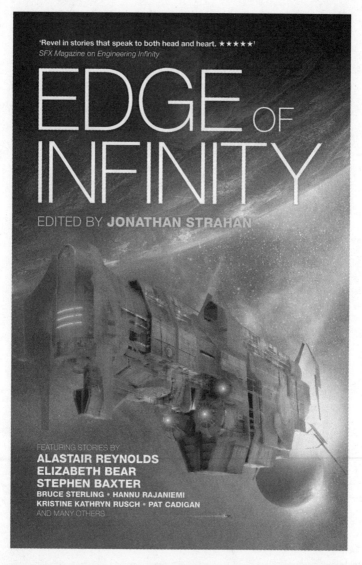

'Revel in stories that speak to both head and heart. ★★★★★'
SFX Magazine on Engineering Infinity

EDGE OF INFINITY

EDITED BY JONATHAN STRAHAN

FEATURING STORIES BY
ALASTAIR REYNOLDS
ELIZABETH BEAR
STEPHEN BAXTER
BRUCE STERLING • **HANNU RAJANIEMI**
KRISTINE KATHRYN RUSCH • **PAT CADIGAN**
AND MANY OTHERS

Edge of Infinity is an exhilarating new SF anthology that looks at the next giant leap for humankind: the leap from our home world out into the Solar System. From the eerie transformations in Pat Cadigan's "The Girl-Thing Who Went Out for Sushi" to the frontier spirit of Sandra McDonald and Stephen D. Covey's "The Road to NPS," and from the grandiose vision of Alastair Reynolds' "Vainglory" to the workaday familiarity of Kristine Kathryn Rusch's "Safety Tests," the thirteen stories in this anthology span the whole of the human condition in their race to colonise Earth's nearest neighbours.

 WWW.SOLARISBOOKS.COM

Follow us on Twitter! www.twitter.com/solarisbooks

FEATURING STORIES BY **KEN MACLEOD** • **PAT CADIGAN** • **ELLEN KLAGES**
ALASTAIR REYNOLDS • **KAREN LORD** • **GREG EGAN** • **LINDA NAGATA**
ADAM ROBERTS • **HANNU RAJANIEMI** • **ALIETTE DE BODARD** AND MORE

REACH FOR
INFINITY

EDITED BY **JONATHAN STRAHAN**

"One of the most respected editors in the genre."

What happens when we reach out into the vastness of space?

What hope for us amongst the stars?

Multi-award winning editor Jonathan Strahan brings us fourteen new tales of the future, from some of the finest science fiction writers in the field.

The fourteen startling stories in this anthology feature the work of Greg Egan, Aliette de Bodard, Ian McDonald, Karl Schroeder, Pat Cadigan, Karen Lord, Ellen Klages, Adam Roberts, Linda Nagata, Hannu Rajaniemi, Kathleen Ann Goonan, Ken MacLeod, Alastair Reynolds and Peter Watts.

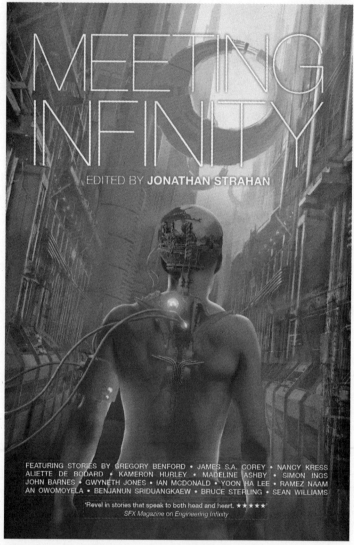

MEETING INFINITY

EDITED BY **JONATHAN STRAHAN**

FEATURING STORIES BY GREGORY BENFORD • JAMES S.A. COREY • NANCY KRESS
ALIETTE DE BODARD • KAMERON HURLEY • MADELINE ASHBY • SIMON INGS
JOHN BARNES • GWYNETH JONES • IAN MCDONALD • YOON HA LEE • RAMEZ NAAM
AN OWOMOYELA • BENJANUN SRIDUANGKAEW • BRUCE STERLING • SEAN WILLIAMS

'Revel in stories that speak to both head and heart. ★★★★★'
SFX Magazine on *Engineering Infinity*

The world is rapidly changing. We surf future-shock every day, as the progress of technology races ever on.
Increasingly we are asking: how do we change to live in the world to come?

Whether it's climate change, inundated coastlines and drowned cities; the cramped confines of a tin can
hurtling through space to the outer reaches of our Solar System; or the rush of being uploaded into cyberspace,
our minds and bodies are going to have to drastically alter.

Multi-award winning editor Jonathan Strahan brings us another incredible volume in his much praised
science-fiction anthology series, featuring stories by Madeline Ashby, John Barnes, James S.A. Corey,
Gregory Benford, Benjanun Sriduangkaew, Simon Ings, Kameron Hurley, Nancy Kress, Gwyneth Jones, Yoon
Ha Lee, Bruce Sterling, Sean Williams, Aliette de Bodard, Ramez Naam, An Owomoyela and Ian McDonald.

 WWW.SOLARISBOOKS.COM

Follow us on Twitter! www.twitter.com/solarisbooks

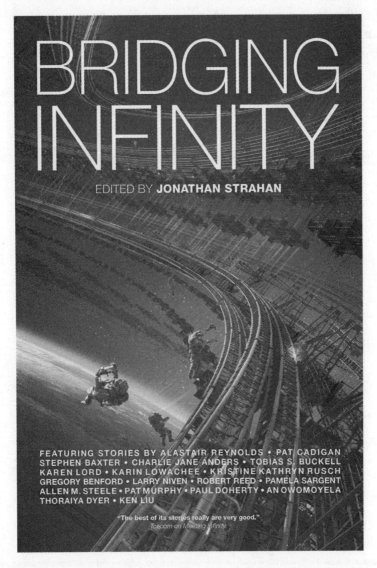

BRIDGING INFINITY

EDITED BY **JONATHAN STRAHAN**

FEATURING STORIES BY ALASTAIR REYNOLDS • PAT CADIGAN
STEPHEN BAXTER • CHARLIE JANE ANDERS • TOBIAS S. BUCKELL
KAREN LORD • KARIN LOWACHEE • KRISTINE KATHRYN RUSCH
GREGORY BENFORD • LARRY NIVEN • ROBERT REED • PAMELA SARGENT
ALLEN M. STEELE • PAT MURPHY • PAUL DOHERTY • AN OWOMOYELA
THORAIYA DYER • KEN LIU

"The best of its stories really are very good."
Tor.com on Meeting Infinity

Sense of wonder is the lifeblood of science fiction. When we encounter something on a truly staggering scale - metal spheres wrapped around stars, planets rebuilt and repurposed, landscapes re-engineered, starships bigger than worlds - the only response we have is reverence, admiration, and possibly fear at something that is grand, sublime, and extremely powerful.

Bridging Infinity puts humanity at the heart of that experience, as builder, as engineer, as adventurer, reimagining and rebuilding the world, the solar system, the galaxy and possibly the entire universe in some of the best science fiction stories you will experience.

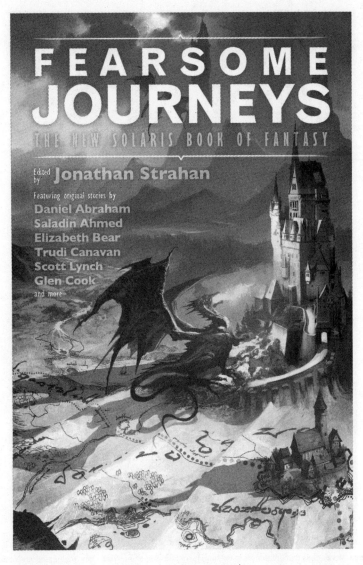

How do you encompass all the worlds of the imagination? Within fantasy's scope lies every possible impossibility, from dragons to spirits, from magic to gods, and from the unliving to the undying.

In Fearsome Journeys, master anthologist Jonathan Strahan sets out on a quest to find the very limits of the unlimited, collecting twelve brand new stories by some of the most popular and exciting names in epic fantasy from around the world.

With original fiction from Scott Lynch, Saladin Ahmed, Trudi Canavan, K J Parker, Kate Elliott, Jeffrey Ford, Robert V S Redick, Ellen Klages, Glen Cook, Elizabeth Bear, Ellen Kushner, Ysabeau S. Wilce and Daniel Abraham Fearsome Journeys explores the whole range of the fantastic.

From sorcerous bridges that link worlds to the simple traditions of country folk; from the mysterious natures of twins to the dangerous powers of obligation and contract. Laden with perils for both the adventurous and the unsuspecting, magic is ultimately a contradiction: endlessly powerful but never without consequence, and rigidly defined by rules of its own making.

Award-winning Jonathan Strahan brings together some of the most exciting and popular writers working in fantasy today to dig into that contradiction, and present you with the strange, the daunting, the mathematical, the unpredictable, the deceptive and above all the fearsome world of magic.

Includes stories by Garth Nix, K J Parker, Tony Ballantyne, James Bradley, Isobelle Carmody, Frances Hardinge, Nina Kiriki Hoffman, Ellen Klages, Justina Robson, Christopher Rowe, Robert Shearman, Karin Tidbeck, Genevieve Valentine and Kaaron Warren.

 # WWW.SOLARISBOOKS.COM

Follow us on Twitter! www.twitter.com/solarisbooks

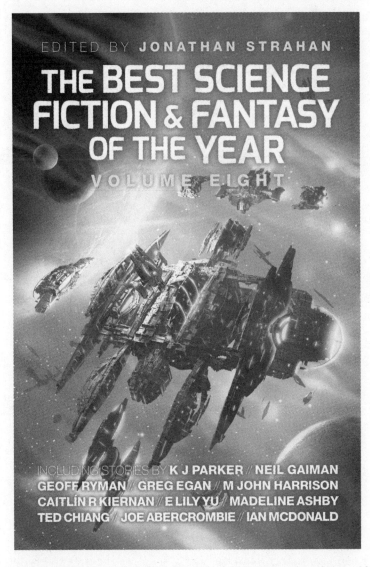

EDITED BY JONATHAN STRAHAN

THE BEST SCIENCE FICTION & FANTASY OF THE YEAR

VOLUME EIGHT

INCLUDING STORIES BY **K J PARKER** // **NEIL GAIMAN**
GEOFF RYMAN // **GREG EGAN** // **M JOHN HARRISON**
CAITLÍN R KIERNAN // **E LILY YU** // **MADELINE ASHBY**
TED CHIANG // **JOE ABERCROMBIE** // **IAN MCDONALD**

From the inner realms of humanity to the far reaches of space, these are the science fiction and fantasy tales that are shaping the genre and the way we think about the future. Multi-award winning editor Jonathan Strahan continues to shine a light on the very best writing, featuring both established authors and exciting new talents.

Within you will find twenty-eight incredible tales, showing the ever growing depth and diversity that science fiction and fantasy continues to enjoy. These are the brightest stars in our firmament, lighting the way to a future filled with astonishing stories about the way we are, and the way we could be.

EDITED BY **JONATHAN STRAHAN**

THE BEST SCIENCE FICTION & FANTASY OF THE YEAR

VOLUME NINE

FEATURING STORIES BY
LAUREN BEUKES
PAOLO BACIGALUPI
JOE ABERCROMBIE
K. J. PARKER
KEN LIU
GARTH NIX
ELIZABETH BEAR
KAI ASHANTE WILSON
RACHEL SWIRSKY
CAITLIN R. KIERNAN
GENEVIEVE VALENTINE
AND MANY MORE

Science fiction and fantasy has never been more diverse or vibrant, and 2014 has provided a bountiful crop of extraordinary stories. These stories are about the future, worlds beyond our own, the realms of our imaginations and dreams but, more importantly, they are the stories of ourselves. Featuring best-selling writers and emerging talents, here are some of the most exciting genre writers working today.

Multi-award winning editor Jonathan Strahan once again brings you the best stories from the past year. Within you will find twenty-eight amazing tales from authors across the globe, displaying why science fiction and fantasy are genres increasingly relevant to our turbulent world.

 WWW.SOLARISBOOKS.COM

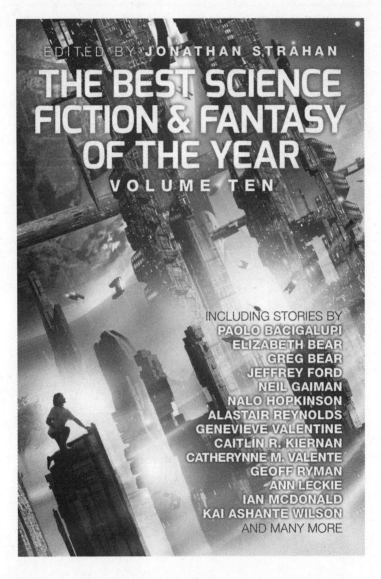

EDITED BY JONATHAN STRAHAN

THE BEST SCIENCE FICTION & FANTASY OF THE YEAR

VOLUME TEN

INCLUDING STORIES BY
PAOLO BACIGALUPI
ELIZABETH BEAR
GREG BEAR
JEFFREY FORD
NEIL GAIMAN
NALO HOPKINSON
ALASTAIR REYNOLDS
GENEVIEVE VALENTINE
CAITLIN R. KIERNAN
CATHERYNNE M. VALENTE
GEOFF RYMAN
ANN LECKIE
IAN MCDONALD
KAI ASHANTE WILSON
AND MANY MORE

Jonathan Strahan, the award-winning and much lauded editor of many of genre's best known anthologies, is back with his tenth volume in this fascinating series, featuring the best science fiction and fantasy from 2015. With established names and new talent, this diverse and ground-breaking collection will take the reader to the outer reaches of space and the inner realms of humanity with stories of fantastical worlds and worlds that may still come to pass.

 WWW.SOLARISBOOKS.COM

Follow us on Twitter! www.twitter.com/solarisbooks

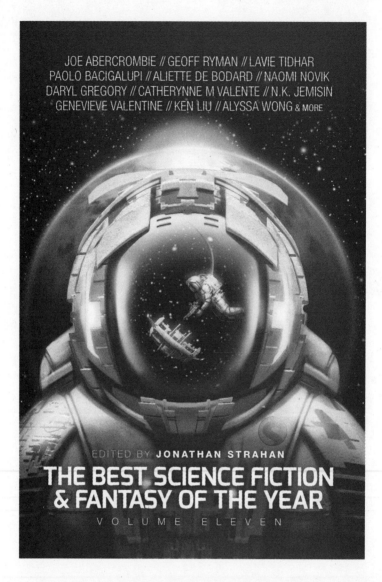